# 'Why do you need a fake fiancée? And why me?' Rebel asked, stunned.

Draco shook his head. 'The "why" will be explained after you accept my proposal. The "why you" is because you happen to be in my debt—literally.'

Rebel jerked away from him. 'Not even a million pounds and a dozen acting awards could make me pull off pretending to like you.'

His grey eyes gleamed. 'I'm not a man you want to cross, so I suggest you give serious thought to giving me what I want.'

'In what universe would *anyone* believe we were engaged to be married?'

He lowered his head and her breath lodged in her lungs. The mouth that was tantalisingly close drifted past. His breath warmed her jaw, then the sensitive skin beneath her earlobe.

'You don't think we have chemistry?'

'N-no,' she forced out.

'Then why is your pulse jumping? Why does your breath catch every time I touch you?' he said huskily in her ear. 'Do you want me to kiss you?'

**Maya Blake**'s hopes of becoming a writer were born when she picked up her first romance at thirteen. Little did she know her dream would come true! Does she still pinch herself every now and then to make sure it's not a dream? Yes, she does! Feel free to pinch her, too, via Twitter, Facebook or Goodreads! Happy reading!

Visit the Author Profile page
at millsandboon.co.uk for more titles.

# A DIAMOND DEAL
# WITH THE GREEK

BY
**MAYA BLAKE**

First Published in Great Britain 2016
By Mills & Boon, an imprint of HarperCollins*Publishers*
1 London Bridge Street, London, SE1 9GF

© 2016 Maya Blake

ISBN: 978-0-263-92110-6

Our policy is to use papers that are natural, renewable and recyclable products and made from wood grown in sustainable forests. The logging and manufacturing processes conform to the legal environmental regulations of the country of origin.

Printed and bound in Spain
by CPI, Barcelona

# A DIAMOND DEAL
# WITH THE GREEK

To Carly, my editor, for being the instrument
that gives my words true meaning.
Thank you!

# CHAPTER ONE

ARABELLA 'REBEL' DANIELS stood at the back of one of the many lifts that served the giant glass and steel masterpiece that was the Angel Building, and waited for the group of four to board. Swallowing down the lingering taste of the second double-shot macchiato she'd given in to this morning, she took a deep breath to calm herself. Although she'd needed the boost very badly at the time, the effect on her nerves now prompted a bout of regret.

Caffeine and panic did not mix well, and, after two long weeks of subsisting on both, she was more than ready to ditch them.

Her heart pounded with trepidation, but, thankfully, she couldn't hear it above the loud music playing in her ears.

Grappling with what would greet her once the lift journey ended was consuming enough, although there was also the real and present albatross of having lost her biggest sponsor three weeks ago and the resulting media frenzy, to deal with. Of course, far from the wild speculation that she was using booze and drugs to cope with her problems, the media would've been shocked and sorely disappointed to know the strongest substance she'd touched was coffee.

She stared unseeing before her, the words of the letter that had been burning a hole in her bag for the last two weeks emblazoned in her mind.

*Arabella,*
*First of all, happy twenty-fifth birthday for Wednesday. If you're surprised at this out-of-the-blue communication, don't be. You're still my daughter and I have a duty of care to you. There's no judgement on*

*my part for the way you've chosen to live your life.*
*Nor are there any strings attached to the enclosed*
*funds. You need it, so put pride aside and use it. It's*
*what your mother would've wanted.*
*Your father.*

Steeling her heart against the lance of hurt at the stark words, Rebel shifted her mind to the banker's receipt that had accompanied the letter.

The five hundred thousand pounds deposited into her bank account was a little less than what her sponsors would've donated had she still been on their books, but it was enough to get her to the Verbier Ski Championships.

This time she couldn't stop her insides from twisting with guilt and a touch of shame.

She should've tried harder to return the money.

Too much had been said between her father and her that couldn't be unsaid. Even after all these years, the pain and guilt were too vivid to be dismissed. And nothing in her father's letter had given her cause to think his views weren't as definitive as they'd been the last time she'd seen him.

He still laid the death of his wife, her mother, firmly at Rebel's feet.

Suppressing her pain, she tried to ignore the pointed looks from the lift's occupants. At any other time she would've turned the music down, but today was different. Today, she would be seeing her father again for the first time in five years. She needed a full suit of armour in place but the music was all she had.

When another suited businessman sent her a scathing look, she mustered a smile. His eyes widened a touch, his ire rapidly morphing to something else. Rebel looked away before her attempt to excuse her music's loudness turned into anything else. Keeping her eyes on the digital counter, she exhaled as the lift reached the fortieth floor. According to what she'd been able to glean from their very brief, very stilted conversations over the last week, her accountant father worked for Angel International Group as their CFO. He hadn't volunteered any more information when she'd asked. In fact, any further attempt to pave a reconnecting road with her father had been firmly blocked. Just as he'd firmly blocked her initial attempts to give back the money he'd given her.

The deeply wounding knowledge that her father was only doing his duty to the wife he'd loved and lost so cruelly should've driven Rebel's actions, not her manager's insistence that the money was the answer to all their prayers.

But it was her father's insistence that the money was hers no matter what that had led her to finally confessing the money's existence to Contessa Stanley. Her manager had had no qualms about Rebel using the funds. Especially since Rebel had recently lost yet another big sponsor due to the continued domino effect created by the sensational reports splashed all over the media. Even her retreat from the spotlight had been looked upon negatively, with wild speculation as to whether she was finally in rehab or nursing a broken heart.

With her chances of finding new sponsorship dwindling by the day, and the championship deadlines racing ever closer, Rebel had finally given in to Contessa's arguments.

Which left her not just in a state of confusion about why her father was now avoiding her after reaching out, at last, with his letter, but also having serious qualms about using money she hadn't wanted to touch in the first place.

'Excuse me?'

Rebel started as the man closest to her touched her arm. Plucking out one earbud, she raised an eyebrow. 'Yes?'

'Did you not want this floor?' he enquired, interest flaring in his eyes as he held the lift doors open and avidly conducted a study of her body.

Groaning inwardly, Rebel wished she hadn't let impulse drive her here until after she'd gone back home to change from her yoga pants and vest top after her morning training session. Muttering her thanks, she slid through the throng.

Hitching her yoga mat and gym bag firmly onto her shoulder, she turned the music volume down as she stepped out of the lift. Plush grey carpet, broken only by a set of massive glass doors, stretched as far as the eye could see, with complementing grey walls interspersed with wild bursts of colour in the form of huge flower arrangements. On the walls along a wide hallway, high-definition images of some of the world's most gifted athletes played on recessed screens.

The whole placed smelled and looked hallowed and expensive.

Rebel frowned, wondering whether she'd walked into the wrong place.

For as long as she'd been aware her father had worked as an accountant for a stationery company, not a slick outfit whose employees flitted past in expensive suits and wore futuristic-looking earpieces. Unable to accept that the father who'd vociferously voiced his hatred of her chosen sporting career would have anything to do with a place like this, Rebel moved towards the set of glass doors and pushed.

Nothing happened. Pushing firmer, she huffed when the door refused to budge.

'Uh, you need one of these to enter,' a voice said from behind her. 'Or a visitor's pass and an escort from downstairs.'

Turning, Rebel saw the man from the lift. His smile stretched wider as he waved a matte black card. The unwillingness to prolong the stomach-churning meeting with her father dragged another smile from her reluctant cheeks. 'Damn, I guess I was a little too impatient to get up here. I'm here to see Nathan Daniels. You couldn't help me out and let me in, could you? I'm Rebel, his daughter. We had an appointment and I'm running late…'

She stopped babbling and gritted her teeth as he took his time looking her up and down again. Fingering the sleeves of the sweater tied around her waist, Rebel waited for his gaze to meet hers again. 'Of course. Anything for Nate's daughter. Awesome name, by the way.'

Pinning the smile on her face, she waited for him to pass the card over the reader and murmured, 'Thank you,' as he held the door open for her.

'My pleasure. I'm Stan. Come with me, I'll show you to Nate's office. I haven't seen him today…' he frowned '…or this week, come to think of it. But I'm sure he's around somewhere.'

Rebel couldn't stop her heart from sinking further at Stan's news. Although now she was here, she realised she'd only *assumed* her father would be at work today. The hurt she'd tried for so long to keep at bay threatened to over-take the small amount of optimism she'd secretly harboured these past two weeks.

Pushing it back, she followed Stan along a series of hall-ways until they reached the first of two brushed-metal doors in a long, quieter corridor. 'Here we are.'

Stan knocked and entered. The outer office was empty, as was the inner office once Rebel followed him in. Frown deepening, he turned to her. 'Looks like he's not here, and neither is his PA…'

Sensing what was coming, she pre-empted him. 'I'm happy to wait. I'm sure he won't be long. If he's not back soon, I'll give him a call.'

Stan looked uncertain for a moment, then he nodded. 'Sure.' He held out his hand. 'I'd love to take you out for a drink some time, Rebel.'

Rebel barely stopped herself from grimacing. 'Thanks, but I can't. My social calendar is booked up for the fore-seeable future.' She had no intention of dating anyone any time soon, either casually or otherwise. At this time of year, she had her hands full dealing with her harrowing guilt and grief.

The press liked to speculate why Rebel Daniels loved to

party hard in the weeks leading up to Valentine's Day. She'd deliberately tried to keep that façade of wild child in place. The last thing she wanted was for anyone to dig beneath the surface, find out the truth about what had happened in Chamonix eight years ago. Besides protecting her beloved mother's memory, the guilt she had to live with was monumental enough without having it exposed to prying eyes.

Now that her dreaded birthday was out of the way, her sole focus was the upcoming championship.

Smiling to take the sting out of the refusal, she breathed a sigh of relief when Stan gave a regretful shrug and left.

Rebel slowly turned and stared around the glass-walled office that belonged to her father. Exhaling, she allowed herself to scrutinise the expensive polished-leather chair and mahogany desk, upon which items had been laid out in the meticulous way her father employed. Insides shaking, she approached his desk, her eyes on the single personal item that stood to the right side of it.

The picture, set in a childish pink and green frame, was exactly as she remembered it when she'd given it to her father on his birthday twelve years ago. At thirteen years old, laughing as she rode a tandem bike with her mother in the picture, Rebel had had no idea her family was about to be ripped apart a few short years later. Or that the decimating of her family would be her fault.

She'd had no cares in the world, secure in the love from a father who'd adored his wife and daughter, and a mother who had encouraged Rebel to pursue her dreams, regardless of any obstacles that stood in her way.

It was that relentless pursuit of her dream that had shattered her family. She knew that. And yet, she'd never been able to walk away from her dreams of pursuing a ski-jump championship. Deep in her heart, Rebel knew walking away would be betraying her vivacious and hugely talented mother, who'd never been quite able to achieve a championship win of her own.

Her heart ached as she passed her hand over the picture. Her father had never understood her need to keep chasing her dream. He'd been harsh and critical to the point where they hadn't been able to stay under the same roof without endless vicious rows. But even then, Rebel had never imagined walking away would mean losing her father for this long. She'd never thought his condemnation and lack of forgiveness would be set in stone.

She dropped her hand. She was here now. She was about to undertake the most important challenge of her career. Before that happened, she needed to know whether there was a way to reconcile with her father.

Forcing the nerves down, she looked around, seeking clues as to his whereabouts. His computer was turned off, but his desk calendar was still set at a date two weeks ago. Unease spiked as she recalled Stan's words. Deciding not to read too much into it, she walked to the far side of the vast office, and set her yoga mat and gym bag down. Another half an hour of pacing, and her nerves were screaming that something wasn't quite right. After leaving yet another message on her father's voicemail stating that she wasn't leaving his office until he called her back, she put her phone on the coffee table along with her sweater, and rolled out the yoga mat.

The situation with her father, a bandaged but far from healed wound, had been ripped open by his letter, bringing fresh anguish. That anguish was affecting her concentration, something she could ill afford. Greg, her trainer, had commented on the fact today, hence the addition of yoga to her exercise regime.

She'd made it through the trials to secure herself a position on the championship-seeking team. She couldn't afford to take her eye off the ball now, no matter how unresolved her issues were with her father.

Dropping onto the mat, she plugged her earphones back in, stretched and closed her eyes. Legs crossed in front of her, she took several breaths to centre herself, then began to move through her positions.

The first few tingles she attributed to her body dropping into a state of relaxation. One she welcomed after the turmoil of the past few weeks. But when they persisted, growing with each breath, Rebel rolled her shoulders, mildly irritated and more than a little anxious that she would truly find no avenue of relief until she spoke to her father.

Then the scent hit her nostrils: dark, hypnotic, with traces of citrus and more than a hint of savagery. At first she believed she was dreaming its complexity. But with each breath, the scent wrapped tighter around her senses, pulling her into a vortex of sensation that increased the tingling along her spine.

Slowly lowering herself from downward dog, she lay flat on her stomach and extended her left leg behind her, hoping the taut muscle stretch would dissipate the strange feeling zinging through her body. She repeated the exercise with her right leg, welcoming the burn.

But the distraction wasn't sufficient. Her concentration slipped further.

Gritting her teeth, she sat up and stretched her legs wide, perpendicular to her body. She aligned her torso to one leg, then the other, then leaned forward on her elbows and slowly raised her pelvis off the floor.

The curse was thick and sharp enough to pierce the cocoon of her music.

Rebel's eyes flew open.

Sensation hit her like a charging bull. The air knocked clean from her lungs, Rebel gaped at the imposing man who sat with one leg hitched over the other and his arms crossed over a wide, firm chest.

Steely grey eyes pinned her in position. Not that she would've been able to move had her life depended on it. Frozen on the floor, she could only stare as the most arresting man she'd ever seen uncoiled himself from his sitting position and stood to a towering, dominating height. His navy three-piece suit was sharp and stylish, and drew attention to broad shoulders, a trim waist and strong thighs, but even without those visual aids, his sheer beauty was potent enough to command her attention.

Her muscles strained, lactic acid building in a body that screamed for relief, but Rebel couldn't heed it.

The man advanced, bringing the scent that had so thoroughly shattered her concentration even closer until it fully encompassed her. There was a vague familiarity about him, like a stranger she'd caught a glimpse of a lifetime ago. But the sensation passed as he drew closer.

Her chest tightened, her lungs struggling to work as he crouched down in front of her and jerked the earbuds from her ears. Flinging the wires to the floor, he leaned forward until every inch of her vision was crowded with him.

'You have exactly three seconds to tell me who the hell you are, and why I shouldn't call Security and have you thrown in jail for lewd conduct and trespassing.'

# CHAPTER TWO

DRACO ANGELIS WASN'T a man overly prone to emotion or volatile impulses. And yet as he stared at the woman before him he wanted to curse again. Loudly and far more filthily than he had in a long time.

He told himself it was because the floor show she'd been giving his male employees for the last fifteen minutes was losing him money with each second her sinuous body undulated. More than that, she was drawing attention to a matter he wanted to keep under wraps by performing said floor show in Nathan Daniels' office. In a business often accused of being shady and underhanded, Draco had striven to keep Angel International above reproach. He'd succeeded beyond his wildest dreams by keeping all his dealings professional, above board and strictly private. None of his clients were permitted to publicise details of their relationship with his company save for a carefully prepared press release at the time of signing.

Draco kept that same stranglehold on his personal life.

But with the sudden disappearance of Nathan Daniels and the suspected reason behind it, Draco knew it was only a matter of time before the whispers grew to wild speculation and brought unwanted attention to both facets of his life.

And this…siren performing moves fit for a certain type of gentlemen's club right here on his CFO's office floor was the last thing he needed.

As to the pull he'd experienced in his body and especially in his groin as he'd watched her… Well, he could deal with the reminder that he was a full-blooded male.

What he wasn't prepared to deal with was her interrupting his—

'Lewd conduct?' A sultry laugh detonated his thoughts, slamming him back to the room and the sensual vision still frozen in position before him. 'I think that's a bit of a stretch, don't you?'

A thick bead of sweat trickled down her earlobe and over her jaw. He tracked it, unable to drag his gaze away as it rolled over her heated skin to disappear between small but lush breasts. He ruthlessly suppressed the growl that rose in his chest and clenched his jaw.

'You think it's a stretch to perform lasciviously in front of a window to the clear view of everyone in my company?'

Her back bowed as she flexed her hips, a smile curving her full lips. 'I wasn't aware what I was doing was so distracting. Do you mind stepping back?'

'Excuse me?' Irritated surprise held him rigid.

'I'm almost done. If I stop now, I'll have to start all over again. Sorry, I'm a little OCD like that. I need room for the last two positions, so if you don't mind...?'

Draco was sure it was pure shock that propelled him to his feet, not the secret need to see her complete her set. All the same, he stepped back, his jaw clenched harder as he folded his arms and stared down at the lithe body sprawled at his feet.

She balanced on her elbows, her torso straightened. Slim muscled legs slowly lifted off the floor, maintaining the perpendicular position for several seconds, before meeting in the middle in a sleek upside-down formation. Draco watched her stomach muscles delicately vibrate as she centred herself, her skin bathed in a sheen of sweat as her toned body achieved the perfect line.

As a former athlete himself, Draco appreciated the discipline it took to hone one's body into the ultimate competitive instrument. And while part of him approved of the level of skill being displayed before him, the greater part was eyeing the delicate, muscled perfection of her body.

And detesting himself for it.

Whoever this woman was, she had no right to be here.

About to step forward and end this nonsense, he halted mid-step as she dropped one leg to the floor behind her. The sexy agility in her body arrested him, drying out every flaying word he'd meant to deliver as he stared.

*Thee mou.*

Anyone would think he hadn't seen a female body before. He'd dated sportswomen at the peak of their careers and slept with more than his share of them. And yet something about this woman drew him as no other had done in a very long time.

That thought sent another bolt of anger through him. Rousing himself, he stepped forward, just as she lowered her other leg and straightened.

She wasn't very tall, only coming up to his chest. But her deep blue eyes sparked with a fire and attitude that made her appear six feet tall. Her chin, pointed and determined, and her mouth, still curved in that sultry, albeit slightly wary smile, made him think thoughts that had no room in this space.

'Now, where were we?' she asked, her voice reminding him of smoky rooms in gentlemen's clubs.

Draco dragged his mind from images of unwanted decadence to a far more appropriate ire. 'We were addressing your unsolicited presence in my building.'

'Ah, yes, you wanted to know who I was?'

'I see you've skilfully avoided my trespass charge.'

'That's because I'm not trespassing. I have a right to be here.'

'I seriously doubt that. Sanctioning half-naked women to perform acrobatics for my employees as part of their busy workday isn't part of my business model.'

'We're talking about my supposed floor show, right?'

She glanced behind her. Catching sight of the group of men staring avidly through the glass from a few offices away, she smiled and waved.

A glowering look from Draco sent his employees dispersing, although a brave buck, Stan Macallister, dared to wave back.

Deciding it was time to bring this farce to an end, Draco strode to the desk of his AWOL CFO and snatched up the phone.

'This is Mr Angelis. Send Security up to Daniels' office. I have an unwanted guest who needs to be removed from the premises. And inform my head of security that I want a report on my desk as to why this breach has happened before the day is out.'

He slammed down the phone with more force than was needed.

'Wow, was that really necessary?'

He turned to find her standing in the same position before the window, her hand on her curvy hips and her head tilted to one side. The loose knot of her silky black hair fell lopsided as she stared at him with one eyebrow raised mockingly.

'I have a client meeting in less than half an hour. I'd throw you out myself but I don't have time to take a shower before then.'

Her expression slipped at the thinly veiled insult. Draco felt childish satisfaction at scoring a direct hit. Absurdly, he'd been off balance since he'd seen her from his office next door. His need for transparency in all things had transmitted to his office layout, and with the open-plan setting and see-through glass windows across the floor he could keep an eye on most of his employees. Although he liked to believe it was unnecessary where his employees were concerned as he'd earned their loyalty, he'd learned the hard way that loyalty came at a cost.

The alternative career he'd had to choose was a cutthroat

one at best. He'd made a few hard bargains along the way to get him where he was.

What he hadn't bargained for today was seeing a decadently curvy woman on display on his CFO's floor. He'd stopped an important call mid-conversation, a move he'd never made before. Now he had an irate, egocentric client waiting for him to call back. And a snarky stranger openly mocking him.

'I hope you don't feel too silly when you find out who I am,' she said in that voice that snagged his senses, made him strain to hear her every word.

'I'm not interested in who you are. My security will furnish me with that information if I need it. What I am interested in is you being escorted off the premises—'

'Okay, this is getting ridiculous. My name is Rebel Daniels, Nathan Daniels' daughter. I'm here to have lunch with my father. I forgot to sign in downstairs so Stan let me in. My dad wasn't here. I assumed he was in a meeting or something, so I thought I'd wait for him. The yoga thing was just to relieve a little bit of stress.'

Several questions stormed through Draco's mind. Was his security so lax that someone could just *forget* to make themselves known downstairs and still make it up here? She was Daniels' daughter? Why was she stressed?

'Your parents named you *Rebel*?' Mildly disconcerted at the least relevant question that had chosen to fall from his lips, he watched a smile twitch at the corners of her mouth.

'Hardly, although my mother did wonder why she hadn't thought of that when I started using it at fifteen.'

Draco waited, wondering at the shadow that crossed her face a moment later. When she continued to stare at him, he pursed his lips. 'So your *real* name is?'

'I thought you weren't interested.' She turned and bent over to pick up her yoga mat.

He forced his gaze from her delectable behind to her bare feet, then away from her altogether when he realised he was even growing fascinated with her peach-painted toenails. 'I'm only interested in you if it helps me locate your father.'

Her head jerked up, the rolled mat held against her body as she frowned at him. 'What do you mean locate him? Isn't he here?'

'Did you have any reason to think he would be?' he countered.

'Of course I did. Why else would I have come here?'

Draco spotted two burly men rushing towards the office. His head of security looked extremely nervous. As he should be. He held up his hand when they reached the door. 'When did you last speak to your father?'

Her gaze darted from the men back to him, a tiny flash of nervousness darkening her eyes. 'Why, what does it matter?'

'Because I would very much like to speak to him too.'

Her eyes widened, again a minuscule motion that he otherwise would've missed had he not been watching her closely. 'So he's not here?' she pressed.

'I think we've established that, Miss Daniels. Now are you going to answer me, or shall I hand you over to them?' He jerked his head at the security men.

She frowned. 'What exactly is going on here? If my father's not here and you want me to leave, I will. There's no need to throw your weight about. And I certainly don't need to be escorted out.'

'But you were in here on your own for over fifteen minutes. Who knows what information you've made yourself privy to?'

'Are you accusing me of *stealing* something?' she snapped.

'Did you?'

'Of course not!'

'I'll leave them to be the judge of that. I'm sure you'll be released in a few hours once the security footage has been analysed, your belongings searched, and your alleged innocence confirmed.' Draco motioned for his men to enter.

His head of security entered, followed by his assistant. Draco ignored their contrite expressions. 'Take Miss Daniels' bag—'

'You can't be serious!'

'And the yoga mat. Make sure she's not in possession of anything that doesn't belong to her—'

'Okay, fine. I'll answer your damn questions.'

The men paused.

Draco shook his head. 'Take them. Leave her shoes. I'll let you know when I'm finished with her.'

She sent him a look filled with pure vitriol and her fingers clenched around the yoga mat as the younger guard stepped towards her. Eyes flashing blue fire, she released her hold on it, slipped her feet into her knee-high boots and propped her hands on her hips.

'Shall we get this ludicrous inquisition over with?'

Sparks virtually flew off her. In another time, Draco would've enjoyed stoking that fire just to see how high her conflagration burned. It'd been far too long since any emotion besides bitterness, guilt and the rigid control he'd put in place ruled his life. Anything beyond that was a luxury he could ill afford.

It was the same control that dictated he take hold of this situation before it blew up in his face. He'd allowed his suspicions about Nathan Daniels to go unquestioned for far too long as it was.

He straightened. 'Come with me.'

'Where are we going?' the question was snapped back immediately.

'My office.'

'Uh…sir?'

He turned to his security chief.

'We need the lady's full name in order to log her into the system.'

Draco raised an eyebrow at her.

Her mouth pursed, bringing his reluctant attention back to her plump lips.

'It's…my name is Arabella Daniels,' she muttered reluctantly.

It took less than a second for Draco to place her. Arabella Daniels had once been a promising cross-country skier until she'd abruptly changed disciplines to become a ski jumper. Although she'd remained in the top ten for the last few years, the twenty-five-year-old woman had never risen above fifth in competitions. Probably due to her off-piste antics.

His mild shock subsided into a heavy dose of distaste, but he kept his expression neutral as he dismissed his men and strode to his office.

He waited until she entered, then activated the privacy setting on his windows. Once the glass was frosted, he perched at the edge of his desk and watched her pace warily in front of him. The burn in his groin as he followed her lissom figure made him kick out a chair.

'Sit down.'

'No, thanks. I thought you had an important meeting? Or was that just a fib rolled up as an insult?'

'It wasn't a lie. But the party concerned will understand. I tend to surround myself with reasonable, rational individuals.'

She paused in her pacing, her eyes narrowing. 'Is that supposed to be some sort of dig?'

'I know who you are, Miss Daniels.'

'Well, since I told you my name, I should hope so. I wouldn't like to think you were thick or anything, seeing as you seem to be the head honcho in this glass playhouse.'

'So the rumours are true.'

'What rumours?' she asked, her expression growing more wary.

'You take pride in being deliberately offensive and exhibiting wild behaviour.'

'And you don't seem to like being told things the way

they are. In fact your actions reek of more than a touch of melodrama. Why is that? Are you overcompensating for something?' Her gaze conducted what started off as a mocking perusal. But a trace of heat flared up her cheeks when her eyes dropped below his belt.

When her gaze darted away, Draco allowed himself a stiff smile. 'I've never needed to overcompensate for anything in my life, Miss Daniels. If I had time to waste and felt so inclined, I'd give you a demonstration.'

'You assume that *I* have the time to stand around listening to your rubbish. Keep your veiled threats, ask me what you want to know and let us both get on with our lives.'

'You seem a little off balance. Is it because you feel out of your depth?' he drawled.

She jerked the hair band from her hair. Thick, silky jet waves fell over her shoulders and down her back before she started combing her fingers through the tresses.

'Why would I feel like that? Just because you're being disgustingly unreasonable—'

'Or is it because you don't find me as gullible as you do the men you like to associate with?'

'I don't know what you think you know about me, but if these absurd questions are why you brought me in here—'

'You like to dominate your men, do you not?'

She tossed her head. 'Only when they beg me to. Do you want me to dominate you? I'm fresh out of horse whips but I'm sure I can get inventive with a pair of boot laces.'

His gaze dropped to her knee-high boots. 'I'm sure you can, in the right circumstances, but I'll pass.'

She wrinkled her nose and Draco's temperature rose, along with his irritation. 'Why? Because you always wait for the right circumstances? How boring. Giving in to your impulses might just surprise you.'

Draco bared his teeth in a smile that had been described by the tabloids as his dragon smile. He knew its effect well enough to know it'd made its mark when her agitation escalated.

'I find that people like you easily confuse the reckless with the impulsive. Personally, I find the wait builds the anticipation.'

Her gaze held his for one bold heartbeat, then she glanced away. Although she engrossed herself in his office decor, Draco was certain she wasn't as bored with him as she pretended to be. The colour in her cheeks was more pronounced and the pulse beating at her throat had increased. His own blood thickened as he followed her figure. He assured himself, now he knew who she truly was, this mild fascination with her would swiftly abate.

'Well, as interesting as this all is, I'm one hundred per cent sure you know very little about me. And I have to insist you either get on with your ever-so-important questioning, or tell your guards to return my things.'

'You're attempting to compete in the Verbier Ski Championships this year. Shouldn't you be training instead of making an exhibition of yourself and taking extended lunches?'

She inhaled sharply and turned towards him, all pretence at being bored vanishing from her expression. 'You know who I am?'

'I make it my business to know people like you.'

'What do you mean, people like me?'

'Reckless athletes, who try to buy their way into the big leagues.'

She stalked to where he leaned against his desk, her whole body bristling with anger. 'How dare you? That's a ridiculous and totally unfounded allegation.'

'I know enough. The rest I don't intend to bother myself with.'

Her hands clenched. 'Just who the hell do you think you are?'

'I'm the man who intends to make sure all the sponsors

you've been chasing the last month drop you from their books. People like you paint talented and dedicated sportsmen and women in a bad light, not to mention your reckless behaviour on and off the ski slopes needs to be stopped once and for all. You have three measly sponsors left, who probably, mistakenly, think your notoriety will bring their products the attention they crave. Perhaps I'll let you keep them.'

Her eyes had been widening with each condemnation. Slowly, shock replaced her anger. And this time, when she looked around at the trophies and pictures that decorated his office, her interest was genuine.

Draco knew the moment the penny dropped.

Her lustrous hair flew as she whirled back to him. 'You're Draco, the super-agent.'

'I'm Draco Angelis, yes.'

She swallowed. 'You represent Rex Glow.'

'Your former sponsors? Yes.'

She inhaled sharply, but the next question wasn't what Draco had expected it to be. 'And my father *works* for you?'

'You're surprised by that.'

A frown clamped her brows. 'Well…yes, to be honest.'

'Why?' he fired back, his need to probe the reason behind Nathan Daniels' disappearance returning.

'Because…' She hesitated, a trace of pained bleakness flitting over her features. 'Let's just say the world of competitive sports isn't his first love.'

He folded his arms, alarm bells clanging loudly. 'Well, he was my chief financial officer up until two weeks ago, when he seemed to fall off the face of the earth.'

'And you're looking for him because…?'

'There's a small matter of a half a million pounds that seems to have evaporated from my company's accounts. I would very much like to speak to him about that,' Draco replied, his eyes narrowing at the mixture of guilt and trepidation that froze on her face.

# CHAPTER THREE

REBEL KNEW SHE'D given herself away a split second before Draco straightened to his imposing six-foot-plus height and took the single step that brought him to within a whisper of where she stood. His broad shoulders and the cloak of power draped around him eclipsed her every thought and action. But even without them, the expression on his face as he stared down at her dried the words that rose to her lips.

This man was responsible for Rex Glow dropping her. While a significant part of her was enraged by the blatant admission, the greater part of her was shocked by the other information he'd imparted.

He was her father's boss. A father who, for all intents and purposes, had disappeared. Along with the uncomfortably *exact* amount of money that had landed in her bank account. The shock of it rendered her attempt to keep a neutral expression hopelessly futile.

'Tell me where your father is,' he pressed.

In that moment, Rebel understood why this man was named The Dragon. His steely grey eyes were cold and deadly enough to freeze the Sahara. And yet his nostrils flared with white-hot anger that promised volatile, annihilating fire.

'I…I don't know where he is.'

Black eyebrows clamped darker. 'You expect me to believe that?'

'You can believe what you want. It's the truth.'

'You admitted to having been in touch with him lately. And you came here to meet him, did you not?'

'We spoke briefly on the phone a couple of days ago. Lunch was mentioned, and I thought I'd surprise him today...' She trailed off, unwilling to elaborate that she'd done most of the talking, while her father had remained stonily monosyllabic. Rebel struggled to hide the hurt that lanced her heart from knowing her father would've probably rejected any firm plans had he known she'd intended to come here today.

'I urge you to come clean now, Miss Daniels, before things get worse for you and your father,' Draco Angelis threatened.

The first tendrils of fear clawed up her spine. 'If you must know, we didn't make any firm plans. It was a spur-of-the-moment decision to stop by and see if he was free for lunch. I haven't seen him in a while and I thought—'

'How long is *a while*?'

'That's between my father and me, and none of your business.'

Firm, sinfully sensual lips pursed. 'You don't think my CFO's sudden disappearance and you turning up unannounced in my building is any of my business?'

'So he's taken a brief vacation. So what?' she speculated wildly, her unease growing as suspicion mounted in Draco's eyes.

'Considering he hasn't taken one in the five years he's worked for me, you'll pardon me if I find his sudden need for one, without speaking to me first, more than a little suspect. Besides, we have a procedure for absences. My employees don't make a habit of just not turning up to work when the mood takes them.'

'Because that would guarantee them an on-the-spot sacking?'

'Perhaps not on the spot. I would demand an explanation first before the sacking ensued.'

Rebel forced an eye roll, which was far from the nonchalance she tried to project. 'So you're not just a dragon to work for, you're an ogre as well? Congratulations.'

Sharp grey eyes, surrounded by the most lush eyelashes

she'd ever seen on a man, lasered her. 'You find this subject amusing?'

Anger surged through her. 'About as amusing as discovering that you seem to have a personal vendetta against me when we've never even met before.'

His face tightened, his expression growing even more formidable. 'We didn't need to meet before I knew exactly what sort of person you are. Your antics in the last half an hour have only confirmed it.'

'Really? Would you care to share it with me or should I take a few wild guesses?'

'You've barely scraped through into ski finals for the last few years because your work ethic is average at best. You're more concerned with headlining in the tabloids with your extracurricular activities than putting in the hard work to secure yourself a position in the championships.'

She swallowed hard before her temper got the better of her. 'I'll have you know I was an under-twenty-one record holder for two years.'

'But you haven't placed higher than fifth in the last six years. Your position in the rankings has fallen in direct proportion to the rise of your notoriety. It doesn't take a maths genius to work out where your true interests lie. Which is why I wonder why you even bother.'

Anger gave way to bewildered hurt, but Rebel locked in her emotions, determined not to show him how his words affected her. 'I'm still at a loss as to how all of this or anything in my *private* life concerns you.'

'If it concerns my client, it concerns me. Besides, it's only a matter of time before your reckless actions have a direct impact on another athlete,' he retorted pithily, his gaze boring harder into her, condemnation stamped in every pore.

Draco Angelis' reaction was too strong for Rebel to believe his motivation stemmed from concern for his client alone. But she was too busy struggling not to react to the accusation of recklessness to pay it much heed.

The only thing Rebel wanted was to leave his office and his oppressive presence. She needed the head space to ponder exactly what her father was up to. And whether the money he'd sent her was indeed embezzled funds as her every instinct shrieked it was. The enormity of what that would mean struck cold dread inside her.

'I think we're done here, Mr Angelis. Rex Glow is no longer my sponsor, so I don't have to listen to you or your groundless accusations about my life. If you choose to believe whatever nonsense you read in the papers, then that's your problem, not mine.'

He made no move to stop her as she headed for the door. She knew why the moment she tried to pull it open and found it unyielding.

'Open this door now.'

Cold steel eyes pinned her in place. 'I'm not finished with you.'

'But I am with you,' she replied, a vein of panic rising in her belly. She rattled the door harder, but the reinforced glass didn't budge an inch.

'You can leave once you tell me where your father is hiding.'

She whirled at the hard demand. He was less than a foot from her, his stance even more imposing than before. His scent attacked her senses a second later, once again cutting a dangerous swathe through her thought processes.

The man wasn't just a dangerous dragon. He was a precariously beautiful creature, his face and body an alluring, breathtaking combination designed to trap helpless prey.

Not that she was one!

'Do you jump to conclusions about every single subject or are my father and I being singled out for special treatment?'

'You think I want my company exposed to the fact that my CFO has embezzled from me?'

Renewed panic gripped her insides. 'Where's your proof that he has?'

'The evidence isn't concrete yet, but what I've found so far doesn't look good. It's only a matter of time before we trace where the funds ended up. His not answering my calls or emails doesn't exactly look promising.'

'What…what would you tell him if he answered?'

Draco's narrowed eyes scoured her face. 'He's served me well for five years. I'd be prepared to listen to his explanations.'

'Before throwing the book at him?'

'You think I should let him go scot-free if he's guilty?'

Her heart lurched. 'Since we haven't established that he's done anything wrong, I think this is a moot point.'

'Sadly, your poker face isn't as flawless as you think. You know where he is. Tell me now and I'll consider not pressing full charges.'

'I don't know where he is. I swear,' Rebel answered.

Draco took the last step that separated them and grabbed her bare arm. The hand still clutching the door handle dropped as raw electricity raced across her skin. Intense tingling tightened her every cell, straining towards the point of contact with a severity that stole her breath. Her lips parted as she fought to get air into her lungs.

Above her, Draco inhaled sharply. The expression on his face reflected her bewilderment for a second before the cold façade slid back into place.

'You may not know where he is, but you know something. I suggest you come clean now.' He repeated his earlier threat.

Rebel shook her head. If her father had truly embezzled the money he'd deposited in her account from the Angel International Group, there was no way she could get it back. And right now, Rebel couldn't be sure which was worse—confessing her suspicion of her father's guilt, or informing Draco Angelis that she had used the funds to secure her place in the Verbier tournament. From Draco's censorious reaction to her as an athlete, Rebel knew he wouldn't hesitate to condemn her as an accessory to the crime and have her thrown in jail.

'Arabella, this is your last chance.'

The sound of her name on his lips sent shafts of disconcerting fire through her belly. The sensation was so powerful it weakened her knees, and the secret place between her legs was dampening with each second his hand remained on her.

God, what was wrong with her? She'd heard her girlfriends confess to growing wobbly at the knees when some hot guy glanced their way at a nightclub. She'd secretly rolled her eyes at that implausible statement, knowing she'd never be one of those women. The shocking sensation ramming through her right now filled her with horror and more than a touch of anger.

She parted her lips, but Draco shook his head, his other hand rising to clamp her other arm.

'Think carefully before you speak.'

She pulled in a deep, sustaining breath. 'No,' she stated firmly.

'Just so we're clear, to what exactly are you saying no?' he breathed softly, dangerously.

Rebel ignored the warm breath washing over her face and raised her chin. 'To answering any more of your stupid accusations. To being kept prisoner in this office. To you having your hands on me. No to everything. Now, let me go before I scream this place down.'

'Scream all you want. This room is soundproof.'

'How very convenient. Do you do this a lot, then?' she taunted.

'Do what?' he sliced at her.

'Drag women in here and hold them against their will?'

A muted curse in a language she didn't understand

spilled from his lips. 'No woman has been in here who didn't want to be.'

The images his words conjured up jarred her into squirming before she forced her muscles to lock tight. 'So you admit to seducing women in your office during the workday?'

A chilled smile parted his lips. 'You assume that I do the seducing.'

'So women not only stage floor shows in your offices, they also seduce you behind closed doors into the bargain. Your poor thing. How on earth do you get any work done?'

'You have a reckless, smart mouth, Arabella.'

Another zing went through her, but she fought it tooth and nail. 'Along with a smart brain. So if you think anything's going to happen here other than me walking out the door in the next minute, think again.'

'You set too high a premium on yourself, I think.'

'Ah, so if I were to strip right here right now, you'd turn me down?'

'You won't. You like to pretend otherwise, but I'm willing to bet, deep down, you're less Lady Chatterley and more Miss Prude.'

The droll observation brought heat to her cheeks. Dear God, he was making her blush *again*?

'Well, sadly for you, you'll never find out.'

'I will. If I wish it, you'll get your chance to strip for me in the very near future. At a time and place of my choosing when I know we won't be interrupted in any way.'

'Wow, you must tell me where you acquired your crystal balls. I'm running out of ideas for Christmas presents.'

*Dear Lord. Was she truly standing in front of him, discussing his balls?*

He freed one arm. Rebel was about to exhale with relief, but her breathing stuttered as he curled his long fingers over her nape and tilted her chin with his thumb. She'd never imagined the skin along her jaw was sensitive until experiencing Draco Angelis' branding touch. Now every nerve in her body screeched as her heart raced and her blood heated.

His head lowered a fraction and his gaze dropped to her lips. He was about to kiss her. And she couldn't move.

Rebel grew frantically aware of every desperate breath that passed between her lips, her own gaze unable to shift from the mouth drawing ever closer to hers.

'I don't need crystal balls. My human ones are more than adequate to deal with challenges from the opposite sex. But we're straying from the subject. Tell me what you know, Arabella.' Again that smile peeled back a layer of her skin and exposed her to sensations as alien as a distant galaxy.

'For the last time, take your hands off me. I don't know where my father—'

The buzz of an intercom from his desk froze her words. Draco tensed, the flex of his jaw exhibiting his displeasure at the interruption.

'Mr Angelis, I'm so sorry to disturb you, but I have Olivio Nardozzi on the line again. He refuses to leave a message or be put on hold. He says you promised to call him back fifteen minutes ago.'

He raised his head, but he didn't let her go. Nor did his gaze move from her lips as he answered, 'Tell Olivio I'll speak to him in two minutes. Tell him he can either hold or wait for my call.'

'Yes, Mr Angelis.'

The intercom clicked and silence once more engulfed them. Draco didn't seem in a hurry to speak, or do anything but hold her prisoner.

Rebel knew she had to move, but for the life of her she couldn't get her legs to work. So she employed her best defence. 'Another one of your angelic, perfectly reasonable, *high-maintenance* clients?' she mocked.

With a slow, deliberate movement, his thumb rose from her chin to pass lazily over her lower lip. 'There will come a time when this delectable mouth will get you into trouble you won't be able to escape from,' he drawled in a low, dark voice that resonated deep within her.

'Tick tock, Mr Angelis.'

His grip firmed, the fire branding her deeper. Then he released her with an abrupt move that spoke of barely leashed emotion. Before she could escape, he caged her in by placing his hands on the glass door either side of her.

'You have until six o'clock tonight to tell me what you know about my money. Trust me, you don't want me to come after you.'

She wanted to dare him to do his worst, but Rebel bit her tongue. Draco Angelis had already demonstrated that he had the power to strip her sponsors from her with nothing more than a hatred of her vivacity. Sure, she'd taken a few risks on the ski slope that had earned her a name in the sport. But they'd all been carefully calculated and had taken into account the injury she'd sustained when she was twenty-two. Without those risks, she'd have fallen even further down the rankings and lost all her sponsorship long before now.

As much as she wanted to tell Draco to take a running jump, if she wanted to get to the bottom of her father's actions, or have a last chance at securing the Verbier championship and laying a few ghosts to rest, she needed to retreat and regroup.

A tug on her Lycra training bottoms drew her thoughts away from her mother and her errant father. She gasped as Draco slid a business card into her waistband. The backs of his fingers brushed her skin and her muscles jumped at the contact.

Before she could form an effective comeback to his audacious action he stepped back. A moment later the frosty glass cleared and a click released the door.

'I assume I'm free to go now?'

He lifted the phone and punched in a series of numbers. 'Provided you're not held by my security, then yes, you may leave. But we both know you're guilty of something, Arabella. Make the wise choice and use my private number. I guarantee you won't like the consequences if you don't.' He sat down behind his desk. The infinitesimal twitch of his chair away from her was as definitive a dismissal as any as he spoke into the phone, 'Olivio, my apologies for keeping you waiting. I hope you're chomping at the bit to speak to me because you've given further consideration to my offer?' His voice rang with charming familiarity, not at all like the ire he'd demonstrated towards her.

Rebel could barely recall stumbling from Draco's office and summoning the lift that raced her back down to the ground floor. She assumed she was free to leave when the Angel head of security met her on the ground floor with her belongings. Thankful that she wouldn't be required to answer any more questions, Rebel took her bag and yoga mat and hurried out into the weak February sunshine.

The light breeze that whispered over her skin brought a little clarity, but her senses were too focused on the card burning against her skin, and the grave certainty that the money she'd used to secure her place in the Verbier tournament was indeed money stolen from a man who seemed to have the lowest, blackest opinion of her, to feel the cold.

Plucking the card out of her waistband, she stared at the black and gold inscription and the private number etched into it.

Rebel wanted to rip it into a dozen pieces and scatter them to the four winds. But deep in her heart she recognised the foolhardiness of doing so.

She might not understand why her father had chosen to help himself to money that didn't belong to him and then pass it on to her. Their last few rows had been awful enough for her to imagine he was done with her as long as she chose to keep competing. For him to have followed her career closely enough to know when she needed help at once lifted her heart and plunged it into despair. Not in a million years would she have wanted him to help in this way.

Jerkily, she searched for her phone and dialled as she hurried away from Draco's building. The moment the line connected, she rushed to speak. 'Contessa, have the cheques we paid out to the tournament organisers cleared?'

Her manager snorted. 'Well, hello to you too. And the answer to your question is yes, the cheques cleared this morning, so did the money we paid for your travel, accommodation and equipment. We only need an extra fifteen thousand for incidentals, but I'm sure your remaining sponsors will front you that. I was going to pop round to your flat tonight with a bottle of champagne to celebrate. I know you don't like to drink during training, but I thought a sip or two wouldn't hurt...' Her voice trailed off for a moment. 'Rebel? Is something wrong?'

Rebel exhaled shakily, her vision hazing as she fought panic. 'And there's no way we can get any of it back?'

'*Get it back?* Why would we want to do that?' her manager demanded, her voice rising.

'I...I just...it doesn't matter.'

'Obviously it does. Tell me what's happened.'

Unwilling to drag Contessa into her problems until she confirmed the depth of the trouble she was in, she forced lightness into her voice. 'Ignore me. Just last-minute nerves. You can come over, but can we give the champagne a miss, though?'

'Of course...are you sure you're okay?' the older woman pressed.

'I'm sure. Talk to you later.'

She hung up and immediately dialled her father's number, already suspecting it wouldn't go through. When the mechanical voice urged her to leave a message, Rebel cleared her throat. 'Dad, it's me...again.' She paused, a new fear chilling her heart. Draco Angelis wasn't above having her father's phone traced. Until she got answers for herself, Rebel didn't want to lead the man who made her spine tingle with dread and other unwanted emotions straight to her father. 'Call me. Please. I need to talk to you.'

Feeling helpless for the first time in a very long time, she hung up. Plugging her earphones in, she ramped up the volume and hurried to the Tube, all the while willing her focus away from the card she'd tucked back into her waistband, hoping against hope she wouldn't be forced to use it.

# CHAPTER FOUR

DRACO READ THE bullet points in the report for the second time and closed the file. He spared a thought as to why his CFO hadn't bothered to cover his tracks, then dismissed the useless thought. The *why* didn't matter.

The inescapable fact was that a crime had been committed. By Daniels and his daughter.

Draco didn't doubt for a second that she was neck deep in this theft. Her guilt had been written all over her face, despite her trying hard to hide it. Her racing pulse had condemned her just as definitely, no matter how much her smart mouth had tried to distract him.

A muscle ticced in his jaw as he remembered the velvet softness of that mouth…the smoothness of her skin. Arabella Daniels didn't use just her mouth to distract. She used her whole body. The need to remind *his* body hours later of that potent tactic irritated Draco as his car raced through the wet, lamplit streets towards the Chelsea address his investigators had supplied him with.

Another bout of irritation welled inside him.

He'd known Arabella wouldn't honour the deadline he'd given her. Six o'clock had come and gone three hours ago, and, despite the conclusive, almost cynical evidence of theft he held in his hands, the daughter of his CFO had remained silent.

Closing the electronic file, he opened a thick manila envelope that held a completely different set of problems. While Draco was satisfied that months of hard work were poised on the edge of finally reaping rewards, he couldn't believe the seemingly inescapable strings Olivio Nardozzi had attached to the contract in his hand.

But he hadn't come this far to lose.

Carla Nardozzi, champion figure skater, number one in the world, was a prize every sports agent wanted. Hardworking, charismatic, almost virginally shy, she would be the jewel in his agency's crown…if her father weren't leveraging an unthinkable condition to signing his daughter with the Angel International Group—

'Sir, we're here,' his driver interrupted his thoughts.

Draco alighted from the car and stared at the two-storey Victorian façade. While he hadn't been surprised Arabella lived in Chelsea, he'd expected her to inhabit a glitzy condominium, not a homey dwelling on a leafy suburban street. Mounting the shallow steps to the door, he pressed her intercom.

The door released half a minute later. Draco told himself he didn't care if she didn't bother about her security, but by the time he arrived in front of an open doorway on the first floor irritation had given way to anger.

Loud music pumped from what seemed like a hundred speakers, although he couldn't immediately see them as he went down a short hallway and arrived in a sizeable living room painted snow-white, and decorated with splashes of purple and pink.

He didn't have time to be offended by the jarring decor because he was once again confronted by a scantily clad Arabella Daniels, who didn't bother to look up as he walked into the room.

Draco dragged his gaze from her cross-legged figure enough to take in the fact that she was packing for a long trip. Escaping with the proceeds of her ill-gotten gains, perhaps?

He gritted his jaw and waited.

A moment later her head snapped up. Blue eyes met his, widened, before her mouth dropped open. 'You're not Contessa,' she shouted above the pumping rock music.

'No, I am not.'

Her eyes darted from him to the darkened hallway and back again. She set aside the sleek, specialist, lightweight skis that Draco knew cost several thousand pounds, and rose lithely to her feet. 'You…I wasn't expecting…what are you doing here?'

'Do you always answer your door without checking to see who you're letting in?' he bit out.

She shrugged. 'I thought you were Contessa, my manager. She's the only one who knows where—' She stopped and waved her hand. 'Let's get back to *my* question. What are *you* doing here?'

'If you insist on playing this game, I'll give you one guess, *after* you turn that racket off.'

Her pointed chin tilted and she folded her bare arms. 'No. If you don't like my taste in music, feel free to reuse the front door.'

Stopping his gaze from conducting a full scrutiny of her body, clad in vest top and hot pants, Draco stalked to the entertainment system set on top of an artsy-looking vanity unit and stabbed the off button.

'Hey, you can't do that!'

He turned and faced her, willing himself not to react to the mingled scent of peach shampoo and delicate perfume that infused his senses now his eardrums weren't being shredded.

'Did you forget the time, Arabella? I'm willing to give you the benefit of the doubt on the off-chance that my deadline escaped your notice because you don't possess a watch?'

Her frowning gaze slid from the silent music system to his face. Her arms tightened and her stare grew bolder. 'I have a watch. Several, in fact. I know exactly what the time is.'

The cold blaze of anger chilled his insides. He welcomed it far more than he welcomed the lick of fire that had flamed in his groin at the sight of her bare, shapely legs. 'I can only conclude, then, that you thought my last words to you were a joke?'

She made a humming, almost accommodating sound under her breath. 'Not quite. You don't seem the joking type. I don't imagine you'd appreciate a joke if it reared up and bit you hard.'

'So that's how you live your life? On the edge of reckless jokes?'

She shrugged. 'You know what they say…if you're not living on the edge, you're taking up too much room.'

The urge to grab her, drag her close, just as he'd done in his office, assailed him. He stabbed his hands deep into his pockets to curb the impulse. Arabella Daniels took pleasure in flaunting her risqué behaviour. Draco wasn't here to be riled. He was here to do the riling. To let her know she wouldn't be getting away with stealing from him.

'But if you insist on a definition,' she continued, 'I'd say I considered your words more of a suggestion…perhaps an invitation? As you can see, I opted to reject both.'

Draco drew in a breath, unable to accept that anyone could have so very little self-preservation. Back in his office, he'd considered her careless attitude a front, but now he wasn't so sure. But then why was he surprised? He knew first-hand the sort of person he was dealing with. Wasn't such a creature the same one responsible for reducing his sister's dreams to dust? He'd trusted his precious Maria's well-being and burgeoning talent to someone he'd thought would treasure and harness them. Instead, his sister's life had been irrevocably destroyed.

The rock of guilt and bitterness that resided in his gut pressed hard and punishing. He'd taken his eye off the ball, relentlessly pursued his own dreams, and his sister had suffered for it. Continued to suffer for it. Draco absorbed the expanding pain he'd become used to bearing. He was grateful for it, in fact. The reminder of the past was as timely as it was bracing.

He looked past her to the suitcases, clothing and equipment strewn on the living-room floor. 'Going somewhere?'

'Yes, as a matter of fact,' she replied. 'And you're interrupting my packing, so…'

Draco sauntered forward, his gaze narrowing on the two skis already wrapped in protective binding and the third one that she'd been wrapping when he walked in. 'Your equipment looks new. Expensive. Have you come into a windfall perhaps?' he enquired.

She tensed. 'It's none of your—'

He slashed his hand through the air. 'Enough. I have irrefutable evidence that every single penny your father misappropriated ended up in *your* bank account. Whatever his motives were for taking the money, he didn't seem inclined to cover his tracks. I've already given you enough time to come clean, but it looks like you prefer to wallow in lies and snarky banter. My time is valuable, Miss Daniels. I refuse to waste any more discussing your guilt. Now, are you prepared to take this seriously or shall I cut my losses and let you explain to the authorities how you came to be in possession of half a million pounds belonging to me?' He took his phone out of his pocket and gripped it, fingers poised over the buttons.

Her arms dropped from their belligerent position. As he'd spoken she'd grown paler, but there was still more than enough fight in her eyes for Draco not to be under the misconception that she'd seen the light of true contrition. 'I wasn't lying. I don't know where my father is, and I didn't have anything to do with the taking of the money.' Her brows clouded. 'Are you sure this isn't just some misunderstanding?'

He bared his teeth, cold amusement making him shake his head. 'I'm not in the habit of *misunderstanding* the whereabouts of my company's funds.'

She paled further. 'I told you, I don't know where my father is.'

'Have you tried calling him?' he fired back.

'Several times.' Her fingers spiked into her loose hair, and for the first time Draco witnessed her undiluted distress. Satisfaction lanced through him. He was finally getting through to her. Herding her into a position where she couldn't fail to see that he wouldn't be swayed from seeking restitution. 'He hasn't answered my calls.' The tiny note of bewilderment in her voice suggested she wasn't lying.

'Be that as it may, the funds ended up in your bank account.'

Her full lips firmed for several moments before she nodded. 'Yes.'

He exhaled. 'So, are you willing to answer my questions now?'

She nodded again.

'The championships don't start for several weeks. The training grounds in Verbier won't be open for another month. So where were you going?'

'I have a friend with a chalet in Chamonix. I was going to stay there while I train.'

'You mean you were fleeing the country with your ill-gotten gains?' he sneered. 'Perhaps meet up with your father and celebrate getting one over on me?'

She flinched. 'No.'

'Just…no? You're not going elaborate?'

'What more is there to say? You say you have evidence that the money ended up in my account. Will you believe me if I say I didn't know it was coming in the first place? That when it arrived I tried to return it?'

He lifted a brow before staring at the expensive items on the floor. 'Really?'

'Look, I know what you're thinking—'

'I seriously doubt that. Picking up the phone and instructing your bank to return the funds was too much effort, but spending it wasn't?'

'I didn't spend it. Not immediately.'

He placed the phone back in his pocket and stared at her until her gaze dropped. 'I'm sure you're going to explain that.'

'The money arrived after Rex Glow and the rest of my sponsors started dropping like flies, thanks to you, I'm guessing.' Her white-hot glare threatened to thaw the edges of his icy anger. 'My father must have realised what you were doing…' she paused…but it was already too late.

'So you're saying your father not only took my money, he also breached my company's confidential secrets?' He couldn't stop the growl that accompanied the question.

'No! I don't know.'

'You keep saying that, and yet all signs point to you hiding something.'

Her mouth worked for several seconds, before she blew out a breath. 'Fine, if you must know, I hadn't spoken to my father in years before I heard from him two weeks ago.'

He tensed. 'Why not?'

'*That* is definitely none of your business,' she snapped, her fingers spearing into her hair again and tossing the heavy tresses over her shoulder. 'But I did try to find out about the money the few times we spoke afterwards. He assured me there were no strings attached. That it was mine to use. And when a few more sponsors dropped me…'

'You went ahead and used it, without a single thought as to its true source?'

'You might automatically suspect everyone you meet to have nefarious motives, but the father I knew before we… lost touch was hard-working and *honest*. I don't know what you did for him to—'

'Excuse me?' Her audacity stunned him. 'Are you trying to wheedle your way into somehow blaming me for this?'

'My father isn't here to account for what's happened, is he?'

'No,' Draco muttered, a daring solution to the conundrum he'd been toying with taking root and firming in his mind. 'He's not. But you are.'

Her eyes widened. 'What's that supposed to mean?'

He stared into the clear depths, unable to pull his gaze away. 'It means the sins of the father will have to be paid for by the daughter. Especially when she's turned out to be a direct beneficiary.'

'Right. Hold that thought for a second.' She turned and walked to the sound system. She toyed with a few buttons before pressing one. About to warn her against restarting the ear-bleeding music when they weren't finished talking, Draco stopped when low, sultry, Middle Eastern fusion music flowed into the room. He stared, his gaze compelled by the sinuous movement of her body as she returned to where he stood. 'I'm afraid I'm not interested in whatever plans you've concocted, Mr Angelis.'

His fists balled harder in his pockets. 'By all means refuse if you feel you're in a position to. I'll bring myself to wait.'

Her mouth curved in a ghost of a smile. 'No need to wait. I have a plan in mind for how you can get your money back.'

Not what he'd been expecting. Or what his new plan entailed. But… 'I'm listening.'

'My manager has received a request for me to star in a reality TV show after the championships are over. I wasn't going to accept, but, since I now have no choice, I'll hand over the proceeds from the gig to you—'

'No.' The word shot out of him with a brevity that rocked him.

She blinked. 'Umm…what?'

'I said no.'

'I heard you. I just don't understand why you'd refuse, seeing as it's my life and I can do what I want with it. Also, I thought all this posturing and threatening was so you'd get your money back?'

'Not in three months' time. And not after you'd whored yourself in front of a camera to repay me.'

She inhaled sharply. 'You did not just say what I think you said.'

'Isn't that what it amounts to? You opening your life to intense scrutiny until every dirty scumbag out there knows what brand of toothpaste you use and what you wear to bed at night?'

'It isn't that type of show—'

'They are all *that type of show*. If you think otherwise, you're naive as well as stupid.'

'And you're an arrogant ass, who's under the illusion he can dictate to me. I don't doubt that you wield a lot of power in the sports world.' She laughed self-mockingly. 'You've already shown you can strip me of my sponsors, although I'm still not completely sure why, but I'm damned if I'm going to give you power over my personal life. You don't agree to my proposal, then fine, have me thrown in jail. Although how that gets you back your money is beyond me.'

Draco looked down at her, a small part of him unwillingly intrigued by her relentless fire. It spoke to a part of his nature that wasn't relevant any longer. These days he harnessed his cold passion to controlling his empire. And to ensuring Maria wanted for nothing. Any other emotion was superfluous.

The reminder of his sister brought him back to reality.

'You're bluffing. People like you love the good life too much to bravely accept a jail term, but before you deny it, tell me, are you willing to risk your father going to prison for his crimes?'

She froze, her eyes widening. 'My father? I thought you said *I* would repay the money?'

'That doesn't absolve him of wrongdoing. My company is being audited at the end of the month. Regardless of who repays the funds after that, the crime will be discovered.'

'But…I can't pay back half a million pounds by then,' she blurted.

'I know,' he replied with more than a drawl of satisfaction.

The shadow he'd glimpsed earlier settled over her face, her eyes darkening as she stared at him. 'You have the power to stop this. If you want to. That's what you've been hinting at all along, isn't it?'

'That depends on whether you're prepared to meet my demands.'

She shook her head. 'If you expect me to pull out of the championship, then the answer's no.'

'You want to compete that badly?'

She bit her bottom lip, then released it. Her mouth trembled slightly before she exhaled. 'Yes.'

Draco wasn't aware his hands had left his pockets until they cupped her shoulders. Delicate bones and soft, silky skin registered along his senses, even as he spoke. 'Are you willing to can the bravado and listen to me for five minutes?'

'If you insist.'

He drew her closer. He told himself it was because he needed her close so she didn't misunderstand what he planned to say to her. 'I insist.'

Her gaze dropped to his mouth for a moment before sliding away. 'Fine. I have training at five in the morning, so if you don't mind, can we just get on with it, Mr Angelis?'

'Draco.'

Her eyes flew back to his. 'What?'

'For what I have in mind, you'll need to start calling me by my first name. Try it.'

'Umm…no—'

He slid a finger beneath her chin to hold her steady. 'Say my name, Arabella.'

Her nose wrinkled. 'I prefer Rebel.'

'I think we've established that what you prefer is low on

my priority list. I will call you Arabella. And you will say my name, without the snark or the attitude.'

'Fine… Draco.'

His fingers tightened. 'Once more, with feeling.'

'This is *truly* absurd… *Draco*.'

The sultry decadence of his name on her lips arrowed straight through his rigid control, reminding him unequivocally that his libido was alive and well. For a hot second, Draco spied himself from the other side of the room, observing the unfolding scene with growing astonishment.

Was he really contemplating this insane course of action?

Then he reminded himself why he was doing this.

For Maria. For the sister he'd let down so severely. For the sister whose eyes filled with pain each time she looked at him, and yet was determined to rise above bitterness. To *forgive*.

Draco hadn't quite mastered that particular technique. Wasn't sure he wanted to. Bitterness and pain were his correct penance for letting his sister down, for ruining a life that had once held so much unbridled potential.

If he could get back even a shadow of joy for his sister, he would do whatever it took.

'Earth to Draco?'

The sinful drawl brought him back to himself. To the room where low decadent music thrummed to a sensual rhythm, and where a reckless siren in hot pants could well be the answer to what he needed.

He really was going crazy…

He jerked as soft fingers grazed his jaw. The touch was gone a second later, but its earthy power streaked fire across his senses.

'If I haven't turned you into a zombie, can you tell me why me calling you by your first name is necessary in this grand plan of yours?'

He stared into her flawless face. With her wide eyes and parted lips, she perfectly emulated innocence. Except he knew she was duplicitous to the core. She was wild, totally remorseless and disturbingly reckless with well-documented antics both in her professional and personal lives.

Those heinous traits would guarantee that he would remain sexually and emotionally detached—not that the latter was in doubt—from the plan he intended to carry out.

This was for Maria. And Maria alone.

'If you want to keep your father and yourself out of jail, I need you to pretend to be my fiancée for the next three months.'

# CHAPTER FIVE

REBEL'S FIRST THOUGHT after the shocked laugh that erupted from her lips was, 'I'd rather skydive naked. Twice.'

She knew the words hadn't remained mere thoughts when Draco's features tightened with formidable displeasure. His mouth twisted in a cruel yet fascinating line that drew her gaze to the sensual curve she'd warned herself not to keep staring at.

'If you think that's your worst nightmare, then you haven't experienced hell.'

'I'm sorry…were you serious?'

If anything, she succeeded in angering him more. Although he barely moved, his overpowering presence filled the room with an oppressive aura that strangled the breath in her lungs. 'Did you not guess that I wasn't the joking type?'

'Yes, but…why on earth do you need a fake fiancée? And why me?' she tagged on, stunned that the absurd questions were falling from her lips.

Again his mouth twisted and he shook his head, as if he was having trouble accepting the very subject he'd initiated.

'The *why* will be explained after you accept my proposal. The *why you* is because you happen to be in the position of being in my debt, literally. And because your reputation fits what I need.'

She couldn't stop the lance of hurt that stabbed her. 'My reputation?' she asked, even though she knew she was inviting further hurt.

'You have a loose relationship with the truth, and you steal. Why not add pretence to your repertoire?'

Rebel jerked away from him. Or she tried to. Draco held on easily, taking firmer hold of her shoulders. Despite the sensations shivering through her at that contact, she forced herself to speak. 'Because not even a million pounds and a dozen acting awards could make me pull off *pretending* to like you. Let me go.'

Grey eyes gleamed dangerously. 'I'm not a man you want to cross, Arabella. So I suggest you give serious thought to giving me what I want.'

'And I suggest you give serious thought to what you're asking me to do. In what universe would anyone believe we're even remotely *attracted* to one another, let alone engaged to be married?'

He didn't answer her immediately. Instead his hold loosened until his fingers merely brushed her skin. Slowly, they left her shoulders and trailed down her arms. Light. Barely whispering. Electrifying. Rebel had thought his forceful grip was bad enough, but the light caress of Draco's fingers along her skin started fires in places that stunned and alarmed her.

The pads of his fingers grazed the inside of her wrists. Rebel couldn't have stopped the wicked shiver that raced through her any more than she could've stopped breathing. Despite telling herself to step away, to stop this disturbing assault on her senses, she remained rooted to the spot as he traced her racing pulse.

A half step closer and one scant inch separated them. This close, she could see the tiny gold flecks in his eyes that added an extra layer of dynamism to Draco Angelis she wouldn't have thought impossible. His rich scent blanketed her with dark, dangerous promise as the music she'd stupidly thought would clear her thoughts added to the thick, sensual pool she was drowning in.

He stared down at her, eyes piercingly direct, reading every emotion she desperately tried to hide. Then he lowered his head.

Her breath lodged in her lungs as, for the second time that day, the belief that Draco Angelis was about to kiss her shook her. Wild anticipation roared through her, shocking her with its intensity. Surely she couldn't want this?

The brief, superficial liaisons she'd had in the past had always left her cold. To the extent that no man had been allowed to go beyond a few kisses, despite the tabloids' wild speculations about her sexual antics. She'd been content being a virgin with no thought as to what her first sexual encounter would be like simply because it hadn't been a concern.

Now with every atom in her body screaming at the mere thought of being kissed by this man, the reality of her sexual innocence hovered like a time bomb above her head.

Would he think her some sort of freak? Would he laugh his head off?

*Pull yourself together!*

What on earth did it matter what Draco Angelis thought? He would never place high enough in her life to ever find out. Just as she would never allow this kiss to happen…

About to step away, Rebel found herself captive once more when he shackled her wrists. The mouth tantalisingly close to hers drifted past. His breath warmed her jaw, then the sensitive skin beneath her earlobe.

'You don't think we have chemistry?'

'N-no,' she forced out.

'Then why is your pulse jumping? Why does your breath catch every time I swipe my fingers across your skin?' he husked in her ear. 'You've been staring at my mouth for the last minute and licking yours in anticipation of my kiss. Do you want me to kiss you, Arabella?'

'No. No!' This time when she jerked out of his hold, he let her go. Striding to the other side of the room, she crossed her arms over her chest, keenly aware of the tightness in her breasts and the telltale pearls of her nipples. 'I don't know where you're going with this—'

'You doubted our ability to pull off an authentic attraction. I've just proved you wrong.'

'You've just proved that we're both half-decent actors. I'll grant you that much. It still doesn't answer my question as to why I'd ever think of indulging you in this absurd caper.'

His eyes darkened dramatically. Coupled with his glare and the stubble gracing his firm jawline, Draco's 'fallen angel' demeanour ratcheted up her already racing heartbeat. He clenched his fists at his sides, his nostrils flaring briefly before he inhaled control back into his body. The whole process was fascinating to watch and Rebel found herself following every subtle movement.

'It seems you were right. I wasted my time coming here.' With an arrogant shrug, he cast another condemning glance around the room, then strode to where she stood. 'I'll be reporting you and your father to the authorities the moment I leave here. I suggest you save yourself a few hours of unwanted attention, and don't try and make a run for it. No doubt the press will get hold of the story by morning anyway. I'll also be pursuing civil charges to recover the stolen money so make sure you hire a good lawyer.'

He was leaving. Just as she'd wanted.

He would be pressing charges against her and her father. Killing her chances of reconciliation or putting her nightmares behind her so she could finally lay her mother's ghost to rest.

Just what she didn't want.

As he walked past her and disappeared through her living-room door, Rebel knew she needed to stop Draco. But what had happened between them minutes ago had struck a vein of irrational apprehension in her heart. Whatever his ultimate plan was in seeking a fake fiancée, she was instinctively convinced she would come out the worst for it.

But the alternative…

Ice drenched her as her front door was pulled open.

The alternative for her father was unthinkable. She'd already deprived him of the love of his life. Could she sit by and watch him be deprived of his freedom as well?

'Wait!'

He froze in the doorway. The hand gripping her door handle tightened, but Draco didn't turn around. Fear climbed up her throat, the thought that he might carry on walking a live wire snaking through her.

'Can we talk about this some more?' she addressed his silent frame.

He released the door and faced her. 'No. You're under the impression that you can bargain with me. You can't. Either agree to my demands or face the charges.'

She swallowed. Leaning against the hallway wall, she speared her fingers through her hair, seeking rationality in a world gone wildly askew.

'I don't even know what I'm agreeing to exactly.'

'I've given you the broad parameters of what I want from you. The finer details will be ironed out once I have your agreement.'

She chewed on her lower lip. 'So I agree to be your pretend fiancée for three months and you call off the search for my father and drop all charges?' she verified.

His jaw flexed for a moment. 'Provided you play your part right, yes.'

'And nothing I agree to will interrupt my training programme?'

'Your training will proceed as you wish, but you have to be prepared to accommodate a travelling schedule. Considering you were attempting to relocate, that shouldn't be a problem. I assume you're doing your dry-land drills at the moment?'

She gave a surprised nod. 'Yes, I've been alternating the on-site training and dry-land training. I return to the snow next month.'

'We'll work out a different schedule when the time comes.'

'I…okay.'

They stared at each other, Rebel unable to believe what she was a hair's breadth from agreeing to. Draco's expression remained shuttered, but he stared at her with an intensity that pierced her to the soul.

'I think you'd better tell me exactly what you want from me. I can act it up with the best of them, but I'm not sure I can pull off wide-eyed innocent if that's what you require.'

Draco stepped back into the hallway and she released a breath she hadn't known she was holding. With an agile foot, he kicked the door shut. Sauntering back, he leaned one shoulder on the opposite wall. 'Since that's the type of woman I'm trying to avoid, my suggestion is that you be yourself with one or two modifications.'

'Just so we're clear, what do you think I am?'

'A reckless pleasure seeker with very little regard for anyone's feelings but her own.'

Rebel wasn't sure why her stomach dropped and rolled or why disappointment cut so deep. She had nothing to prove to Draco Angelis. His opinion of her didn't matter. All that mattered was her father was safe from whatever hellhole had been intended for him. She still had a chance at closure, might even dare to seek absolution for the wrongs she'd done.

'And the modifications you seek?' she asked past the hard lump lodged in her throat.

He straightened from the wall, his height and breath dominating the space so she was aware of nothing else but him.

'You will not see any other guy while you're with me. Any past liaisons are officially over as of tonight. As far as the public is concerned, you're mine and mine alone.'

The possessive throb in his voice rammed home his acting ability. 'Is that all?'

'For now. We'll discuss any further addenda as and when they come up.'

'How democratic of you,' she murmured under her breath. 'Who exactly are we faking all this for?' she asked curiously.

He thrust his hands in his pockets and rocked on the balls of his feet. 'Do we have an agreement?'

Rebel swallowed hard, a chasm opening up before her she couldn't see a way out of. 'Yes.'

Draco gave a single nod before he strode back into her living room. By the time she followed him in, he'd taken a seat on her small white sofa. The sight of him, dark and imposing, on her dainty sofa sent another fissure of alarm skittering through her. But there was no backing out now. She'd agreed to this.

'Sit down.'

She curbed the snarky comment that tripped on her tongue and sat down on the armchair opposite him. Draco had nearly walked out and doomed her father to criminal prosecution. While she didn't know why her father had done what he'd done, she wasn't about to risk dicing with Draco again. Instinct warned he wasn't prone to giving second chances.

'Do you know of Carla Nardozzi?'

Rebel frowned. 'The three-time champion figure skater? Of course. Everyone knows who she is.' The twenty-four-year-old was stunningly beautiful, with a talent that had seen her soar up the figure-skating rankings halfway through her seventeenth year. She was the darling of the sports world, with sponsorship deals that had made her one of the richest sports stars by the time she was twenty-one. Her talent and success, coupled with her shy and innocent demeanour, had given her an unattainable, almost royal-princess allure that only added to her appeal.

'I want her.'

An unpleasant zing jerked Rebel in her seat. Viciously unwilling to examine the feeling, she stared back at Draco. 'Then I'm at a complete loss as to why you're sitting in my lowly Chelsea flat when you should be somewhere on the Upper East Side in New York courting her. That *is* where she lives, isn't it?'

'She divides her time between there and her training facility in Switzerland. But at the moment, she's at her father's estate in Tuscany.'

'Even better. You could be reunited with her in less than two hours. I'm sure she'll eventually see past your... interesting traits to a happy ever after with you.'

A dark frown clamped his straight brows. 'Happy ever after? What the hell are you talking about?'

She shrugged. 'You just said you want her...oh, is she playing hard to get? Is that what this is about? You want to use me to make her jealous?'

His frown deepened, then he shook his head. 'You misunderstand. She's playing hard to get, but not in the way you think. I want her as a client, but her father's standing in my way.'

Rebel despised the relief that poured through her. It pointed to an interest in Draco's private life that shouldn't be piqued. In any shape or form.

She straightened her back and cleared her throat. 'Right. I'm still at a loss as to why you need a fiancée.'

Draco sat forward and planted his elbows on his knees. 'During our last few meetings, Olivio Nardozzi hinted heavily that he'll let me sign his daughter only if I brought something...more to the table.'

'More? He wants you to date his daughter in order to secure a business deal?'

A whisper of disdain crossed his rugged face. 'I suspect he has something more permanent than dating in mind.'

That unpleasant zing returned, harder than before. 'So you intend to beat him at his own game, all for a business deal?'

Disdain morphed into something darker. Bitterness edged with pain. His features cleared a second later, but the image lingered in Rebel's mind, sparking a different interest altogether.

'I have other reasons for pursuing this.'

'Such as?' she asked before she could stop herself.

His eyelids dropped. The hands dangling between his knees slowly clenched into fists and bleakness settled over his face. Rebel was certain he wasn't aware he was exhibiting such a strong and telling reaction to her question. Her breath stalled in her lungs as she watched him battle to get his emotions under control.

By the time he raised his head, his expression was once again formidably neutral. 'My other reasons are private.'

She shook her head. 'I don't like surprises. I heard you on the phone yesterday. There was familiarity between you.'

'And your point is?'

'I hardly think Papà Nardozzi would be hell-bent on pairing you with his daughter if you two hated each other's guts.'

His eyes gleamed. 'I've known Carla since she was a teenager.'

'And…?' she pressed, disconcerted by the need to probe deeper.

'And our past bears no relevance to this deal. Your role is to help me convince Nardozzi that I'm already taken.'

Pushing aside the burning need to know more about his past with Carla, she asked instead, 'Will he sign his daughter with you if you don't give him what he wants?'

'He's on the brink of achieving the biggest endorsement deal any sports personality has ever acquired, through my company,' he replied. 'Javier Santino, the sponsor, is growing tired of the unnecessary delays. Nardozzi needs to be made aware of where I stand once and for all.'

'A simple *no* to him won't suffice?'

His eyes turned hard. 'Some people don't understand the word. They believe it's their right to have what they want simply because they want it.'

The direct taunt stabbed her deep, but she managed to

keep her composure. Standing, she folded her arms. 'Okay, I get it. So we're talking a few outings with me on your arm to convince Papà that he needs to find another suitor for daughter dearest?'

'It requires a little more than that. Nardozzi is hosting a charity gala in Italy this Sunday. He's invited me to stay at his Tuscany estate the day before the gala. He's made it clear he won't be discussing the deal, which means he intends to push his personal agenda instead.'

'So I'm expected to come to Tuscany with you this weekend?' she asked, feeling a curious dredging in her abdomen at the thought of sharing her private time and space with Draco Angelis.

'Yes. We'll fly out on Saturday and return on Monday morning.'

Rebel paced the short distance to her window and settled her agitated body against the sill. 'I still don't get why you're humouring him if you don't think he'll walk away from a deal he clearly wants.'

Draco remained silent for a full minute, prompting her to think she'd misstepped without knowing. When his face tightened again, she was sure she'd hit a nerve somewhere.

'I don't just want to represent Carla for this deal. I want her to change training teams. I want to be in charge of her training.'

The sense that she was missing a key element in this scenario nagged at her. The idea that it might be far from platonic was another notion she couldn't dismiss. But Draco had made it clear he wasn't prepared to share that side of his plan with her. 'I wasn't aware agents had a say in which training teams their clients took on.'

'They don't. Not normally,' he said abruptly, before rising to his feet.

About to ask him to elaborate, she bit back her words when he swerved towards her. 'Before we leave for Tuscany, we need to ensure our relationship attracts the appropriate public attention.'

'Won't it raise suspicion for us to be suddenly engaged?' she queried.

'I'm an intensely private man. I'm not in the habit of broadcasting my liaisons. It won't be a problem to let slip that we've been dating for a while. A few might find it hard to believe that *you* haven't publicised our association, but hopefully we'll convince them that some of my good traits have rubbed off on you.'

She rolled her eyes. 'If I didn't know better I'd think you just attempted a joke.'

His grim lips twitched, but his face remained stoic. 'I'll have my PA email you a list of restaurants I prefer to dine in. If you have any objections, let her know. Please provide her with your training schedule, and I'll try and work around it.'

Rebel supposed she ought to be grateful he was accommodating her needs. But having her time monopolised so completely stuck in her craw. 'You need anything else? Like fingerprints or a sample of DNA?'

His eyes travelled with acute intensity from the top of her head to the tips of her bare toes and back again before he met her gaze with a raised brow. 'Such invasive procedures won't be necessary, but perhaps you'll make an attempt to address your wardrobe issues for the next three months?'

'What wardrobe issues? I thought you preferred me the way I am?'

One corner of his mouth lifted in a shadowed sneer. 'Consider this another minor modification. Skin-tight leather hot pants and see-through tops have their place somewhere on the fashion landscape, I'm sure. My PA will furnish you with a reputable stylist's details. Make use of it.'

'Wow. Do you make a habit of issuing orders like a drill sergeant or am I just special?'

'It seems to be the only way I can get through to you.'

'Really? I don't recall getting the honey treatment, just the rancid-vinegar one.'

He crossed the floor to stand before her. Rebel watched, heart leaping to her throat as he raised his hand. His thumb traced her lower lip as it had done in his office. Except this touch was slower. Deadlier in its intensity.

'You'll get the honey when you deserve it. In the meantime, I'll leave you to practise giving *me* the honey. We're dining out tomorrow night. Make sure you bring your A-game. Remember what's at stake here, Arabella. Fail me and all bets are off.'

She was still slumped against the windowsill when he walked out. Even the firm click of her front door didn't rouse her from the fevered daze rushing over her.

Rebel had no idea of when she finally moved, although she managed a quick call to Contessa begging off her manager's visit, and also to inform her of the change of travel plans. Then she returned her clothes and skis to their rightful place, and made herself a cup of light cocoa.

It was another treat her trainer would no doubt chastise her for, but cocoa had always helped her sleep better. And she needed to sleep.

She needed the escape of slumber to help her *not* think about Draco Angelis. She needed to *not* think about honey or sinful caresses or A-games. Or the dark hunger veiled behind his censure and bitterness.

For one thing, the danger that accompanied the man held a mesmeric quality that spelled doom for any self-preserving creature.

For another, Rebel had always been recklessly attracted to danger.

# CHAPTER SIX

THE FLOWERS ARRIVED at eight a.m., just as she was donning her gym gear. Greg, her trainer, who'd arrived at her door five minutes earlier for their run to the gym, raised an eyebrow as he walked in with an armful of the most exquisite arrangement of calla lilies Rebel had ever seen.

Besides the flowers, the black sculptured vase holding the stems was equally breathtaking.

Greg whistled as he set it on her small dining table. 'Flowers from Gilla Rosa. Someone's all out to get your attention.'

Rebel, still taking in the stunning delivery from the florist who only catered to A-list celebrities, attempted a smile. 'I guess so.' Spotting a card, she plucked it, her nerves jangling alarmingly as she opened it.

*Château Dessida.*
*Eight o'clock tonight.*
*Can't wait.*
*D*

'Château Dessida, huh? I thought you weren't dating anyone?' She started as Greg moved away from where he'd been reading the card over her shoulder.

As her trainer, he was one of a few people who knew how dedicated she was to making the championships. He also knew her occasional outings to nightclubs were coping mechanisms so didn't give her grief about it.

About to confirm that she wasn't actually dating, Rebel bit her lip. There were twelve hours before she had to begin her performance as Draco Angelis' fiancée, but it seemed her acting debut was about to commence. 'I wasn't…until fairly recently.' She dropped the card on the table and propped her foot on a dining chair to finish lacing her trainers. Then she went through her stretching routine.

The six-foot ex–body builder eyed her. 'Don't mean to judge but—is it wise getting involved with anyone so close to the championships?'

Rebel tossed out a laugh that was a million miles from genuine. 'Probably not, but isn't there a cliché about not being able to help who you fall for?'

His dark blond brows spiked. 'It's that serious already?' The brotherly concern in his eyes made her feel a heel for the subterfuge, but Rebel forced herself to remember why she was doing this.

'Cliché number two—I guess when you know, you know?' She grabbed her water bottle and tucked her phone and keys into her pockets.

Greg glanced at the flowers before he followed her out of the door. 'Here are a few more—hard work is its own reward. You've worked hard to get where you are. So don't take your eye off the ball.'

Rebel rolled her eyes, but kept the smile pinned on her face. 'As if there's any chance you'll let me. Besides, you never know. True love might be the extra-special ingredient I need to win this thing.'

She set off before he could reply. Although he caught up with her easily, he refrained from speaking, for which Rebel was grateful. But cranking up her earphones to near maximum didn't stop her mind from reeling at the full assault Draco seemed to have mounted. It was obvious he was setting the scene for their fake relationship to achieve maximum publicity in minimum time, but she would've welcomed a little more time to get used to the idea before being hit over the head with it.

Sadly, the pummelling came at an even more frantic pace the moment she returned from her morning training.

She'd barely stepped out of the shower when her doorbell rang. The courier delivered a five-page document that detailed Draco's schedule for the next fortnight and boxes to tick as to her preferred sources of entertainment. Her mouth dropped open when she read the extensive list and the final bullet point that told her the courier would return in an hour to retrieve the answered document.

Irritated, she started to tick random boxes, but by the next page a cheeky smile twitched at her lips. Crossing out several lines of questions, she scrawled one answer across the page. Then proceeded to do the same on the following pages.

She answered the courier's knock with a smile, which turned into a scowl when she spotted a sleek estate car pulling up behind the courier's van.

The six outfits and matching accessories the stylist delivered fitted perfectly, and the quirky but stylish edge to the designs made them ones she would've picked out for herself, had she come across them in a boutique. With the only exception that the delivered items had featured a designer way out of her price tag.

Deciding going with the flow was better than raising unnecessary hell, she was stepping out of a sleeveless white jumpsuit when her phone buzzed.

She sprawled across her bed to get it. 'Hello?'

'I hope your intention isn't for the next three months to be a tedium of modifications to our agreement.'

Rebel tried to ignore the tingling along her spine that Draco's deep voice elicited. 'Umm, I don't do well with cryptic. What did I do wrong now?'

'Crossing out questions about your personal interests and giving one inappropriate answer isn't acceptable.'

'Oh, right. You don't like pole dancing?' she quipped, tongue firmly in her cheek.

'Or bungee jumping. Or eating blindfolded in a blacked-out room. Skydiving—with my clothes on—might be a consideration if we had the time. We don't.'

Rebel rolled over and contemplated her black polka-dot ceiling. 'Are you sure you've got the balls for skydiving? Not everyone does.'

'Is that a dare?' he growled.

'Maybe. I'll answer the rest of your boring questionnaire if you agree to skydive with me once the championships are over. If you have the stones, that is.'

'I don't need my stones to skydive. They're for a specific purpose.'

Rebel was thankful she was on the phone when her face flamed at his words.

'Yeah, whatever. Do you accept?'

'No, Arabella. I don't accept your invitation. Not everything in life needs to be attacked with adrenaline-fuelled ferocity. And I prefer to see how you fare in the coming week before I make plans for months down the road.'

The bite in his voice erased any trace of mirth left in her. Rising, she shifted to the edge of her bed and stared at the delicate tissue paper and couture boxes strewn on her bed and floor. Suddenly, the sight of the expensive clothes produced a whiff of unease inside her. Try as she might, she couldn't dismiss the insane idea that Draco Angelis was somehow marking her with an indelible stamp of possession.

'Have I rendered you speechless for once?' he drawled.

Rousing herself, she answered, 'I answered the first page of your document. I think that should get us through this first week, don't you?'

'You ticked only one activity that interests you for every posed question.'

'So I like nightclubs. What's wrong with that?'

A faint growl rumbled down the line. The muscles in her stomach quivered as an image of a rousing dragon flashed through her mind. 'We will discuss it further tonight. I'll be there at seven-thirty. Make sure you're ready.'

He hung up before she could reply. Which was just as well since the answer on the tip of her tongue would no doubt have released the fire-breathing monster on her.

Rebel chose to wear the white jumpsuit simply because her afternoon training session overran and it was the only item of clothing that didn't need careful ironing. Slipping her feet into black and gold heels, she accessorised with a long gold necklace and chunky bangles, then caught her hair up in a loose knot before completing the look with gold chandelier earrings and a white clutch.

She was waiting on the kerb by the time Draco drove up in a gleaming black sports car. Pulling the door open, she slid into the soft leather bucket seat. And immediately clocked his tight-jawed irritation.

'Are you in the habit of hanging out on street corners waiting for your dates?'

She took her time to secure her seat belt, which didn't go as smoothly as she wanted because her every cell had grown hyperaware of the powerful and arresting man behind the wheel. He'd swapped yesterday's three-piece suit for a darker set, minus the waistcoat and tie. With the light grey shirt unbuttoned at the neck, she glimpsed a few wisps of dark silky hair that had her quickly averting her gaze.

Once she got the belt's metal housing to click, she drew a breath. Then wished she hadn't when his clean, spicy aftershave attacked her senses. Draco smelling good enough to devour wasn't a thought she intended to dwell on. 'I only came down to save you time. Please don't tell me I've offended your gentlemanly sensibilities?'

His mouth pursed. 'I'd prefer our association not to begin with hints of impropriety.'

'I was standing outside my flat, Draco, not in a red-light part of town.'

He pulled up to a red light and locked cool grey eyes

on her. 'It wouldn't have been too much trouble for me to walk to your door.'

Rebel wasn't sure why his solicitous remark robbed her of breath. Competing in a high-octane sport meant lady-like sensibilities were often mocked. She'd trained herself a long time ago to be one of the boys or risk acquiring a sneering nickname. She'd thought herself immune to needing gentle consideration. And yet the thought of Draco treating her with the tiniest deference caused a lump to rise in her throat. Her father had worshipped her mother that way, bending over backwards to grant her smallest wish.

Her mother had grumbled, but she'd always done so with a teasing smile. The memory thickened the lump in her throat, even as the acute lance of pain pierced her heart.

Struggling to retain her composure under Draco's intense stare, she cleared her throat. 'Noted. I'll do better next time.'

Surprise lit his eyes, but he turned away without response as the light turned green. The rest of the short journey passed in silence.

Château Dessida, located in a side street off the King's Road, was tiny and extremely exclusive. It was renowned for its French fusion-themed dishes, the three-Michelin-starred chef who ran the kitchen rumoured to personally select which customers patronised his establishment. He also reserved the right to publicise who dined in his restaurant, with famous photos making his millions-strong social-media following green with envy.

Draco tossed his car keys to the waiting valet and guided her through the canopied doorway.

'It's show time,' he murmured in her ear.

Before she could grasp his meaning, he pulled her close and settled a hand over her hip. Despite the layers of clothing separating them, Rebel felt his touch as keenly as if he'd branded her bare skin with a hot iron. Biting back a gasp, she stumbled. Draco's other hand shot out to grasp her waist.

'Steady, *agapita*. You okay?'

Held immobile, she stared up at him, then grew dizzy all over again as his mouth stretched in a dazzling, captivating smile. Rebel knew she was gaping, but for the life of her she couldn't look away from the stunning transformation on Draco's face. Gone was the fire-breathing ogre who seemed to find fault with every word that spilled from her lips.

In his place was an Adonis who oozed charm and attentiveness as the hand on her hip rotated in a slow caress and his other hand gripped her tighter.

'Arabella? Baby, are you okay?'

Absurdly, it was the combination of her name and the endearment that tossed her out of her stupor. Sucking in a long, restorative breath, she summoned a bare-toothed dazzler of her own. Leaning closer, she tiptoed her fingers up his chest.

'Laying it on a bit thick, aren't you, *baby*?' she remarked through clenched teeth.

The hand on her waist drifted up her arm, leaving a trail of goose bumps. 'Your neat little stumble attracted the right attention. We're now the spectacle for a few dozen pairs of eyes to feast on.' With a little too much practised ease, he lifted her faux-fur wrap from her shoulders and handed it to a cloak attendant.

Irritation jerked through her. 'I didn't do it on purpose.'

'Then it's a good thing your lover is here to catch you when you're adorably clumsy, isn't it, sweetheart?' Light fingers framed her cheek, his smile continuing to blind with its fake brilliance.

Rebel was about to snap for him to ease off with the false charm, but her words dried in her throat when Draco's name was boomed from over her shoulder.

François Dessida, a short, wiry man with thick, flowing brown hair, greeted them with a short but effusive torrent of French, which Draco answered flawlessly. Introductions were made, a few Gallic shrugs thrown in the mix, then

François clicked his fingers. As if by magic, the maître d' appeared with a discreet camera.

Rebel found herself wedged between the two men, Draco's hand back on her hip as he dragged her close enough for there to be no doubt as to their intimacy. Resurrecting her smile, she held her pose through several snaps, then exhaled in relief when François clicked his fingers again.

Wishing them a pleasant evening, he disappeared back into his domain.

By the time the maître d' showed them to their table, having stopped at a few tables when Draco returned greetings, Rebel felt as brittle as glass and just as transparent.

Her smile was fracturing at the edges and with each brush of Draco's hand on her—a gesture he seemed bent on repeating often in this insane charade—her insides clenched tight.

The moment they sat down and he'd dismissed the maître d' with their wine order, he leaned forward.

'What's wrong?' he breathed smoothly, but she caught the steely edge in his voice.

'Can we dial down the touchy-feely stuff, please?' she whispered.

'The idea is to exhibit that we're utterly besotted with each other. That involves a degree of contact.'

Thankful they'd been seated at an intimate table away from the nearest guests, she replied, 'But not three thousand degrees of it. Can we not be a couple who are discreet about their PDA?'

'To all intents and purposes, I'm about to propose to you tonight. We're starting what will become one of the most memorable nights of our lives. And you expect me to keep my hands off you?'

Her mouth dropped open. 'You're about to propose?'

'That's generally how engagements happen,' he replied.

'No, I meant…you're going to do it *here*?' Her gaze darted around only to confirm they were still the subject of great interest. Anxiety clawed up her chest. Which was absurd because all this was make-believe.

'You don't seem pleased about it,' he quipped.

Struggling for composure, she threw on a mock pout. 'I guess because you've ruined the surprise. Now I have to sharpen my acting skills even more.'

He reached across the table and took her left hand. 'I'm sure you'll rise to the occasion admirably.' Raising her hand, he kissed her ring finger.

The flash of a phone camera a second later confirmed the reason for the gesture. But it didn't stop her belly from flipping over with a mixture of anxiety and dread. The moment he set her free, she drew her hand into her lap and curled it into a fist. She was fast becoming aware that she wasn't as immune to Draco Angelis' touch as she'd assured herself she was. The chemistry she'd denied so vehemently last night was alive and well, and growing with each passing second.

Draco's stellar performance continued throughout their appetiser and main courses. He tucked into his plate of braised veal and roasted vegetables soaked in red wine sauce, while she pushed her truffled chicken escalope around her plate, taking the occasional bite when he sent her a speaking look. By the time the course was over, the food had congealed in her stomach.

'Something on your mind?'

'You asked for my A-game. I don't think I can bring it. I'm not sure I can pull this off,' she blurted once their wine glasses had been refilled.

He inhaled sharply, his eyes snapping with displeasure. 'I suggest you find a way to make it happen. We've set the ball rolling on this. It's too late to change your mind now. Even if your father makes a triumphant return and you somehow find yourself with another windfall, you still have an agreement to fulfil.'

The remnants of wine she'd just swallowed turned sour

in her mouth as she twisted the wine-glass stem between her fingers.

The sensation of falling deeper into a bottomless chasm grew. She jumped when Draco leaned closer. 'He hasn't returned, has he?' he enquired.

Pursing her lips, she shook her head. 'No, he hasn't.' Despite her calling him every free moment she'd had today, her phone remained silent.

'Has he done this before? Disappeared without a trace?'

Pain dredged through her. With every fibre of her being, Rebel wished she could answer in the negative. 'Yes, he's done it before.'

Draco's gaze sharpened. 'When?'

'When…when my mother died. After her funeral, he left home. He didn't return for three months.'

He frowned. 'How old were you?'

'I was seventeen.'

'And he left you alone?' The bite was back, the charming façade he'd worn all night slipping to reveal the ruthless man beneath. Absurdly, Rebel felt a tiny bit of relief at seeing the real man, even though this version of Draco remained a formidable force that battered at the foundations of her existence.

Rebel shrugged. 'He had my aunt look in on me every once in a while, but I was pretty much independent by then.'

'And that excuses his actions?' Anger laced his every syllable.

Unable to risk him seeing her guilt, she stared down at her plate. 'He'd just lost the love of his life. He…he was grieving.'

'While he had a responsibility to you? Were you not grieving too?'

Her gaze snapped up. 'Of course I was!' Swallowing, she shook her head and continued. 'But…there's more to the story, Draco.'

His mouth twisted in a cynical grimace. 'Isn't there always? Sadly, more often than not, *more* is just an excuse for shirking responsibility or seeking blanket absolution.'

'We all deal with our issues in different ways.'

'Yes. And your father's way seems to be doing a runner and leaving you with the smoking gun,' he drawled pithily.

'Don't—!'

'More wine, *madamoiselle*? *Monsieur*?'

They both started. Draco recovered first, reaching out to take the bottle from the waiter and dismissing him. When she shook her head, he set the bottle down without refilling his own. Silence cloaked them for several minutes, with Rebel trying hard to stem the tremors charging through her body.

She couldn't believe she'd spilled her guts to Draco, given him further ammunition against her and her father.

'You gave me your word. You will not back out of this,' he stated with unmistakable gravity.

For myriad reasons, she wanted to take back her promise. But each and every reason that tumbled through her head was a selfish one. And they all centred around how Draco Angelis made her *feel*. Unbalanced. Apprehensive. An all-encompassing excitement each time he touched her. A craving for more of that touch.

But her feelings didn't matter here. Winning the championship in order to keep her mother's memory alive and ensuring she found a way back to her father were the two most important reasons to stick with this. She couldn't do either from a prison cell.

After a brave sip of wine, she set her glass down. 'I won't back out. From this moment, I'm all in.'

# CHAPTER SEVEN

Draco exhaled the breath locked in his chest and nodded. He refused to acknowledge the anxiety that slowly seeped out of him as he stared at Arabella. 'And I have your assurance that this is the last time I'll have to deal with a change of heart?'

A shrug lifted her smooth, bare shoulder. 'I'll try not to make a habit of it, but I reserve the right to throw a mini wobbly if this charade gets a little too much. I'm human after all, not a robot.'

Had she been a robot, she would've earned the title of sexiest robot created. Her gold accessories highlighted her perfect, vibrant skin, drawing his gaze to her slim neck, delicate collarbones and the delectable shadows between her breasts. The spark that had started in his groin when he'd pulled her close at the door surged into a flame. He shifted in his seat, his trousers growing uncomfortably tight as she lifted her water glass and drank from it.

Setting it down, she sent him a furtive glance.

'This is really important to you, isn't it?' she probed.

Draco guessed that this was her attempt to steer the conversation away from her father. And while residual fury burned in his blood at the realisation that the man whose integrity and hard work he'd relied on for the past five years had turned out to be untrustworthy to the extent of abandoning his own family when he'd been needed most, Draco was content to let the matter rest. For now.

He took his time to answer, relaying their coffee orders to the waiter before he responded, 'Yes, it's important.'

She continued to toy with the crystal goblet. 'Why? And

before you say so, I think I can accurately guess it's not about the money.'

He tensed, debated for a moment how much to divulge. Maria's privacy was of the utmost importance to him. As long as he had breath in his body, his sister wouldn't know the slightest pang of further suffering. He hadn't been able to protect her when it counted. But he intended to do everything he could to ease her tiniest worry.

'No, it's not about the money, although, as a businessman, it's in my interest to protect my and my clients' assets.'

'Of course, but there's more.' It wasn't a question. It was a statement of unwavering certainty.

Normally, prying from his date was a turn-off. But he found himself answering her, while reminding himself that this wasn't a proper date. This was a charade to get him what he wanted. What Maria wanted.

'Carla Nardozzi and her father are thinking of renewing her contract with Tyson Blackwell for another three years. I intend to make sure that doesn't happen.'

Surprise sparked her blue eyes. 'But Tyson is one of the most highly sought-after trainers out there. I worked with him in a group programme myself a few years ago.'

Renewed fury flamed through him, but he banked it down. He was supposed to play the part of a besotted lover, not an angry one, exhibiting bewildering signs of jealousy. 'I'm aware of that. Why did you part company?'

She shrugged. 'I think he had his eye on bigger fish. Carla Nardozzi, I expect.'

'Consider yourself lucky. He's known to push his trainees beyond their limits.'

She smiled at the waiter who delivered her coffee, before she met his gaze once more. 'And that's a bad thing?'

Regret and bitterness locked a vice around his chest. 'It is when they eventually break.'

Her eyes shadowed with sympathy, an emotion Draco wouldn't have associated with the flighty, self-obsessed creature he knew her to be. 'This happened to someone you know?'

The vice tightened. 'Yes.' He forced the word out.

She nodded, then picked up her coffee and blew gently on it. A different sort of tightening took hold of Draco. He wasn't sure whether to be resentful of the reminder that his libido was alive and kicking or welcome the distraction from trying to grapple with the diverging personalities of the woman sitting across from him. A sympathetic listener and narcissistic thief. Was there such a thing?

'I'm sorry that happened to them. Were you close to this person?' she pressed.

Draco decided that he preferred to tackle the subject of his libido. Discussing matters that ploughed through rough and disturbing memories wasn't what he'd intended for this dinner. And yet the box that resided in his jacket pocket remained there as he lifted and tossed back his double espresso.

'Did you take care of the matter of your other liaisons as you promised?'

Mocking laughter spilled from her lips. 'First of all, I made no such promise. Secondly, where on earth did you get the idea that I had *liaisons*, plural?'

His teeth ground until pain lanced his jaw. 'There have been several photographs of you cavorting with a certain rock band for the last few weeks.'

An emotion flicked through her eyes, one that resembled hurt. 'And that automatically means I'm dating all of them?'

Tension gripped him. 'Are you?'

'No. Cole, the lead singer, used to be into snowboarding when we were younger. I met him again at an event a few weeks ago, and we just hung out for a bit.'

'In the pictures you seem to be hanging out in his lap.' The words emerged in a rumble that thoroughly irritated him.

Arabella shook her head. 'I swear, if I didn't know better, I'd think you were jealous.'

His tension increased, along with the irksome need to probe this subject. 'This is nothing more than due diligence to ensure there are no surprises down the road.'

She held his gaze, hers bold and clear. 'There won't be.'

For the second time in under an hour, tension eased out of Draco. For whatever reason his instinct was to believe her. Or perhaps on a subconscious level he knew this was a minor problem, easily resolved once the world knew she belonged to him. His gaze dropped to her bare fingers, a sudden need sparking through him.

Confirming she'd finished her coffee, he stood and held out his hand.

After a tiny hesitation, she slipped her hand in his and stood. The few diners remaining glanced their way. One or two acquaintances tried to catch his eye, but he avoided them. He'd achieved what he came here for. He wasn't sure why he'd decided to take the next step away from prying eyes but he was tired of being on show.

The maître d' materialised with Arabella's wrap. Draco draped it over her shoulders and caught her faint shiver as his fingers brushed her skin.

He'd effectively debunked her denial of their chemistry at her flat last night. But little had he known that he would be caught in the tangle of chemical reaction so strong that he'd spent the night fighting lurid dreams.

She murmured her thanks and walked beside him, her hand once more clasped in his. He stared down at her profile, forcing himself to stay removed from the ever-growing tendrils of attraction grabbing at him.

A cold, rational part of him insisted that the attraction would make their fake relationship more believable. While the part of his anatomy that refused to remained unstirred urged him to change the parameters of their agreement. To make certain sections of it real.

He suppressed that urge and led Arabella to his car.

Even if he were on the market for a brief dalliance, Arabella Daniels wouldn't be his choice of partner. Her wild, brash approach to life would never gel with his, even for the weeks-long period his affairs usually lasted. Besides, she'd all but admitted to being as unscrupulous and lacking in integrity as her father.

There was no way he could risk exposing such a person to Maria.

Satisfied with his decision, he saw her into the car and slipped behind the wheel. The return journey back to her flat went much faster. When she went to open the door, Draco growled, 'Stay.'

As before, she seemed surprised by his gesture as he rounded the bonnet and opened her door.

'Thank you.'

Taking her by the elbow, he walked her to the front door and waited as she dug through her clutch for her keys.

Another furtive glance at him prompted a twitch of a smile. She was nervous.

'Invite me up.'

Nerves turned to surprise. Then suspicion. 'Why?'

'Because there's one more thing to address before we end the evening.'

Her eyes rounded before she caught his meaning. 'Oh, the engagement ring. I thought you wanted to do that in front of an audience?'

He shrugged. 'We lost our audience while we were discussing…other matters. And I don't intend to place my ring on your finger on the steps of your flat. Invite me up.'

The breath she inhaled was a shaky one. 'Umm…okay.'

She opened her front door and he held it wide for her, then followed her up the flight of stairs to her flat. In her living room, Draco waited as she turned on lamps and straightened cushions. Then watched, bemused, as she twisted her fingers and eyed the entertainment centre.

'You seem nervous.'

She laughed and shrugged. 'Not sure why I am. I guess I've never been genuinely fake-proposed to before.'

The idea that she'd been proposed to at all sent a thin vein of tension through him. He dismissed it and reached into his pocket. As his fingers closed over the velvet box, tension mutated to something else. Something Draco faintly recognised as trepidation for this moment. The kind that ran parallel with monumental tasks he didn't want to fail at. Frowning, he pulled the box from his pocket. There'd been no words to practise because this wasn't a prelude to a love union. They were each playing a finite role with a clear endgame in mind. The moment shouldn't contain as much gravity as was moving through him.

'If you want dramatic music to draw out the suspense, just say the word. I have tons,' Arabella quipped, one perfectly shaped eyebrow raised.

He fisted the box for a brief moment. 'That won't be necessary.'

Striding to where she stood, he held it up and pried it open.

She gasped, then frowned. 'It's real. I mean, I'm not a gem expert, but that looks…real!' Blue eyes met his, alarm swimming in the depths.

His teeth gritted. 'You thought I would supply you with a fake ring?'

'Well…yes. To go with the fake engagement? I don't know why you look so offended, but that would make sense, wouldn't it?'

'It would also announce our engagement as a sham to the whole world.'

Her gaze dropped down to the box. 'But this is probably worth more than I owe you. You're sure you trust me with it?' she murmured. 'What if I lose it?'

'It's insured against loss. And theft.' Draco wasn't sure why he added that. When she raised her gaze and he spotted the hurt she tried to hide, a tiny spark of remorse burst through him. Which was absurd because this situation had come about because of her collusion with her father's duplicity. Brushing aside the feeling, he growled, 'Give me your hand.'

She hesitated for one moment. Then two. At the back of his mind, Draco faintly wondered if this was what the average man felt like when he got down on one knee. If so, then he pitied them. Her unnecessary hesitation was irritating in the extreme. And he wasn't even on one knee. Nor did he intend to be.

'Arabella. Your hand.'

Rebel slowly held out her left hand, nerves eating her alive. 'Damn,' she muttered under her breath.

Draco's gaze rose from where he held the ring poised. 'What's wrong?'

She shrugged. 'If I'd known I'd be sporting a rock like this, I'd have made more of an effort with my nails.' She kept them trimmed short for training, but a little gloss wouldn't have gone amiss. She swallowed as she caught his frown. 'Sorry, I didn't mean to ruin the moment.' Realising she was babbling, she pressed her lips together.

'There isn't a moment to ruin,' he rasped. Rebel felt the cold tug of platinum over her knuckle. Then the ring slid into place. 'And your nails are fine.'

The rectangular-cut diamond was flanked by baguette diamonds, which connected to the platinum band. In the low lights of her flat, the ring glinted and flashed as her fingers trembled. It was a perfect fit. Just how he'd achieved that was a mystery, but Rebel couldn't take her eyes off the ring's sheer perfection. Nor could she divorce her mind from wandering down a senseless road of how she would've felt if this moment were real.

Not that the man she'd have chosen would've been Draco Angelis. He was far too arrogant and domineering for her to even consider him as—

'Is it my turn to ask whether we need melodramatic music? Or do you not like the ring?' Draco drawled with a slight edge in his tone.

'It's…' *beautiful.* Wondering why the word stuck in her throat, why so many different emotions darted through her, Rebel dragged her gaze from the stunning ring. 'It's fine. It'll probably get the job of convincing Nardozzi to back off done all on its own.'

His mouth twisted. 'I think you need to put in more personal effort than that.'

Before she could answer, his phone buzzed. Slipping it from his pocket, he stared at the screen for a moment, a hint of satisfaction flitting over his features. 'Dessida has done what I requested of him.'

Why was she surprised that Draco could get men with bloated egos like François Dessida to bend to his will? 'Great,' she responded, even though an added ball of uncertainty churned in her stomach. 'We're all set, then.'

'Not quite.' He stared down at his screen for a few more seconds before his steely gaze pierced hers. 'Your body language needs a little work.'

'Excuse me?'

He turned the phone towards her. The chef had posted a picture of them on his social-media site. 'This doesn't quite do the trick.'

She flicked a glance at the picture, suddenly unwilling to look closely at it. 'Our picture has already had over half a million views. I fail to see what the problem is.'

'The problem is we're supposed to be lovers. Your posture indicates otherwise.'

Rebel forced herself to look past Draco's firm, proprietary hand on her hip. Or the fact that it sparked a fizz of unwanted sensation through her. Clinically, she perused her slightly stiff posture and the neutral expression she'd forced her features into in reaction to Draco's touch. Her gaze slid to the dominating presence beside her.

'You could've done with cracking a smile too, don't you think?' she countered.

He slid the phone back into his pocket. 'The next time we're seen together in public you'll be my fiancée. Your performance needs to be stellar.'

'Fine. I promise to fawn all over you.'

He shook his head. 'No, I'm not risking you going overboard either.'

She threw up her hands. 'What, then? You should know, I'm not the here's-a-cute-selfie-of-us-cuddling-while-walking-our-dog type.'

'Neither am I. But we need to achieve the right balance.'

'And how do you suggest we do that? Take a compatibility test?'

'Of sorts.'

He stepped forward and gripped her waist. The unexpected move, and the blistering heat from his touch, made her whole body clench tight. 'What are you doing?' Her voice rose several octaves higher than it'd been a moment ago.

'You just tensed up. If you do that every time I touch you, we might as well declare this thing a failure.'

'You surprised me, that's all,' she replied, her voice still unlike her own.

He dragged her closer and her tension mounted. 'Arabella, relax,' he rasped, his voice deep and frighteningly hypnotic.

'Said the snake charmer to the snake.'

One corner of his mouth lifted in a shadow of a smile. Then the pads of his thumbs pressed into her hip bones.

Electric sensation blasted through her. The secret place between her legs tingled wildly before singeing her with a fiery need that robbed her of breath. Draco stared at her as his thumbs continued to play over her covered skin, the direct gaze adding a potent layer of awareness to the one already blanketing her.

Just when she thought she couldn't stand it any more, his gaze dropped to her mouth. A rough sound rumbled from his chest, but she was too caught up in what was happening to her body to pay it much heed.

But she heeded the unrelenting descent of his head, and the mouth that took hers a second later.

Every single atom in her body strained to that point of contact, to the pressure that teased at first, then turned into a deeper, more breath-stealing exploration.

Rebel had been kissed before, but the expertise Draco brought to his kiss, even mere seconds into the act, melted her senses. Warm, firm lips bruised hers, the feeling of being devoured drenching her before she succumbed to it.

His hand strayed from her hip to the small of her back, compelled her closer still. Her arms moved, almost of their own accord, twined around his neck. Silky hair teased the back of her hands and Rebel gave in to the temptation to slide her fingers through his hair.

His tongue breached her mouth, the bold swipe as he shamelessly tasted her knocking the strength from her knees. Desire blistered her, tightening over her skin until her breasts ached and her nipples were needy little buds straining against her bra. Needing to relieve the ache, she rubbed herself against him.

A groan erupted from him. Lost in sensation, Rebel barely acknowledged being lifted off her feet. Or laid down on the sofa. Every frantic heartbeat begged for more of what she was experiencing. The kiss. The man. The potent smell of him that filled her nostrils and the hands moulding her body. She wanted it all with a desperation that defied logic.

When he gripped her leg and angled it over his hip, she twisted to accommodate him, the move settling him snugly between her thighs.

The unmistakable power of his erection brushed her clothed core. Lightning zapped at the contact, electrifying and so strong, they both froze. She opened her eyes to find grey eyes, dark with volatile hunger, staring into hers.

Hunger that had no place whatsoever inside the parameters of what she'd agreed to.

With a shocked, garbled cry, Rebel wrenched her mouth from his. Disengaging the fists locked in his hair, she slammed them on his shoulders and pushed.

'Get off me. Now.' Her voice was a shaky mess, light years from confident, and nowhere near rational.

Draco lifted his imposing body off hers, his control back in place as if that wild hunger she'd seen in his eyes had been a figment of her imagination. 'Calm down, Arabella.'

She jumped up and fled to the other side of the room. One shaky hand sliced through her hair as she noted she'd lost her shoes along the way to insanity. 'God, I can't believe that just happened,' she muttered under her breath.

He took his time to straighten his cuffs, then shrugged. 'We needed to be familiar with each other. Now I know what you taste like, and you won't jump whenever I touch you in public.'

'Not if you're going to paw me like you did a moment ago.'

He raised a mocking brow. 'You reciprocated in kind, *glikia mou*. I'm sure I can locate a claw mark or two on my person should I feel inclined to do so.'

Heat rushed up her face at the reminder of her wanton behaviour. Folding her arms to still her body's betraying tremble, she glared at him. 'Are we quite finished? Only I'd like to get some sleep. I have an early start in the morning.'

He sauntered past her and paused at the door. 'We are for now. Don't forget we do this again tomorrow night. With added public scrutiny thrown in.'

Her heart tripped over itself as unpleasant images of being in a goldfish bowl tore through her mind. 'Are you sure all this is just to save Carla? From where I stand, she seems to be doing just fine.' Rebel hated herself for probing, but all day she hadn't quite been able to shake the feeling that there was more to his motives where Carla was concerned than Draco was letting on. And she hated herself even more that the prime emotion when she thought about the two of them felt alarmingly like jealousy.

Draco's face hardened into a steel mask. 'I've learned to look beneath the surface, Arabella. If you bother to do the same, you'll see that things aren't always as they *seem*. Goodnight.'

She stayed rooted to the spot as he left her flat. Although his words echoed through her mind, it was the depth of feeling in his voice and wave of vivid pain that had crossed his face that stayed with her.

# CHAPTER EIGHT

'*YOU'RE DATING DRACO ANGELIS?*'

Shock lined every inch of Contessa's face as she stood in Rebel's doorway. Her mop of red hair and electric-blue dress should've clashed horribly, but somehow the ensemble worked. Probably because her unapologetic, no-nonsense attitude dared anyone to criticise her wardrobe style.

Not that Rebel would've done so as her manager brushed past her and headed for the kitchen. She plunked the bottle of champagne in her hand on the breakfast counter and turned to her.

'Your email was a little vague as to why you weren't going to Chamonix any longer, but I'm guessing this new development has something to do with it? Tell me it's not true—' She gasped as her gaze fell on the rock adorning Rebel's finger. Rushing forward, she caught up Rebel's hand. 'What's this?'

'Umm…want to take a wild guess?'

'An engagement ring? You're *engaged*? To Draco?'

Rebel bit her lip and gave a sheepish nod.

A deeper bewilderment etched Contessa's face. 'When? And why? Damn it, what's going on, Rebel? I had no idea you'd even met the guy, never mind were dating him!'

'It sort of just happened.'

'A serious rock like this doesn't *just happen*. You've been evasive these past few weeks.' She dropped Rebel's hand, her green eyes wary and hurt. 'I thought you trusted me?'

'You know I do.'

Contessa's gaze dropped to the ring, then back up. 'Then why won't you tell me what's going on?'

Rebel didn't know Draco well enough to speak with cer-

tainty as to how he'd react to her divulging details of their
agreement. And she had too much to lose to risk it. 'Because I can't. I'm sorry.'

Contessa's eyes narrowed shrewdly. 'It's something to
do with your father, isn't it? And the money he gave you?'
She snapped her fingers. 'You wanted me to get it all back
but you never said why. Does this Draco thing have something to do with it?'

Shame and anxiety engulfed her. 'Please, I can't really
talk about it. And I'm sorry to have to cut this short but
Draco will be here in a minute.'

On cue, her door intercom buzzed.

'Why? Doesn't he want you to have friends?' Contessa
snapped. 'Or are you suddenly ashamed of me?'

'Don't be absurd. Of course I'm not ashamed of you. I…
we're going out, that's all.'

The older woman's gaze drifted over the moss-green
beaded dress and platform heels Rebel wore. 'I can see that.'
She hitched her stylish tote handbag higher on her shoulder,
then sighed. 'Be careful, Rebel. You're more than a client
to me. And I'd hate myself if you got hurt. You know he
represents Rex Glow now? Have you stopped to think he
may have had something to do with them dropping you?'

'Yes, I—'

Contessa shook her head. 'This engagement…well, all
I'm saying is, a man like Draco can give you a lot. But he'll
take more than you'll want to give.'

Rebel frowned. 'I know exactly what he wants from me.
I don't intend to give him more than that.'

'The sport agents' business is a small world. He's discreet, I'll grant him that, but I know a few of the women
he's been involved with in the past. They always believe
they're incapable of being hurt by him, but things always
end the same way. With the women emotionally and professionally shattered, and Angelis walking away without a
backward glance.'

'It's a good thing that you're in charge of my career, then, isn't it?' Rebel said with a forced smile.

'What about your heart?'

'I'm fully in control of it. I know you're worried, but please trust that I know what I'm doing,' she replied, choosing not to recall the sleepless night she'd spent thinking about Draco, the kiss they'd shared, and the unfurling heat in her belly each time she relived it. Assuring herself it was a simple chemical reaction and therefore didn't warrant further thought had lost its credibility somewhere between dawn and sunrise. As had telling herself she didn't really want to know the reason behind Draco's anguished look when she'd asked about Carla in the moments before he'd walked out.

Both subjects had stayed with her all day and, the closer the time came for her date with Draco, the more uneasy she'd grown.

The intercom buzzed again, ending with a snap of impatience.

Schooling her features, she smiled at Contessa. She knew her friend and manager wasn't buying her assurances when Contessa stalked past her to the door she'd walked through minutes ago. Collecting her black purse from her bedroom, Rebel rushed after her, cursing as she stopped to lock her front door.

She caught up with Contessa as she was pulling the main door open.

Contessa and a just-arrived, smartly dressed Draco eyed each other. Despite her warning, Rebel watched her friend's eyes widen a little as she took in the full impact of the man before her. A second later, Draco glanced past her to capture Rebel's gaze.

'Good evening, Arabella.'

The sensual curl of her name from his lips sparked a higher charge in her belly. Doing her best to ignore it, she came down the last few steps and stood next to Contessa.

'Are you going to introduce me to your friend, *glikia mou*?' he asked, his voice deep and low.

The endearment reminded Rebel of Draco's Greek origin, reminded her that she knew next to nothing about him besides the circumstances surrounding the situation they found themselves in. And even then, Draco was hiding far more than he'd divulged.

Making a note to do something about it, she summoned a smile. 'This is my manager, Contessa Stanley. Contessa, meet Draco Angelis.'

Draco held out his hand. 'A pleasure to meet you.'

'Good to meet you,' Contessa replied, then her sharp looked morphed into glazed astonishment when Draco smiled. Witnessing the transformation from a few feet back, Rebel couldn't stop herself from staring at the dazzling effect of his smile. It took several moments for Contessa to regain her composure. 'I believe congratulations are in order.'

'Thank you,' he drawled. 'I'm a very lucky man.' The heated, adoring look he sent Rebel could've knocked her off her feet, had she not known it was an act.

Contessa stared at him for another long second, before she cleared her throat and turned to Rebel. 'I'll call you tomorrow. Have a good evening.'

Without another glance at Draco, she headed to the white hybrid parked in front of Draco's sports car.

Draco watched her depart with a faintly amused expression. 'Any reason why she doesn't like me?'

Rebel shut the front door and fell into step beside him, cautioning herself against walking too close. 'She's a sport manager. She suspects you were involved with my sponsors walking. She also believes the women you get involved with end up on the used and discarded heap, both professionally and emotionally.'

Any semblance of amusement vanished from Draco's face. He caught her wrist and glared down at her. 'You didn't tell her about our agreement, did you?'

'Of course not.' She pulled her hand away. 'Although I trust her implicitly,' she added.

'Be that as it may, I'd prefer it if this thing remained between only you and me,' he commanded.

'I'm not stupid, Draco. I don't want this to get out any more than you do.'

He observed her for a moment, grey eyes narrow and intense. 'Good.'

Striding to his car, he held the door open for her, his movements tense as he rounded the bonnet and slid behind the wheel.

After several minutes of silence, she glanced at him, unable to smother the question that had been bubbling at the back of her mind. 'Why *did* you talk Rex Glow into dropping me?'

She'd told herself she didn't care. That she was better off without the demanding apparel and footwear sponsor. But she held her breath as she waited for Draco to answer.

His jaw flexed for a moment. 'I didn't. They'd already made the decision to drop several athletes by the time I joined their board. Yours was just a name on the list.'

Rebel knew it was true because Contessa had informed her of others who'd been dropped. 'And you did nothing to stop it?'

Draco shrugged. 'I didn't know you. And you weren't exactly trying very hard to convince them of your dedication to your sport. You switched disciplines from cross-country to ski jumping after almost five years. Since then you haven't risen above fifth in the rankings.'

'I know you think I'm whimsical about my career, but I'm not. It wasn't an easy decision, especially with the intense training involved.'

He switched lanes suddenly, and her eyes were drawn to his powerful thighs. Recalling them cradled between hers, she turned her heating face to the window.

'Did you grow up skiing?' he asked after a few minutes.

She answered only because talking took her mind off the lurid images unreeling through her head. And perhaps because she wanted him to know that she was more than the superficial pleasure seeker he thought her to be?

'Yes. My mother was a ski jumper. She never made it past the juniors but she excelled in amateur tournaments. She taught me how to jump when I was ten. I loved it but I was stronger in cross-country skiing so it was a natural choice to do that professionally.'

'That makes sense. Less so is why you changed disciplines.'

'I stopped loving cross-country.'

'I'm guessing the reason behind is more emotional than professional?'

She wanted to hate him for the cynical edge to his observation, but how could she when it was the truth? Pain slammed through her as she glanced at his profile and replied, 'Does my mother passing away count?'

He exhaled, a look of regret lining his features. 'It counts. Unfortunately death and tragedy arrive before clarity lights our paths,' he murmured, then seemed to slip into deep thought. Expertly handling the powerful vehicle, he didn't speak until they were a few streets from the restaurant. 'But you didn't change disciplines until a few years after you lost your mother. And yet you won more cross-country competitions in that time.' The statement held a ton of questions. Questions that, should she answer, would expose the state of her hidden anguish to a man whose ruthlessness she was very much privy to.

But not answering would risk leaving him with the belief that she was shallow. Wondering why that mattered so much to her, Rebel decided on a not too revealing answer. 'I was trying to prove a point.'

'To who?'

'To myself. To my father.'

His mouth compressed, disapproval back in full force.

'You disapprove? No matter what everyone else thinks, an athlete needs a better support system than just agents and trainers. I thought I could function without one, and, yes, I was at the top of my game during that time, but in the long run it didn't work for me. So I chose to do something different. It probably doesn't mean anything to you, but I found more fulfilment in jumping.'

Draco parked the car on a quiet lamplit street in Fulham amid several late-model sports cars and SUVs. The restaurant he'd chosen tonight was another exclusive one, frequented by the crème de la crème of celebrities. A discreet security presence ensured the patrons could dine without intrusive media presence, although somehow information usually leaked out.

He helped her out, but held onto her as he shut the door. After clicking the lock, he stood in front of her, effectively pinning her against the car.

Tensing, Rebel tilted her face to look at him, expecting more of the disapproval that had bristled from him. Instead, she read a jagged understanding in his eyes. He looked almost uncomfortable as he stared down at her.

'I understand the need to find fulfilment in what you do. But I believe that it should go hand in hand with attempting to be the best you can be. You have the potential to be number one again, but you've let your emotions and superficial things get in the way of that goal for far too long.'

Draco's view of her might have altered slightly, but he still believed she wasn't committed enough to what she'd dedicated the past five years of her life to. The pang that accompanied the observation triggered alarm. How could the view of a man she hadn't known three days matter so much?

'You should really stop thinking you know all there is to know about me,' she replied.

His eyes dropped from hers, his gaze roving her face before locking on her lips. 'Everything you've told me so far has only confirmed my opinion of you.'

She swallowed, wishing the hurt in her chest and the sudden tingling of her mouth away. Forcing lightness to her voice, she said, 'Whereas I know next to nothing about the man who I'm supposed to be madly in love with. Perhaps we should rectify that before I slip up and commit a faux pas?'

'We will do that over dinner,' he replied. Then his gaze dropped past her shoulders to the unsteady rise and fall of her chest. Pushing back from the car, he completed a full scrutiny before he trapped her hand again. Lifting her ring finger to his mouth, he kissed the knuckle above the stone. 'You look incredible, by the way.'

Her breath caught, her heart tripping over itself before slamming hard against her ribs. 'Thank you. You don't look so bad yourself.' She made a show of perusing him from head to foot, secretly revelling in the freedom to look her fill of the lean masculinity that inhabited the dark suit and black silk shirt. Having experienced the power of that body up close, she found her breathing was decidedly unsteady by the time her gaze rose to meet his.

His smile wasn't as show-stopping as it'd been when he'd unleashed his charms on Contessa. But it had more genuine depth, making it even more dangerous to her equilibrium as she found herself smiling back, her senses singing as his eyes warmed and his thumb rubbed over her knuckles.

'Now that we've established our appreciation of each other's dress sense, let's go eat.'

He linked his fingers through hers and walked her into the modern decor of the Italian restaurant. Unlike before, there wasn't a chef to fawn over them or pose for pictures, for which she was glad. Although their presence wasn't brazenly acknowledged, Rebel caught a few discreet glances as they ate their first course.

But even that small disturbance disappeared as Draco furnished her with his history. His flawless English had made her think he'd been brought up in England despite his Greek name. Finding out he'd only relocated from Athens to England five years ago came as a surprise. But not as much a surprise as discovering he, like her, had lost his mother during his teens. And that he'd been a champion cross-country skier.

Rebel frowned. 'I know the name of every skier who's won a major competition for the last fifty years.'

One sleek eyebrow rose, giving him a rakish look that she strenuously resisted gawping at. 'Are you accusing me of lying?'

Lowering her gaze to the less interesting subject of her water glass, she shrugged. 'I know what I know.' And she definitely would've remembered him.

'I competed under my mother's maiden name of Christou.'

Her head snapped up. 'The only Christou I remember— you're Drakos Christou! Five-time world champion?' Rebel wasn't aware she'd grabbed his hand until he traced his thumb over hers. She started to pull away but he held her tight. And because she liked it, she stayed.

'Yes.' A lopsided smile accompanied the acknowledgement.

Knowing she was risking fan-girling over him, she reined herself in. 'Wow. You look…different.' He'd sported longer hair and a full beard during his competitions years, and although his build had been leaner, more streamlined, it had suited the sport he'd excelled in. No wonder she hadn't recognised him, despite the faint feeling of familiarity she'd experienced in his office when they'd first met. 'Why the change of name?'

The air thickened, sucking dry the easy banter that had eased their preceding courses. 'My father disapproved of my chosen career. He would've preferred it if I'd joined the family real-estate business and succeeded him. He made it clear I wasn't his son until I came to my senses and gave up skiing.'

'But you didn't give it up.'

His features tightened. 'Not until I was forced to anyway.'

With the realisation of just who Draco Angelis was, the worldwide sensation that had surrounded his departure from cross-country skiing came flooding back. 'You trained yourself for the last competition, but your knee blew out before you could win your sixth trophy.'

The hand now curled around hers tightened. 'Discovering that my trainer had been pushing me past my limits just so he could gamble on my winning the tournament left me no choice.'

A soft gasp left her lips. 'No way. What happened to him?'

His nostrils flared as he dragged in a breath vibrating with quiet fury. 'He faced game throwing and other charges, but by the time the case went to trial and the extent of the gambling ring was discovered, it was too late.'

Sympathy welled through her. 'Your knee injury ended your career.'

His lashes swept down to their joined hands. Slowly his grip loosened and he withdrew from her. Rebel missed the contact with an acuteness that stunned her. Drawing her hand from the table, she lowered it to her lap and balled it.

'Amongst other things. But the most important lesson I learned was to always look beneath the surface. I knew things weren't right, but I chose to ignore them because I was determined to win that final championship.' His words held raw self-condemnation that struck a vulnerable place inside her.

Self-condemnation was an emotion she'd lived with and knew well. But Draco's case was different. He hadn't rushed recklessly into a situation through selfishness. He'd been deceived by someone he'd believed he could trust.

The urge to comfort him snowballed through her, but the rigid control once more clamping his features dissuaded her.

The rest of the meal passed in near silence, and Rebel was thankful when Draco asked for the bill.

She was sliding back into his car when her phone started pinging. Digging it out, she read the congratulatory emails flooding her inbox, almost all of them from people she barely knew.

It wasn't until she clicked an attachment that she saw the first headline.

*Super-Agent and Sports Star Engaged!*

Rebel didn't bother to read the article, knowing this time round the carefully crafted story within was from source. About to click off her phone, she stopped as another picture from a social-media account lit up her screen, along with the history of how many times it'd been viewed.

She gasped.

'Is something wrong?' Draco asked, his gaze spearing her as he paused in the act of securing his seat belt.

She showed him the picture taken of them earlier, as he'd kissed her hand outside the restaurant. The quality of the photo was much too good to have been taken with a discreet phone camera. 'Did you know the paparazzo was there?'

Shrugging, he pressed the ignition and the car roared to life. 'Of course. That was the whole point of the act, wasn't it?'

For a moment, Rebel couldn't speak. Her hand trembled as she tucked her phone back in her bag. She called herself a thousand kinds of fool for each dart of hurt that lanced her. She'd dropped her guard for a handful of moments. So what?

If the figures were to be believed, the public were lapping up the image of a loved-up 'Drabella'.

'Yes, I guess it was,' she replied quietly.

'Then we'll chalk up the night as a success. Put on your seat belt, Arabella.'

Woodenly she complied, then lapsed into silence. After all, what else was there to be said?

Draco left her at her door with instructions to be ready for his chauffeur on Saturday. The announcement that they would be travelling via his private jet to Tuscany was carelessly thrown over his shoulder as he returned to his car. He seemed in a hurry to get away, so Rebel nodded through it all, then hurried inside.

Keeping a tight leash on the ball of emotions that had lodged in her chest, she climbed the stairs to her flat. Her feet froze on the last step as she saw the figure standing in her doorway.

Time and age had taken their toll on the man whose profile was visible in the hallway light, but Rebel would've recognised him anywhere. 'Dad?'

He jerked upright from his slumped position. The eyes her mother had insisted were the exact shade of her own widened a touch before dimming with wariness.

'Arabella.'

Her avid gaze sprinted over him, took in the pertinent details of weight loss pronounced by his baggy clothes, his thinning hair and unshaven face, before meeting his shadowed eyes.

'What…what are you doing here?' Considering she'd been frantically calling him every day for the past two weeks, the question was absurd, but the shock of seeing him again after so many years battered her thought processes.

'I came because of this.' He held up a copy of the latest edition of the evening newspaper. The picture on her phone was blown up on the broadsheet. Rebel's gaze darted away from the picture of her face as Draco bent over her hand, and took a step closer, her insides clenching with hurt as she stared at her father.

'I call you every day for weeks and you don't answer, but you turn up because of a picture in the paper?'

'It's not just any picture, though, is it?' he replied, that trace of condemnation she'd prayed never to hear again underlining his words. 'You need to end whatever this is, Arabella. Now.'

Shakily, she approached him and indicated the door. When he moved away, she inserted the key, opened it and thrust it wide.

She went inside, then didn't breathe until she heard his footsteps behind her.

Looking over her shoulder, she asked, 'Would you like a cup of tea?'

'Arabella—'

'I'm going to boil the kettle. You're already here. You might as well stay for tea.'

She hurried to the kitchen, kicked off her shoes and turned on the kettle. Her father walked in a few seconds later. After giving the room a once-over, he dropped the newspaper on the counter, pulled out a stool at the breakfast bar and sat down.

Struggling to contain her anxiety, Rebel got busy fetching mugs. Once the kettle boiled, she made the tea and slid a cup to him. 'Can I get you anything with it? Biscuits? A sandwich?'

He cradled his cup but made no move to drink it. 'You can tell me what this is about.' He indicated the paper.

'Can we forget about that for a minute, please?' Before he could respond, she rushed on. 'Where have you been? *How* have you been?'

'Away. Fine.' He continued to avoid her gaze, and with each second that ticked by Rebel's heart broke all over again.

'I'm sorry, Dad,' she whispered. 'I don't know how many more times I can say it.'

His breath shuddered on a deep exhale. 'The apology doesn't matter, Arabella. It never did. You're my child. Forgiving you was never a problem.' He pointed to the picture.

'But this is a problem. We spoke a few days ago, then overnight you go and do this?'

Her fingers clenched around her mug. 'You make it sound as if we have long talks on a regular basis. You may have known where I was and what I was doing, but I had no idea where you were. Until two weeks ago, I hadn't heard from you in *years*! And when I did try to talk to you after that, you barely said a handful of words to me. So, no, it hasn't been overnight for me, Dad, but years. Years during which you've watched over me, apparently. How else would you have known I'd been dropped by my sponsors?'

His fingers clenched around the mug. 'I had to.'

Pain clawed deeper. 'Because it was your *duty*? That's what you said in your letter, wasn't it? Was it your duty to deposit stolen money in my account?'

His head jerked up. 'You know?'

'Of course I know. According to Draco you didn't do a great job of hiding your tracks.'

He pushed away the tea and stood. 'Is he threatening you? Is that what this *engagement* is about?' He lurched towards the door. 'I'll turn myself in.'

Slamming her own cup down, she launched herself in the doorway. 'You can't!'

He frowned at her. 'Why not?'

'Because…it's too late. I've used the money and Draco knows it. If you go down, so do I.'

'But you didn't know it was stolen.'

'That doesn't matter. If Draco decides to press charges, I'll automatically become an accessory.'

Her father's throat worked as he swallowed. His head bent forward, and she glimpsed weariness in each movement.

Hesitantly, she placed a hand on his arm. 'Why did you take the money, Dad?' she asked, because deep down she knew he hadn't really changed from the upright, hard-working man she'd grown up admiring. 'Surely you must have known you wouldn't get away with it? That I'd be in the frame too if you were caught?'

He veered away from her, heading back to the stool. His rejection cut deeper but she stood her ground.

'I wasn't…' He stopped and shook his head. 'I wasn't thinking straight. I thought I could sell our old house and replace the money before he found out.'

'Why? Why was this so important to you?' she demanded, desperate for some indication that this hadn't been just duty for him.

'I promised your mother I'd look after you. It was one of the last things I said to her before…' He stopped again.

Rebel swallowed the sob that stemmed from her soul. 'She's gone, Dad. But I'm still here.'

Her father's head slowly rose from its heavy slump, then he speared her with haunted eyes. 'You took her from me. Then you began to turn into an exact copy of her.'

Her heart shrank. 'You hate me for that, don't you?'

He shook his head, his blue eyes swimming with sorrow, sharp and ocean-deep, even after all these years. 'I don't hate you. I could never hate you. But…I can't stand to look at you. Not when you were twenty and we fought constantly until you left home. And not now.'

The stark declaration wrenched a sob free as a part of her died.

'Where do we go from here, Dad?'

'I don't know. You've always known how I feel about your skiing. I always knew it wouldn't end well. And it didn't, did it?'

'Dad—'

'You don't need to talk me round. I know you'll do as you please, like always. But I know this thing you're doing with Angelis isn't the answer. The man is a predator.'

She wanted to refute the allegation. But really, what evidence had she apart from one evening's conversation where a small part of his life's story had tugged at her heartstrings? Draco had reverted to type soon enough.

Besides, she had even less of a choice now. After seeing her father still locked in grief after all this time there was no way she could stand by while he suffered for something he'd felt compelled to do because of her.

Heart in her throat, she shook her head. 'I can't, Dad. Like I said, it's too late.'

A full minute passed before he stood. He paused beside her by the kitchen door, but made no move to touch or even look at her. 'Goodbye, Arabella.'

Her tears came thick and fast long before he shut the door. And it was only through sheer exhaustion that sleep finally overtook her in the early hours.

# CHAPTER NINE

THEY LANDED AT Pisa Airport mid-morning, before being flown by helicopter to Olivio Nardozzi's estate in northern Tuscany.

Draco alighted first before helping Rebel down. Guiding her beneath the rotating blades, he draped his arm around her waist and steered her to the path that led up to the sprawling mid-twentieth-century villa.

Although her mint-green sundress and matching sweater did nothing to alleviate the deep sizzling sensation his touch sent through her body, Rebel was too numb to do more than stay at his side as they approached the wide terrace that overlooked an aqua-tiled Olympic-sized pool.

She'd woken up raw and aching, unable to relive the conversation with her father without experiencing a hopeless, consuming pain at the thought that there could be no easy reconciliation. Not if her father couldn't look at her without—

'Whatever is wrong with you, Arabella, I suggest you get it under control right now,' Draco slashed in a fierce undertone. 'Now is *not* the time to drift into a trance.'

Rebel dragged herself back from the edge of the abyss, thankful that the unseasonably warm weather provided her with the perfect cover of her sunglasses as she blinked back rising tears.

'Not even a love trance with you in the starring role?'

He sent her a glance filled with combative censure, and a touch of disappointment. Reaching down, he plucked the sunglasses from her face and tucked them into his tailored trousers.

'We both know I've been far from your mind since you

boarded my plane in London this morning. I don't expect to be the subject of your thoughts night and day, but I expect you to be both physically and *mentally* present for this to work.' His voice was a low, hard throb so they wouldn't be overheard, but each word held unmistakable warning.

'Cool your jets, Draco. I haven't suddenly taken leave of my senses,' she whispered. Then in a pseudo Marilyn Monroe voice, she added, 'I'm still besotted with love for you and can't wait to tell our hosts what a lucky woman I am to have captured your elusive heart.'

They rounded another sun-dappled terrace and came face-to-face with Carla Nardozzi. Dressed in a pale yellow, clinging sundress, she stood next to an older man Rebel guessed to be her father, Olivio. Judging from their frozen expressions, it was clear her last words had carried. Before embarrassment could kick her hard, Draco strode to the middle of the terrace, where their hosts waited.

'Olivio, good to see you again.' He clasped the older man's hand in a firm greeting, then turned to his daughter. 'Carla, a pleasure, as always.' Draco's smile was warm as he leaned down and kissed the stunning, model-thin figure skater on both cheeks.

Rebel fought the acid-tipped spears that attacked her insides as she watched the scene.

Carla Nardozzi's limpid green eyes stayed on Draco for a second longer than Rebel thought was necessary before both father and daughter turned to her.

Returning to her side, Draco caught her hand in his. 'Allow me to introduce Arabella Daniels.'

Olivio was the first to greet her, eyes a shade lighter than espresso measuring her shrewdly. 'Welcome to my home, Miss Daniels. I look forward to making your further acquaintance,' he said in a thick accent.

'Thanks. And I'm sorry if you overheard me just then.'

'Nonsense. A woman should shout her love for her man from the rooftops. If it is genuine, that is,' Olivio declared.

His eyes dropped to her engagement ring, his scrutiny long and intense before he smiled at her.

Rebel forced her own smile wider. 'Oh, I'm glad you think so. Not everyone approves of public displays of affection.'

Carla came forward, her hand outstretched. Her caramel-streaked, chocolate-brown hair was pulled up into a severe chignon, the effect showing off the sleek lines of her jaw and neck. 'A pleasure to meet you.'

Rebel shook her cool hand, but before she could reply, Carla continued, 'So, it's true, then, what the papers are saying? You two are really engaged?' Her eyes drifted briefly over Rebel before they returned to Draco. Seeing the almost imploring look in the other woman's gaze, a boulder wedged in Rebel's midriff.

'Yes, it's true. I've finally succumbed to my heart's desire.' Molten grey eyes met Rebel's in a look designed to fool the most hardened heart.

Feeling him about to lift their linked hands and kiss hers as he had on Wednesday night, Rebel tensed her arm. Moving closer, she draped her hand on his chest and rose to kiss his cheek. His muted exhalation was the only exhibition of surprise at her move.

'But…didn't you two meet only recently?' Carla pressed, her eyes darting searchingly between them.

Rebel laughed and shook her head. 'We only chose not to make our relationship public before now since Draco is a *monster* when it comes to his privacy.'

Carla's smile was a little stiff. '*Sì*, I haven't forgotten.'

The boulder in Rebel's chest grew. 'Anyway, it's all out in the open now. Which is just as well because from the moment I met Draco, I knew my life would never be the same again. Fortunately, he felt the same and now doesn't mind shouting it to the world. In fact, he wouldn't leave my flat earlier this week until I'd accepted his ring and everyone knew I belonged to him. Isn't that right, darling?' She let her gaze drift over his face, stopping to linger at his mouth before meeting his eyes.

His eyes gleamed without a trace of mockery as his head angled towards hers. 'Only because my heart insisted you were mine, and I wasn't about to let you get away.'

A delicate throat-clearing fractured the moment. And yet Rebel couldn't look away from Draco, despite the astonishing evidence of his superb acting skills.

He broke the connection first. Rebel slowly sucked in a restorative breath before facing their hosts.

'Apologies for being sceptical. We wanted to be sure the media wasn't playing tricks on us,' Olivio stated. 'But now that you have confirmed this news, we must celebrate.' He snapped his fingers and a member of his staff rolled forward a serving trolley. At Olivio's nod, the server plucked a bottle of vintage Pol Roger champagne from a silver ice bucket and popped the cork.

'Not for me, thank you,' Carla said when she was offered a glass. 'I have another training session in an hour.'

'Ah, *sì*.' Olivio smiled indulgently. 'My daughter, she's the ultimate perfectionist. Never resting until the gold crown is on her head. And then she gets to work again the very next day.'

Carla paled slightly, a trace of anxiety passing over her face before she regained her composure.

Beside her, Draco tensed and a momentary trace of anger pursed his lips. But he lifted his glass at Olivio's prompt.

'To your future union. May it last for as long as there are stars in the sky.'

Carla excused herself as soon as the toasts were done, walking away with a painfully erect posture. As soon as he'd finished his drink, Olivio summoned another member of staff.

'This is Stefano, your personal butler. He will show you to your rooms and give you a tour of the grounds and facilities when you're ready. I have a few more guests arriving today, but tonight we're doing things a little informally. Food and drinks will be ready whenever you are out here on the terrace. There's nothing more special than dining al fresco on a cool Tuscan night.' Although he smiled, the warmth didn't quite reach his eyes.

The men shook hands, and Draco steered her out of the room.

The interior of the villa was opulence personified, with marble the dominant feature gleaming on the floors and walls. Followed a close second by Carla. Her pictures and trophies were displayed proudly on every surface. On the walls, several portraits and pictures with world leaders and dignitaries documented her from childhood to womanhood. It was clear Olivio regarded his daughter as his prized possession.

Rebel batted away the desperate envy she felt towards the other woman as the memory of the scene with her own father threatened to cut her off at the knees. Locking it away at the back of her mind once more, Rebel focused instead on the endless stream of Carla-mania, experiencing a touch of unease as she realised how extensive the displays were.

She was forcing herself not to think about the more disturbing interaction between Draco and Carla when she entered their designated suite and stumbled to a halt. Peripherally, she heard Draco dismiss Stefano and shut the door behind him, but she couldn't look away from the bed.

It was huge. Set on a pedestal made for lovers. With no other bed or divan in sight.

'Staring in horror at the bed won't let it magically dissolve into twin beds, *glikia mou*,' Draco drawled as he walked past her, pulling his shirt from his trousers as he crossed to what she assumed was a dressing room.

She stared, dry-mouthed, as he unbuttoned his shirt and shrugged it off. Discarding it on the centre island, he toed off his shoes as he went to a shelf and selected a white polo shirt. Barefooted, he strutted back into the room, then paused, one eyebrow raised at her.

'Are you staring at me in horror now because you want *me* to disappear?'

Rebel knew she was gaping at his contoured chest. The expanse of golden, vibrant skin made her tingle from head to toe. Which was bad. Really, really bad.

'I…we didn't discuss sleeping arrangements,' she blurted.

'Because it was inevitable that we would have to share a room with one bed in it for obvious reasons.'

The fever that had gripped her spiked. 'Well, you should've told me so I was better prepared, seeing as I'm not as well-versed in fake engagements as you seem to be.'

'Keep your voice down,' he warned as he sauntered towards her.

'Oh, please. You don't really think Olivio's skulking outside, eavesdropping on us, do you?'

He stopped in front of her. Still shirtless. More devastating to her senses. 'You tell me. Do you think our performance convinced him?'

'I don't think anything convinces Olivio that he can't hold physically in his hand.'

Grey eyes narrowed at her. 'What makes you say that?'

'Most people keep their trophies in a cabinet in a special room. He keeps Carla's trophies and pictures within easy view and reach, as if he needs a visual reminder of his and her success. I bet he's framed every endorsement he's negotiated on her behalf too. So I guess you were right about this.' She wriggled her ring finger. 'If nothing else, the fat diamond should work for us. Can you put your shirt on?' she snapped, forcing her knees to lock so she didn't retreat from the sinful temptation that was his bare torso. Or worse, lunge at him!

Both his eyebrows arched and a wolfish grin curved his lips. 'Why, Arabella, you'd think you'd never seen a half-naked man before.'

'Whether I have or not isn't the question here. It is whether the visual…situation is my choice, or whether it's imposed on me.'

'I see you've regained your smart mouth. If nothing else, I suppose it's better than your sullen mood this morning.'

Draco watched her eyes dim as if a switch had been turned off. For the first time in his life, he wanted to curse himself for stating a truth when discretion would've been the better part of valour. Truth be told, he hadn't enjoyed sharing space with a silent Arabella. He hadn't on Wednesday night either on the drive back from dinner. But *then*, he'd been reflecting on their dinner conversation, a part of him wondering whether he'd taken leave of his senses somewhere between the first and second courses. No other explanation made sense as to why he'd divulged intimate details known only to his closest family. Even the trial he'd mentioned had been held behind closed doors to protect Maria.

He'd eventually reasoned his behaviour away as a necessary evil in the task he'd undertaken. In the grand scheme of things, what did it matter if Arabella knew a few more details about him than he was comfortable with? He seriously doubted that she would step out of line with the threat of criminal charges hanging over her head.

He'd expected things to resume as planned, only to be met with a woman who, while he'd felt a modicum of satisfaction that she wasn't jumping at his touch any more, didn't seem inclined to engage with him on any level whatsoever.

And that had been before he'd seen the heavy traces of anguish shadowing her eyes this morning. He'd spotted the evidence of tears beneath her cleverly applied make-up the moment she'd stepped on the plane that not even the sunglasses had been able to disguise. Her mournful posture when she didn't think she was being observed had added to the mounting evidence that something had happened between Wednesday night and this morning.

'Arabella? Is something wrong?' he prompted when she remained silent.

A burst of laughter tripped from her lips but her gaze refused to meet his. 'Right at this moment, nothing that a quick chat about our sleeping arrangements won't fix.'

She was being evasive, but, short of shaking the truth out of her, Draco had no choice but to bite down on his frustration. 'You're that concerned about sharing?' He glanced at the bed. 'The bed is big enough for two. Or are you afraid you'll attack me in the middle of the night?'

She shrugged. 'I already have a few black marks against me. I'd rather leave grievous bodily harm off my list of sins.' Her tone was light but held a brittle edge that sliced at him. He searched her expression, his fingers itching to catch her chin and make her look at him so he could see beneath the snarky surface.

Draco wasn't entirely sure why he didn't. Perhaps he was wary of exposing a different set of problems. Where Arabella was afraid of close contact with him, was he craving it with her? More than that, was he craving more of the closeness he'd felt when he'd opened up to her about his past?

He stepped back abruptly. The questions were absurd in and of themselves. They were both playing a part. Closeness was a given. But not to be mistaken for anything he needed, never mind craved.

'If you're that worried about it, you take the bed. There's a living room through there with a comfortable enough sofa.'

He tugged his polo shirt over his head and returned to the dressing room to don his loafers.

'Do you want a tour of the training facilities?'

Her nod held relief. 'If you hang on a sec, I'll change into my trainers.'

When she joined him a few minutes later, she'd tied her hair into a ponytail. Stefano showed them where several golf buggies were parked in a neat row after Draco refused a personal escort.

He took the path that curved west of the villa, then aimed the buggy towards the domed building that sat atop a small hill. 'You seem to know your way around.' Her tone was neutral, as if she didn't care whether he answered or not.

When he glanced her way, her face was angled away from him.

His jaw clenched for a tight second. 'Yes. I've been here a few times. I advised Olivio during the training-facility build five years ago.'

She frowned. 'That implies a friendship. But you don't react to each other as friends do.'

'Probably because over the years we haven't seen eye to eye on a few issues.'

Her gaze flitted to him, speculated, then drifted away. 'But he still wants you to marry his daughter.'

Draco shrugged. 'Purely for dynastic reasons.'

Her mouth firmed and minutes ticked by as they crawled up the hill.

Bringing the buggy to a halt before large studio doors, he stopped her as she went to get out. 'I don't like it when you're quiet. If there's something on your mind, spit it out.'

Dull blue eyes met his. 'I thought you didn't like it when I used my smart mouth?'

His gaze dropped to the plump lips in question and heat dredged through him. 'I'm finding that I prefer it to your silence.'

She froze. They stared at each other for several charged seconds, the atmosphere growing thick and sultry, until she broke the connection and jumped from the buggy. 'Be careful what you wish for or I may never shut up again,' she said over her shoulder.

Deciding that it wasn't a scenario he was completely dissatisfied with, Draco followed her into the facility. The main feature was the enormous ice rink, around which several specialist gyms and sports-health centres had been installed. He found Arabella in the weights room, inspecting the state-of-the-art equipment.

She looked up as he entered. 'I'm in charge of my own training this weekend so the bench press is out of the question.'

'What are you swapping it with?'

'Free weights.'

He shook his head. 'You can't switch this far into the training.'

'It's only for this weekend. I talked it over with my trainer.'

'A small change can go a long way to hurt you. If you don't need to change it, don't. I'll spot you.'

Her eyes widened. 'Don't you have other stuff to attend to?'

'They will be dealt with. But not at the risk of neglecting your training.'

She blinked at him, her mouth dropping open to form responses that never emerged. Again he felt the gravity of unspoken words.

When minutes ticked by, he gritted his teeth. 'Are you happy with that?'

A shrug lifted her shoulders. 'Sure. If you want.'

As they left the gym the sound of blades cutting across ice filled the hall below. They both paused and watched as Carla, dressed in a white leotard, glided across the frozen surface.

She moved with effortless grace, years of practice making her fearless as she executed jumps and pirouettes that had seen her rise to the top of her game.

As he watched her, the wretched pain that came with wondering what Maria could've been slammed into him. Gripping the railing, he stared at the figure below and saw the image of his sister, her wide, infectious smile lighting her face as she did the only thing she'd ever dreamt of doing.

'She's breathtaking.'

He heard the voice from afar, lost as he was in torment-ing memories. 'Yes, she is,' he breathed, still unable to take his eyes off the figure. Draco wasn't sure how long he stood there, wishing he could change the past. Know-ing he couldn't.

When he resurfaced, Arabella had moved a short dis-tance away, facing away from the railing with her arms folded. Her face was averted, but he caught the pain etched deep into her profile.

About to call her name, demand that she tell him what was wrong once and for all, he froze as a dark tingling seized his nape. A door slammed shut at the far side of the rink and he watched a figure glide to where Carla had stopped in the middle of the ice.

Every nerve in Draco's body tightened as he recognised the man.

'Draco?' Rebel's voice came from a tunnel of darkness.

'Hmm?'

'Are you okay?'

'No,' he bit out.

'What's going on?'

'That man Carla's talking to. That's Tyson Blackwell.'

Arabella turned around, glanced down at the ice. 'Did you know he was going to be here?'

'No. Olivio chose not to inform me of that fact.' His grip tightened around the smooth railing, the urge to rip it from its moorings clawing at him.

'Right. As devious as that sounds, unless you intend to stare Tyson to death, can we get out of here, please?' Her voice trembled, her features pinched in misery.

Without waiting for an answer, she vaulted out of the door and rushed down the stairs.

He emerged into sunlight, fury still burning in his chest. Draco had never felt inclined to cause bodily harm. Not when his trainer had sent him down a path that had ruined his dream. Not even when he'd surfaced from his nightmares to find his sister's life equally ruined.

But seeing Blackwell here, preparing to sink his teeth into yet another victim, Draco had to fight hard to resist the urge to march back in and rip the man to pieces.

Instead, he forced one foot in front of the other. Reaching the buggy, he slammed on the ignition, wishing he had an engine far more powerful than a battery-packed one.

Beside him, Arabella sat in silence once again, her hands folded in her lap, her features remote. The volatile emotions churned harder inside him. A roar mounted in his head.

With no outlet, hopelessness closed over him, dark and devastating. In that moment, Draco knew his only choice was to drive. So he let the silence reign.

# CHAPTER TEN

'COME THIS WAY. I know a back way to the suite,' Draco said, his voice a gruff command.

From the moment she'd seen his face as he watched Carla skate, Rebel's world had turned dark and her misery had bloomed. Like toxic smoke, it'd sped through her veins, insidious and inescapable, until her body was steeped in it.

Up until that moment, she hadn't realised she'd been using Draco as a balm against the gaping wound of her father's rejection since she'd stepped on his plane this morning. It didn't matter that the man was often times cold and ruthless, or cutting and dismissive. It didn't even matter that, when it came right down to it, she was an unwitting criminal, who dangled between jail and freedom at the sole discretion of the man she was relying on to drag her from her nightmares.

All she'd cared about was that she was with him, and not at her flat, reliving each word her father had said. She'd been sure it was why the thought of a history between Draco and Carla chafed as much as it did.

Draco's face as he'd watched Carla glide over the ice had hammered home a different truth—her reasons for relying on Draco weren't wholly for the sake of avoiding thinking about her father.

The level of her misery had forced her to acknowledge another truth. Draco obviously cared for Carla beyond platonic or business interests.

'The sight of Carla with that man upsets you that much?' she forced herself to ask, because she couldn't *not* know.

'Yes, it does,' he grated as they mounted stairs that ended in two wraparound terraces.

Her heart dipped, along with her ability to think straight. She followed almost robot-like as he took the left wrap-around terrace, which brought them to a set of French doors. He thrust it open and they entered the hallway that led to their suite.

She stepped in front of him as he was about to head to the living room.

'Carla means more to you than just getting her away from Tyson Blackwell, doesn't she?' she challenged, absently wondering why she couldn't stop herself from probing a point that seemed to lance her with arrows of bewildering pain.

Draco frowned. 'Of course. You think I'd go through all this for someone I didn't care about?'

Rebel's hand shook as she lifted it to her temple. 'Sorry, I'm confused. You care enough about her to want to save her from Tyson, but it's just the marrying her that you're against?'

'I'm against being manipulated, period,' he snarled. 'Somewhere along the line, Olivio has obviously concluded he can leverage my private life to suit him. That's not going to happen. Now if you're done with your questions, I'd appreciate not being interrogated further about this. You know your role. Just play it and we'll be fine.'

He went to the drinks cabinet. Grabbing a bottle of single-malt whisky, he pulled the cork and poured two fingers into a crystal tumbler.

He knocked it back in one clean swallow. Then he slammed the glass down and clenched both hands in his hair.

Several Greek curses fell from his lips as he paced the floor.

Chest tight with emotions she refused to name, she eyed him. 'You do realise that if you insist on continuing this façade and you don't do anything about the state you're in, you're going to blow this charade wide open, don't you?'

He paused mid-stride. 'Why do you think I'm in here knocking back drinks instead of out there, punching Blackwell's face in?' he growled.

Rebel flinched. She needed to walk away, leave him alone to handle this on his own. She wasn't equipped to deal with anyone's emotional fallout; not when she was actively hiding from her own. But she'd also never seen anyone care this deeply…not since witnessing the unstinting adoration between her parents. She'd deeply missed the overflow of warmth from that special bond. So even though a physical ache lodged in her chest as she watched Draco try to wrestle his emotions under control, she remained rooted to the floor beside the armchair.

'Are you going to talk to Carla about this?'

'I'll have to. I can't let this go any further. Olivio might not listen, but I hope she will.'

He dropped his hands from the back of his neck and then stared at his trembling fingers. He seemed fascinated with his body's reaction. Then slowly he clenched his fists and exhaled. Although his body calmed, the Draco who walked past her with a curt, 'I need a shower,' possessed eyes so bleak they were almost black.

She instinctively reached out and grasped his arm. He jerked to a stop, his gaze going to where she held him, then back to her face.

'Arabella, I'm not thinking very rationally right now,' he rasped. Residual fury vibrated off him, emotional aftershocks that threatened to bury her the longer she stayed this close.

'I know, and I'll be quick. I just wanted to say, if you can help it, don't let this eat you up too much.'

'As long as that bastard is sniffing around her, it'll eat me up.'

'But—'

His hand shot out to grip her arm, the other coming up to hover over her mouth. His thumb slid across her mouth.

'Enough, *glikia mou*. I don't want to think about Black-well any more. So enough. Okay?' Bleak eyes searched hers, pleading.

At her nod, he dropped his hand. And replaced it with his mouth. Shock held her still long enough for him to delve between her lips. Then pure, unadulterated sensation took over. Her moan rose up from her soul, excavating every yearning she'd tried to suppress since Wednesday night. Her hands gripped his bare arms, the fierce joy of touching him somewhere else besides his nape and face piercing her. She strained up, plastering her needy, super-charged body against his, and earning herself an answering groan in return. One hand trailed the length of her back to her behind, then splayed open to drag her even closer. She ground against his erection, her nerves tingling, the secret place between her legs dampening, readying itself for this man...

This man who didn't belong to her.

He nipped at the corner of her bottom lip just as she jerked away from him. They parted and she was left with a coppery taste in her mouth. Draco's eyes zeroed in on the spot, a hiss issuing from his lips. 'Arabella *mou*...your lip.' He reached out. She danced out of his way.

'It's okay, I'm fine.' She licked at the spot again, and he groaned.

'Sweetheart, let me—'

'No. You can't do this, Draco.'

He stared at her for a frozen second, his breath shuddering in and out. With another curse, he threw his head back and closed his eyes for a brief moment. Exhaling one last time, he stared straight at her. 'No. I guess not. But next time, tell me which body part you want me to cry on before I go thinking everything is available to me.'

'How about we agree right now that *none* of it is available to you?'

His gaze dropped to her mouth. 'So I get your *words* and nothing else?'

'Wasn't that what you wanted?' she replied.

A stiff smile twitched one corner of his mouth. 'Thanks for the reminder.'

He strode out of the room with long, angry strides. Rebel waited till she heard the faint sound of running water before she hurried to the dressing room. She swapped her trainers for heels that would elevate her attire back to smart casual. Combing out her hair, she sprayed perfume on her wrists before grabbing her bag and slipping out onto the terrace. She reclined on the shaded lounger, willing her racing pulse to subside as she plucked her phone and earphones from her bag. Cranking up the music, she tucked up her legs to her chest.

Much as she'd have liked to escape the suite totally, she didn't want to risk running into Olivio or any of his guests without Draco in case the agitation bubbling beneath her skin showed. If Draco wanted to stay, he would need his acting skills to get them *both* through tonight and tomorrow.

Rebel grew drowsy as her pulse finally calmed and her thundering heartbeat stopped roaring in time to the music.

The feeling of a soft blanket being draped over her roused her from sleep. Draco sat on the twin lounger, his eyes a lot less volatile than they'd been. In fact, he looked downright solemn and perhaps even a touch contrite.

'How long have I been asleep?' she asked around a dry mouth.

He handed her a cool drink, which she accepted and sipped gratefully. 'Long enough for your cycle of crazy music to play three times.'

So just over two hours. 'It's not crazy music. It calms me down.' She bit her lip as she said it, wondering if she would unwittingly set him off.

But he remained seated, his gaze steady on her. 'I owe you an apology. You were trying to help and I...took advantage.'

A knot she hadn't acknowledged unravelled inside her.

'You warned me you weren't thinking rationally. I should've let you go, not insisted on saying my piece.'

His mouth twisted. 'Your piece, brief as it was, was very welcome. It saved the shower wall from getting a pounding.'

'Yikes. Not sure you'd have come off without serious battle scars, what with *all* that marble.'

He grinned, then sobered after a few seconds. 'While you were asleep, I spoke to Olivio. He won't discuss his business with Blackwell, but it turns out he's not staying at the villa. I guess Olivio wasn't prepared to risk one of us walking out.'

'Did you get a chance to talk to Carla?' she asked.

He shook his head. 'She was resting after her training.'

Rebel twirled the straw through her drink. 'So what now?'

'We can go down to dinner. Or we can stay here and have dinner brought up to us. We are newly engaged, after all.'

The thought of not having to put on a show in front of strangers was hugely appealing. She'd fallen asleep before she'd worked things through and now the events of the afternoon came flooding back.

Setting her half-empty glass down, she braced her elbows on her knees and massaged her temples.

He frowned. 'Are you all right?'

'I'm trying to wrap my mind around all this.'

Draco sighed, a wave of cold misery rushing over his face before he schooled his features. Then he released a breath. 'Perhaps a further explanation would help?'

'Please,' she murmured.

For almost a minute, his jaw clenched tight. 'After my knee blew out and my career ended, I shut everyone out. I was angry with myself for not seeing what Larson and his team were up to. I just gave my statement to the police and let them handle it. What I didn't know was that they'd missed one crucial member of the team. Larson's nephew.'

Her heart leapt into her throat as she made the connection. 'Tyson Blackwell?'

Draco nodded grimly. 'He was in charge of my sister's training.'

'Your *sister*?'

'Yes.' He blew out a ragged breath. 'Maria was a figure skater. She and Carla are best friends. They don't see each other as regularly any more, but she idolises Carla. Watching Carla's videos was the only thing that pulled her from the brink after the accident.'

'What happened to Maria?'

'What always happens when Blackwell's in charge. He pushed her past her limit. She was doing a quadruple rotation she was woefully unprepared for when she fell and hit her head on the ice. She fractured her third vertebrae and lost the use of her arms and legs.'

A sob strangled Rebel's chest. 'No!'

'By the time I got my head on straight after my own accident, Blackwell had covered his tracks. He stood trial but he only got an eighteen-month ban for two of his trainees missing doping tests. He got off scot-free for what he did to Maria.' Bitterness and anger twisted his face.

The same expressions he'd exhibited this afternoon as he'd watched Carla skating…

Had she got it wrong? Had she attributed a different spin on Draco's feelings for Carla? The pressure eased in her chest. Surely he wouldn't have gone to the trouble of engineering a fake engagement to put off a woman he could have had if he felt so inclined? From the first, it'd been Olivio's manipulation and Tyson Blackwell's presence in Carla's life that had enraged Draco.

Relief punched through her, startling a laugh from her throat.

'What?' Draco demanded.

'I…nothing.' She sobered and reached out, curling her hand around his jaw before the action fully registered. 'I know it's hard to believe, but what happened to your sister wasn't your fault.'

He shook his head. 'It was. Larson didn't broadcast it but I knew he had a nephew. I was so focused on my career, I didn't pay attention to the team my father had hired for Maria. If I'd been around more, I would've noticed that things weren't right.'

'Sorry to break it to you, but if you couldn't see it in your own team, how would you have noticed it in your sister's team?'

Raw anguish propelled him to his feet. 'I was her older brother. I was supposed to look after her!'

The weight of her own guilt crushed down on her. 'Blind spots when it comes to our family are dangerously common.'

He stopped and stared down at her. 'Your father?'

She shrugged, her chest clamped in a steel vice. 'Me. My mother. We all have our faults. Some are a little more unforgivable than others.'

Exhaling sharply, Draco strode to the terrace railing a few feet away and gripped it hard. The muscles in his back bunched as tension gripped him harder. 'I had you investigated—I'm sure you understand why. Your mother died in a skiing accident. You weren't responsible for her death.'

The blood drained from her face, and her lungs closed up. Dropping her head forward, she desperately tried to get her blood pumping again.

Sound faded in and out as she tried to breathe.

'Arabella!'

A moment later, Draco swung her into his arms and strode back into the suite. The sofa was the closest comfortable surface. He placed her there and drew the blanket over her and crouched before her. 'I shouldn't have left you in the sun for so long.'

'I'm fine.'

'You're not. You didn't eat on the plane and you haven't

eaten since we got here,' he huffed. Rising, he headed for the door. Rebel heard him issuing instructions to Stefano before he returned to the living room.

Despite the guilt eating her alive, she couldn't look away from him as he sat on the coffee table and leaned towards her. Brushing her hair from her face, he tucked a strand behind her ear. The side of his finger smoothed over her cheek to her jaw before repeating the caress.

The gesture was so sweet, she wanted to relive it over and over. 'Are you going soft on me, Draco?' she murmured.

'Only until you're back on your feet,' he murmured back. 'Then it'll be all-out war again.'

She sighed. 'War is exhausting.'

'Who have you been fighting, *glikia mou*? Besides me, that is?' he asked, his voice a gentle rumble that lulled her from the secret place she'd inhabited for far too long.

'My father.'

'You've seen him?'

Her gaze clashed with his. 'Will you hate me if I say yes?'

He stilled, his finger dangerously close to her pulse. 'Family is complicated, I get that. Besides, I gave my word that if you fulfilled your part of the agreement, I'd forgive the debt.'

Relief flooded her. 'All right, then. He was waiting for me when I got in on Wednesday night.'

Draco frowned. 'At your flat?'

'Yes. He'd seen the news of our engagement in the paper.'

One brow rose. 'Let me guess—he came to warn you off me?'

She nodded. 'He's not a fan of yours.'

His mouth twisted. 'I don't have many of those these days who aren't contracted to me in some fashion or other.'

Her eyelids felt heavy again, but she fought them open. 'I was your fan way before you turned into Draco the Dragon.'

'*Efkharisto*, Arabella.'

'I love the way that sounds.'

'What?'

'The Greek…and my name.'

She stared up at him, her breath catching all over again at the sheer dynamic beauty of his face. Then she shut her eyes when his image swam. 'Why am I drowsy again?'

'Probably because you haven't slept well recently.'

'Hmm. You're bad for my health.'

His mouth twitched. 'You were telling me about your father.'

'Yes. He offered to turn himself in so I wouldn't be engaged to you any longer. I refused.'

She wasn't sure whether the sharp exhalation came from him or her, but she pressed on. 'I told him it was too late. I'd given you my word. Besides, I don't think prison dungarees would suit me, do you?'

'You'd look good in anything, but perhaps prison gear shouldn't be on anyone's wish list.'

'I agree. Anyway, he accepted that there was nothing he could do so…' She tried to shrug, but couldn't quite pull it off. Sorrow clawed at her, her father's words still fresh, and deep, and anchored into her heart. Tears brimmed and rolled down her temples.

This time Draco's hiss was audible. 'What did he say to you?'

'I asked when I'd see him again. He said he…he couldn't look at me without seeing my mother…and that it hurt too much that she's no longer alive, so he intends to stay away.'

He surged to his feet. '*Thee mou.* What sort of man is he?' he raged.

Rebel struggled up. When he tried to stay her, she grabbed his hand. 'You don't understand, Draco. He loved my mother. I mean *really* loved her. It shattered him completely when she died.' Another tear rolled down her face. She swiped at it with her free hand.

'It still doesn't excuse his treatment of you.'

Her heart ached that she couldn't tell Draco the last piece

of her life's puzzle. But after hearing him condemn himself and anyone who'd been responsible for his sister's injuries, Rebel knew he would never forgive her for causing her mother's death. 'Does it hurt? Sure. But I don't want him to be in pain because of me. If he can find some peace away from me, then…'

Draco made a rough sound at the back of his throat. Raising her head, she met his laser-sharp gaze. 'You'd sacrifice that? A lifetime's relationship just so he could be happy?'

Her tiredness was receding. But with more clarity came harrowing pain. 'As opposed to him being miserable with me? Yes, I would.'

'You're…extraordinary,' he husked out.

She raised one eyebrow. 'You seem surprised.'

The knock on the suite door stopped their conversation. Draco stared down at her for several heartbeats before he called out for Stefano to enter.

The trolley was heaving with meats and sausages from the barbecue going on by the poolside, Stefano informed them. Warm focaccia bread, with olive oil and garlic sauces, and an assortment of salads were unearthed from beneath domed dishes.

Dismissing Stefano, Draco heaped a plate with food and set her tray down on her lap. After seeing to his own, he sat down next to her. They ate in companionable silence, for once at ease with each other's company.

Her insides clenched momentarily at the thought of the tight secret lodged inside her. She'd thrown caution to the wind and told him as much as she could about her relationship with her father. Despite Draco's harsh views, she knew he wouldn't go after her father as long as she kept up her end of the bargain.

She was used to flying through the air without a safety harness or a net to break her fall. Ski jumping was one of the riskiest sports out there, and yet she'd thrown herself into it without a backward glance.

She glanced at Draco and found his gaze, direct and intense, on her.

Perhaps it was time to take a different, equally exhilarating, risk.

# CHAPTER ELEVEN

THE SOUND OF the door shutting woke Rebel in the early hours. She'd said goodnight to Draco shortly after their meal last night with an arrangement to head out to the gym at five a.m.

Turning over in bed, she stretched her limbs, groaning with relief at the most restful sleep she'd had since her father's letter had brought her nightmares about losing her mother surging back. She hadn't even needed her earphones to drown out the demons.

Glancing at the clock, she noticed it was only four-fifteen. Had Draco headed out to get his own training in before he trained with her? Pushing aside the covers, she sprang out of bed. On the off-chance she was mistaken, she peeked into the living room. The sofa bed had been tucked away and the sheets folded up.

Deciding to join him, Rebel changed into her exercise gear, caught up her phone and earphones, and left the suite. Knowing she would get lost if she tried the shortcut, she went through the villa, unease striking all over again at the gratuitous display of Carla Nardozzi's pictures and trophies.

She stepped out into the crisp air, thankful that the whole estate was well lit. After stretching her arms and legs, she placed her earphones in and struck out in the direction of the facility.

The studio door stood ajar when she reached it. She slipped in and muted her music.

The cry from the direction of the ice rink froze her steps.

Changing direction, she entered the room to witness the tail end of an argument between Carla and Tyson Blackwell.

He had her gripped by the arms, Carla's whimper echoing across the room.

'You want to win another glitzy trophy? Then do what I tell you to do!'

'A triple axel into a death spiral sounds insane!'

'Damn it, maybe I am wasting my time with you. All your competitors are doing it. Fail to master it and you can kiss your career goodbye.'

He flung her away from him. Carla tried to catch herself but went sprawling onto the ice.

Rebel stepped into the light. 'Hey, you can't talk to her like that!'

Tyson whirled from his fallen victim. 'Who the hell are you?'

'Someone who can see that you're pushing her way too hard.'

He shooed her away. 'The way I run my training programme is none of your business. Now, I suggest you clear off.'

'I'm not going anywhere. Unless Mr Nardozzi decides to throw me out, of course.' From the corner of her eye, she saw Carla drag herself up and totter on her blades.

Turning, shock slammed through Rebel at the full blast of the younger girl's glare before Carla carefully schooled her features.

'She's my father's guest. She's here with Draco Angelis.'

Even from several dozen feet away, Rebel saw malicious interest spark in his eyes. Leaving Carla's side, he slid across the ice to her.

'So you're Angelis' little piece on the side I've heard so much about this past week.' His head tilted. 'You look familiar. Do I know you?' A suggestive leer draped his face.

'Yeah, in your dreams.'

The leer evaporated. 'This is a training session, not a spectator event. Please leave.'

Rebel looked past him to where Carla stood, a forlorn

figure in the centre of the ice rink. About to call out to her, she spun at the sound of thundering footsteps.

'Arabella!'

The urgency in Draco's deep voice sent a delicious spark down her spine. 'In here,' she called out.

He surged into the room a second later, his eyes narrowing as they zeroed in on her. 'You were supposed to wait for me—' He froze as he spotted Tyson Blackwell. Then he looked past him to where Carla was poised.

When Draco's eyes clashed with Rebel's, his rage had quadrupled. 'What the hell's going on here?'

'I'm conducting a training session. Have you been out of the game so long you've forgotten even the basics, Angelis?' Tyson sneered.

Draco ignored him. Striding to the edge of the ring, he called out, 'Carla. Come here.'

'Hey, what the hell—? Stay where you are, girl,' Tyson countered.

After a moment's hesitation, Carla skated to Draco. This close, the finger marks where Tyson had gripped her were visible against her pearly skin.

Fury flared through Draco's nostrils. 'Did he do this to you?' he grated out.

Hesitantly, Carla nodded. Draco pointed a finger at Tyson. 'You're finished. If you know what's good for you, find a deep dark hole and disappear inside. If I see you around one more skater, the only place you'll be heading to is jail to join your bastard uncle.'

'You have no authority here, Angelis. I have Olivio's full support. If you think you're going to change that, forget it,' he snarled. Glancing at Carla, he added, 'We'll pick this up later.' Tyson rolled back to the other end of the ice rink, kicked off his blades and stormed out via another entrance.

Holding out his hand, Draco helped Carla down. 'Take off your blades. I'll take you back to the villa.'

With a dazzling smile at Draco, Carla replaced her blades with heeled boots and tucked her hand through his arm.

Despite choosing to believe that there was nothing romantic between Draco and Carla, Rebel's stomach still contracted with irrational envy as she watched them disappear through the door.

'Right. Guess I'll see you when I see you,' she muttered, unprepared for the renewed misery snaking through her. Just as she was unprepared for Draco to suddenly reappear as she mounted the stairs to the weight room.

'What do you think you're doing?' he snapped.

She paused on the second step. 'Umm…going training?'

'Not without me, you're not.' Taking her arm, he walked her out and sat her on the remaining unoccupied passenger seat of the buggy, which happened to be behind a less-than-happy-looking Carla.

Draco walked Carla to the villa door once they arrived, his low murmuring voice eliciting several nods from her before she went in and shut the door behind her.

His demeanour changed as he strode back to the buggy. Sliding behind the wheel, he flicked her a glance. 'Get in the front.'

She complied, simply because she wanted to be closer to him. She was barely seated when the buggy surged forward. The five-minute journey felt like hours, the easy silence they'd shared last night a smoky figment of her imagination.

As they crested the hill she cleared her throat. 'Are you upset with me?'

His jaw clenched hard before he spoke. 'Damn right. You were supposed to wait for me. Instead I returned to find you gone.'

'I woke up early and thought you were here, at the facility.'

'I'd just gone to get a drink of coffee. We agreed to come here together. At five. Instead I found you here, in the cross hairs of a man I wouldn't trust with my goldfish.'

'Then we should be thankful I'm more substantial than a goldfish, shouldn't we? And for the record, I pack a hell of a punch when threatened.'

His eyes narrowed. 'Is that jibe aimed at me?'

'Unless you plan to attack me, no.'

His hand slashed through the air. 'I don't like this. In case you've forgotten we're still playing a role. One Olivio is keeping a close eye on.'

'Being engaged doesn't mean we're joined at the hip. You were worried about overcooking things. You not letting me out of your sight runs the risk of doing just that. You can frown all you want, but it's the truth.'

'I hardly think not wanting to be parted from you sends that message. Certainly not at four o'clock in the morning when you should be in bed with me.'

Rebel sighed. 'You found me, Draco. I'm okay. Let's chalk it up to a win because my getting here early stopped Tyson from manhandling Carla more than he did.'

Fury detonated. The vibrations from him threatened to flatten her. 'What if you'd been on your own with him?' he seethed.

'I wasn't,' she stated simply.

He fisted his hair for a charged second before he jerked out of the buggy. 'You wanted to train so badly? Let's get to it, then.'

Rebel followed him in, her senses surging higher as she followed his ruggedly lean body up the stairs to the weights room.

Over the next hour, he set a blistering place, his commands bullet fast and relentless.

'Faster!' he shouted over the sound of the treadmill.

'Lower!' he boomed from behind her as she sank into another excruciating squat.

'Damn it, lock your elbows.'

'Damn it, they *are* locked!'

He leaned over the weight bar vibrating with the tension in her triceps. 'Are you being smart with me?' he snarled.

'I don't have a single smart left in me, Drill Sergeant,' she ground out.

Their eyes met. Battled. Then his stormy grey eyes moved over her sweat-drenched body as she lowered the bar and pressed it back up.

'Ten,' he rasped, without taking his eyes off her bare midriff. 'Nine,' he supplied helpfully after another shredding lift.

'Draco…'

'Eight.'

'Stop,' she gasped.

'Seven. Stop counting?'

'Stop…staring.'

'No.' His gaze moved to her breasts and his breathing altered. 'Six.'

*'Grrruuuugh!'*

'Is that even English? Five.'

'I hate you!'

'I hate you back. Four.' He squatted and brushed back the wet tendrils at her temple. 'Three.'

'You're…touching me, Draco. You want me to fail,' she panted.

'Never. Almost there, *glikia mou*. Two.'

Pain rippled through her body as lactic acid surged through her system. 'One!' she shouted.

He stood over her and took the weight from her trembling grip.

Rebel stood and shook her hands, relief pouring through her wrists and biceps as her pumping heart settled. 'Piece of cake.'

Draco came up behind her, and held a bottle of water to her lips. She drank thirstily, then, just because she could, she relaxed against him, rubbed her back against his front.

His breath hissed in her ear. 'Why do you drive me crazy like this?'

'Umm…you make it too damn easy?'

Dropping the bottle, he flipped her round. '*Thee mou*, your mouth!'

'Is all the workout you need?'

With a pained grunt he smashed his mouth on hers. Strong arms banded her waist and she linked her arms around his neck as he picked her up and walked forward to the martial arts area. Her body hit the mat none too gently, but Rebel didn't care. Draco was kissing her and her senses were on fire. This time when he parted her legs, she welcomed him, holding her breath until he rolled his hips against her.

'Oh!' She thrilled to the shudder that rolled through her.

'Damn, you're so responsive,' he groaned against her mouth.

'Complaint?'

'Compliment.'

'Okay. Proceed.'

He consumed her, each lick, bite and pinch twisting them higher, until they broke apart, desperate for the sweet sustenance of oxygen. Weaving her fingers through his hair, Rebel just gloried in the weight of him and the hand sliding up and down her calf.

'Arabella?'

'Drill Sergeant?'

His mouth stretched against her cheek. Her heart flipped over at the thought that she'd made him smile. Turning her head, she stole a kiss. He groaned again. 'We can't do this here.'

'In this room, this villa, or this country?'

'Definitely not in this room. I'd prefer a different bed and a different villa to one owned by Olivio Nardozzi. How would you feel about leaving a day early and switching to a different country?'

'What about Olivio?'

A hard smile curved his lips. 'My wanting to be alone with you away from this place should serve as a further convincer.'

Her breath shuddered. 'And do you?'

He fused his mouth to hers in a hard kiss. 'Enough to put my pilot on standby to leave immediately after the gala tonight.'

'So…where would you take me?'

His nostrils flared as his eyes darkened. 'I have homes in most of the major sports-orientated cities around the world. But wherever you want to go, I can make it happen.' He leaned down and brushed his growing stubble against her cheek before placing an open-mouthed kiss on the racing pulse at her throat.

'Do all your homes have what I need to train?'

'Of course,' he murmured.

'What about Greg?'

His head jerked up, blazing eyes piercing hers. 'Who's Greg?'

'My trainer.'

He relaxed a touch. 'Get him to send me your training schedule. I'll take care of you until your dry-land drills are over. He can take over again when we get to Verbier.'

Her heart leapt. 'You're coming to the championships?'

'You're my fiancée. How would it look if I'm not there by your side?'

Rebel told herself the lurching of her heart was a good reminder that all of this wasn't real. That what they were doing had a coldly calculated purpose and a finite conclusion, no matter that she'd decided to risk making it a little bit more than the platonic undertaking they'd agreed.

Mentally shaking off the voice that probed the wisdom of changing the parameters of their agreement, she grimaced at him. 'I'm not sure I want you as my trainer if every training session is going to be like this.'

'It's not going to be like this,' he returned. 'It's going to be worse.'

Her eyebrow shot up. 'Worse?'

'I've seen what you're capable of. You protest at every drill, yet you can easily achieve so much more.' A frown locked between his eyebrows. 'It's almost as if you don't want to achieve your full potential.'

Her gaze dropped from his probing look.

He caught her chin in his hand. 'Arabella?'

'I…it's not that. I want to win this championship. More than anything.'

'But?'

'But I'm afraid after that there'll be nothing else. Nothing to strive for. My father is gone, Draco. I don't know if I'll ever see him again. Once the championships are over, I'll have nothing.'

His frown dissolved, but his jaw clenched. 'Why were you doing it in the first place?'

'Mostly for my mother. I want to honour her memory.'

'But not with a win? How is coming fifth when you can be champion truly honouring her?'

'It wasn't so much the winning, as just participating in the sport she loved.'

He shook his head. 'I don't buy that. And I don't think you do either. This still has to do with your father, doesn't it? What is it?'

She swallowed the rock that lodged in her throat. 'He didn't want me to become a professional skier. Like your father, he wanted me to do something else. My mother and I talked him around with…with a promise that I'd give up once I won a major championship.'

Fury roared through his eyes. 'So you've been deliberately holding yourself back because of a promise you made when you were…how old?'

'I was fifteen.'

'You were a child!'

'But old enough to understand what promises meant.'

A scalding curse ripped through the room. He levered himself off her and stood glaring down at her.

'So that's what you're going to do for the rest of your life, always achieving a little less than your potential because of a father who doesn't have a problem betraying you?'

Pain bit deeper. 'Draco…'

'What would your mother have wanted for you?'

She closed her eyes, her insides a churning river of sorrow. 'For me to compete. And win.'

He crouched down and lifted her to her feet. 'And what do *you* want, Arabella?'

Sharp tears prickled the backs of her eyes. 'I want everything. To keep my promise to my father. To honour my mother. And to win multiple championships.'

He shook his head, a tinge of bleakness in his eyes. 'You're realistic enough to know that we never get everything we want. And by fruitlessly hanging onto one dream, you're jeopardising everything else.' He let go of her and took several steps back.

Rebel wasn't sure why that deliberate withdrawal sent a wave of panic through her. 'Draco?' She reached for him, but he stepped farther away.

'Choose, Arabella. Either you're in this all the way or you're not.'

Her hand balled into a fist, the vein of shame she'd always felt when she'd held back instead of going all in during competitions thickening uncomfortably. 'Why? What is it to you?'

'I'm not asking you to choose for me. I'm asking you to choose for yourself.' He paced in front of her but still kept out of reach. 'Imagine yourself thirty years down the line. Is this the legacy you'd want to leave? That you deliberately fell short of reaching for your goals?'

'No.' The word charged out of her, fired from a place she'd deliberately closed off because the desires that resided there were too painful to dream about. Being forced to confront them sent a wave of sadness through her. Because in order to achieve what she truly yearned for, she would be throwing away any chances of reconciliation with her father. But then what were the guarantees that they would reconcile when he'd stated plainly that the very sight of her wrecked him? Was she in danger of throwing out one dream to follow another that might never come true?

The memory of her mother pierced her thoughts, of her beautiful smile and ecstatic cheering when Rebel had won her first junior championship. All the way home Susie Daniels had babbled her pride and hopes for her daughter's future to anyone who would listen. That day had been one of the happiest days of Rebel's life. She wanted to relive that day again. And again. She wanted that memory of her mother to never fade. Never cease to inspire her. With a shaky breath, she looked at Draco. 'No, I don't want that.'

He breached the gap between them and caught her face in his hands. His eyes glowed with a fire she wanted to believe was pride. But then he angled his head and kissed her, and her every sense coalesced into pleasure. He didn't let up until the need to breathe drove them apart.

This time the look in his eyes when their gazes met was one of pure predatory hunger. Sliding his hand down her arm, he laced their fingers and tugged her to the door.

'Come. Let's go and get this day over with so I can begin kicking your ass into gear,' he drawled with unabashed relish.

'Just remember, I kick back.'

He laughed. 'How soon you forget yourself. Insubordination of any kind will only make things worse for you.'

'How did I know you'll try to get your way with threats?'

'Those aren't threats, *glikia mou*. They're golden promises.'

# CHAPTER TWELVE

Rebel was still hiding a smile that threatened to split her face when they returned to their suite. The look in Draco's eyes as she walked away to take her shower could've buckled steel.

All through the day as they mingled with guests whose names she forgot almost as soon as Olivio made introductions, she felt the weight of Draco's hungry stare. Not that he left her side for more than a few minutes at a time. By the time they returned to their suite to get ready for the gala, Rebel was sure she would spontaneously combust if he glanced at her one more time.

But he did more than glance at her when she emerged from the dressing room at a few minutes to eight.

'I'm good to go,' she addressed a tuxedoed Draco, who was nursing a small whisky as he gazed out into the Tuscan night.

He turned. He froze. His scrutiny was thorough, taking in every inch of her white Greek-style gown, cinched in at the waist and collared at the throat with gold metal. At her wrists her favourite gold bangles clinked as she moved nervously beneath his intense…increasingly frowning gaze.

'Draco…?'

'*Thee mou*, you look breathtaking,' he rasped.

'Maybe next time, lead with that, instead of the frown?' she suggested with a nervous but pleased laugh.

He discarded his drink on a nearby surface and came towards her, the frown still in place. 'I've seen the guest list. More than half of them are male sports stars with overblown egos and the impression that they can have anything, or anyone, they want.' He captured her hand, his grip tight. 'Just remember, you're my fiancée. I'll kill anyone who dares to make a pass at you.'

Rebel had ceased trying to fight the insane chemical thrill that his touch and his words brought. She was firmly immersed in whatever was happening between them. So what if a part of her had taken more than a moment or two during the day to wonder what it would be like to be truly engaged to Draco? *That* was the part of her she needed to control.

Now that she'd decided to fight all out for her dreams, she couldn't afford to get emotionally tangled with Draco. Walking away from this charade without emotional loss was imperative. The physical side, the potent chemistry that wrapped them in its own formidable force field, she could handle. And as she'd seen with so many of her friends and acquaintances, the chemistry didn't last for anyone, once explored.

'Well, I hope you'll keep the bloodletting at a distance. I don't want my gown ruined,' she replied.

Exhaling, he muttered something under his breath about her mouth, then tugged her after him to the door.

The ballroom holding the gala was themed like the rest of the villa—an exhibition of marble and Carla Nardozzi. The event, purportedly to raise money for children's sports in Third World countries, was in danger of being overshadowed by the Olivio and Carla Nardozzi Show.

The woman in question, dressed in a white and silver gown that moulded every inch of her skin from throat to feet, her face impeccably made up and her hair caught up in her signature chignon, glided forward on her father's arm to greet them. Compliments were exchanged, but Rebel noticed Carla's gaze barely stayed on her before it returned to Draco. And this time there was no disguising the keen interest in the younger woman's eyes. An unpleasant sensation coiled inside Rebel.

'Carla told me what you did this morning,' Olivio said,

his gaze on Draco. 'She was lucky to have you there to intervene for what I'm sure was just a misunderstanding with Tyson. But I owe you my thanks nevertheless.'

Draco's gaze hardened. 'It wasn't a misunderstanding. And Arabella was there too. In fact, she stopped the situation from escalating.'

Carla laughed. 'Hardly. I had things under control.'

Shock froze Rebel for a second. 'He was manhandling you, and trying to force you to do a dangerous move you weren't ready for!'

Carla's mouth pursed. 'You were there for only a few minutes, Miss Daniels. I only meant I wasn't prepared to do that move at that time of the morning when I'd barely warmed up.'

'A dangerous move is a dangerous move, no matter the time of day it's performed,' Draco inserted with unmistakable gravity. Although his bleak expression cleared a moment later, Rebel's heart squeezed at the naked pain and guilt he carried for what had happened to his sister.

'Then you'll be pleased to know I succeeded in my attempt this afternoon,' Carla said.

Olivio smiled with smug satisfaction. 'Now that we've cleared that up, perhaps we can get on with the evening? Draco, Carla has a few people she's dying for you to meet. I promise to take care of your beloved while you're away.'

Short of offending their host—a move she didn't doubt Olivio would hold against Draco—she had no choice but to slide her hand through Olivio's proffered arm.

Draco's gaze dropped to the point of contact, his nostrils flaring slightly. Olivio's laughter held a touch of edgy mockery. 'She's only going across the room, not to the ends of the earth.'

When Draco's eyes gleamed dangerously, Rebel smiled, thinking it wise to defuse the situation.

'He told me before we left our suite that he'll kill any man who strays too close to me tonight. Perhaps I ought to level the playing field by stating that I'll gut any woman who looks at him the wrong way. Does that help, darling?'

Draco's gaze caught hers, the promise of retribution echoing clearly, before dropping to her mouth. 'It helps.'

'Such passion,' Olivio drawled.

Rebel placed her tongue firmly in her cheek. 'You don't know the half of it.'

Carla slipped *both* her hands through Draco's bent arm, her gaze daring as it met Rebel's. 'Come on. It's almost time for us to take our seats and I may not have time later.'

Rebel walked away, the smile pinned on her face hopefully disguising the fact that her insides were still knotted with an unhealthy mix of anger and jealousy. Draco might not have romantic intentions towards Carla, but the younger woman clearly had other ideas.

'So when is the big day?' Olivio enquired in between playing the attentive host to his mingling guests.

Rebel frowned, dragging her eyes from where Carla was plastered to Draco's side as they chatted with a basketball star and his wife across the room. 'Big day?'

'The wedding. Surely that's what every woman thinks about the moment she's proposed to?' His brown eyes drilled into hers, as if hoping to catch her in a lie.

'A wedding takes time to plan. Besides, I have a championship to think of before we get round to setting wedding dates.'

'Ah, yes. I understand you dabble in cross-country. Or is it jumping?' His teeth were bared in a semblance of a smile, but his eyes were slowly hardening, a hint of a sneer in the espresso depths.

Rebel tossed her head. 'I'm sorry, is there an insult in there somewhere? Only I despise insinuation.'

Another guest approached. Olivio slipped into charming host mode, chatting and smiling until they were once again alone. Then he turned so his back was to the room.

'My Carla needs a man like Draco in her camp to keep her at the top of the game.'

'Isn't she already at the top? And isn't Draco's offer of representation going to achieve what you want?'

'The sort of contract he's offering is one that can be broken at any time. What I need from him is a firmer commitment.'

Rebel arranged her features into fake astonishment. 'What are you saying? That you want me to give up the man I love to your daughter?' Her voice caught, her whole body clenching hard with a stormy sensation that had nothing to do with the role she'd agreed to play.

'I'm in a position to make sure it's worth your while.'

Struggling with the sudden pounding of her heart, she lifted her hand to her throat in a dramatic pose. 'And how much is ripping out one's own heart and throwing it under a bus worth these days?'

Olivio assessed her shrewdly. 'Will a million euros do it?'

Over his shoulder she spotted Draco and Carla, now standing alone. His head was bent towards her shorter form as she murmured in his ear. Rebel couldn't dismiss the evidence that they made a striking couple.

Looking away from them, she stared at Olivio. 'Sadly, I don't think you've thought this through properly. You want me to walk away from a dynamic, wildly successful man, whose net worth I'm guessing eclipses yours many times over, and who I also happen to be in love with, for a mere million euros?' She injected as much sarcasm into her voice as possible. 'And even if I was crazy enough to consider your offer, you forget, there's nothing between Carla and Draco.'

Olivio made a dismissive gesture. 'Romance just needs the right circumstances to be rekindled.'

Rebel's breath locked in her lungs. *'Rekindled?'*

His superior smile widened. 'I see he chose not to tell you.'

'Perhaps he didn't think it important enough,' she replied, although her voice lacked the conviction she'd been able to project thus far.

'Or perhaps his male pride still smarts from the fact that I put a stop to their dating three years ago because my Carla was too young for that kind of intensity and didn't need the distraction. I don't apologise for looking out for her best interests. But Draco should be made to see he's letting his bruised ego get in the way of a perfect union.'

The poisoned knife that seemed to have impaled her sternum wasn't easing up, no matter how much she tried to breathe through it. In fact, with every second that passed, numbness spread through her body. 'Again, I don't see how any of this interests me. Draco put his ring on my finger. I need a little more than a second-hand tale of infatuation to discard it.'

The soft background music that had accompanied the pre-dinner drinks faded and the lights blinked, indicating it was time to take their seats. Rebel saw Draco and Carla head their way.

'You don't want to make an enemy of me, Arabella,' Olivio warned.

'Oh, I don't know if that'll make a difference, Olivio. This one seems to take pride in collecting enemies,' an intruding voice suggested.

She tensed as Tyson Blackwell stopped beside them, a glass of champagne in his hand. From across the room, Draco's face contorted with barely contained fury as he swiftly headed back towards her.

'What can I say? Meek and mild have never been friends of mine. And I find it hard to bite my tongue at the best of times when someone is being mistreated right in front of my eyes.'

'Maybe you should learn,' Tyson ground out.

'Where's the fun in that?' she fired back.

'Everything okay here?' Draco's icy voice joined the

conversation. In the light of what Olivio had just imparted, Rebel found she couldn't look at him. Not without betraying herself. And now more than ever, knowing how much she wanted to win the championship—ironically thanks to Draco helping her admit the truth she'd been hiding from— she couldn't afford to let her mask slip.

Tyson smiled indulgently at Carla before he shrugged. 'Your girl seems to need convincing about what she saw this morning. As I explained to Olivio, I get passionate every now and then in my quest for excellence. Carla knows she has nothing to fear from me, don't you, *bella*?'

The look that passed between them made Rebel wonder if they were sleeping together, but the younger woman's gaze immediately returned to Draco. With the knowledge of their full history, she could no longer stop the arrows that pierced her heart as she watched them. With a heavy buzzing in her head, she took in Draco's almost protective shielding of the figure skater from her trainer, and Carla's proprietorial hold on his arm.

Pain lanced sharper her as the lights blinked again.

'We need to take our seats,' Carla said without answering Tyson's allegation.

The trainer's face hardened. Glancing away, Rebel caught Draco's enquiring gaze. Unable to deal with it, and not wanting to, she turned away, and followed the usher who stood ready to guide them to their table.

Her breath caught painfully as Draco took over pulling out her chair. 'Arabella?'

'Everything's fine,' she said lightly, flashing an empty smile before reaching for her water glass. Expecting him to take the seat next to her, she glanced up to find him walking away.

Discovering she'd been placed as far away as possible from him with Carla and Olivio on either side of him shouldn't have come as a surprise. Inhaling shakily, she summoned a smile for the tennis star and his expectant wife to her left and introduced herself to the soccer star on her right. Beyond him, Tyson Blackwell smirked at her as he took his seat.

As the courses were served and practised speeches given, Rebel picked at her meal and tried to make conversation, even as a part of her was staggered at how drastically different the evening had turned out from how she'd imagined when they'd left their suite. Just from the simple disclosing of one small fact she hadn't been privy to.

A fact Draco had deliberately neglected to mention.

As if compelled, her gaze lifted from her plate. Across the table, steel-sharp eyes met hers, and, despite the charming smile gracing his lips as he nodded at something Carla was saying, Rebel saw the unyielding questions lurking and the grim warning wrapped around each of them.

Tyson Blackwell laughed loudly at a joke and Draco's jaw tightened. Rebel didn't doubt that Draco's motivation for wanting Tyson Blackwell banned from training was genuine. The man was dangerous. For that reason alone, she had to keep this up. As to why Draco had kept his prior relationship with Carla from her…

She vowed to ask him the moment they were alone.

Looking up, she caught his gaze again, the deeper warning in his eyes tensing her spine.

He didn't need to remind her they were playing a role. Letting go of her glass, she tucked her hand beneath her chin. Allowing her gaze to grow languid, she puckered her lips and blew him a kiss.

His smile evaporated. His fist tightened around his poised knife until his knuckles gleamed white.

Beside her, the tennis star's wife laughed. 'That certainly caught his attention.'

Rebel forced a giggle. 'You think so? A girl has to use whatever weapons she has in her arsenal these days.'

The pregnant woman leaned in closer and nodded. 'I hear ya. Especially when there are shameless predators around who feel they have more rights to your man than you do,' she whispered conspiratorially.

Rebel swallowed, wincing inwardly as the words struck bone. Humming in agreement, she battled her way through further conversation, making sure not to glance Draco's way again.

At the stroke of midnight, the gala ended with a closing speech from father and daughter.

Rebel was saying goodbye to the tennis couple when Draco arrived at her side. 'Arabella, we need to—'

'Draco? You said you wanted to talk to me after the gala?' Carla joined them, expertly insinuating herself between them. 'I've done my bit for the night, so I'm all yours.'

'Carla, I'll come and find you in a while—' He stopped as she shook her head.

'It's been a long day and I want to get to bed soon,' she said softly, her eyes wide and limpid. 'And since you insist on leaving right away, I hope you don't mind if we talk now or I risk falling asleep mid-sentence.' Her smile was wide and perfect.

Draco responded to her smile with one of his own, but Rebel saw the tension that gripped his shoulders when he turned to her.

She pre-empted him with a fake smile and a hand on his chest. His muscles contracted and she dropped her hand. 'It's fine, darling. I'll go and take a shower, and warm your side of the bed. I know how much you love that.'

The look Carla sent her could've shattered granite. Rebel walked away before her smile slipped, holding her head high and avoiding eye contact with the guests drifting out of the ballroom.

She made it to the suite with only Stefano approaching to ask if she needed anything. Thanking and dismissing him, she shut the door behind her, relief mingled with a heavy dose of raw trepidation welling inside her.

Rebel didn't think she'd lost sight of what she was doing

at any point in the shockingly brief time since she'd crashed into Draco's world. So how had she arrived here, deeply unsettled by emotions she could barely explain?

She was in lust with him, that she couldn't deny. But why did her heart ache this much at the thought of Draco having dated Carla? Putting it down to anger over the deliberate trap Draco had let her walk into with Olivio earlier, she lurched from the door, tugging off her shoes as she entered the dressing room. Their cases had been packed and stood neatly by the centre island.

Realising she couldn't shower without having to repack, she left her shoes by the cases and went into the living room. The urge to pour herself a drink and numb the disquieting emotions surging beneath her skin was strong. But stepping up her training meant no alcohol, even for emotional-crutch purposes.

Snorting beneath her breath, she plunked down on the sofa, only to jump up again as Draco's scent curled around her. Heart leaping in her throat, she crossed the living room and sank into the armchair. Grabbing the remote, she turned on the TV.

She was channel-surfing, ignoring the antique fireplace clock that announced that Draco had been gone for an hour, when the door opened.

'Arabella.' Her name was a curt demand.

She muted the TV and stood, cursing the renewed anxiety swirling in her stomach. 'In here.'

He entered the room. Every cell in her body felt as if it'd been zapped with liquid nitrogen when she took in his dishevelled state.

'Wow. You know you can't forcibly save her if she doesn't think she needs saving, don't you?'

A muscle in his jaw flexed. 'What are you talking about?'

She walked to him, caught the betraying scent oozing from him and her heart dropped further.

*Keep walking.*

She went to the dressing room. Tugging on the handle of her case, she dragged it behind her, only to stop short when he filled the doorway.

'What are you doing?'

'I assume this charade is over, since you stink of her perfume, your hair's all over the place and your jaw is covered in peach lipstick—seriously, though, that "lipstick on the collar" thing is so last-century soap opera. Anyway, I'm guessing either your talk was wildly successful or she refused to take you up on your role as saviour. Judging from your scowl I'm guessing it was the latter.'

'Arabella—'

'By the way, thanks for making me look like a fool tonight. You told me you were trying to get her father to drop his matchmaking. You never said anything about the daughter being head over heels in love with you.'

His scowl deepened. 'Carla has had a crush on me since she was a teenager. It's nothing.'

'Oh, believe me, it's something. A very big something. Especially since you two *dated*.'

He looked momentarily disconcerted, then he shrugged. 'I took her out a few times when she lived in London a few years ago. So what?'

She laughed. 'Only a man like you would ask that ridiculous question.'

'What's that supposed to mean?'

She sighed. 'Never mind, Draco.' She moved forward, expecting him to get out of her way. He didn't. 'Oh, right. I guess you want this back.' Letting go of her case, she tugged the ring off and held it out to him.

'What the hell do you think you're doing?' he growled, his voice jagged ice chips.

'Come on, you can't surely want to prolong this farce! You're wearing another woman's lipstick on your skin, for heaven's sake. Stay. Leave. Do whatever you want. But here's where I step off this crazy train.'

She stepped forward, intending to shove the ring in his pocket. He caught her wrist, trapping it against his chest in a tight grip. Underneath her fist, his heart slammed hard and fierce.

'Put the ring back on,' he sliced at her.

She jerked at her hand. He held on tight.

'God, what do you want, Draco?' she railed, knowing she was inches away from losing control.

'You, Arabella. I want you.'

# CHAPTER THIRTEEN

'EVER SINCE I walked in on you performing that ridiculous yoga pose, I've thought of little else but having you beneath me in my bed. Did I not make that perfectly clear this morning?'

Rebel clawed at the strands of sanity blissfully fleeing her mind. 'Again. The lipstick on your face tells a *very* different story.'

With a thick curse, Draco released her, but kicked the door shut. 'Stay here. If you walk out that door I'll make you regret it.'

'Oh…charming.'

He stalked to his case and flung it open. Extracting a fresh pair of trousers and a clean shirt, he slammed it shut.

Rebel stared in disbelief as he jerked his tuxedo jacket off, followed by the dress shirt and trousers. Her mouth dropped open at the sight of him in his black briefs, a picture of ripped, bristling, male perfection, using the shirt balled in his fist to swipe at the lipstick on his face. Stunning was a woefully inadequate description of Draco Angelis' male stature, his perfectly proportioned body overlaid with smooth dark olive skin that just begged to be touched. Worshipped.

From somewhere she regained the use of her vocal cords. 'Umm… Draco—'

He flung the shirt away. 'Shut your mouth and listen for once in your life. I didn't kiss Carla. She kissed me.'

Rebel let her rolling eyes speak for her.

'And before you call it a convenient excuse, no, I didn't see it coming.'

'So you spent the last hour fighting her off?'

He glared pure fire at her. 'I spent the last hour *talking* to her. This—' he flicked impatient fingers at his face '—happened as I was leaving her.'

'Okay, if you say so.'

He glared harder. 'I do say so,' he ground out.

Her stomach quivered. 'And?'

He pulled his clean clothes on, then spiked his fingers through his hair. The silky strands settled, but not by much. He still wore a tumbled-out-of-bed look that was at once heart-throbbingly perfect and deliciously indecent. Snapping up the suitcase, he crossed to her and took her bag. 'She knows what she stands to lose if she carries on using Tyson Blackwell as her trainer. The ball is now in her court. I just hope she doesn't take too long to make her stand.'

A harrowing bleakness threaded the edge in his voice. Her hand on the door, Rebel glanced back at him. 'You tried. Isn't that enough?'

His eyes were a raw, turbulent gunmetal; the skin around his mouth was pinched. 'No, it isn't. Should Maria see on the news one day soon that a tragedy has happened to Carla and I hadn't done everything I could to stop it, it'll finish her. And with Blackwell in charge, it's not a case of if but when. I can't let that happen to either of them.'

Rebel let out a shaky breath. 'So…this engagement *is* really about helping Carla through forcing her father's hand, and not a male-pride thing to get back at Olivio because he stopped you from dating her three years ago?'

Already dark brows clenched in a thunderous frown. 'I see Olivio has filled your head with nonsense. Open the door, Arabella. We're leaving. I can't stand to stay in this place another minute. The moment we're on my plane, you'll tell me what else that bastard filled your head with. I didn't think it was possible, but you've grown even more insufferable since the damned gala.'

Purely for self-preservation purposes, she opened the door and walked out of the suite. Stefano waited in the hallway and took charge of their bags. The walk to the helipad was swift and they were lifting off within minutes.

They boarded Draco's plane and took off with Rebel having no clue where they were going since Draco had disappeared to take a shower. On his return, he clamped the phone to his ear, and conducted several conversations in rapid-fire Greek. A solid hour after take-off he finally hung up and flung his phone on the table between them.

He dragged his hands down his face, but she thought the look he levelled at her was a little less incandescent.

'Is it safe to ask where we're going now?'

He blinked at her, then his gaze dropped to the ring, which had somehow found its way back onto her finger. 'I was going to take you to my water villa in the Maldives. It's secluded and beautiful and rainbow-coloured fish swim up to you to say hello. But after the stunt you pulled tonight—'

'Which stunt are we talking about?'

Narrowed eyes sizzled at her. 'The getting-your-head-filled-with-lies part, followed by the part where you tried to dump me.'

'Oh. Right.'

'Yes. Right. You don't deserve the Maldives. And I don't want to be stuck on a plane for half a day with a woman who drives me insane, and yet who I want to make love to more than I want to breathe.'

Rebel was glad she was seated. His powerful, enthralling words buffeted her like a freak storm, raising her heart rate and melting her insides. 'I guess that's completely rational. So do I get a destination?'

'No. You'll find out when we get there. Tell me what else Olivio told you,' he commanded.

She told him, leaving nothing out. Draco shook his head once and uttered a curse. She grimaced. 'Sorry. But on a positive note, now he thinks I'm not going to step aside easily or be bought off, he might rethink his plans?'

'I doubt it. Men like Olivio rarely change their ways. But

I have to try something. Maria will never forgive me if I don't,' he said grimly.

'Surely you understand that you don't have total control over this?'

He didn't reply and several minutes passed before she asked, 'So, what now?'

His gaze rested on her, scrutinising her from face to midriff and back again. 'I have my investigators digging deeper for anything they can find on Blackwell. Come here.'

Temperature spiking from an infusion of wicked excitement, she rose and rounded the table.

He drew back and patted his lap. 'Sit.'

She hitched her gown up and swung one leg over his thighs. His breath hitched as she lowered herself and settled onto him. Shaking his head, he gave a low, deep laugh. 'I should've known better than to expect you to sit side-saddle with your legs daintily crossed,' he teased.

Face flaming with embarrassment, Rebel drew back. 'Sorry, I'm fresh out of dainty,' she quipped. Bracing her hand on the table, she started to rise.

He clamped his hand on her hips. 'Stay. How is it that your relentless mouth hasn't seen you thrown into an institution long before now?'

Heat rose higher, but this time from the blatant presence of his arousal between her legs. 'Umm…I'm nice to little old ladies and I don't walk under ladders?'

His hands slowly travelled up to shackle her waist. Leaning forward, he stopped a hair's breadth from her lips. 'I want you like crazy, Arabella Daniels.' His voice was a warm, whispered rumble over her lips. 'Nothing has changed since this morning. So tell me you want me too.'

'I want you too,' she delivered, although she couldn't accept that nothing had changed. Tonight's events had unleashed emotions she didn't want to brave uncovering just yet. Hell, she might leave that box sealed for ever.

He stared at her for endless seconds. One hand came up

and teased the hoop that formed the neckline of her dress. When it reached her pulse, he traced it, a light, delicate touch that lit a flame on every nerve ending and concentrated it at her core.

His touch, still light, still tormenting, drifted up to her eyebrows, her cheek, then over her lips. A pained groan ripped from his throat.

'I want to kiss you. *Thee mou*, I want to kiss you so badly.'

'And you're holding back because…?'

His hand dropped back to her waist and his head jerked back to the headrest. 'We're landing in three minutes.'

Cutting disappointment warred with the need to know where they were. Knowing she could do nothing about one and maybe something about the other, she looked out of the window onto a black, inky landscape with only a set of runway lights breaking the vastness.

'You've brought me to the middle of nowhere?'

'Indeed. No one can reach us unless I want them to, or they're prepared to swim a hundred miles in every direction.'

'We're in the middle of the ocean?'

'On my island in the Aegean.'

'How long are we staying?'

'That depends entirely on you. Play nice and I won't fly us north and dump you in a Gulag.'

He rose with her in his arms and walked them to the sofa. Setting her down, he secured her seat belt, then settled down away from her. Glancing at him, she witnessed the strain in his features and bit her lip against a smart quip as his fists bunched on his thighs.

The second they touched down he released his belt and hers, then stood with her.

'Arabella?'

'Yes, Drill Sergeant?' she responded, trying her utmost to stem the anxiety flooding her.

'I'm going to have you. The moment we're alone again, I intend to make you mine. Speak up now if that isn't what you want because you won't be using that smart mouth for talking later.'

Every sharp retort evaporated from her head as erotic images flooded her. 'I want it. I want you.'

His breath shuddered out and he nodded once before moving to the door. An SUV stood a short distance away and he guided her to it before sliding behind the wheel. More lights than she'd seen from above lit their path, but all she could see was vegetation and a profusion of flowers.

'You'll get the grand tour tomorrow after your training,' he rasped, his gaze not moving from the road ahead.

Two long roads and corners later, Rebel sat forward in her seat, her widening gaze on the villa ahead. It was built into the side of the hill, with multi-layers she stopped counting after five. In the dark, welcoming golden lights lit up the vast property, pitching it against the night sky like a wonderful masterpiece.

'Draco, it's stunning.' She craned her neck to see more of it as they neared.

'It's not the Maldives, but it's one of my favourite homes.'

'Water villas and brightly coloured fish are overrated.'

He drove past a pillared entrance with double doors, and through a giant, arched trellis. He stopped before a square wooden gate and entered a code. The gate glided back on a smooth rail and they drove along a narrower drive that led to another pillared entrance. It wasn't until Draco parked and she alighted that her gaze was drawn upward. 'That's a pool. A see-through pool,' she blurted, blown clean away.

His mouth curved. 'You get to have your water villa after all.' He walked round to her, swung her up in his arms and whispered in her ear, 'You can swim naked in there if you want to. In fact, I insist on it.'

He was striding forward as she fought her way through a blush. Codes were entered along the way, a lift accessed that shot them up and spat them out on an upper level. Then they were in Draco's bedroom. He slid her down his body, slowly, torturously, not bothering to hide the thick evidence of his arousal. It nudged her belly as he tugged her even closer. The hands that had shackled her on the plane were twice as hard, twice as demanding, as Draco finally unleashed the ferocious hunger that screamed for satisfaction. He devoured her mouth, muttering words in Greek she didn't understand in between long, ardent kisses. Their groans mingled as each kiss fed the hunger and need for a greater assuaging.

He fisted her hair, his fingers holding her tight as he trailed his tongue over her jaw to the pulse racing at her throat. He lapped at it, his moan deep and primeval. '*Thee mou*, you taste like paradise. And sin. And every forbidden thing in between.'

Her hands, frantically exploring his covered back, bit into his flesh as he nipped at her collarbone. Never having imagined that area to be an erogenous zone, she felt her knees threaten to buckle as Draco explored her. Her eyes grew heavy, drawing half closed as sensation arrowed south and pooled between her thighs. Desperate to discover as much of him as she could before her faculties melted beneath the fierce onslaught of desire, Rebel pulled his shirt up and dragged her nails over his heated skin.

The hiss that heated her cleavage was followed by another savage curse. He dragged his head upward. 'You mean to torment me, don't you?' he rasped thickly.

Slightly shocked by the allegation, she blurted, 'I'm only touching you. You want me to stop?'

His laugh was darkly amused. 'Not even on pain of death would I wish that.'

Stepping back, he yanked his shirt over his head. The chest she'd glimpsed from across the dressing room was now within reach. Rebel's ability to breathe became severely compromised as she glided her hand over his pectoral muscles. As she felt them quiver lightly under her touch a bold, feminine power filled her. She explored south, hesitated, then went lower and grasped him.

Her mouth parted on a silent gasp as the full thickness of him registered.

'Arabella.'

She heard her name from afar, her senses completely overcome by the power and heat of him.

'Arabella.' His voice was more strained, almost guttural as he captured her hand in his.

A sound erupted from her throat that sounded very much like a whimper. 'Draco…'

He spun her round and trapped her with one hand on her abdomen. The other slowly gathered up her gown, the slide of hot silk against her skin delicious, decadent torture. 'Play with me all you want later. But I need to take you…be inside you, right now, before I lose my head.'

She shuddered at the inflamed words. Then shuddered some more, when his clever fingers brushed her naked hip and skated along the edge of her panties. Her legs sagged and parted, the hunger between her thighs desperate for satiation.

A cry ripped from her throat when his fingers finally found her. Pulling aside the wet lace, he caressed her, muttering earthy words that drew her deeper into a sensual stupor.

He toyed with for her several minutes, then one finger slipped inside her, testing her, tormenting her. 'So wet, *glikia mou*. And mine,' he growled.

The hand on her belly tugged open her belt before reaching up to tackle the neck fastening. When it came open, Draco pulled away and spun her around. Rebel gasped at the sheer magnificence of the passion stamped across his face.

Keeping his gaze locked on hers, he pulled the dress off her shoulders. It pooled at her feet, leaving her exposed in her strapless bra and panties. Still trapping her gaze, he reached round and unclipped her bra.

Cool air hit her breasts, puckering the tight tips to harder points. Rebel wanted to cover herself, gain back a little of the control that had long fled.

At the same time she wanted Draco to look at her, drown in her as she was drowning in him. So she kept her hands down.

His eyes dropped. He made a sound that could've been her name or a curse. She didn't care because he reached out and touched her. Specifically her panties, which were torn from her body between one breath and the next. Then the world blurred as he lifted her and tossed her on the bed. The primitiveness behind the act had her shuddering wildly. She was struggling for breath when he fully undressed and prowled closer.

Anxieties she'd pushed to the back of her mind flooded forth. She'd never viewed her virginity with the sacred awe some women did, but Rebel couldn't dismiss the profundity that gripped her as she stared at the magnificent man who would be her first lover. Nor could she ignore the physical evidence of his manhood.

He was impressive. Almost a little too impressive. Apprehension clawed higher. She bit her lip to keep it down as he reached into the bedside drawer and extracted a condom.

Stretching out beside her, he glided his hand from her neck to her midriff. She arched into his touch, forcing her mind away from the power between his legs.

'I didn't desire smart talk, but I admit to being disconcerted by your complete silence.'

She bit her lip harder. 'Hmm.'

He raised his head. 'Was that English?'

Her breath burst from her lungs. 'Draco…please?'

'Begging, Arabella?' His head dipped, and his mouth grazed one nipple. He rotated the bud between his lips before flicking his tongue against it. 'Whatever next?'

When she didn't answer, he raised his head.

She blew out a shaky breath. 'Okay…fine… I'm worried. You're big…I think?'

'You think? I guess there's only one way to find out.'

She gasped as he performed the same decadent torture on her twin nipple. Unable to stand it any longer, she tugged her fingers through his hair. He continued to suckle on her even as she faintly registered the rip of foil.

Pressing her back against the bed, he levered himself over her and took her mouth with his. The thrust of his tongue was a precursor to the thick head that breached her core. She gripped his neck as he probed deeper, then withdrew. Strong arms stretched her legs wider and Draco raised his head.

Grey eyes locked on hers, he thrust inside her.

The deep flash of pain ripped a cry from her lips and drove her nails into his flesh. With her shaky gaze on his, Rebel first witnessed puzzlement, then shock, before fury glazed his eyes. 'You think…' he seethed as understanding dawned. *'You think?'*

'I…know?' she supplied on a gasp, her flesh struggling to contain his thick girth as new, delicious sensations flowed through her.

He moved, perhaps to withdraw. The drugging sensation heightened. She moaned, her fingers digging in deeper.

*'Thee mou.* Arabella—' he muttered as she rotated her hips, chasing more of the feeling. She tried it again. With a thick curse, he slid one arm behind her back, grabbed her waist and held her still. 'Why…?' He stopped to breathe. 'You didn't tell me you were a virgin. Why?'

'Because it was no big deal. Until it literally was.' Her hips twitched, the need to move consuming her. 'Please, Draco, if you still want me, then take me.'

'If I—' He exhaled in disbelief, his eyes squeezing shut for a long tense moment. Then he released her waist. He let her experiment for a scant minute before he took over.

Eyes pinned on her face, gauging her every reaction, he set a steady rhythm, the tension slowly draining out of him as helpless moans spilled from her lips.

Pleasure as she'd never known exploded through her as Draco filled her, stretched her to her limit, over and over. Her back arched with each thrust, an alien storm raging deep inside.

The earthy scent of their union rose to mingle with all the different, wondrous sensations. Lost in delirium, Rebel didn't know whether she was dying or being reborn.

'Arabella, look at me.'

The rough, fierce command fused her back to him, to see the look in his eyes raw and unashamedly carnal. He let her see how she affected him, let her hear each hoarse gasp and guttural groan as he took her higher until she was consumed by the need to jump off the edge of the precipice.

'Oh, God… Draco!'

'Now, Arabella. Let go.'

Rebel soared as she'd never done before, her world unfurling in a white-hot blaze that wrapped her soul in pure joy. Time stood still, granting her the gift of basking in the breathtaking experience. But eventually, her senses returned to her, albeit on a soft haziness that could only absorb the sound of the man whose thickness still registered deep inside her.

Draco watched her eyelashes lift, an indescribable feeling striking him as he traced the flush of pleasure staining her skin. The fervent need for release gnawed at him, but he held it back. He wanted to stretch out this moment for a while longer. Why, he wasn't exactly sure.

His gaze roved over Arabella's face once more. She was breathtaking.

*And she'd been a virgin.*

The feeling he'd been holding at bay rushed over him again. Stronger. Heavier.

She'd been a virgin. And she'd chosen him to be her first.

Was he that primitive that it turned him on more than he'd ever thought possible?

He felt himself thicken even further inside her in answer. Her eyes widened as he stretched her. Unable to deny himself any longer, he pushed deeper inside her. Her slick channel welcomed him in a tight embrace. Her back arched, presenting her perfect breasts for him to feast on. He gave himself over to sensation, the new and mind-numbing bliss sweeter than anything he'd ever experienced.

Soft, feminine arms slid around him, holding him through the buffeting storm he never wanted to subside. Inevitably it did.

Burying his face in her neck, he inhaled her sweet scent, then rolled them over. Her hand splayed on his chest.

'How long do I have before the Gulag train gets here?'

The sound of her voice sent another unfamiliar thrill through him. Draco lay there, unable to believe he was perfectly content to engage in post-sex banter. Normally, he would be dressed and out of the door before the hint of familiarity approached anywhere near contempt.

But he wasn't even thinking of drawing away now as his arms tightened around her.

'They can wait. I haven't had my fill of you yet.'

'Ah, reprieve.'

He reversed their positions, tucking her beneath him once more. 'No, not total reprieve. You didn't tell me about Olivio's attempts to bribe you until I demanded it, and you neglected to mention your virginity. Don't hold back anything that important from me again. Are we clear?'

Her eyelids dropped and she swallowed.

Unease trickled down his spine.

A moment later, she blinked. Then smiled. 'Yes, Drill Sergeant.'

Her familiar snark was lacking its signature bite. Draco tried to push away the disquieting sensation that she was hiding something else, but it lingered, cautioning him not to revel in this moment too long. Nirvana could become addictive.

Dropping his guard was foolish. This was just sex, a side bargain struck with his libido as the sole benefactor.

He would move on once his goal was attained.

# CHAPTER FOURTEEN

REBEL FELT AS if she'd been asleep for only minutes before being woken up. Probably because she had. They hadn't made love again after the first time last night, but dawn light had already been tingeing the skies as they'd gone to sleep.

'Move it, Arabella. You don't want the sun to get any hotter before your run.'

She dragged her head from the pillow. Draco stood beside the bed, a tray in one hand and her gym gear in the other. He was dressed in running shorts and a body-hugging T-shirt. The sight of his body—the body she'd had the freedom to touch at will last night—sent a pulse of heat through her. Dry-mouthed, she tried to divert her gaze elsewhere as she sat up and accepted the tray. She needed to get her thoughts to coalesce so she could say something that didn't sound completely embarrassing.

But her gaze climbed his frame, lovingly exploring it until she reached his face. And the arrogant smile that graced it.

'You ogling me so hungrily isn't going to get you out of training. In fact for every minute you stay in bed, you get to do another vertical jump.'

Since vertical jumps were her favourite of the exercises, Rebel contemplated staying put. One look at his face told her it was the wrong move.

He set the bowl of muesli in her lap. 'Eat your breakfast. I'll be back in ten minutes.'

He was back in five, just as she was about to get out of bed. She froze. 'Can you…turn around, please?'

'No.' He shook out her training gear. 'You get to wear

this while you train. The rest of the time clothes won't be necessary. You might as well get used to it now.'

She bit her lip and frowned. 'If I'd known your island doubled as a nudist colony, I'd have taken my chances with the Gulag.'

He grinned, then dropped the clothes next to her. 'You'll wish you hadn't said that by the time I'm finished with you. Up.'

She'd made love with him—was still not quite sure how she'd survived that transcendental experience—and yet the thought of him seeing her naked made her whole body flame with self-awareness.

Gritting her teeth, she flung the sheets back and stood. About to reach for her shorts, she gasped when he caught her wrist and yanked her close.

His grin had disappeared, his face a taut mask of hunger and desire as his sizzling gaze burned down her body. 'First, you need to greet me properly,' he commanded.

Rebel told herself it was unwise to give in so easily, to reach so greedily for what she wanted. But she was already surging close, curling her arms around his neck and raising herself on tiptoe to reach his mouth. His slanted across hers the moment they touched, his ravenous possession of her mouth making her senses sing. He fisted her hair, angled her head for a deeper exploration, while his other hand moulded her bottom.

They were both groaning, their breathing harsh, when they parted. Rebel licked her lower lip, already mourning the loss of his kiss. 'Good morning, Drill Sergeant,' she husked out.

'Good morning, Arabella *mou*,' he replied, his face an unsmiling mask reflecting all her cravings. 'Now you can get dressed.'

A full-body tremble raking her, she turned, picked up the shorts and stepped into them. She was sliding them up when she felt his gentle touch on her lower back, just above her right buttock.

Rebel froze. She'd forgotten about her scar.

'What happened here?' he murmured.

She kept her face averted. 'An accident,' she replied, injecting as much lightness into her voice as possible.

'During training?' She heard the frown in his voice. She knew why. The scar wasn't extensive, but the wound had been deep, the scar tissue pronounced. But far deeper was the secret scar she carried on her heart. The one she couldn't tell him about because he would hate her, condemn her as no better than someone like Tyson Blackwell.

'No, it was a long time ago.' Hurriedly she snapped the waistband into place and reached for the top. Yanking it on, she schooled her features and turned. 'I'm ready. You can do your worst now.'

The eyes that met hers held lingering questions. Rebel's breath caught in her lungs; she was hoping against hope he'd let it go. She wasn't ready for the sheer magic she'd discovered last night with him to be over. And it would be if he forced the secret out of her.

After another contemplative look, one corner of his mouth lifted. 'That invitation is way too hard to ignore.' Grabbing her hand, he marched her into the lift, and pressed the button for Level Three.

Rebel read the buttons on the panel. 'There are seven levels?'

He nodded, then pushed her back against the lift wall, his hand bracketing her. 'Guess what's on the seventh level?' he murmured, his lips brushing her temple.

It felt like the most natural thing in the world to slide her hands around his tight, trim waist. 'Umm… Draco the Dragon's lair?'

His mouth twitched. 'Close. I look forward to showing you.'

The lift stopped and they stepped out onto a wraparound

terrace wide enough to fit her Chelsea flat four times over. Her breath caught as she saw the view for the first time. The Aegean glistened like a moving jewelled tapestry, meeting a sky of unmarred blue. Perfectly framing it was the white beach below and the red cliffs that formed the foundations of Draco's villa.

'It's so beautiful.'

He smiled and nodded as he guided her across the vast terrace to stone steps that meandered out of view. 'This is where I come to get away from the world. I had it built seven years ago.'

'Before your accident?'

He trotted down the stairs and she followed. 'Yes. I wanted a private place to train when I didn't need to be on the sports sites. This was the perfect place. When I became an agent, this part of the property became a good place to decompress. The other side of the villa is where I entertain.'

'How big is the island?'

He reached the bottom of the stairs and stretched. While he waited for her to do the same, he adjusted the timer on his watch. 'Four kilometres across. Which you will run twice with three minutes shaved off your usual average. Go.'

He set off through an archway of trellised bougainvillea, disappearing out of sight before she'd taken the first step. She caught up and managed to keep up by the skin of her teeth. Sweat poured off her body by the time they finished the second course, the sun hot on her face as she rehydrated. Her gaze caught Draco's as she swallowed the last drop, and she almost choked at the heat that blazed from his eyes.

'Let's get you inside,' was all he said as he took the bottle from her and disposed of it.

The seventh level was just as she'd suspected. A vast area, twice the size of a basketball court, held gleaming exercise machines in all shapes and sizes. There was even a boxing ring tucked into one corner.

Rebel turned a full circle. 'I was wrong. This is more like Dante's seventh circle of hell.'

He smiled and led her to an exercise mat. 'Hell is good. It helps you appreciate heaven more.'

She found out just how much he relished putting her through hell over the next three hours. He upped her regime by thirty per cent, then grunted with satisfaction each time she achieved her target.

Pride burned in her chest as she pushed her body to the limit. And just for the hell of it, when he called time, she did another ten vertical jumps more than he'd instructed her to.

'Fine, you've made your point. Don't get cocky,' he growled.

She laughed and swiped at the sweat pouring off her temples. 'Yes, Drill Sergeant.'

Turning, she braced her foot against the wall and stretched her arches. She was about to step back when she sensed him behind her. All through training she'd seen the banked hunger in his eyes. Even without looking at him now, Rebel knew he'd finally released the tight grip on his restraint.

'Keep your hands on the wall.' His voice was a deep, primitive rumble that took complete control of every nerve in her body. She shook just from the power of it.

She felt him drop into a squat behind her. A moment later, he grasped one ankle and took her trainer and sock off, then did the same to the other. Standing, he slipped his hands into the waistband of her shorts and peeled them down her legs.

'Draco,' she murmured hesitantly as he widened her stance.

'Yes?'

She shut her eyes with a tiny grimace. 'I'm sweaty.'

'Yes, you are,' he agreed with a decadent relish that tightened her skin and increased the tempo beating at her core.

His hands slid up to her breasts and he lowered the

front zip of her top. Leaving it hanging open, he cupped her breasts on a deep groan.

She shuddered as he tweaked her nipples, her whole body a receptive vessel eagerly absorbing the expert attention being lavished on it. Several mindless minutes later, she felt him drop low again.

Rebel wasn't prepared for the sensation that blazed through her next.

'Draco!' Her eyes flew open and she glanced down to see the source of her pleasure. Molten eyes met hers as his tongue lapped at her nether lips. The view alone was enough to send her into orbit. He grounded her with a firm hand on one thigh, then parted her flesh with his other hand to reach the bundle of nerves that ripped a scream from her the moment he flicked his tongue against it.

He might have caressed her for seconds. Or hours. Time ceased to exist or matter. All she could process was the encroaching tide of bliss that rushed over her and pulled her under.

She resurfaced to find herself still upright but caught in his arms.

'You're exquisite, Arabella *mou*. Truly exquisite,' he rasped against her ear. 'And all mine. Why did you let me believe all those things said about you in the media?' he added gruffly, his tone holding a touch of contrition.

Senses still swimming, she tried to find the right words to reply. 'Umm…you seemed blissfully wedded to the idea that I was a wild, wicked siren. But it was just the…white noise I needed to…to forget.' She bit her lip, wondering if she'd gone too far. Rushing on, she added, 'I told you, you didn't know everything about me.'

He grunted, his hand cupping her core in a shockingly possessive hold. 'From now on *I* will be your white noise. You get to be the wild, wicked siren only with me. And no more hiding important stuff from me. You'll be straight with me on everything. Understood?'

Her heart lurched. 'Draco…I…'

His hand moved between her thighs, melting away the apprehension and budding guilt, and leaving nothing but fevered anticipation behind.

When he picked her up, and walked over to the weight bench, Rebel gave up trying to formulate a single thought.

He arranged her over the bench. The rasp of the condom being ripped open barely registered against her buzzing senses before he was once more in control of her, his hands on her waist, his power at her throbbing centre. He took her higher than he had last night, almost rough in his possession as he drew every ounce of pleasure from her. His guttural shout as he followed her into bliss echoed in her ears as she lost her mind to sensation once more.

For the next three weeks they fell into a rigid routine. Intense training twice a day, six days a week. In between training, they made love, picnicked at various spots on the island, or ate their meals on whichever breathtaking level of Dante's villa took their fancy. On her first rest day, he took her out on a launch to his yacht moored on the other side of the villa. Rebel had seen the impressive vessel on their morning runs, but nothing had prepared her for the beauty of the *Angelis*.

Draco had smiled indulgently as she rhapsodised over the vessel, then let her take the wheel as they sailed around the island.

By some unspoken agreement, their conversation didn't stray into too personal territories, as if they were both emotionally wary, having bared their innermost cores to each other in the first week of meeting.

Of course, Draco didn't know of the last layer, the one she feared would be uncovered each time his gaze lingered on her scar and she pretended not to notice. Or when he kissed it during lovemaking and she felt the question on her skin.

Although, more and more, an equally insidious fear

trickled through her each time her gaze caught her engagement ring. The craving for everything happening between them to be real had taken permanent root in her heart. She couldn't shake it off, and with each day that passed it embedded itself deeper into her heart.

It was there, silently clamouring for attention, when she woke from an afternoon nap on their last week on the island and went in search of Draco. His expansive office was located on Level Two. It was the only place in the private villa besides the gym that she went into with clothes on, having refused point-blank to risk entering a room while Draco was on one of his many videoconferences.

She heard his dark, smoky voice now as the lift doors parted, and heard his deep laugh before she saw him, the sound so beautiful her footsteps slowed. In contrast her heart leapt, then filled with a powerful emotion that threatened to knock her to her knees.

She stepped into the sunlight as he threw back his head and laughed again. The clear joy in his face caught her breath as a certain knowledge pounded through her.

She had no time to process it because Draco turned his head and saw her. She expected him to wave her to the sofa at the far end of the room where she usually waited for him to finish; her eyes widened as he held out his arm to her.

Warily, she stepped forward, then gasped when he jerked her into his lap. Face flaming, she glanced at the wide screen.

The woman bore a striking resemblance to Draco, her dramatically beautiful face and the headrest of what could only be wheelchair announcing who she was.

'Maria?'

She smiled. 'So I finally get to meet my brother's fake fiancée.'

Rebel's gaze flew to Draco's. He shrugged. 'Maria and I don't have secrets. Not any more.' A hint of regret washed over his face, but it was gone a moment later when his sister replied.

'Enough of that, brother. So we had to learn our lesson the hard way. We got through it,' she admonished gently. Then her gaze swung to Rebel. 'But he still didn't tell me about you until the story hit the papers.'

Draco's hand curled over Rebel's hip as he peered at his sister. 'I was trying to protect you.'

Maria rolled her eyes. 'I live in an ivory tower, Draco, guarded twenty-four-seven by security and private physicians. A scandal or two wouldn't hurt to get the blood pumping.'

Rebel laughed. 'I tell him that all the time.'

'And let me guess, he does the "dragon breathing fire" thing—yep, there it is.'

They both turned to see the deep scowl marring Draco's face, and dissolved into laughter.

He reached up and tucked a strand of hair behind Rebel's ear before cupping her nape in a possessive hold. 'Very funny.'

'He makes it so easy, doesn't he?' Rebel chuckled.

Maria sighed. 'Almost too easy.'

'Enough from you two.' He pointed at his sister. 'I'll see you next week.'

Her grey eyes softened. 'I can't wait. And I know you're doing your best with Carla, but please remember that not everyone who needs help necessarily wants it. I love you no matter what.'

Beneath her, Draco tensed for a second. Then a weight seemed to lift off his shoulders. The smile he sent Maria positively glowed. 'You stay out of trouble.'

Maria rolled her eyes again before her gaze swung to Rebel. 'It was nice to meet the reason for my brother's bigger smile. I hope we meet in person one day.'

She signed off and the screen went blank. Draco turned his monitor off and an awkward silence descended.

Unable to stand it, Rebel cleared her throat. 'I'm the reason for your bigger smile? Does that mean I get an extra half hour's sleep tomorrow morning?' she teased, praying her heart's wild leaps wouldn't show on her face.

Draco snorted. 'In your dreams. Maria's a hopeless romantic who sees hearts and happy ever after in every cloud.' His grip tightened. 'You want an extra half hour's sleep? You *earn* it.'

She managed to keep her expression composed, despite the hollow that caved in her stomach. 'And how do I go about earning my sleep? Scrubbing all seven levels of your villa?'

'The only manual labour I require from you besides your training is on my person,' he replied.

Like a flame on gasoline, the air erupted with desire. The hand around her nape caressed with rough insistence. Then he pushed her off him. 'Take off that dress,' he growled.

She took it off, but before he could grab her she dropped to her knees. Draco froze, giving her the precious time she needed. Before her nerves could get the better of her, she reached for his waistband and lowered his zipper. A hiss erupted from his lips but he raised himself up to help her ease off his shorts and briefs.

She grasped him, emitting a soft gasp as the power and steel of him sent a thrill through her. She caressed him from root to tip and back, lazily, worshipping him. Then she took him in her mouth. Quickly learning what pleased him most, she teased and sucked with just the right amount of pressure for the vocal sounds of his pleasure to fill the room.

At some point his fingers fisted her hair. For an alarming second, she feared he'd pull her away. Her gaze raced up to find his locked on her, his face a tortured mask of brutal hunger. Whatever he read in her face made him nod. Absorbing every expression on his face, feminine power roaring through her, she revelled in owning him as he succumbed greedily to her ministrations.

Afterwards, he caught her beneath her arms and tucked

her up into his lap. Depositing an almost reverent kiss on her temple, he said gruffly, 'For that, *glikia mou*, you can have a whole extra hour in bed tomorrow.'

Draco watched Arabella sleep the next morning, thankful for the reprieve of not having to keep his guard up. He wasn't even sure what he was guarding. The emotions crowding through him had snuck up on him, slipped in and taken up residence while he'd been busy making love to Arabella. Or had it been when she'd met and exceeded his expectations each time he'd set her a physical challenge? Or the times when he'd found himself living for her fearless, smart mouth to draw laughter from him?

However it'd happened didn't even matter.

Maria's observation about his obvious contentment had rocked him, planted the evidence firmly in his lap, before she'd signed off, blissfully unaware of the wreck she'd left him with. But it was a wreck shrouded in fog on a black night of lies. He knew in his gut Arabella was hiding something big from him. She tensed and evaded him far too often for that not to be the case.

He despised himself for not confronting it head-on, for giving himself leave for one more day with the excuse that the investigative report he'd done on her had provided him with enough pertinent details about her. Everything else she'd revealed so far had been harmless.

She couldn't hurt Maria, and that had been enough.

*But she could hurt you.* His chest tightened, and he pushed the thought away. He could only be hurt if he let this thing spin out longer than their agreed time.

So far his investigators had found nothing on Tyson he could use and Olivio remained intransigent. Draco hated to rely on no news being good news, but more and more he was accepting that the choice might not be his as to whether Carla remained out of danger. She might have been partly responsible for his sister turning a corner during the bleak years after her accident, but Maria was much stronger than he'd ever given her credit for.

He would protect Carla as much as he could, but Draco was beginning to realise that some things were indeed out of his hands.

Arabella rolled over in her sleep, straight into his arms. He was pulling her close even before caution kicked in. She opened her stunning blue eyes and smiled, and he kicked caution to the kerb.

Sliding her arms around his neck, she stretched against him. 'Thank you for my extra hour. It was *heavenly*.'

'You're welcome. Now let's see if this is equally heavenly.'

He lowered his head, took what was his and silenced the clamouring of his instincts.

# CHAPTER FIFTEEN

THE PACE CHANGED drastically over the next three weeks. Although she was fully installed in Draco's chalet in Verbier, Rebel barely saw him. Her training had stepped up another gear with Greg and a team Draco had hired now in charge of her on-site drills.

She hadn't realised how much she'd missed the snow until she stood at the top of the ramp on the first day. Breathing in the frigid air, she felt peace settle over her as her mother's smiling face wove into her mind. She suffered a moment's regret for the years she'd wasted being less than she could've been. How could she have ever believed she could go through life like that?

'Ready?' Greg's voice piped from behind her.

'Ready.' She adjusted her goggles a final time and planted her skis, the sheer joy of being here, doing what she loved, firing through her.

Greg counted down and sounded the klaxon. She grimaced as she pushed off a millisecond later than she'd intended.

She could already imagine the conversation with Draco later that night in her head.

Blocking it out, she poised her body for the lift-off. Exhilaration burst through her as her feet left the ramp. The elation her mother had felt and passed down to her wrapped around her as she soared.

Her mother had loved her beyond her own life. Rebel knew that had she survived the accident that had claimed her life, she would've forgiven Rebel's part in it.

It was time to forgive herself. Time to come clean to

Draco. If for nothing else, for the chance to take the risk of baring her heart to see if there was a future for them.

Although things had remained the same on the surface, Rebel had felt a shift in Draco the day after she'd met Maria via video link. He hadn't smiled as widely at her jokes, nor lingered in bed with her when they'd both had a little time on their hands. By the time they'd left the island, the only time she'd felt fully connected to him was when they'd made love.

She couldn't let it carry on. He'd helped her achieve life-changing clarity, the least she could do was give him the complete truth about herself in return. What he chose to do with it was up to him.

Her heart squeezed as the ground rushed up to her. Bending her knees, she executed a perfect landing and skied to the bottom of the hill.

'You know you're going to hear about that take-off, don't you?' Greg said via the mic in her ear.

She grimaced and made a face at the camera that was recording all her jumps for Draco to review later.

'I'm not scared of the dragon,' she quipped, lying through her teeth.

Greg laughed. 'You're in the minority, then.'

Grinning, she skied to the edge of the enclosure, toed off her skis and got back on the escalator for another test jump. She had three days before the championships began, and Draco had found less and less to criticise her about as she'd perfected her jump.

She didn't doubt that he would chew her out for the millisecond delay. But he would be doing so while in the same room with her. And after four days without him, she didn't care if he berated her for half the night. As long as she got to spend the other half in his arms.

She was showered and in bed, anticipating Draco's arrival, when her phone rang. She saw his number, and her heart sank.

'Unless you're calling me from the living room, consider your entire accumulation of brownie points docked.'

'I'm calling you from the emergency room,' Draco replied, tersely.

She jerked upright, her heart slamming hard against her ribs. 'Are you okay?'

'I'm fine, Arabella. Unfortunately, Carla isn't. She's in intensive care as we speak.'

'No! What happened?'

'She fell, hit her head. She hasn't suffered any spinal injuries, but the doctors aren't taking chances. The air ambulance brought her to Rome from Tuscany this morning.'

Rebel's hand tightened around the phone. 'How is Maria taking it?'

'She's being exceptionally strong,' he responded, his voice reflecting a quiet pride. 'I flew her down this afternoon.'

'I'm glad she's there with Carla.'

'Yes. Arabella, I don't know when I'll be able to come to Verbier.'

Her stomach hollowed, bringing with it a tinge of shame for her selfishness. 'It's fine,' she mustered with as much grace as she could. Then, remembering her vow this morning, she added, 'When you do get here, though, we need to talk.'

Tense silence greeted her. Wondering whether the line had dropped, she glanced at her phone. She was still connected. 'Draco?'

'I'm here. We will talk as you wish.' Voices murmured in the background. 'I have to go.'

'Umm…okay—'

He hung up before she could stumble through telling him she'd missed him. Or, even more, that she loved him.

Because she did.

She'd agreed to stage a flawless performance of make-believe love. Instead she'd fallen in love for real.

The irony didn't escape her as the phone dropped from her numb fingers into her lap. Looking down, she caught sight of her engagement ring. Her heart cracked open at the real possibility that she might have to take it off in the very near future. After all, even if Draco saw past her role in her mother's death and forgave her, she had no guarantee that he would want to be with her, never mind on a permanent basis.

Her heart shuddered at the phantom loss even as it contemplated the real one. Desperate to flee the bleakness snaking through her, she grabbed the remote and flicked on the TV.

Every channel carried the news of Carla Nardozzi's accident, with the blame laid firmly at Tyson Blackwell's feet. Footage of the moments before the accident had been leaked to the media, and the trainer had been arrested.

Relief for Draco and Maria for the delayed justice and closure surged through her. Turning the TV off, she lay back in bed, sending up a silent prayer that she and Draco would be granted a chance for a fresh start.

Carla Nardozzi was put into a medical coma the day before the opening ceremony of the Verbier Ski Championships.

Draco called with another terse apology—one that was becoming a common occurrence. And one that Rebel brushed off with a light tone and a heavy heart.

Her first competition took place that afternoon. With Greg and Contessa and the rest of her team in her camp, Rebel should've been ecstatic when she placed second by the end of the first day. Instead she kept her phone on her lap all through dinner with the team, her heart jumping each time she felt a ring that turned out to be her imagination. Tuesday and Wednesday were even better days. By Thursday she was leading the women's ski-jump category, with her name suddenly on every sports commentator's lips. Contessa excitedly booked interviews and negotiated with new sponsors who wanted to be associated with the new and improved Rebel Daniels. Rebel nodded and smiled through it all, but inside she was dead with complete misery.

She was getting ready for her final afternoon session on Friday when Greg walked into the recreation room. 'I've just had a note that there's someone wanting to see you in the VIP hospitality box.' His dark frown spelled his displeasure. 'They won't tell me who it is and I can't bring them back here. I'm going to have to come with you.'

Her heart leapt into her throat, her whole body revving into invigorating life as she jumped up. Draco had arrived!

'It's fine. I have my personal official here with me.' Rebel waved at Greta, the woman who'd been assigned to her.

Greg's lips pursed as he handed over the note. 'Are you sure?'

'I'm sure,' she insisted, rushing towards the door.

Rebel asked Greta to point her in the direction of VIP box number sixteen. The older woman struggled to keep up as Rebel sprinted ahead. The box was at the far end of the luxurious championship course, directly overlooking the ski-jump platform. Slightly out of breath, she entered the semi-lit room, leaving Greta in the hallway. Spotting the figure looking out to the course, she hurried towards him.

'Drac—Dad!' she amended as her father faced her.

'Hello, Arabella.'

'What are you doing here?' The question emerged like an accusation.

She was happy to see him, of course she was, but the scything disappointment of not finding Draco here raked her raw without the numbness to protect her.

'I'm sorry for the cloak-and-dagger stuff. But I wasn't sure you'd want to see me. Not after the way we parted.'

Pain she'd thought she'd grappled under control fired through her. 'You were the one who didn't want to see me any more, remember?'

He sighed. 'I should never have said that.'

'Why not, if you meant it?'

'I didn't *mean* it. It was wrong, but that was just my grief talking.'

Weariness weighted her shoulders. 'It's okay, Dad. I get it now.'

His light blue eyes widened. 'You do?'

'Yes, I do.'

*We need to talk.*

Draco had lost count of the number of ways he'd dissected those four words, hoping to disembowel every worst-case scenario they might represent. Each time, a new one had reared up stronger, more venomous than before.

What good thing had ever come from those words? Hell, weren't those same words his own lead-in to a break-up with a girlfriend who suddenly grew too clingy? Or an underperforming employee who needed to be kicked into touch or kicked out? He'd never been at the receiving end of them, of course.

Until now.

He read the box numbers as they flashed past, the location Greg had given him stuck in his brain. He wanted to reach his destination yet he dreaded what would happen when he got there. That dread was partly why he'd stayed away. Sure, Olivio Nardozzi had finally wised up to the fact that the daughter he'd viewed as little more than an asset he'd kept too tight a grip on was in danger of slipping away from him and had begged for Draco's help. But everything he'd done for them could've been done from his Verbier chalet, within touching distance of Arabella.

Except he hadn't been sure Arabella would wish to be at his side.

The *not* knowing had finally got to him. He needed to know where he stood, whether her request to talk was a precursor to her walking away from him.

He neared box sixteen and flashed his Access All Areas card at the stout woman guarding the hallway. A few steps away from the door he froze at the sound of Arabella's voice.

'You lost the love of your life because of me.'

'Arabella, don't—'

'No. Don't try to mince your words. If I hadn't disobeyed you both and gone out skiing on my own, she'd still be alive today. She'd be here with you and we'd still be a family.'

Horror clawed up Draco's spine.

'We tell everyone it was an accident, but it wasn't, Dad, and we both know it. I rebelled against my parents. You warned me not to go skiing when there was a blizzard warning. I waited until you'd gone to the village to do the grocery shopping, then snuck out. I wanted what I wanted and it ended up killing her.'

A ragged breath echoed out into the hallway. 'You'll never know what coming back to see the note that she'd gone after you did to me. To have never got the chance to say goodbye…'

'Because of me. I know, Dad. You'll never know how much I wish I hadn't—'

Draco didn't realise his feet had moved until he was standing in the room. Twin pairs of blue eyes swung his way, one narrowing in wary dislike, and the other rounding with the same horror spiralling through him.

'You had a direct hand in your mother's accident?' he rasped, blinding rage eclipsing everything else.

She swallowed, her eyes pools of dark horror. 'Draco… I…'

'After agreeing we'd be up front with each other, you didn't think to tell me you selfishly and irresponsibly put your own mother's life in danger?'

'Draco—'

He waved her silent, her voice a bleak implication he didn't want ringing in his ears. Shaking his head, he laughed. 'But then you didn't exactly agree to the *up-front* part, did you? I was too caught up in…other things to recognise that you avoided that particular stipulation.'

She stepped towards him. 'I wanted to tell you. Draco, please believe me—'

He silenced her with a slash of his hand. 'I let you into Maria's life. She already thinks you're the most incredible woman to walk the earth. And you've turned out to be no better than the man who put her in the wheelchair.'

She gasped.

Nathan Daniels stepped forward. 'Now hang on there, Angelis—'

'Save it. I have no time for either of you. If I never see either one of you again in this lifetime, it'll be too soon.'

Rebel watched Draco walk out, her ashen world turning a soulless, all-encompassing black. From far away, she heard her father call her name. She probably responded, because the worried look in his eyes receded.

'I know this probably wasn't the best timing, but I didn't want to do it after the fact.'

Struggling to think past the pain slashing at her heart, she frowned. 'Do what?'

'Tell you that your mother would be proud of you and what you've achieved. Whether you win today or not, we're *both* proud of you. And I sold our old house. I'm sure you'll agree we need to make new memories?'

Her breath shuddered. 'Yes.'

'I'm seeing a grief counsellor. And I also intend to pay back the money, Arabella. I don't care how long it takes, I'll make things right.'

Tears welled in her eyes. 'Dad—'

'Miss Daniels, it's time to go,' Greta said from the doorway.

She glanced at her father. He nodded. 'We have a lot to talk about, I know. But you need to go and see all your hard work pay off.'

She blinked the tears away. 'Will…will you come and watch me?'

He swallowed hard before he nodded. 'Yes, I will.'

She walked back with Greta, picked up her skis and made her way to the waiting area. She was the first to jump, which helped because once again blocking everything and keeping her mind blank were imperative.

This time it wasn't just her mother's face that spurred her on. Her father's solemn eyes and quiet pride flashed too. Her timing was laser-perfect, and she soared higher than she ever had. But as the snow-white ground rushed up to meet her, a piercing realisation lanced through her.

*It's not enough. I want love too.*

Unbidden, Draco's words from weeks ago when he'd made her realise she was holding herself back from winning popped into her mind.

*We never get everything we want.*

Her feet crashed to the ground and she cartwheeled into the barrier. A collective gasp rushed through the frigid air. Officials nearby rushed to her aid, but Rebel was already struggling to her feet.

Draco might believe they never got what they wanted, but she had proved otherwise.

She wanted him. She loved him. She'd never got the chance to tell him. No way was she willing to accept what had happened in the VIP room as her fate until she'd stared him in the eye and said her piece.

She was toeing off her skis when an excited Greg and Contessa rushed towards her. 'Did you see?' Contessa screeched. 'You jumped two *metres* farther than the world-record holder!'

'My God, Rebel, what happened up there?'

*I got my heart smashed into a million pieces.*

She smiled and shrugged. They waited in the pen for the remaining competitors to jump. With each one that didn't make it as far, Greg and Contessa squealed. If they noticed she wasn't as excited, they refrained from commenting.

Then her name erupted in lights as the winner. Tears welled and her whole body shuddered as she imagined the spirit of her mother wrapped around her in a warm, comforting glow.

Half an hour later, Rebel stood on the podium and waved to the crowd, an even harder determination burning in her chest. Returning to the dressing room, she entrusted her trophy to Contessa and her skis to Greg, then hurried into the shower, with a promise to meet up later.

Slipping on jeans and a long-sleeved top and layering it with a hoodie and beanie to finish off her disguise, she left the grounds and walked to a taxi stand. Whether Draco had left Switzerland or not she still had to collect her belongings from his chalet. But she prayed he would be there. She pulled her phone from her bag and brought up the text app.

When I said we needed to talk I actually meant that I would talk and you would listen. So you owe me another 'We need to talk' minus the fire-breathing antics. Where are you?

She pressed *'send'* with her heart in her throat, and waited.

An answer pinged a second later.

Behind you.

Rebel whirled, her foot slipping on the ice before she righted herself. A black limo crept towards her, its back window slowly winding down as it neared.

Draco's molten grey eyes pierced hers as the car drew to a stop. He alighted and held the door open for her.

She stayed on the pavement. 'You were creeping behind me on the off-chance that I would text you?'

'No, Arabella. My hopes have dropped to nil where you're concerned.'

Her heart stumbled, but she'd come this far. She needed to see this through. 'I need to get my things from your place.'

His eyes shadowed, but he nodded. 'I'll take you. You can talk on the way.'

She slid into the plush interior and retreated to the far side. He regained his seat and slammed the door, sealing them in semi-dark silence.

They travelled a mile with Rebel trying to find her nerve. 'You missed my victory dance on the podium.'

'No, I didn't.'

Her breath caught. 'You were there.'

'I couldn't leave.'

'Too many potential clients to schmooze?'

'The farthest thing from my mind.'

She bit her lip and looked out of the window. When she saw how close they were to Draco's chalet, she cleared her throat. 'Everything you heard me say to my father I'd planned to tell you. Yes, I should've told you when you asked me about my scar, or afterwards. But I'm not perfect. I made a mistake.'

He exhaled. 'Arabella—'

'No, I'm not quite finished. What I did in my past doesn't give you the right to act like an ass. I made a horrible mistake when I was only seventeen that tortured me and which I was still paying for when I met you. But you know what? I've learned to forgive myself, ironically, thanks to you.' She pointed a finger at him. 'But you decided to heap on me anyway—why, because you think I haven't suffered enough?'

A wave of regret washed over his face. 'No. You've suffered more than enough.'

She sagged back in her seat, bewilderment and pain eating at her. 'Then why?'

'I knew what you were keeping from me was big. I just didn't realise how I would feel to know you had a secret like that you couldn't trust me with. I despise secrets and knowing something this monumental had happened in your life and you were hiding it from me... I lashed out without thinking.' He turned suddenly and lunged for her hand. 'Everything I said in that room was inexcusable. I'd braced myself for something else—'

'What?'

'You, breaking up with me. And not the fake engagement either. You said we needed to talk—'

'And you immediately slid into complete-bastard mode?'

'I'd had too much time to dwell on a few worst-case scenarios.'

She didn't want to get her hopes up, not when his words still stung so deeply. 'And the worst was me breaking up with you?'

He slashed a hand through his hair, his breathing ragged. 'I'm in love with you, Arabella. Deeply. Completely. The past few weeks have been hell when each time I wanted to say it, I knew you were keeping something from me. Something that might mean the end of us. Going along with the charade just to keep you close felt like the safest option, but I hated it, and so I overreacted when I finally heard the truth.'

With supreme effort, Rebel regained her power of speech. 'You're...in love with me.' Parts of her were coming alive that she wanted to send back to sleep. Until she was completely certain she wasn't dreaming this.

'You forgot the deeply, completely part.'

She shook her head. 'I still don't understand why you were so mean to me. As for my father...what he did was inexcusable, I know, but he intends to make amends. He did what he did because he loves me. He lost his way for a while, but I think he deserves a chance to make reparations.'

Draco nodded. 'He does, and I intend to give him one. We've already agreed a payment plan for the money he took.'

Her eyes widened. '*What*? When?'

'I went back to the VIP room to beg you to let me take back my words. He was still there. We talked. Then we watched you win together.'

Her hand flew to her mouth as she choked back a sob. 'That does not touch me in any way.'

A hint of an arrogant smile curved his mouth. Then his face turned solemn again. 'I will do better, if you give me a chance. Please, Arabella.'

'You really love me?' The words shook out of her.

He cupped her face, his gaze contrite and direct, and filled with an emotion that caught at her hard. 'Deeply. Completely. You challenge me, you make me feel alive. I give you hell and you laugh in my face. I want that every day for the rest of my life.'

Rebel leaned into him, unable to be this close and not want more of the man she loved more than life itself.

'I hope you realise I'm going to live off this grovelling for the next sixty years?'

He tensed but replied, 'And I will fall at your feet every time and beg forgiveness.'

'Wow. Okay, that sounds like a plan.'

'Does that mean what I think it means?'

'You're in love with me. I'm in love with every infuriating inch of you. I hate you for breaking my heart and making me sad on the day I won my major trophy, but I love you for agreeing to be mine for the rest of our lives.'

He squeezed his eyes shut and dropped his forehead to hers. '*Thee mou*. You wreck me, Arabella. I love you.'

When they reached the chalet, he dragged her inside, then sealed his lips to hers in a fervent reminder of what had brought them together and what was in store for them.

Finally letting go of the fear and letting joy in, she closed the gap between them and slid her arms around his neck. 'I love you, too. Oh, and don't bother getting yourself fixed. I plan on wrecking you every day for as long as we both live.'

\* \* \* \* \*

*You can read Carla Nardozzi's story in*
*SIGNED OVER TO SANTINO.*
*Available June 2016!*

**'This is not a game, Nicole.' Rigo's voice took on a dangerous tone. 'I made it clear the last time we met that I am not a man to mess with.'**

'I would have been quite happy never to lay eyes on you again.' She narrowed her eyes, the anger she felt finally rising to the surface.

Rigo took a step forward, a half-smile breaking across his harsh features. 'Now, *this* is interesting. So far I've witnessed Nicole the innocent temptress, followed by Nicole the damsel in distress.' He raised one brow. 'But I think this passionately angry version is my personal favourite.'

Nicole was speechless. The idea that they had ever been anything so romantic as lovers was poetic nonsense. Once upon a time she might have thought they shared a connection. That for one night in his bed she had somehow been special.

She had been a fool.

'My silence is the most you're going to get. I don't deal with the press any more.'

'You will make a public statement that the child is not mine, Nicole.'

She fought the emotion welling up in her chest. It was ridiculous to feel hurt at his words after so long. After all, he had made his position on fatherhood quite clear. But still, a part of her had always hoped he would come in those weeks afterwards.

Indignation won out over the sadness, and she stood up a little taller, meeting his gaze head-on. 'I will *not* publicly tell lies…'

# *Secret Heirs of Billionaires*

*There are some things money can't buy…*

Living life at lightning pace, these magnates are no strangers to stakes at their highest. It seems they've got it all… That is until they find out that there's an unplanned item to add to their list of accomplishments!

Achieved:

1. Successful business empire

2. Beautiful women in their bed

3. *An heir to bear their name…?*

Though every billionaire needs to leave his legacy in safe hands, discovering a secret heir shakes up his carefully orchestrated plan in more ways than one!

Uncover their secrets in:

*Unwrapping the Castelli Secret* by Caitlin Crews

*Brunetti's Secret Son* by Maya Blake

*The Secret to Marrying Marchesi* by Amanda Cinelli

Look out for more stories in
***Secret Heirs of Billionaires*** series in 2016!

millsandboon.co.uk

# THE SECRET
# TO MARRYING
# MARCHESI

BY
AMANDA CINELLI

MILLS &
BOON

First Published in Great Britain 2016
By Mills & Boon, an imprint of HarperCollins*Publishers*
1 London Bridge Street, London, SE1 9GF

© 2016 Amanda Cinelli

ISBN: 978-0-263-92110-6

Printed and bound in Spain
by CPI, Barcelona

**Amanda Cinelli** was raised in a large Irish/Italian family in the suburbs of Dublin, Ireland. Her love of romance was inspired after 'borrowing' one of her mother's beloved Mills & Boon novels at the age of twelve. Writing soon became a necessary outlet for her wildly overactive imagination. Now married, with a daughter of her own, she splits her time between changing nappies, studying psychology and writing love stories.

**Books by Amanda Cinelli**

**Mills & Boon Modern Romance**

*Resisting the Sicilian Playboy*

Visit the Author Profile page at millsandboon.co.uk.

For my grandmother Anne.
Who taught me to always have a pile of good books
by my bedside.

# CHAPTER ONE

SHE WAS DEFINITELY being followed.

Nicole tightened her grip on the stroller's handlebar and picked up her pace. The same black Jeep had already made its way past her three times as she took her morning walk through the village. Two men sat inside, their dark sunglasses doing nothing to disguise the fact that their attention was focused entirely on her. As the vehicle slowed to a complete crawl a short distance behind her, she felt the familiar prick of ice-cold terror in her throat. It was officially time to panic.

The cobbled laneway that led up to her farmhouse was still slippery from the light April drizzle. Her ballet flats scraped against the stone as the breath whooshed from her lungs with effort. A gleeful squeal sounded from within the cocoon of pink blankets as the stroller bounced and swayed. Nicole forced herself to smile down at her daughter through tight lips, summoning an inner calm she wasn't quite sure she possessed. They were nearly home. She would lock the door and everything would be fine.

As she rounded the last bend that led to La Petite, she

slowed to a stop. The gateway was filled with vehicles, and a line of cars stretched further up the lane. A dozen figures stood in wait with cameras slung around their necks. Nicole felt a humming begin in her ears as her blood pressure instantly skyrocketed.

They had found her.

Thinking fast, she pulled off her light jacket and draped it over the stroller's hood. They descended quickly, the crowd of men forming a circle around her as the cameras began to flash. She kept her head down, and the air seemed to stretch her lungs to breaking point as she tried to move forward. They seemed to gather more tightly around her. Apparently the addition of a child made absolutely no difference to the paparazzi's definition of *personal space*.

A man stepped forward, blocking her way. 'Come on—a quick photo of the young 'un, Miss Duvalle.' He smile was shark-like, sharp-toothed and dangerous. 'You've kept this hidden quite well, haven't you?'

Nicole bit down hard on her bottom lip. Silence was the key here. Give them nothing and pray that they went away. The sudden jarring sound of a car horn was just what she needed as the black Jeep appeared in the lane behind her. The vehicle began pushing its way through the crowd, forcing the photographers to scatter. Taking advantage of the distraction, she moved as fast as she could, pushing hard through the throng.

It seemed like a lifetime before she crossed the gateway onto her own private property. They couldn't enter without breaking the law, but she wasn't so naive to think that she was somehow out of their reach.

She would never have privacy here again. The thought brought a choking sob to her throat.

She resisted the urge to look over her shoulder and focused on retrieving her keys from her handbag with trembling hands. Once she was finally inside, she slid the deadbolt into place and scooped Anna up into her arms. Her daughter's warm cotton scent soothed her nerves, giving her a small moment of relief through the haze of blind panic. The sun shone through the windows, brightening the room and filling the space with light. Anna's sparkling blue eyes smiled up at her, so peaceful and unknowing of the situation they were in.

She needed to find out what was going on. *Now.* She gently settled her daughter on a soft mat surrounded by toys, then quickly got to work. It wasn't an easy task to fire up the ancient computer that had come with the farmhouse. One of her first resolutions upon moving to the French countryside from London had been to throw away her smartphone and stop checking the showbiz news. Still, she made sure to keep a phone charged for emergencies. One that only made and received calls—that was all she needed.

It seemed like hours before she could finally type a few keywords into the search engine on the dusty screen. She immediately wished she hadn't bothered.

'Billionaire Marchesi's Secret Love Child Uncovered!'

Seeing the words in black and white filled her with ice-cold dread. She scanned through a few lines of the anonymous interview before turning away from the screen in disgust. Was her life always going to be sordid entertainment for the masses? She bit her lip hard as she dropped her head into her hands. She wouldn't cry.

This wasn't supposed to happen to her here. The tiny village of L'Annique had been her sanctuary for more than a year now. She had fallen in love with her kind neighbours and the quiet, almost humdrum atmosphere. Unlike in London, where her name was synonymous with scandal, here she had been free to raise her daughter in peace. And now this quiet village would be overtaken by the storm of her old life catching up with her.

Every penny from the sale of her London town house had been poured into her new beginning. Uprooting herself again would bankrupt her. And if she ran they would follow her—of that much she could be sure. She didn't have the kind of power it took to protect her child from the media.

There was only one person she knew who did. But the man she was thinking of didn't deal with idle tabloid gossip. Rigo Marchesi wouldn't even *think* of trying to help her. She was surprised the media had even dared to cross him with the sheer power of his family name. Luckily for him he had a whole team of PR people to deal with this. Nicole would be left, alone once again, to pick up the pieces and deal with the aftermath.

She parted the curtains to peer out at the crowd, frowning at the sight of the men and their cameras being herded further down the street. Two police cars full of officers had arrived and they were quickly moving all the people and vehicles down the lane and out of view.

A second black Jeep had joined the first, this one

with blacked-out windows. A handful of men in dark suits stepped out and began fanning across the premises and down each side of the laneway.

Nicole felt her breathing slow to a dangerous pace, and the air rushed in her ears as she watched the last man step out of the vehicle. He was tall, wearing a sleek suit and dark sunglasses. She bit her bottom lip hard as he finally turned to face her, removing the glasses from his face. A moment of utter stillness passed before she released her breath in one slow whoosh.

It wasn't him.

For a moment there she had honestly thought… Well, it didn't matter what she'd thought. Right now the tall, suited man was walking up to her front door.

Pushing her hair behind her ears and clearing her throat, she opened the door with the latch in place, so that she might survey the imposing stranger through a comfortable three-inch gap. Something about him was vaguely familiar.

'Miss Duvalle?' He had a hawklike gaze and spoke in her native English, albeit with a strong Italian accent. 'My name is Alberto Santi. I work for Signor Marchesi.'

She felt cold humiliation prick at her memory. This was the man who did all the jobs that Rigo wouldn't lower himself to do. He wore the same disapproving glare now as he had the night he'd guided her across a crowded room, away from his employer's mocking laughter.

'I am here to help you.' He spoke calmly.

'You have some nerve, showing up at my door.' She

shook her head, moving to close the gap, but found the door blocked by a polished leather shoe.

'I have orders to bring you under the protection of the Marchesi Group.'

'I don't take orders from Rigo Marchesi.' She crossed her arms in front of herself. She knew whom these *orders* were from. Knew the kind of ruthless power she was faced with here.

'Perhaps I phrased that poorly.' The man forced a smile to his thin lips. 'I have been sent to offer you assistance. May I come in so that we can speak privately?'

Nicole thought on it for a moment. It wasn't as if she had a whole lot of other options. Perhaps at least he could organise some sort of protection for them. She stood back, unclipping the latch and motioning for him to come inside.

He moved through the doorway and took in the surroundings of her simple home with quick, disapproving efficiency. He looked back down at her. 'Miss Duvalle, my team has already contained the area, as you can see.' He gestured to the men standing guard at the gateway to her property. 'We would prefer it if you had no more contact with the media until we have a chance to resolve the matter privately.'

'That's kind of difficult, considering they are camped out on my doorstep.'

'Which is why I am here. A meeting has been arranged in Paris to address this…situation. If you choose to cooperate you will be offered every assistance.'

The way he called it that—a 'situation'—made it sound like such a nuisance. A minor fender-bender in the Marchesi fashion empire's shipshape working schedule. These people had no appreciation of the fact that her entire life had been upended for the second time in less than two years.

'I have no control over this *situation*, Mr Santi, as you can see. So I doubt that I can help anyone to resolve it. All I need is to keep my daughter out of this mess.'

'The media will not relent—you know this,' he said gravely. 'Surely you expected the attention?'

'Why on earth would I expect *this*?'

The man shrugged and looked away, making it clear what he meant. Nicole felt cold shame wash over her. Just as she had on the last occasion this man had passed on a message from his employer. She shook her head in disgust. Of *course* Rigo would think that she had willingly pawned her child off to the tabloids. She was Goldie Duvalle's daughter after all, wasn't she?

Shaking off the hurt and anger, she forced herself to speak. 'Just to be clear—if I decline to come with you will the police stay to protect my privacy?'

'I'm afraid not.'

Well, there it was. She felt the skin on her arms prickle. It was clear she was being given an ultimatum. Get in the car and go and make a deal with the devil or stay put and be trapped in her home while the vultures circled.

Sure, she could always leave and find some new place. But with this much attention on them she and Anna would never live a normal life again. They hadn't managed to get a clear photograph of her daughter yet, but they would. And with the scandal of her parentage she would become infamous.

She knew what that life was like. She had lived it. And she would never put her child under that kind of microscope. But now…would she be able to ensure Anna's privacy with this scandal surrounding them both? She didn't have the kind of financial power it took to control the media, to keep her daughter's innocent face off the front pages.

Her chest tightened. Anna was too young to be aware of the drama unfolding around her. But Nicole knew better than anyone that awareness would come with age. Memories of her own childhood threatened to surface. She could almost feel the familiar stifling pressure to perform for the public.

She shook her head and paced to the window once more. The thought of those men outside, wrestling with each other to take photographs of her daughter to sell to the highest bidder… It stirred something deep and primal inside her. This was exactly why she had walked away from her old life in the first place.

She didn't want Rigo's help, but she wasn't stubborn enough not to recognise that she was in desperate need of it. She was certain he would want this whole episode erased as soon as possible. He had made his stance on fatherhood abundantly clear once already, hadn't he?

She would go to Paris. She would sacrifice her pride and ask him for help. The story would be silenced and they could all return to normality.

The European headquarters of the Marchesi Group was a gargantuan chrome-and-glass tower in the heart of Paris. It was a relatively new building, and its acquisition had been one of the first changes to his family's historic fashion brand that Rigo Marchesi had made upon taking his seat as CEO five years previously.

There had been outrage when he had moved the company's flagship building from Milan to Paris. But Rigo had a vision for the future of his company, and that vision required change.

Keeping his finger on the pulse of the modern business world was what made him a great leader, along with his razor-sharp negotiating skills and a clean-cut, dependable reputation. His unconventional choices had already seen profits skyrocket, and his family name restored after the steady downward decline of the business during the decade preceding his rise to CEO.

Great leaders were never caught by surprise. Rigo glowered at his computer screen as he stirred a spoonful of organic sweetener into his double espresso. Great leaders were not waylaid by a scandal that had apparently already been live on the internet for several hours. Above all, great leaders did not get publicly vilified by the world's media mere weeks before the biggest deal of their company's history was about to be completed.

Downing the hot coffee in one go, he stood up and paced across to the window.

Nicole Duvalle had been a blip. A moment of madness that had somehow bypassed his usually crystal-clear judgement. Rigo did not *do* mindless pleasure. He made sure that the women he took into his bed had their own careers to take up most of their time, just as he did. He was selective in his affairs and had no time for the kind of woman who was simply attracted to his net worth.

And yet when it had come to Nicole his logic had failed him. He'd got caught up in the blinding attraction between them and thought to hell with the consequences.

Well, the consequences were here now, and Miss Duvalle had no idea what she had just started.

Rigo turned as the glass door to his office opened and Alberto entered. His right-hand man looked rumpled and nothing like his usual pristine self.

'I trust your day has gone to plan?' Rigo raised a brow in question.

'She walked out after less than five minutes.' Alberto exhaled harshly. 'They offered her the deal and she point-blank refused it.'

Rigo was silent for a moment, leaning back against the desk. He'd be lying if he said he hadn't expected this outcome. If Nicole was as money hungry as her mother she would hardly accept the first pay-off she was offered. He had only offered the money to get the story settled quickly, out of the courtroom.

The deal he was currently negotiating with French jewellery icon Fournier was time sensitive. The family-owned company had been initially reluctant to merge with such a large corporation, and it had already taken months to get to this point. Rigo gritted his teeth, feeling his jaw tighten with frustration. How could one interview cause this much mayhem?

Already he had been notified of shareholders jumping ship and rumbles amongst the board members. His late grandfather had left a black spot on the Marchesi name that had almost bankrupted their eighty-five-year-old brand. After his own father's tireless work to put the business to rights, there was no way Rigo would let this shake them.

If his own shareholders were nervous, then he was damn sure Fournier were nervous, too. And he didn't blame them. Eighty per cent of their market was female. A new CEO who had apparently left his conquest pregnant and out on the street was bad for business.

Even if was a blatant lie told by a ruthless gold-digger.

'Where is she now?' Rigo asked.

Alberto looked uneasy for a moment. 'The child needed to sleep, so we put her in one of the company apartments on Avenue Montaigne.'

'She rejects the deal and you immediately set her up in luxury accommodation?' He raised a brow. 'Alberto, you are a soft touch.'

'We couldn't risk the press getting wind of her location yet,' Alberto said hurriedly.

'Forget about it. I will just have to fix this myself,' Rigo growled, grabbing his suit jacket.

It was time for him to reinforce what he apparently hadn't made clear enough to her the last time.

He would not be made to look a fool.

Ignoring the uncomfortable burn in her stomach, Nicole scraped the rest of her half-eaten meal into the bin and poured a small glass of white wine. She needed to unwind and get rid of this nervous energy so that she could formulate a plan. A plan that did *not* involve being holed up at the top of a fancy apartment tower like a scared defenceless princess.

She walked over to the windows, looking at the lights of Paris twinkling in the dusk.

Her old life had been filled with nights like this, drinking wine and gazing out at the lights of countless beautiful cities. But no city had ever felt like home—not even London. 'Home' was what she had been trying to create in L'Annique. A stable, solid place where Anna could grow up, go to school, have her first kiss. All of those normal things that young girls were meant to go through. And instead they'd been forced to flee, to accept help from the one man she had promised herself she would never turn to, no matter how hard things got.

She sank down onto the suede sofa and closed her eyes. It had taken over an hour to get Anna to sleep in the absence of her usual routine. She needed to pull herself together. After all, children felt their mother's anxiety, didn't they? Their entire life had fallen to pieces and she only had herself to blame.

She took a long sip from her wine and gazed anxiously out the window at the dark street below. Alberto had assured her that they were guaranteed privacy here, that they would be safe from the press until they came to an agreement. And that was all that Nicole needed right now—until she figured out what the hell her options were.

The luxury apartment was on the third floor of an exclusive building not far from the Champs-Elysées.

It was all high-gloss modern minimalist furniture and white walls—not very child friendly or lived-in.

Honestly, what on earth had she been *thinking* to come here? Of course they wanted to pay her off, she cursed silently, kicking off her shoes and tucking them underneath herself. She had expected to be met with a gag order of some form, but not an outright pay-off in return for her lies. She needed help, but the deal she had been offered came at a price much too high for her to pay.

She had barely thought about Rigo in the weeks before all of this. That had been no mean feat, considering she looked into her daughter's cobalt-blue eyes every single day. It had been more than a year since she had looked into the identical blue eyes of her one-night lover.

Maybe on some level she had half hoped he would be there today. She wasn't sure she would have been able to be quite so calm if he had been.

A knock sounded on the door to the apartment. Nicole stood slowly. Alberto had said no one would know her location here except for him…and his boss.

'Who is it?' She stood in front of the closed door, feeling her heartbeat pound against her ribcage.

'You know who it is, Nicole.'

She felt the deep baritone of his voice vibrate right down to the soles of her feet. She fought the sudden need to turn tail and run. She stood frozen, amazed at her own ridiculous nerves. Her stomach seemed to be flipping over in circles as she reached out and laid her hand on the doorknob.

She swung the door open and there he was. Six foot two of pure Italian male, his short dark hair perfectly coiffed to match his immaculately tailored suit.

'May I come in?' he said, the subtle hardness of his tone belying the seemingly polite request.

Nicole stepped back, opening the door wide and gesturing for him to enter.

She was aware of his cobalt-blue gaze sweeping over her as he moved into the apartment. His eyes still had the ability to make her breath catch. No doubt he was taking note of how much she had changed since they'd last met. She became acutely aware of the fact that she was about ten pounds heavier, her plain brown hair hadn't seen a stylist in over a year and she had stains from Anna's supper all over her jeans.

She self-consciously tugged the hem of her plain white cotton shirt down lower on her hips.

Rigo leaned casually against the bar in the open-plan kitchen. His arms were crossed over his impressive chest and he continued to stare at her, waiting.

'Nothing to say, Nicole?' he asked.

'I would say it's nice to see you again, but we both know that would be a lie.' She avoided his gaze, staring at a point to the left of his shoulder. 'I suppose I should be honoured that you've even bothered to speak in person.'

His brows raised a centimetre. 'Believe me, I have a thousand things I would much rather spend my time doing than this.'

'At least we're being honest.' She shrugged, telling herself not to be hurt by that statement. She had no reason to be hurt. They were practically strangers. He might be her daughter's biological father but they had only ever spent one night together. She felt heat reach her cheeks as she thought of what that night had involved.

Rigo didn't seem to take any notice of her heightened colour. 'Oh, I wouldn't say we are being honest at all, Nicole,' he drawled. 'If you're angling for more money, then I am afraid you are wasting your time. You're lucky I am offering you anything at all and not dragging you into court for slander.'

'I don't want a single cent from you.' Nicole crossed her arms defensively. 'All I want is for the press to back off and give me back my privacy.'

Rigo let out a harsh bark of laughter. 'Oh, that's your play, is it? We both know you threw away any right you have to *privacy* the moment you dragged my name through the mud.'

'I had nothing to do with this.' She met his eyes without hesitation.

'This is not a game, Nicole.' His voice took on a dangerous tone. 'I made it clear the last time we met that I am not a man to mess with.'

'I would have been quite happy never to lay eyes on you again. Your ego is so large it's amazing you can even get out of bed in the morning.' She narrowed her eyes, the anger she felt finally rising to the surface.

Rigo took a step forward, a half-smile breaking across his harsh features. 'Now, *this* is interesting. So far I've witnessed Nicole, the innocent temptress, followed by Nicole, the damsel in distress.' He raised one brow. 'But I think this passionately angry version is my personal favourite.'

Nicole was speechless. The way he looked at her, his eyes filled with such disdain… It made the hair on the back of her neck prickle. How had she ever thought that this man had felt anything close to what she'd felt that night? He was a complete stranger right now. The idea that they had ever been anything so romantic as lovers was poetic nonsense. The harsh reality was that they were simply two people who had had sex.

Once upon a time she might have thought they shared a connection. That for one night in his bed she had somehow been special.

She had been so naive.

'Rigo, you are threatening to sue me because of gossip that I have no control over.'

'Then, why have you not tried to deny it?' he countered.

'My silence is the most you're going to get. I don't deal with the press anymore.'

'You will make a public statement that the child is not mine, Nicole.'

His mere presence was so commanding that she would be a fool not to feel intimidated by the demand. She fought the emotion welling up in her chest. It was ridiculous to feel hurt at his words after so long. After all, he had made his position on fatherhood quite clear. But still, a part of her had always hoped he would come in those weeks afterwards.

Even as she'd lain in hospital, terrified to hold her tiny premature daughter, she'd held hope that his world had shifted as profoundly as hers had. That he would instinctively know he had become a father.

Indignation won out over the sadness, and she stood up a little taller, meeting his gaze head-on. 'I told you that I was pregnant with your child. You chose not to be a part of it, and that is fine. But I will *not* publicly tell lies and go against my principles as a mother just to protect your damn family name.'

He shook his head with disbelief. 'Do you honestly think I would have let you run off like you did unless I was completely sure that I was *not* the father of your child?'

Nicole walked to the kitchen counter and began digging down to the bottom of her handbag. Her fingers finally closed on the object she sought, and she turned back to meet his cold gaze once more.

'I'm telling you that you were wrong, Rigo.' She held out the photograph. 'Anna is your daughter and here is the proof.'

# CHAPTER TWO

RIGO LOOKED AT the woman standing before him. She was so different from what he remembered. Gone was the carefree, uninhibited temptress and in her place was this formidable tigress of a brunette, wearing torn jeans. He always went into negotiations prepared, with adequate knowledge of his opponent. But it seemed that his previous knowledge no longer applied.

He took the photograph from her, holding it between his hands as she watched him. The picture was of a baby with soft brown curls and fair skin. He looked back down at Nicole.

'This is not proof of anything.'

Hurt flashed across Nicole's pale features for a brief instant before she shook her head and snatched the photograph from his hands. 'I don't know what else to say. I have been completely honest with you from the start. I told you that I was pregnant, and I didn't cause a scene when you chose not to be involved.'

Rigo bit his lip with frustration. She was determined to stay her course. That much was becoming brutally clear. He had known she was an actress as a child, but

he had never expected her to be this stoic in her performance.

'You make me out to be such a villain in this production of yours,' he said, keeping his tone deliberately calm.

'Rigo, right now all I'm asking of you is that you use
your power and influence so that I can go back home
with my daughter and never bother you again.'

'And am I to presume you don't want a single penny
from my heartless hands?'

She sighed audibly. 'Ask yourself this. Why would
I wait almost six months of my child's life before leak-
ing a story if I was so desperate? It doesn't make sense.'

She looked so maternal right now, so innocent. It was
likely she meant to look that way—to play the victim.
He shook off the feeling of unease after seeing the photograph of the child. He was here to finish this.

'You're right. It doesn't make sense.' He shrugged.
'But I am not in the least bit inclined to make sense of
what goes on in your brain. Whether or not you leaked
the story is of no consequence to me right now.'

'You just want me to clear your name.' She bit her
lip. 'I can't do that, Rigo. I won't lie.'

Rigo fought the urge to growl. 'Nicole, I might be
able to gag the media and prevent further stories, but I
can't undo the damage that has already been done. The
public cannot be gagged. And the only way to stop them
talking is for the scandal to be disproved.' He paused
for effect, watching as her eyes narrowed. 'I am willing to increase the offer that was made to you today by

twenty per cent. I'm asking you to do the right thing for everyone involved.'

All trace of softness seemed to disappear as she took a deep breath, shoving both hands into the pockets of her jeans. 'As much as I want my privacy back, I can't compromise my integrity and tell a lie that will affect my daughter forever. I vowed that I would never come to you, Rigo, and I haven't until now. But right now her privacy means a lot more to me than my pride.' She looked at him, her caramel-coloured eyes wide and deathly serious. 'Do a paternity test. If it proves negative I will make whatever statement you like.'

'I fail to see the point in performing a test when I already know what the outcome will be.' He fought the urge to raise his voice. Performing a test would mean more time, and every day this scandal was out there was another day of plummeting shares.

'If you are completely sure that she is not your daughter, then you have nothing to lose.' Her voice was quiet.

'Fine—I will arrange for the damned test. But, Nicole, once the negative result is confirmed, you *will* make a statement to the press.'

'If it's negative, you have a deal.' She nodded.

'Good, then we're done here.' He made to move towards the door.

'Wait!' she called, stopping him midstride. 'We haven't discussed the details of what will be done if the test is positive.'

Rigo shook his head. 'If the test is positive...' he said, looking down again at the picture of the child briefly. Her eyes were a deep cobalt blue. If he wasn't so sure that he was sterile he might almost call them Marchesi blue.

Nicole was looking at him intently. He tore his gaze away and walked over to open the door, very intent on leaving all of a sudden.

'It would be nothing short of miraculous,' he stated plainly. 'I'm pretty sure a paternity test isn't going to change what I already know.'

With that, he closed the door behind him.

The executive boardroom of the Marchesi Group headquarters was on the forty-fifth floor. Nicole sat alone at the end of the black marble conference table while various men and women in designer suits sat around her in complete silence. No one addressed her or looked her way. She suddenly wished she could trade places with Anna, who lay happily chewing on her toes in the stroller by her side.

An elderly white-haired gentleman sat at the top of the table, watching her. Nicole cleared her throat, sitting up a little straighter in her seat. A slim leather folder was laid out in front of her. She hesitated for a moment before opening it, aware that all eyes in the room were suddenly trained upon her. The cheque inside had so many zeroes she felt her breath catch.

The white-haired man sat forward, clearing his throat. 'As the most senior member of the board present, I am presenting you with our final offer, Miss Duvalle.'

'This can't be right...' she breathed, the figures swimming in her vision.

'The Marchesi Group is offering you a generous deal

in return for your public statement that Rigo Marchesi is not the father of your child.'

'This wasn't the deal.' She began to pick at her nails under the table, a familiar sense of entrapment setting in. This wasn't a meeting at all. It was an ambush.

'Understand this, Miss Duvalle. We will not be negotiating the figure on that cheque, so if you want the payout I would advise you to take it now.' The man sat back in his seat, openly surveying the neckline of her blouse.

Nicole crossed her arms over her chest, feeling very small and very alone in the room full of suits. It would be so easy just to do what they asked. To deny the truth and run away would be the easier option in some respects. The truth was inconvenient—just as she and her daughter were. A press release would take less than ten minutes and then she could escape. She could forget all about Rigo Marchesi and start over again somewhere new.

And what would happen when her daughter became old enough to understand? What about when she asked why her father had never played a part in her life? Her daughter would eventually find out that her mother had lied to the world and denied her the right to her true parentage.

She thought of her own mother, of her countless lies and manipulations. All for money. What kind of role model would she be if she lied to her own daughter about something so important?

She took a deep breath. These people wouldn't cow her. 'I won't be signing a thing without speaking to Mr Marchesi first.'

A woman in a beige suit spoke, her hawklike eyes spitting fire across the room. 'I'm aware that you probably grew up observing a certain level of…legal negotiations through your mother. But are you really prepared to go toe to toe with a multi-billion-euro corporation in a courtroom?'

Nicole felt her skin prickle. These people made her feel cheap and utterly worthless.

Suddenly every other person at the table avoided her eyes, seeming very focused on the door behind her.

Nicole turned to see Rigo's hulking frame silhouetted in the doorway.

She stood, anger steeling her resolve. 'This is unacceptable. I won't be bullied.'

'I did not agree to this meeting, Nicole.' His voice was deeper than usual, and his gaze dropped momentarily to where Anna was growing rapidly more tired in her stroller. 'Go and wait in my office, I'll be there in a moment.'

Rigo stood dangerously still at the top of the table and waited for Nicole to leave before he spoke. 'Somebody had better tell me right now why this meeting was arranged without my knowledge.'

The man at the top of the table sat forward. His uncle Mario was a white-haired oaf in his late fifties, with a penchant for contesting his nephew's authority at every turn. 'We have already got agreement from the rest of the board. You have been outvoted in your plan. Swift, heavy-handed action is in the best interests of the company.'

Rigo cleared his throat, eyeing the leather-bound folder on the table and closing it with a loud snap that resounded across the table. 'This will not be buried with legal settlements.'

A brave PR executive spoke up. 'You know that this company's past makes it far more vulnerable to the media. Your father always made it clear that private indiscretions cannot be allowed to fester.'

Rigo felt his patience snap. 'My father is no longer CEO of this corporation. *I am*. Everyone who is not a member of the board leave the room. *Now*.'

He turned to the window, taking three deep breaths as the men and women quickly scurried from the room. This afternoon had pumped his adrenaline into overdrive—and only half of it had to do with suddenly finding out about this clandestine meeting.

He turned to face his uncle, the only board member present. 'You don't have the power to make my decisions for me, Mario. If you wanted my job you could have fought for it.'

'I value my free time far too much.' Mario rolled his eyes. 'This is a straightforward pay-off, Rigo.' He stood up, stalking towards him. 'This woman is slandering the Marchesi name out there and jeopardising the entire Fournier deal, for God's sake.'

'It's not slander,' Rigo stated gruffly, hearing the words echo in his mind as he said them. 'I had the DNA analysis confirmed twenty minutes ago. The child is mine.'

Mario was silently stunned for a moment, his mouth agape. 'You agreed to a paternity test without alerting the legal team?' His eyes bulged. 'Are you completely insane? Even your grandfather wasn't that stupid.'

Mario didn't seem in the least surprised at the news itself—which was more than could be said for Rigo. He was still absorbing the information. His brain was working overtime, examining the revelation that, against all the odds, Nicole had been telling the truth. He had never once wavered in his certainty that she was lying. He'd long ago taken very permanent measures to make sure he would never be put in this position again. And yet here he was.

His uncle cleared his throat, looking pointedly at the leather folder. 'Marchesi men have all committed some indiscretions, Rigo. It seems it is a family weakness. My advice is to not let this get in the way of resolving the matter. Everyone has a price. Find hers.'

Nicole paced from one side of Rigo's open-plan office to the other. Her fists clenched by her sides as she weighed up the options in her head.

Plan A was to walk out of there without another word to Rigo Marchesi *or* his goons. She could take her chances with the press and beg for privacy—or, more likely, just give up on her dreams of ever having a normal life again. But her daughter would grow up knowing that her mother had tried her best.

Plan B… Well, plan B was to take every moral she had and throw it out the window.

She sat down on the nearest armchair and tried to clear her thoughts.

Strangely, she wished her mother were here to guide

her through this. No, she corrected herself, she wished that her mother cared enough to try to help. But Goldie Duvalle was a law unto herself, breezing in and out of her daughter's life in between marriages and even then only when she wanted something.

The last time she had seen her mother had been the day she'd told her that she was pregnant. Cold anger made her fists clench tight by her sides, her insides tightening at the memory of having her last thread of hope pulled out from under her. Her mother was not an option—not unless she needed some contacts for a magazine spread.

With her own upbringing to go by, maybe she had been fooling herself to think she could offer her daughter a normal life. Her erratic childhood had been the furthest thing from normal you could get. It seemed that scandal was just destined to follow her around everywhere that she went.

She looked around, feeling small and alone in the iron-and-marble-dominated office space. Anna had fallen asleep in her stroller by the window.

Rigo entered the office with a dull thud of the heavy panelled door behind him. His usually perfectly groomed dark hair was ruffled, and that same formidable expression on his face made her confidence waver.

He stood still, looking around him. 'The child?'

That one question caught her off guard. She frowned, gesturing to where the stroller sat by the window, her daughter now sleeping peacefully inside.

'She won't wake if we speak?' he asked.

Nicole shook her head once, trying not to soften at

his apparent concern. 'She's a deep sleeper, thankfully. She should be fine.'

Rigo nodded brusquely, his eyes lingering on the pale pink blankets for a moment before turning back to her. His eyes held the strangest combination of anger and some other unknown emotion.

They stood there for a moment, facing each other in complete silence, before Rigo finally spoke.

'Let me make it clear that I had nothing to do with that meeting.' His jaw was tight as he held her gaze in earnest. 'The board members were growing impatient and decided to act against me. I'm sorry you were put through that.'

She hadn't expected an apology. It kind of threw her. 'I told you I wouldn't sign anything without the test.'

'You did.' He breathed out heavily. He walked past her, moving across the large office to his desk. He gestured to a leather wingback chair, motioning to her to sit, and taking a seat behind the desk once she had.

With his hands clasped in front of him he looked instantly more powerful and infinitely less approachable. The formidable CEO, taking care of yet another item on his agenda. He was powerful and unyielding, and yet right now he looked off balance somehow.

'I have received a phone call from the laboratory,' he said calmly. He tapped his thumb absentmindedly on the desk. He looked at her. 'The test results reveal a positive DNA match.'

Nicole stared back at him for a moment, unsure of what to say in response to this sterile, emotionless statement. 'I see,' she said quietly, watching as his thumb continued to move of its own volition, beating a steady rhythm.

'That is all you have to say?' he asked.

She shrugged, biting down on her lower lip. 'I already knew what the result would be.'

He leaned back in his seat and watched her thoughtfully for a moment before speaking. 'I chose not believe your claim based on what I believed to be the facts, Nicole. Now that I know I was mistaken… Well, our current situation is regrettable.'

It was like speaking with a corporate drone. Was it simply 'regrettable' that he'd missed the first six months of his child's life? Nicole thought of the countless milestones that had come and gone, the days and nights full of laughter and tears. It seemed as if an entire lifetime had passed between them since the day he had made his *regrettable* choice.

Anger flared in her chest as she took in his solemn expression.

Rigo continued, oblivious to her inner turmoil. 'The media's attention is an immediate concern for us both, but I feel that we can come to an agreement to work it to our advantage.'

She crossed her arms, amazed that he was still talking business when he had just found out he had a daughter. 'I've told you already. I won't lie to the press to save your public image.'

'I am not asking you to lie,' he countered. 'Now that I know she is mine, I do not plan to deny the fact. Publicly or otherwise.'

There it was. The words she had hoped to hear a lifetime ago. Only instead of feeling relief that her daughter would have some sort of relationship with her father, all she felt was cold, icy fear.

She stood up, taking a few paces away from him. 'First of all, she is not *yours*,' she said breathlessly, turning back to face him. 'You are biologically her father, but the rest you have to earn. I am not asking for anything right now other than your help in getting the press off my doorstep.'

He didn't speak. He just watched her with that same intensity she had come to recognise was naturally him.

Nicole crossed her arms, looking down at him. 'There is no obligation for you to play a part in Anna's life if you don't want to.'

'We both know that my walking away isn't an option here.'

She didn't know if that meant he didn't want to walk away or that he knew it wouldn't look good. She had a hard time believing that it was completely the former.

'I would be happy for you to play a part in her life. But if you go public as her father you know that I will be hounded by paparazzi for the rest of my days. Pictures of her will be used to pad out every tabloid on the planet. Is that what you want?'

'You don't want to lie, but you don't want me to tell them the truth?' He sat back, his eagle eyes surveying her with keen interest. 'It seems we have run out of options, then.'

'All I'm asking from you is media protection,' she said calmly. 'I know such things exist with your kind of power.'

'Protective orders are flimsy and easily overturned. The photographers would still come for pictures of you. The story is out there and she will always be a child of scandal. It will stick to her like glue.'

'There has to be a way…' Nicole felt herself weaken with the weight of his words. He was right, of course. The damage had already been done. Scandals like this never truly disappeared.

Had she really been so naive as to think that he could somehow magically make it all go away? She had brought her daughter into this world and made a vow never to let the same things happen to her that she had suffered herself as a child. Being hounded by cameras at the school gates and constantly playing a part for the media. She had grown up far too quickly as a result. How could she let her daughter suffer the same?

Rigo cleared his throat, standing and coming around to perch against the side of his desk. 'There is a way, Nicole. One I'm prepared to offer so that we might work the media to our mutual advantage.'

'How on earth could we do that?' She looked at his serious expression, feeling utterly defeated. She had only made things worse by running away and hiding. Anything she did now would just be damage control. A normal life wasn't something the secret child of a billionaire could ever hope for, was it?

Rigo's voice was cool and businesslike. 'The fastest and most effective way to turn a story on its head is to give the media an even bigger story to salivate over.'

'What could be bigger than this?' She frowned.

'A wedding. To be more precise, *our* wedding.'

Nicole was silent, hardly believing what he was saying. If she had heard him correctly that was absolutely ridiculous and not a real solution at all.

'You want to pretend that we're *married*?' she said incredulously. 'That wouldn't do a thing—everyone would know it was a sham.'

'I am not suggesting a sham.' He looked down at her, some unknown emotion blazing in his eyes. 'Nicole, the only way to end this scandal once and for all is for me to prove that I have not abandoned my child and her mother. To make a grand production of how wrong the media has got it. And the best way for me to do that… is for you to actually become my wife.'

Rigo watched as the colour drained from Nicole's face. She wasn't wearing a scrap of make-up, the dark waves of her hair were tied at the base of her neck, and yet she still looked effortlessly elegant. She was frowning at him, her brown eyes wide with shock.

Not the reaction he had expected.

'You can't be serious,' Nicole whispered.

Rigo crossed his arms, looking down at her pale face. 'That's not what a man expects to hear when he has just proposed marriage.'

'You haven't proposed anything. You've just thrown another deal at me. One that I am not prepared to accept under any terms. I'd rather take the money and run.'

'I assure you that I am completely serious. And this isn't just about business—not now that I know I am a father.' He almost stumbled over the simple word—a word he had never intended to label himself with. 'Nicole, like it or not, you and I and Anna are now irrevocably linked together. I am simply suggesting that we make that link public and permanent so that we might solve all our problems at once.'

'I can't believe that you are actually prepared to marry me to save your precious business.' She let out a single shocked burst of laughter.

'This would be a legal union—a real wedding. What I'm proposing is a way to secure and protect both our interests. Now that I know I have a child, I will want to play a part in my daughter's life.'

'Would that still be the case if your precious shares weren't decreasing?'

Rigo felt the barb hit him and instantly tensed. 'I might not have planned this, Nicole, but I would never turn my back on my own flesh and blood.'

She lowered her eyes, wrapping her arms around herself in that defensive gesture she always seemed to use when she was around him.

Finally she cleared her throat and looked back up at him. 'It *is* possible to co-parent without being married, you know.'

'I was lucky enough to grow up with the love and support of both of my parents in one home. I had private schooling and medical care along with overall financial stability. Are you telling me that, given the choice, you wouldn't want the same for Anna?' He narrowed his eyes. 'What is your alternative?'

Nicole looked down at the ground, biting on her lip. They both knew what her alternative was. Rigo knew after tracking her down that she didn't own a home.

She had already made a big move to a new country in the past year.

'There is a lot more to parenting than money, Rigo. I may not know where my career is going right now, and I may have had to budget, but I am a good mother. I love my daughter more than anything on this earth.'

She swallowed hard and he caught a glimpse of moisture in her eyes before she blinked it away.

'I wanted her from the moment I knew she was there. That's more than I can say for you.'

Rigo had no argument for that. He was trying to convince her to do the best for their child when he had already done the worst thing a father could do by not being a part of her life. He had started this conversation as a means to an end—a way to solve a problem in the fastest and most efficient way possible. But suddenly he felt the weight of his proposal hit him.

He was proposing to acquire a whole *family*, not a company. The thought almost unnerved him, sending shivers down his spine.

Clearing his throat, he hastily continued, 'If we marry she could have the best of both.' He chose his words carefully. 'Nicole, think of this logically. We have a child together and we both need this scandal gone as soon as possible. We need a long-term solution that puts Anna first.'

'Stop with all the business jargon, for goodness' sake.'

She walked away from him, and for a moment he feared she might walk out through the door. But he could tell by the way she glanced at him from the corner of her eye as she stared out the window that she was on the ropes. He was a skilled negotiator. He knew when to go in for the kill and when it was best to let his opponent have some breathing room.

He remained silent as she seemed to wage a battle within herself, her hands wringing together tightly. Eventually she turned back to him, her expression unconsciously giving away all her thoughts.

'I've sacrificed everything to ensure my child has the best life I can give her. And now it will never be the same, no matter what choice I make.'

'Then, you have everything to gain by marrying me.' Rigo took two steps forward—just enough so that he could see her face clearly.

'I can't believe I am even considering this.' She looked up at him, dropping her hands to her sides. 'I don't believe in these kinds of…nonmarriages. It's absurd.'

'Marriage is not a belief system, Nicole. It is a union between two people to protect mutual assets and interests. You told me to stop treating this like business, but that's exactly what this would be.'

'How can you be so cold and logical when you're proposing to shackle yourself to a woman you have already made it clear you see as nothing but a gold-digger?'

'Your past will be forgotten so long as you commit yourself to being a respectable partner for my public image.' Rigo shrugged.

Nicole's eyes widened. 'How utterly romantic.'

'If you imagined flowers and love letters, I'm afraid I won't be that kind of husband.'

'This is all very overwhelming, Rigo. Three days ago I was living a quiet, normal life. Now you are asking me to voluntarily put myself back into the media circus…'

'You would have to deal with their judgement either way. Why not do it on your own terms for once? In this world our lives are just one big game to the public. Sometimes we are forced to choose whether to play or be played.'

# CHAPTER THREE

NICOLE LOOKED UP at the man who was offering both to save her and ruin her all at the same time. What kind of woman would she be if she agreed to such a marriage? She knew exactly what kind she would be. One just like her mother.

Except her mother had never chosen her husbands based on the interests of her daughter. It had only ever been about money and magazine spreads. Nicole had simply been another instrument to use in her love affair with the media.

'If I were to agree to this, I would want your word that Anna will never be a part of your public image. She will never be used for photo ops or anything of the sort.'

'She will be protected. You have my word on that.'

Nicole nodded, swallowing the ever-growing lump forming in her throat. Her hands were trembling. The enormity of what she was agreeing to threatened to unravel what was left of her composure completely.

'We can agree on the finer details in good time. For now, am I correct in assuming that you are accepting my proposal?'

Nicole took a deep breath. 'Yes, I will marry you.'

Triumph gleamed in his eyes and he nodded his head once in approval. '*Bene*. I will call a meeting with my PR team and get the ball rolling.'

He held the door open for her before striding ahead out into the large bustling atrium of the top floor.

Nicole frowned. That was it? She had just agreed to marry him—surely they had more to discuss? Their living arrangements…the backstory for this ridiculous charade.

She followed quickly behind him, all the while feeling as though her head was no longer attached to her neck. She was doing the right thing, surely? This was the best course of action for her daughter. It didn't matter that she was essentially selling her life to this man in return. It was a business arrangement. He would likely be gone most of the time and she would be free to carry on raising her daughter in peace.

'Rigo—wait.' She reached out, bringing them both to a stop. 'I need to know what happens next. This is all very fast.'

'I will take care of it. You just need to worry about playing your part.'

Nicole felt the coldness of his words right down to her toes. Unable to speak, she nodded her head, avoiding his eyes.

Rigo began tapping his phone. 'I'll have you both moved into my apartment immediately. You can give a list of the items you need from your old home to Alberto.'

'We will be living together so soon?' Nicole asked,

dipping down to look in at Anna, where she still slept peacefully in her stroller.

'We will need to get started on our united front right away. We will let the press know that we have nothing to hide.' Rigo turned around, entering into a hushed conversation with his right-hand man and effectively cutting her off.

Nicole tried not to balk at his complete lack of interest in interacting with his daughter. She needed to curb her expectations here. There was no point in expecting anything close to normal from this arrangement. It was enough that Rigo had proposed marriage to protect their child. She wouldn't dare to hope for anything more from him.

Rigo stayed as long as possible at the office before returning to his apartment. The ninth-floor penthouse in the sixteenth *arrondissement* had been his first purchase as CEO five years ago. It boasted a wide-open rooftop terrace and a sweeping view of the Bois du Boulogne. An ideal space for the little leisure time he took—the perfect blend of modern decor and 1930s vintage features to suit his taste. Although almost everything was made of hard edges and high gloss—not exactly the ideal place for a small child to roam about.

Listening for a moment, he was relieved to hear no noise coming from the bedrooms. Nicole and the child had been moved in early in the afternoon and he had purposely waited until well after dinner to return. He'd needed time to think, to process this monumental shift.

The living room held no signs of change at all. Everything lay just as he had left it that morning. It was a bachelor pad of the highest order, with a large black marble bar dominating one side of the dining area and a flat-screen television mounted in pride of place above the fireplace. Had it really only been fourteen hours since he had downed his coffee while watching the morning news? He had walked out through the door just as he had every other day, sure that he had everything in his life under control.

Nothing could have prepared him for those test results.

There had never been a single doubt in his mind that Nicole was chancing her arm at palming her pregnancy off on her richest conquest. Money-hungry admirers came with the territory when you were a Marchesi. He'd had enough experience of gold-diggers to last him a lifetime.

And now he was a father.

The thought hit him on the chest with heavy finality. He could sit there all night and brood, while getting painfully intoxicated, but that wouldn't solve anything. It would only serve to leave him with a raging headache, and the issue of fatherhood would still be there in the morning.

He had long ago made a difficult choice, knowing that one day he would be able to reverse it if he so wished. But he had never once expected it to reverse itself. His doctor had assured him this afternoon that it was extremely rare. 'Natural reversal'—that was what he'd called it. Rigo called it mutiny. He had become quietly accustomed to the idea of never having a child of his own. The decision to have a vasectomy had been both necessary and final.

What were the chances? The one night he had forgotten to use a condom… A night that he had never been able to forget…

Nicole Duvalle was the exact kind of woman he had spent the past ten years avoiding like the plague, and yet he had taken her to his bed without a second thought. That night he had thrown caution to the wind and taken what he wanted for once. For a brief moment in time he had believed that maybe he could be someone other than who he was. Being with her had unleashed a thirst inside him for something more than the rigid confines of his world. And then he had found out who she was and that thirst had disappeared with crushing finality.

She had been like a drug to his numbed senses. In a world of falseness she had seemed so real and pure. He had drowned in the intoxicating attraction that had burned between them, losing track of time. If his right-hand man hadn't intervened and told him who she was…

He walked to the window, looking down at the inky darkness of the Bois du Boulogne. It didn't matter what might have happened. It didn't get much more complicated than this. He was engaged to marry a woman with a reputation murkier than most politicians. She had raised hell through the tabloids for most of her adult life and she was only twenty-five. Nicole swore that she was a changed woman and that she wanted nothing from him or the media. But he knew all too well how a woman could lie.

Feeling tiredness seep into his bones, he made the decision to choose his usual eight hours' sleep over a night of wallowing in the past. He walked down the hall to his bedroom, pausing when he noticed the decidedly feminine articles of clothing draped across his bed sheets. The bathroom door opened and Nicole emerged, her hair wet from showering, covered by only a short bathrobe.

She jumped when she saw him, standing completely still in the doorway.

Rigo's breath hitched. The scent of warm vanilla and honey was reaching across the room to tease his senses.

Nicole pulled the belt of her robe tighter around her small waist, the movement only serving to push her breasts out further against the thin fabric. Rigo clenched his fist by his side.

'They put all my things in here with yours.' She spoke quickly, avoiding his eyes. 'Your housekeeper was very…excited.'

'I see.'

Rigo briefly took in the two perfectly toned creamy thighs below the bathrobe and felt the tension in his muscles increase. His gaze must have given away some of his thoughts, because Nicole cleared her throat and quickly grabbed her clothing from the bed. Without another word, she slipped back into the bathroom to dress, closing the door behind her.

Rigo leaned back against the dresser, feeling his breath hiss out between his teeth. This was an unforeseen complication in an otherwise perfect plan. His staff was from the best agency in Paris, but nothing was truly confidential in his world. They were presenting the media with a whirlwind love story. It was expected that he should share a bed with his new fiancée. As any red-blooded man would.

He had thought that seeing her for who she was would effectively erase whatever it was that had drawn them together that night. Clearly his body had other ideas.

He undid the buckle of his belt, sliding it out from its loops and coiling it up into a tight spiral as he walked across the room. His walk-in dressing room was of the highest specifications, with personalised nooks and cabinets for every little detail. Organisation was his secret pleasure. Seeing everything perfectly lined up gave him a sense of calm.

He opened his belt drawer to find it only half filled with his own items. The second half contained an array of colourful scarves. Frowning, he opened the next cabinet, to find that completely rearranged, too. His housekeeper had clearly taken a shine to Nicole, he thought with an uncomfortable prickle of foreboding. If they were expected to share a bed, of course they would be expected to share closet space. He felt as if he had jumped head first into a rabbit hole and there was no going back.

He abandoned his dressing room with a scowl, returning into the main bedroom to find Nicole dressed in simple pale pink linen pyjama trousers and a white tank top. She was gathering her things into a small case, a frown marring her brow.

'All your things have been put away in my dressing room.'

His voice came out harsher that he'd intended. Nicole looked at him incredulously.

'Is that somehow *my* fault?'

Rigo raked his hand over the growth of hair on his jaw, his mind wrestling with the myriad implications he hadn't foreseen. 'We will need to share a bed until this wedding is over with,' he gritted, removing his tie and folding it up on the antique dresser. 'We can't risk the staff spreading rumours.'

Nicole's brow rose. 'That's not happening.'

'What's wrong? Afraid you won't be able to control yourself?'

He watched as she bit hard on her lower lip, looking away from him. When she looked back he was surprised to find anger in her expression rather than embarrassment.

'This isn't what I agreed to, Rigo.' She stared at him. 'It's not…appropriate for this arrangement.'

'Believe me, I am *not* a threat to you. I'm counting down the days until this wedding is over just as much as you are.'

'Well, then, why on earth would we need to sleep together? Surely you trust your own employees?'

'I make it a rule not to trust anyone.' He began to open the buttons at his neck, noticing how her eyes followed the movement. 'We are supposed to be in a whirlwind love affair here. We will share a bed. End of discussion.'

'It's nice to see that I have some say in this arrangement.'

'About as much of a say as I do, *cara*,' he drawled. 'Sleeping alongside each other is the least of our worries right now.' He removed his shirt, folding it up before moving to unhook his trousers. He looked up to find Nicole watching him.

She cleared her throat as if to speak, but no sound came out. He almost smiled when she averted her eyes, sliding quickly under the covers and pulling them up to her chin. He might have won this round, but who was the real winner when the prize was a night of physical torture?

Rigo finished undressing, opting to leave his boxers on. He usually slept completely nude, but he decided that might be a step too far in this cosy little arrangement. He lay down, crossing his arms behind his head. Her breathing was slow and contained, but he could sense the tension coming off her in waves. They both felt it—the madness they were capable of unleashing if they let their guards down.

He was in for a long night.

It took a moment for Nicole's mind to adjust when she awoke in Rigo's bed the next morning. Holding her breath, she turned to find the other side of the bed empty. The sheets were still warm, so he hadn't been gone long. Sleeping next to a wall of half-naked muscle had seemed an impossible task last night, but in the end she had slept soundly, having been so exhausted from the day's events.

The apartment was quiet. Anna had woken once briefly for comfort in the night but had fallen back to sleep in the crib that Rigo had arranged to be transported from her home along with the rest of her things. While she still slept Nicole took her time to shower and apply light make-up, silently thanking the staff's efficiency in having all of her belongings transferred from La Petite so quickly.

The thought of her beautiful farmhouse being occupied by new tenants made her heart break. All the little homely touches she had added would be removed and painted over...all trace of their time there gone. That life was just a memory now.

She'd agreed to this marriage for Anna—to give her a relationship with her father and a better life than she could offer. But still something plagued her. It was almost as though she had got away from the ever-present threat of the media only to be presented with another, less obvious threat in Rigo.

She was glad when Anna finally awoke so that she could focus on the usual routine of her day and avoid the uncomfortable thoughts that played on her mind. But she soon found that 'normal' wasn't so easy to achieve with a housekeeper anticipating her every need. A breakfast buffet was presented to her, along with an array of freshly prepared baby meals for Anna. Fresh fruit, crêpes, pastries and steaming coffee filled the kitchen island.

Nicole thanked the woman for her thoughtfulness. The food was much better than the simple meals she had learned how to prepare in La Petite. She had never cooked more than toast for herself before moving away from London, having always eaten in trendy restaurants and cafés in order to be 'seen'. But surprisingly learning to cook and bake had been a secret joy of hers while she was pregnant, along with cleaning and just being self-sufficient.

Sitting here and seeing that all of her baby's bottles had been washed and steamed, all of their clothing laundered and pressed… It made her feel strangely redundant. She felt a deep frown settling between her brows and instinctively smoothed it away.

'Nicole, the nannies are here to be interviewed.' Alberto's tall, thin frame appeared in the doorway, startling her.

'Nannies?' Nicole swallowed a mouthful of melon and stood up to face Rigo's right-hand man. 'I never arranged for any interviews.'

'Rigo made a shortlist from the most elite agency in Paris.' He smoothed his shirt absentmindedly, clearly bored with the day's task.

'I didn't agree to a nanny,' Nicole argued. 'This is something he should have cleared with me first,' she said quietly.

'I'm just the messenger. Take it up with him if you have a problem,' he droned.

She bit her lip and picked up her mobile phone. She would call him and calmly tell him that it was not okay for him to commandeer her life simply because they were going to be married. She took a breath, then paused, suddenly realising she didn't actually have her fiancé's phone number.

Alberto rolled his eyes at her request, pressing a button on his own phone and handing it to her. Nicole avoided the older man's cynical gaze. He made her feel deeply uncomfortable any time he was around. The memory of him silently escorting her out of this apartment all those months ago had never truly left her.

She was shaken from her thoughts as Rigo's deep baritone answered with a curt, *'Si?'*

'Did you arrange for someone to care for my daughter without consulting me first?'

A shuffling of papers could be heard in the background, along with hushed talking before he spoke to her again. 'Yes, I arranged for a selection of candidates to arrive this morning. As I'm sure Alberto has already informed you, seeing as you are calling me from his phone.'

'Why would you presume that I need help, Rigo? I've cared for her just fine for the past six months of her life—or do you think me incapable?' She heard the hostility in her voice, but didn't care.

Rigo sighed on the other end of the line. 'Nicole. You will have a handful of events to attend and an entire wedding weekend to get through. I hardly think walking down the aisle with the child strapped to your back will be practical, now, do you?'

Nicole bit her lip, absorbing his words. She had been so caught up in the storm of changes that she hadn't even thought of who would care for Anna. She had never needed anyone to watch her daughter before now, having spent all her time at home with her. Perhaps she *did* need someone trustworthy—just until the wedding was done with…

'I'll take your silence as an apology,' Rigo drawled

on the other end of the line. 'Is there anything else you would like to accuse me of this morning, or will that be all?'

'No, that was it,' she said quickly, her cheeks burning. 'I'm sorry for presuming that you thought—'

'Don't worry about it.' He cut across her, and the sound of voices became louder in the background. 'I have to go, but make sure you are ready at seven this evening.'

'Ready? For what?' She frowned.

'We're going to dinner.'

With that the call ended, and Nicole looked unbelieving at the device in her hand. He had just demanded she be ready at a certain hour—was that how this arrangement was going to go?

Alberto coughed pointedly in the doorway and she rolled her eyes. 'Yes, all right. I'll be in in a moment.'

She handed him his phone and breathed a sigh of relief once she was left alone in the kitchen for the first time. Anna sat in her high chair, happily sucking on a piece of buttered toast and watching her intently.

'What on earth have I got us into, baby girl?' she whispered, brushing a tendril of dark hair behind her daughter's ear.

Anna's answering gurgle was completely incoherent, as expected, and yet it made her smile. She knew that the key to getting through this wedding alive was to focus on her daughter every step of the way and put her own needs last.

If only her future husband didn't seem so intent on making everything so difficult.

* * *

'Isn't this a little flamboyant?' Nicole's eyes widened as she took in the gilded sign above the restaurant door. 'We could have spoken in private in the apartment just as easily.'

'The food is good here, and we need to be seen in public.' He guided her inside, speaking briefly to the hostess and angling them both slightly away from the line of guests at the door.

It shouldn't surprise her that a man with Rigo's taste and reputation would choose to take her to the most exclusive restaurant in Paris. The two-hundred-year-old building was situated right next to the gardens of the Palais Royal and was one of the finest Michelin-starred establishments the city had to offer.

The hostess ushered them to a private dining room and introduced them to their own personal maître d' for the evening.

The restaurant was one of the few in Paris that she had never eaten in before. The waiting list was impossibly long and she'd only ever visited before on short trips. There was no way Rigo could have got in at such short notice, even if he *was* a billionaire. Unless he'd already had this table reserved for tonight...for dinner with someone else. The thought did strange things to her stomach.

Biting her lip, she focused on the stunning decor that surrounded them as the waiter laid down their napkins and filled their crystal glasses with iced water. Ornate golden mirrors lined the walls of the dining room and neoclassical frescoes adorned the ceiling along with stucco garlands and roses.

'I'll admit I've become a little jaded by gourmet food of late, but Le Chef Martin is one of the best in Paris.'

Rigo gestured for Nicole to peruse the menu, and in the end they agreed on a *menu plaisir*—a bespoke sample menu designed by the chef himself.

Nicole allowed her glass to be filled with a fragrant golden wine. She was aware of her empty stomach and limited herself to only one small sip, feeling the smooth liquid warm her insides instantly.

'We will be throwing an engagement party in three days.' His deep voice interrupted her thoughts. 'The process is going to be very fast and intense, so my PR team will want to brief you about interacting with the press.'

Nicole gulped. 'Is there really a need for all this fanfare? It seems to make more sense for an arrangement like this to take place in an office or something.'

'A large wedding is expected in my family. Anything to the contrary would draw suspicion,' he said, making it clear that the issue was not open for discussion. 'We will be married at an exclusive secret location on the first of the month.'

'That's less than three weeks away.' She felt her fingers tighten on her wine glass. This was all of a sudden becoming so much more than the simple solution she had agreed to.

'Why the frown? You will be the star of your very own fairy tale, Nicole. I had thought you would be jumping for joy.'

'Because I'm so fame hungry, right?' Her temper threatened to flare but she curbed it, taking a small sip of wine. 'If it inflates your ego to think I'm overjoyed to be marrying you, then by all means please continue.'

Rigo sighed. 'We will need to find a way to stop this enmity if we hope to convince people this is genuine.'

'I'll just draw upon my mediocre acting skills, shall I?'

'I'm serious, Nicole. There is a lot at stake here for both of us. The press is not going to be gentle.' He raised a brow. 'But I'm sure you've grown a tough skin over the years.'

'I've been given no choice.' Nicole sat back in her chair, crossing one leg over the other and casually smoothing out her dress across her knee.

'So why run away from them in the first place?' he asked. 'Why not sell your story straight away?'

'Instead of selling it now, you mean?' She squared her shoulders at his veiled comment. 'Is that why we're here? For you to try to make me confess my crimes?'

Rigo shrugged. 'I'm just trying to make sense of the woman I'm set to marry.'

'Well, you clearly already have me tarred, so forgive me if I don't feel like pleading my case.' Nicole felt the shame of his accusation wash over her.

'You're not on trial here, Nicole. Whether or not you leaked that story makes no difference to me. I don't *need* to trust you.'

'Good, because I will never trust *you*,' she countered.

'Well, then, this is an excellent start to any marriage.'

His laugh was entirely false as he took a sip of his wine and continued to survey her with that cool blue gaze.

'I'm sure we will live happily ever after,' Nicole said drily. She wished she were back in the apartment watching Anna sleep rather than sitting here under his scrutiny.

'Ah, there's that sarcasm again,' Rigo said harshly. 'We may not be traditionally happy, Nicole, but we owe it to each other to make things tolerable at least. We're in this for the long run after all.'

Nicole sat up straight in her seat. 'Just how long do you plan to stay married?'

'We are barely engaged and you are already planning the divorce?'

She felt his comment like a slap in the face. 'I'm aware that you see me as a cheap copy of my mother, Rigo. Please stop insulting me.' She cleared her throat and looked away from him, refusing to show any sign of the emotion that was bubbling under the surface.

'Look at me. That is not what I meant.'

His hand on her wrist turned her back to him, the contact sending a thrill of electricity up her arm.

'*Per l'amore di Dio*, everything I say is not a deliberate attack on your character.'

'You have made presumptions about my character since the first time we met. At least be upfront about your opinion of me and then maybe we can move on.'

'You want me to be honest? Fine.' He sat back in his seat. 'When I first saw you in that ballroom I pinned you as yet another husband hunter, joining the pack. I didn't know your name but I knew your type. Desperate to be noticed. You were everything I deliberately avoid, and yet…I couldn't take my eyes off you.' He took a sip of his wine, keeping her pinned with his eyes as he continued to speak in that low, husky tone. 'I kept seeking you out in the room, listening for your laugh. It was irritating, and damned infectious, and it made me desperate to know what the hell was so funny.'

Nicole remembered looking up into those deep blue eyes for the first time, being pinned by the infamous Marchesi blue gaze. She had already been far out of her depth and she hadn't even known it.

'You entranced me, Nicole. It's rare that I do anything without a second thought. But with you… I don't think either of us did much thinking after that first dance.'

She felt his gaze sweep over her features, down past the neckline of her dress. It wasn't leering or inappropriate, the way he looked at her. It was the same way he had looked at her that night all those months ago. As though she were a work of art that his eyes needed to worship and savour. As though she was the singularly most beautiful woman on the earth.

She bit her lip, calming the rage of hormones that seemed to have risen within her. It must be a combination of the wine and being out for the first time in a long time, she argued with herself, and nothing to do with the magnetic male presence across the table from her.

'And now look—it seems I've caught myself a husband after all.' She raised her glass in a mock toast, desperate to steer the conversation back to safer waters.

'If that were true you might possibly be the most forward-planning woman in history.'

His words were intended as jest, but Nicole could see a hint of speculation in his eyes.

They were interrupted by the arrival of the first dish: the chef's specialty, *pâté en croute*. Nicole took her first bite and stifled the urge to moan. This was so more than just food. It was a work of culinary art. It made the tension of their conversation melt away as the food took over.

The meal passed slowly from there, with the chef changing the wine with every new dish. In typical French style they took their time—food in France was an event after all.

Rigo asked politely about her life in L'Annique. She told him about her farmhouse, La Petite, and the relatively quiet life she had led. Her heart mourned the loss of the secluded paradise she had created for herself and her daughter. The daughter he hadn't even held yet...

By the time the waiter had finished clearing away their fifth tasting—a dish of succulent lobster claws on a bed of warm rhubarb—Nicole was feeling thoroughly indulged and refused the offer of a dessert platter. Rigo agreed, dismissing the waiter, who removed himself swiftly, leaving them alone.

'I have something to give you,' he said.

Nicole watched as Rigo reached into his jacket pocket and retrieved a small grey lacquered box with a single silver rose painted on top. She had been in Paris on enough occasions in the past to know that the box came from Fournier, one of the most expensive luxury jewellery boutiques in the city. She felt her stomach clench tightly as he laid it on the table in front of her.

Without a word she eased open the top and took a moment to survey the glittering diamond ring that lay within. It was huge. The large white diamond virtually dwarfed the rest of the platinum band, which was encrusted with more sparkling gems.

'This looks…very expensive,' she offered, not exactly knowing what else to say as she laid the box back down on the table.

'I gave it to you to put on, Nicole. Not to decorate the table.'

When she didn't make an immediate move he leaned forward, taking the ring out of the box and offering his hand to her. She placed her hand in his and watched as he slid the band slowly onto her third finger. The stone was so large it bumped her knuckle.

Rigo surveyed the end result before releasing her hand. 'Now. You are officially my fiancée.'

Nicole looked up at the man she had agreed to join her life with and tried to resist the urge to scratch at the band so tightly clamped on her finger. Biting her lip, she swirled the remaining wine around her glass a couple of times.

A phone beeped. Rigo pulled a sleek black device from his pocket and frowned at the screen. 'The press have arrived. I had our location leaked.'

'They're here?' Nicole breathed, looking around as though expecting cameras to start appearing from the walls.

He nodded. 'Outside. It's time for us to leave.' He stood and motioned for the waiter to retrieve their coats.

Nicole wrapped her light jacket around her shoulders, hurrying to catch up with his long strides. Rigo stopped just before the open doorway, turning to her and taking her hand in his. His skin was hard and warm on hers and he stood so close she could smell the scent of aftershave on his skin.

'All you need to do is act naturally.'

Nicole nodded, her insides quivering at the familiarity of the situation. 'Act naturally'—what a paradoxical phrase. There was nothing *natural* about this relationship…nothing to help her feel comfortable by Rigo's side. She had done this a thousand times—waited in anticipation before playing her part for the press. Only this time she wasn't alone.

Rigo stepped forward, and the dull hum of the crowd outside travelled through the air. She barely caught a glimpse of the first flash before Rigo's head suddenly descended, his lips covering hers in a kiss that took her breath away. Momentarily stunned, Nicole didn't dare to move as his scent enveloped her, his warm muscular forearm sliding around her waist to hold her against the hard planes of his abdomen.

His lips grew more demanding as his tongue demanded entrance, sliding hot and hard against hers in a sinfully erotic rhythm. His other hand swept her hair back and rested against her cheek, the heat of his palm seeming to scorch her. She moaned low in her throat as she finally began to give in to the delicious sensation—

only to have Rigo break the kiss just as quickly as it had begun.

His voice was low and husky in her ear as he turned them both to face the wall of cameras. 'Make sure they see the ring.'

# CHAPTER FOUR

RIGO BRACED BOTH hands on the marble countertop of
the master bathroom. Taking a deep breath, he exhaled
in one long burst in an effort to alleviate his tension.
That kiss had been planned because he knew a candid
shot would get them on the front page. But his reaction
had taken him completely by surprise.

He was stressed—that was the only logical answer
for a grown man having to fight off his libido after one
kiss. Even as a hormone-addled teenager in boarding
school he had been the most rational and in control of
his peers.

Scowling at his reflection in the mirror, he decided
a long cold shower was in order, to clear his brain. He
unbuttoned his shirt and folded it neatly into the linen
basket, doing the same with his trousers. He had just
removed his boxer shorts when the door to the bathroom swung open unexpectedly.

Nicole's eyes lowered, taking in his state of undress
briefly, before she spun on her heel to face the other way.

'Oh, God… I'm sorry!' she groaned, covering her
mouth with her hand.

Rigo fought the urge to laugh at her innocent reaction to his naked body. She was far from a shy virgin—that much he knew for sure.

'Nothing here you haven't seen before,' he drawled, taking pleasure from her evident discomfort. 'There's no need to play the maiden.'

'I'm not playing anything.' She breathed in deeply. 'And it's not appropriate for you to keep...alluding to events in the past that we both want to forget.'

'Does it unsettle you to think of our night together?' He took a couple of steps forward, the urge to reach out and draw her against him again was almost painful.

Nicole turned around to face him, crossing her arms over her chest in a gesture that couldn't say have said 'no' any louder if she had screamed it.

'It's better if we don't talk to each other that way, that's all,' she said, keeping her eyes trained firmly above his chin. 'I just need to get my things and I'll go to the other bathroom.' She gestured to the items spread haphazardly across the countertop.

'No, I'll go.' Rigo moved past her in the doorway, noticing her body tense as his arm brushed hers. It seemed she was wound just as tightly as he was.

'Thank you.' She quickly gathered her nightclothes from a drawer, disappearing into the bathroom without another look back at him.

Rigo abandoned his plan for a cold shower, deciding that maybe a cold Scotch might serve him better. He had just eased a pair of loose-fitting sweatpants over his hips when a loud bang came from inside the bathroom.

'Is everything okay?' He paused, his fingers on the handle.

The sound of rustling fabric and a delicate female grunt could be heard through the thin panel of wood between them.

'Do you need help?' he asked, hoping to hell that the answer was no.

'I'm fine,' she called out, but her breathing was definitely laboured.

Moments passed before the door opened and Nicole appeared dressed in a simple pink nightie. Her hair was deliciously ruffled, and Rigo tried to look away—but not before he noticed an angry red welt snaking down her shoulder blade.

'*Madre di Dio*, what happened in there?' Rigo looked past her, noting the bottles of lotions and potions scattered along the counter and on the floor in disarray.

'Nothing, I just slipped. I think I ripped my dress,' she said sheepishly, holding up a pile of red fabric.

He reached out, touching the reddened skin on her shoulder. 'I'm more worried about your arm than the damned dress. Would you honestly rather risk splitting your head open than ask for some help?'

'Who knew independent dress removal was so dangerous, huh?' She shrugged away from his touch. 'I'll survive, I reckon.'

She moved past him, hanging up the torn dress. 'I would try to sew it myself, but I'm terrible at anything that requires precision.'

'That doesn't surprise me.' He pointedly eyed her shoes on the floor.

'What exactly do you mean by that?' She placed a hand on her hip.

'You've unleashed a minitornado in my bathroom, for one.' He gestured to the array of bottles and brushes scattered all around his usually pristine bathroom.

'That's different. I fell. But I just don't care if everything is lined up correctly. I've noticed *you* are freakishly neat. I'm almost afraid to touch anything in the closet.'

'I like organisation.' He shrugged.

'Well, I am more organised chaos.' She grabbed a pair of fluffy pink socks, slipping them onto her feet.

It was strange, seeing her this way. He didn't think he'd ever seen a woman in actual nightwear. But then again, he'd never lived with a woman before. He'd spent the night with former girlfriends, of course. But none had ever gone without make-up, and their nighties had left a lot less to the imagination.

Nicole's cheeks were flushed from her scuffle with the dress zipper, the rest of her skin flawlessly pale against the contrast of the dark waves of her hair. The nightie she wore skimmed just across her knee—hardly an instrument of seduction. And yet the sight of her full breasts curving against the soft cotton made his libido roar to life once more.

'This is the kind of thing that can end a marriage, you know,' Nicole joked, intruding on his less than innocent thoughts. At his puzzled look she continued, grabbing her hastily discarded shoes from the floor and looking for a place for them. 'My mother left her third husband because he chewed too loudly.' She shook her head. 'She said it made her want to poison his food.'

Rigo raised a brow, watching with trepidation as she moved a few items around in the walk-in closet area. 'So my tidiness will be the cause of our divorce?' he asked.

'That's if I don't drive you insane with my mess first.'

'You seem very fixated on the eventuality of our marriage ending,' Rigo said, watching as the smile died on her lips.

'Why would you have had a prenup arranged if you didn't expect a certain outcome?' she countered, stepping out of the closet and closing the door behind her. 'I've been to enough of my mother's weddings to know not to be naive. Marriages end, Rigo. It's just the way things go sometimes.'

Rigo moved towards her. 'And when this inevitably ends, what will you do then?' he asked, surprised that he genuinely wanted to know the answer.

'Will I move on to another rich husband like my mother did, do you mean?' She pondered for a moment. 'Or perhaps you are the beginning and end of my illustrious career?'

He stepped closer, angry at her for once again twisting his words. But he soon realised his mistake. He stood still, feeling the pull of her scent, seeing the telltale dilation of her pupils as she looked up at him. He could just take her to bed and let them both give in to this angry heat between them. She wanted it just as badly. He could tell by the way she moistened her lips with the tip of her tongue.

His hand trailed along her jaw. Their bodies were separated by a mere inch of space. Her hands came to rest on his shoulders, small and pale against his olive-toned skin. He encircled the indentation of her waist, feeling the smooth curve under his fingertips. He wanted nothing more than to tear every piece of clothing off her and see if his memories of her naked body were simply an exaggeration of the brain.

Three long breaths passed with them both standing still before she finally stepped away. He almost groaned with the mixture of relief he felt mingled with crushing disappointment.

She pushed a tendril of dark hair away from her face. 'This is just a result of us being forced into close quarters.' She sat on the bed, tucking her fluffy sock–covered feet underneath her. 'I'm going to sleep.'

Rigo blinked, trying to convince his body to follow the same path as his mind. There was no way in hell he would get to sleep anytime soon. His breathing was still heavy—as was hers. He could see the flush on her cheeks as she lay down and pulled the covers hurriedly over herself.

'I've got some work to do,' he said gruffly, needing to put some distance between himself and her beguiling presence. 'I'll likely be gone tomorrow before you wake, but Alberto will be on hand if you need anything.' He left the room, trying not to dwell on the way her skin looked, so pale and inviting against the black sheets.

Why her ease in laying down boundaries should bother him, he didn't know. He had done the same thing, hadn't he? He should be grateful that she wasn't blatantly pursuing him to try to gain more leverage in their situation…

An impromptu trip to New York had taken longer than anticipated, making it almost a week before Rigo stepped back on French soil. Having already changed into his evening suit on the jet, Rigo entered the apartment with barely ten minutes to spare before they were scheduled to leave for their engagement party.

The middle-aged nanny stood in the living room, holding Anna in her arms. The baby was smiling, clearly content in the older woman's arms.

'Monsieur Marchesi.' With a smile she walked over to him, gesturing for him to take the child from her arms.

Rigo shook his head. 'I've actually got a call to make.' He made to move away, but the woman just smiled and placed the child gently in his arms before he could protest further.

'I'll be back in a moment.' She looked down at the little girl. 'Just look how happy she is to be in Papa's arms.'

Rigo was frozen as the nanny disappeared into the kitchen. His arms felt awkward. The child barely weighed anything and yet he felt as though he held a solid boulder against his chest. What was he doing here? This was exactly why he'd been avoiding the apartment. He should have just collected Nicole at the door, as he'd planned.

Anna looked up at him with blue eyes just like his

own, full of curiosity. She reached out to grab the shining satin of his tie, pulling it out of place and frowning. She was a serious child. Rigo felt an urge to laugh at her tenacity, but breathed out with relief as the nanny finally returned, holding a bottle of milk. He returned the curious blue-eyed bundle to the woman, murmuring something about his call, before stepping out to the peace and seclusion of the terrace.

He leaned forward on the balustrade, feeling the breath hiss out from between his clenched teeth. The evening light was fading and a handful of stars were emerging in the sky above the iconic Eiffel Tower in the distance. Normally this spectacular view would calm him after even the most hectic of days. But at that moment it did nothing to calm the quiet demons of his past threatening to escape from the corners of his subconscious.

He had thought his biggest problem was keeping his own inconvenient attraction to Nicole at bay, but it seemed he had entirely avoided coming up with a plan to deal with the fact that he was a father. His daughter was a Marchesi through and through—that much was now clear. Whether or not he had ignored the similarities at first, he wasn't sure. But in the handful of times he had seen her since she'd arrived in his life he had become increasingly drawn to her.

He had meant it when he'd told Nicole that he planned to play a part in his child's life. But as to how to begin playing that part, he had no idea. How did one apologise to an infant for missing the first six months of her life?

Rigo ran a hand across his jaw, feeling the tension in his muscles weighing down on him like lead in his bones. All he had to do was get through the next few weeks until their wedding was over. Then they could set about living separate lives. Perhaps that would be better for the child than having a virtual stranger unsettle her by trying to play daddy.

He shook his head, banishing all other thoughts from his brain. He had to be on the ball tonight. This engagement party was a chance for the company to publicly put the rumours to rest. Three hundred high-profile guests would be joining them to celebrate their union, and the Marchesi Group would be front and centre, taking the opportunity to capitalise on the exposure.

His plan had been a success from the moment the first picture of their kiss had hit the tabloids. Pictures of Nicole's ring had gone viral and she had been immediately scrutinised, with full spreads about her past as a child star and her subsequent struggles as an actress being dug up. But for the most part the spin had been a positive one. The media was abuzz with this unexpected turn of events, and the company's shareholders had immediately seen dollar signs.

For a fashion house there really was no better publicity than their figurehead's very public no-expenses-spared wedding. His own team had taken full control of the event, with him only having to sign off on venues and entertainment without much of a second glance. The date had been booked and the paperwork prepared. Once tonight was through, the whole world would be on tenterhooks, waiting to follow Europe's most talked-about couple down the aisle.

Having never previously allowed the press access to his personal life, he'd be lying if he said it wasn't intrusive. But it was necessary. Once their wedding had passed they would revert back to making selective outings as a couple, keeping Anna under a complete protection order from the media.

'I wasn't sure you were going to arrive.'

Nicole's voice drifted from behind him and Rigo turned, his eyes widening as he took in the beautiful woman standing in the open doorway. She was breathtaking.

The dark waves of her hair were swept back to one side in a fashion that reminded him of old Hollywood. Her eyes seemed sultry and more intense, and a luscious red colour enhanced her full mouth. His throat slowly dried as he appreciated the way her light blue dress seemed to showcase every single delicious curve of her body. He vaguely recognised it as one of the exclusive pieces from their upcoming haute couture autumn line—an exquisite concoction of powder-blue lace and shimmering crystals. The overall effect was mesmerising.

His pulse quickened as he noticed the provocatively sheer panel that ran from the middle of her thigh to just below her knee. He cleared his throat, realising she was looking at him expectantly and he hadn't yet spoken.

'I would never stand my fiancée up.' He looked down at his watch. 'When I said seven I didn't mean it with military precision.'

'It's hard to be late with a team of make-up artists and hairdressers.' She smiled. 'Thank you for organising that, by the way.'

Rigo shrugged. 'You need to make an impression tonight.' He looked down at those endless legs once again, feeling his jaw tighten in response. 'We need to leave now.' He brushed past her, momentarily surrounded by the sweet scent of her perfume before powering across the living room to the doorway. Nicole took a moment to speak with the nanny before following him with a puzzled look in her eyes.

He didn't care if she was upset at his lack of pandering compliments. This might be their engagement party, but it wasn't a date. And the less comfortable they were around each other until their wedding was over, the better.

Nicole held her breath as the car pulled to a stop. Bright lights flashed rhythmically against the one-way windows. Rigo finally ended the call he had been on for the entire journey just as the chauffeur opened the door.

Plastering on her best smile, she stepped out behind her fiancé, accepting his arm as support as they headed into the fray.

Cameras flashed from all directions as they stopped on the bottom steps of the hotel to pose for the photographers. Questions were fired at them in loud streams of French, Italian and English. Some were innocent, enquiring about their upcoming nuptials and about the dress she wore this evening. But one particular journalist took no time in going in for the kill.

'How does it feel to have nabbed a billionaire, Miss Duvalle?' she asked acidly. 'Your mother must be very proud.'

Nicole kept her smile frozen in place, ignoring the attempt at provocation. Her skin prickled where Rigo's hand lay at the base of her spine. She stole a glance at him. He was effortlessly casual, wearing the same smile he used for all the press. They were directing questions at him, too, mostly about the recent jump in sales of Marchesi prêt-à-porter range and the subsequent rise in stock prices. No one asked *him* about his sexual past, or made assumptions about his character. They treated him like a person. They respected him.

She focused on smiling for the cameras, moving her body so that they got good shots of the dress.

'You seem very covered up, Nicole.' A young male journalist smirked. 'Has your fiancé decided to take your risqué dress sense in hand?'

'Do you still have an alcohol problem?' another called out.

'How do you plan to shed all that baby weight for your wedding?'

Nicole swallowed hard as the barbs kept on coming. The PR team had been clear on the questions they should answer and the ones they should ignore. But it seemed the more that she ignored their assaults, the harder they pushed.

Rigo just sailed through without a scratch, but she felt as if she was fourteen again, being thrust in front of the paparazzi like a juicy steak to a pack of starving dogs. They all wanted a piece of the golden widow's daughter. They wanted her to be just as scandalous as her mother.

'What about the baby, Nicole? Who gets the magazine spread for little Anna?'

Nicole froze.

'Who asked that question?' she called out, unable to control her response.

Her voice was drowned out in the sea of noise. Rigo held her arm tighter, trying to steer her further along the line, but Nicole stood firm.

'Who was it?' she asked again, her voice a little louder. 'There will be no talk of my child—do you understand?'

She was vaguely aware of Rigo's hand sliding around her waist, her body being turned towards him before his mouth was next to her ear.

'Smile and walk, Nicole,' he whispered harshly, his breath fanning against her neck.

She shivered in response, her teeth scraping her bottom lip as she fought the mad urge to nestle against him and drown out the poisonous din that surrounded them.

She gave one final wide smile before letting Rigo guide her away from the flashes and up the wide stone staircase of the hotel. Once they were safely inside and away from prying eyes, he turned to her with barely controlled frustration.

'You almost lost it out there,' he warned, his voice a low rumble. Anyone walking by would think they were lovers, whispering sweet nothings to one another.

'I held it together,' she said quietly.

'Barely.' He reached a hand under her chin, forcing

her head up to look at him. 'You need to practise your poker face.'

'You're saying it doesn't affect you when they speak your daughter's name? When they talk about her as though she is a commodity to be speculated upon?'

'It's their job,' he gritted. 'You need to grow a thicker skin.'

Nicole shook her head in disbelief. Of course he didn't care about Anna. All he cared about was how this sham of a relationship affected his stock prices.

She stepped back from him, letting his hand fall from its place on her chin and regaining a little of her composure. 'I just don't want them talking about my child. I don't care what they think of me.'

She walked past him, powering ahead towards the elevator that would take them to their party on the top floor.

Rigo fell into step behind her. 'Maybe just try to pretend that you're happy to be here?'

Nicole fought the urge to roll her eyes, pinning her best smile back in place and focusing on maintaining as little physical contact with her infuriating companion as was humanly possible.

Once they reached the opulent grand ballroom and greeted their A-list guests, that task became significantly more difficult. With each new introduction Rigo took to draping his muscular arm lightly around her waist in a display of confident possession. His seductive smile and hooded looks were certainly for show, and yet she felt her pulse quicken with every change in the pressure of his fingers through the lace of her dress.

A man stepped casually in front of her, leaning forward to drop a light punch on Rigo's arm. Nicole stepped back, the gesture catching her off guard. Rigo didn't seem fazed at all by the action. In fact he practically beamed as recognition dawned.

'*Fratello!* You made it after all.' He turned to embrace the man, clapping his hand roughly around his shoulders. After a moment he stepped back, circling his arm around her waist once more. 'Nicole, this is Valerio—my brother.'

Nicole offered her hand and a polite smile, trying to ignore the coldness in her future brother-in-law's gaze. Apart from the blue eyes, the brothers were very different. Rigo was tall and athletic, whereas Valerio was more hulking and broad. But they definitely shared the ability to make a woman feel thoroughly disapproved of.

'I thought at least *one* member of our family should be present at your big announcement.' Valerio turned back to Rigo without another glance in her direction.

'Will your parents not be joining us tonight?' Nicole turned to Rigo.

'They're currently on a schooner cruise in the Indian Ocean,' he explained. 'They will return in time for the wedding.'

Nicole nodded, biting her lip. If his brother was openly disapproving, she dreaded to think what his mother would be like.

Nicole looked around at the throng of people staring at them, their hushed conversations and averted looks doing little to disguise their blatant curiosity. They were all wondering the same thing: Why were they here? It was public knowledge that Rigo Marchesi was a self-professed bachelor. Now all of a sudden he had a fiancée and a six-month-old daughter and the world was supposed to not blink an eyelid. The ridiculousness of it suddenly became too much. She needed a drink—or three.

Rigo watched as Nicole made her way across the room towards the bar. She had excused herself politely but he had felt the tension building in her from the moment they'd entered the room. She was on edge—but then so was he.

'So, your fiancée…?' Valerio's smile didn't quite meet his eyes as he took a long sip of his whisky. 'What has it been? A whole week of courtship?'

'What can I say, little brother? When you know, you know.' Rigo shrugged.

'This whole situation is like history repeating itself. Are you sure the child is even yours?' Valerio lowered his voice.

'I'm not even going to grace that question with an answer.' Rigo's jaw tightened.

'I know you haven't told Mamma yet. Just because they're in the middle of the ocean doesn't mean she hasn't got a satellite phone glued to her side.'

'I thought it best to wait until they had finished their trip.'

'You're afraid to tell her.' Valerio smirked. 'I would be, too. After you jumped into proposing to the last one.'

Rigo felt every muscle in his body tense at his

younger brother's reminder of a time when he had been younger and infinitely more naive. He resisted the urge to throw him down and fight it out, as they had as boys. Maybe he would postpone that for the future…in a less crowded place.

'No more talk of that—not tonight.' Rigo motioned to a waiter to bring him another drink. 'We are here to toast my beautiful fiancée.'

He raised his voice so that the men and women surrounding them joined in, thus cutting off their intimate conversation.

Taking a deep breath, Nicole ignored the heat flushing her cheeks and stopped to take a glass of champagne from a passing waiter. It didn't take long for her company to be monopolised by the other guests. Everyone wanted to know more about the woman who had finally snared the elusive Rigo Marchesi.

Rigo's PR team had advised her to stick to the essentials and avoid awkward questions about their time apart. After a few minutes she felt her nerves melt away. Suddenly she found herself almost enjoying the pretence. She talked about her fiancé with the compulsory flowery endearments, referring to their relationship with all of the expected love-struck excitement of a newly engaged woman.

After the third time reciting the story she almost started to believe it herself.

How wonderful would it be if this were actually true? She sipped from a flute of champagne and listened as the group of women surrounding her gushed about her ring. What would it be like to be actually engaged to Rigo Marchesi? If this had truly been a celebration of their love with their closest family and friends? What would it be like to be the woman who held all of his attention?

As she began to describe their fictional proposal story for a fourth time she became aware of a commotion at the doors of the ballroom. A woman burst in, her shrill voice cutting across the soft music of the jazz band.

'This is *my* daughter's party, you buffoon!' she exclaimed in a thick London accent, turning a hasty smile on the crowd of hushed guests. 'Look at your bloody list again.'

A guard quickly appeared beside Goldie Duvalle, speaking in hushed tones into her ear. Whatever he said made her ageing features twist with distaste.

As though in slow motion, her mother's trademark red talons lashed out and struck the guard on the jaw.

Nicole prayed for the ground to open up and swallow her at that moment. She looked across the ballroom to Rigo, watching as he nodded briefly to the security guard. The man backed away, clutching his red cheek, as Goldie scanned the crowd and easily spotted her.

'*There* you are, my love.' She rushed forward in her sky-high heels and her daringly low-cut neckline, crushing Nicole into a dramatic embrace.

'Mother, what are you doing here?' Nicole kept her voice low, pulling away from the obnoxious display of maternal affection.

'I'm here to celebrate your engagement with the rest

of these people.' Goldie smiled brightly. 'I'm going to presume my invitation got lost in the post and speak no more of it.'

Nicole cleared her throat, silently thanking the band for playing a louder tune to smooth over the awkward interruption. 'I didn't invite you, and you know why.'

Goldie's eyes narrowed a fraction. 'Let's not give in to dramatics on such a wonderful occasion, my love.' She took Nicole's hand in her own, squeezing it in a ridiculously maternal gesture. 'I decided it was past time to make up after our little spat. I wouldn't want to miss my only daughter's wedding over a silly misunderstanding.'

Nicole felt her jaw clench. A *misunderstanding*? She strengthened her resolve not to lower herself to her mother's level. She was the hostess tonight after all, and she had to play her part.

'If you want to stay—fine. I'm not going to draw any more attention to you by kicking you out, so enjoy the festivities. You have already disrupted the party more than enough.'

She had hoped to make a calm exit, but she should have known her mother would never make things that easy for her. Her mother's eyes hardened pointedly in a way she knew all too well.

'*Disrupted?*' Goldie raised her voice. Both perfectly plucked brows rose in astonishment. 'I'm hardly a wayward child. I just wanted to see my daughter—is that such a bad thing?'

Nicole felt her control snap. 'It's been more than a year since we last spoke. You've never even met your own granddaughter.'

Her mother grasped her hand painfully to stop her from walking away, her eyes filling with tears. 'You're right, darling, I've been awful. But you need to understand—you wouldn't listen to me.'

Nicole grabbed her hand back, massaging her wrist where her mother's nails had dug in. 'You were angry that I wouldn't sell my story to the press. Nothing more and nothing less.'

'I was *worried* about you! I couldn't have my only daughter throwing away her future. Planning to raise that child alone when you could have lived in luxury.' She shook her head. 'But thankfully that argument is null and void now…'

Her mother took a deep breath, a bright smile breaking across her ageing features.

'Just look at you. My Nicole—engaged to a billionaire, living in his penthouse… I'm glad to see you didn't let your silly principles get in the way of common sense.'

Nicole felt nauseated at the look of approval on her mother's face. 'Are you trying to say that I *wanted* this?'

'Of course you didn't.' Goldie laughed. 'Not openly. You're proud, just like your father was—God rest his soul. You're just lucky you have me looking out for you, making it easier for you to do the sensible thing.'

Nicole looked at her mother's smile, feeling a ball of cold dread sink to the pit of her stomach as it all clicked into place. She had been so blind, not wanting to believe her mother could be capable of something so cold. But no one else knew who Anna's father was.

Goldie continued, unaware of any problem. 'You are

a mother now—you know what it is to only want the best for your daughter.' She nabbed a flute of champagne from a nearby tray, downing it in one go. 'There's no need to thank me for my efforts. Lord knows I never thought the fool would *propose*, of all things, so I can't take credit for that. All I ask is that you hold on to him now that you've got your claws in.'

She winked, and that one gesture sent Nicole over the edge.

'It was *you*.' Her voice sounded hollow and shrill in her ears. 'You gave that interview, didn't you?'

'Don't worry, it was anonymous—not a soul will ever know.'

'*I* will know!' She forced the words out, the emotion building in her throat. 'How *could* you?'

'Don't act as if I'm the villain here.' Goldie wagged a finger in Nicole's face. 'We both know I've done you a favour. I mean, what else could you do with your career history but marry for money? It's like our little family business.' She laughed weakly, stopping when Nicole's expression darkened. 'All I wanted was a normal life for my daughter…'

Nicole swallowed hard. It was futile to try to explain the concept of normality to her mother—a woman who had strived for superstardom from the moment she'd left home to be a model at sixteen. It was always going to be about what Goldie wanted. Nothing else mattered. She couldn't deal with her mother's narcissistic logic right now.

Her mother's smile changed swiftly and Nicole became aware of a warm, muscular hand settling on her hip. A scent that she had rapidly come to identify as his enveloped her, wrapping her in its warmth. She avoided his eyes, finding herself suddenly unable to look at him for fear he might somehow see her shame. Rigo already believed the worst of her, and once he found out that her mother had been the catalyst behind this whole mess he would never believe that she'd had no involvement.

'Mrs Duvalle, I'm delighted to make your acquaintance.' Rigo smiled, taking Goldie's hand briefly.

Nicole was almost sick at the look of blatant female appreciation on her mother's face as she allowed her red-painted fingernails to rest briefly on Rigo's forearm.

'Soon to be *Miss* Duvalle, I'm afraid.' She blinked once. Twice. A sheen of moisture appeared in her eyes. 'Husband number seven was not so lucky after all. Unless you count his getting lucky with anyone *but* his wife.'

'I'm sorry to hear that.' Rigo's voice was sincere, and his hand still splayed casually across Nicole's hip.

Nicole ignored the sensations his hand threatened to evoke and swallowed past the choking lump now forming in her throat at her mother's words.

So *that* was why her mother had waited until now to out her daughter's story to the tabloids. Her private life had been nothing more than a damned insurance policy for when Goldie's latest marriage went belly-up.

'I'm much more interested in *your* good news.' Goldie touched Rigo's arm once more. 'I had hoped that we might all celebrate together privately…as a family.' She simpered.

That was it for Nicole. She couldn't stand there one more moment and listen to her mother's empty words. She removed Rigo's hand from her side and quickly excused herself, walking towards the nearest doors with as much speed as she could muster. The anger she felt, the pain at her mother's betrayal, it was all too much. She needed to escape.

# CHAPTER FIVE

NICOLE WALKED AS far as the elevator bay and exhaled slowly. Seven floors below the ballroom's mezzanine floor she could see hotel staff and guests ambling around the fountain in the lobby. The calm babble of water and the hum of distant voices seemed ridiculously peaceful in comparison to the storm of emotions waging within her.

She would have to tell Rigo. Dishonesty was not a trait that she possessed. It wasn't as if it would come as such a surprise, with what he already knew about her mother anyway. But if she were truly honest with herself she simply didn't want him to know the truth.

She didn't want to tell him that the most pressing reason for her disappearance a year ago had had less to do with him and more to do with her mother, who had even then hoped to use her unborn grandchild for publicity. And, perhaps most embarrassingly of all, that Nicole had chosen to run away rather than stand her ground. Just as she had run away right now.

She watched the progress of an elevator upwards towards her. She didn't even know where she was going, for goodness' sake.

Was she really so weak that she couldn't even be assertive for her own child now? A year ago she had been pregnant and scared. She had turned to Goldie at a time when she'd needed her mother the most, but had been met with nothing but selfishness and greed. 'A baby for a billionaire!' Goldie had practically screamed with delight. And Nicole had instantly known her mistake. She had been a fool ever to think her mother could be relied on for anything other than her own agenda.

She wasn't upset—she had long ago stopped shedding tears over things she couldn't change. She just hated herself for the way she always seemed to let her mother take control of her life. She had played right into Goldie's plan. She hadn't had to go to Rigo for help, and she certainly hadn't had to accept his proposal.

Maybe she *was* just like her mother.

The thought actually stopped her breathing for a moment. Could that be it? Was she that person who thought the entire world was against her when really she was exactly what they made her out to be?

The elevator arrived with a ping and she hastily stepped inside. The doors began to slide closed, only to be stopped suddenly.

'Where do you think you're going?' Rigo's voice was low, his eyes narrowed in question as he moved his shoulder against the elevator door and effectively blocked her escape.

'I don't know...' Nicole breathed. 'I just needed to get out of there.'

'There was no need to hightail it across the ballroom, drawing everyone's attention.'

Nicole groaned inwardly. Of course everyone would have noticed. They were probably all speculating on what the latest drama was. She leaned her head back against the solid marble wall of the elevator. Steeling herself for what she knew had to come next.

'Nicole…?' he said, his voice demanding an answer.

'I can't marry you.' She forced herself to look him in the eyes as his gaze darkened. 'I can't go ahead with this wedding.'

He was completely silent, allowing his gaze to sweep over her features momentarily before he stepped forward into the lift and let the doors swing shut behind him.

She straightened up to her full height, feeling cornered. 'I'm serious, Rigo.'

'I heard you.' He reached behind her to the panel of lights on the wall, tapping a button at the very top. A voice came from the speaker and Rigo replied in fluent French, looking briefly up at the security camera in the corner. The lift shuddered to life and began moving steadily upwards.

'Where are we going?' Nicole asked, holding on to the railing as they continued to rise higher and higher towards the top of the hotel.

'Somewhere we can talk alone.'

The elevator doors slid open, revealing a corridor with three separate double doors with gold plaques bearing the names of past French presidents.

Nicole followed closely behind Rigo, her feet aching

in her high heels, as he led her through the first door. The suite inside was enormous, with stylish dove-grey walls and vaulted ceilings. The antique mahogany furniture looked decades old, with clawed feet and polished silver fittings.

'Do they normally allow you to use the most expensive suite in the hotel for private discussions?'

'They let me do whatever I want.' Rigo shrugged.

'I'd say that kind of freedom is nice.' She bit her lip, feeling the emotions of the past few days threaten to catch up with her.

'We're alone now. So talk.'

Rigo leaned against the side of a dining table, watching her with an intensity that made her insides quake. Where did she even begin to tell him what was going on in her mind right now? All she knew was that her entire being was telling her to run as fast as she could—away from this hotel, their ridiculous plan. Him.

She pressed a hand to her chest, turning away from his scrutiny in the pretence of exploring the suite further. She ran her hand along the ornate back of one of the chairs—another antique, by the looks of it.

The dining table had to be at least ten feet long, she mused. And the room ended in a wall of floor-to-ceiling French windows that led out onto the most spectacular terraced garden. She turned the handle, feeling the cold night air fill her lungs. She could finally take a breath and not feel as if she was drowning.

As she moved out onto the terrace she heard him follow behind her. He wasn't talking, and for that she supposed she should be thankful. She needed to relax if she had any hope of going back to the party. Of course she would go back. She wasn't so cruel as to embarrass him by jilting him in public the way he had rejected her.

The distant memory of him laughing at her in that nightclub threatened the edges of her consciousness. But she didn't believe in giving an eye for an eye, no matter the extent of someone's misdeeds.

'This view is breathtaking.'

She cleared her mind, leaning against the stone wall to peer down at the rooftops of Paris far below. It was like another world up here—so quiet and peaceful. She could stay here forever, just counting the lights on the horizon. If she moved forward just an inch she would be able to see the street where Rigo's apartment was. She tilted her hips, leaning forward just a little more.

Warm, muscular hands settled on her shoulders, pulling her back from the ledge. She could feel Rigo's breath behind her, warm against her bare skin.

'I can admire the view from a distance, but I draw the line at leaning over the edge.'

His voice was like dark chocolate on her frayed senses. His hands still pressed against her bare skin.

'I was just looking.' Her voice came out huskier than she'd intended.

'It's funny, I keep telling myself the same thing.' He moved one fingertip up her arm, tracing her collarbone lightly. 'But then I keep doing this whenever I get the chance.'

Nicole swallowed hard at the sensation his hands on her bare skin evoked. Her shoulders felt tingly and loose, and the feeling was moving steadily downwards.

If one touch could make her feel like this, she wondered what his lips might feel like. The thought surprised her, making her angry at herself, angry at him for starting this.

She turned around.

He took a step closer, his hand dropping back to his side. 'I'd imagine you're used to men acting like fools around you.' His mouth turned down at the corners.

Nicole laughed nervously at the ridiculousness of that statement, pushing a tendril of hair behind her ear. 'Last year in Paris was a first for me. With you.'

He had no idea just how telling that statement was. It *had* been a first. He had been *the* first. Not that she would ever fully admit that to him.

Rigo smiled. 'You're good at telling me what I want to hear.'

She tried not to let her wounds show as he took one single step, bringing the heat of his chest almost flush against hers. What was he doing? Her hands reached up to his shoulders, intending to push him away. He was like a wall of hot steel, moulded against her. She could feel the sheer power of him through his suit jacket, barely contained. She arched her head back, knowing she was inviting more but not managing to care. His head lowered, his lips touching the delicate skin beneath her ear. Nicole shivered, arching her neck to give him better access. He kissed a trail of fire down her neck and along her bare shoulder.

'I've been fantasising about this since I saw you tonight,' he whispered against her ear, nipping the skin lightly. 'Probably long before.'

She wished he would stop talking so that she could give in to this completely. She suddenly wanted nothing more than for him to lay her down on a bed so that she could jump into this delicious fire completely and forget about everything else.

But she wouldn't do that. Still, she knew she wouldn't have an excuse to touch him again after tonight. If this was to be goodbye, then she was going to make it count.

She leaned forward, closing the gap between them, and pressed her lips to his. Her kiss was soft…curious, even. His hands captured her hips, pulling her close against him. She could feel every hard plane of his body through the thin lace of her dress as he held her trapped in the circle of his arms.

She wasn't sure when he began to take control of the kiss, but by the time she realised it he had already gained full steam. She followed his lead, their tongues moving against each other in a steady rhythm. They feasted on each other for so long she almost forgot to breathe, vaguely aware of him guiding her towards the wall behind them, pushing her back flat against it.

His hands cupped her bottom through the lace of her dress as he continued to take possession. She gave as good as she got, holding the front of his shirt in her grip and nipping his lower lip with her teeth. This was fast heading out of her control, but she didn't have the will or the inclination to stop. It felt much too good to walk away just yet. She wanted to see if the reality of him matched up to the memories she had of their night together. It was like stepping back into a dream. She had kissed him first that night, too.

That thought stopped her.

Nicole broke away, pressing her hands against his chest. This was just as bad an idea now as it had been the first time. She wasn't going to make the same mistake twice. She moved away from him, stepping back to the balcony ledge as if the distance might somehow dampen the smouldering heat she could still see blazing in his eyes.

Rigo smiled at her, but it wasn't a smile at all. There was no hint of playfulness in his gaze.

'This isn't a game, Nicole.' He leaned back against the wall, watching her. 'I won't be used as a distraction for whatever is going on in that head of yours.'

'I'll take the blame for that one...' she breathed, straightening the material of her dress and holding her arms around herself in the sudden cold breeze.

She remembered the reason they had come up here in the first place—the conversation with her mother. She felt adrift once again.

'So you were saying you're not going to marry me?' he said coldly.

Nicole bit her lip at his abruptness. 'I can't. Not now that I know...' She shook her head, a shiver running down her bare arms. The temperature was certainly a few degrees lower at this height, but that was only half the reason she felt so cold.

Rigo sighed, shrugging off his jacket in one smooth movement and offering it to her without a word. She accepted it gratefully, draping it around her shoulders and instantly regretting the decision. The material was still warm from his body heat, and it smelled so divine it made her head spin. It was a sin to smell this good… It did funny things to her insides.

'Are you upset about your mother's arrival?' he asked. 'Or is this still about the paparazzi's questions?'

'Just leave it,' she pleaded, feeling cold dread pool in her stomach at the memory of what her mother had revealed. 'It's none of your concern.'

'It is, actually. I can't risk you snapping at photographers when we're trying to build an image together. No matter what they say to provoke you.'

'I wish I *had* snapped, Rigo.' She shook her head. 'All I did was try to stand up for myself for once. And in the end I walked away.'

'In my experience, silence is sometimes the safest option.'

'Maybe I'm tired of being quiet. Maybe I'm *over* having my options taken away from me.'

She thought of her mother's manipulation, cold shame pooling in her veins. They were so different. He had been raised to value his privacy and had always chosen when to disclose his affairs. From the moment she'd been born her mother had used her to promote her own publicity. She had done her first photo shoot when she was four days old, her first solo interview at the age of three. She had been raised at the end of a camera lens.

'Is that actually what you think this marriage is?' His voice hardened. 'Nobody backed you into a corner, Nicole.'

'I cared too much about the implications. I thought I was making the right choice.'

'You cared *too much*?' He laughed—a cruel sound. 'If I had known I was agreeing to marry a martyr perhaps I would have chosen another option.'

Nicole fought against the stinging emotion in her throat. His words were a cruel reminder that this entire relationship was nothing more than a sham. There was no way he could know how much she truly cared. Not just about her daughter, or about what the media said about them, but about what he thought of her, too.

It was ridiculous. After all the times he had hurt her in the short time they'd known one another he still had a strange hold over her emotions. From the moment they'd met she had felt it—that need for him to see her for who she really was. And for a few short hours she had honestly thought he had. But then, as always, reality had come crashing in and he had looked at her with the same scorn that everyone else heaped upon her.

She should just reveal her mother's deception right now. It wouldn't change his opinion of her anyway. No matter how hard she tried to step away from her past it was never going to be enough.

She stepped away from him, bracing her hands on the cold stone balustrade that overlooked the entire city. A tear fell to her cheek and she hastily brushed it away. She wouldn't let him see how deeply his words cut.

Rigo watched Nicole visibly shrink from his words. Even with her back to him he could tell she was hurt. That had not been his intention. He simply didn't understand how a woman who had spent most of her life basking in the limelight of the media could suddenly be so affected by their intrusion.

He laid a hand on her wrist, turning her to face him and noticing the telltale redness in her eyes.

'I have upset you.' He frowned. 'I'm just trying to say that you always have a choice, Nicole. You *choose* to care. You choose to value everyone else's opinion of you more than your own.' He spoke softly, lifting her chin so that she would look at him.

'Their opinions have always had to matter more,' she whispered. 'It's hard to form a high opinion of yourself when you barely even know who you are.' She stepped away from him, hiding her tears from him once more. 'I've played a part for so long, it just became natural to let others dictate who I should be.'

'What are you talking about?'

'I'm talking about *me*, Rigo.' She sighed. 'How could you want to marry me when you have no idea who I am?'

'I know enough,' he said coldly.

'That's just it. You *think* you know enough but really you know nothing at all.' She shook her head. 'Rigo, I've been a walking sham for most of my life. A persona created by my mother and her publicist,' she continued, refusing to look at him while she spoke. 'I've never broken out of rehab, or slept with married politicians, or done half of what the crazy rumours out there say I have. I was publicly provocative, but once the cameras were gone…I could never follow through. I could never trust anyone enough.'

She looked up at him, meeting his eyes for the first time since their kiss.

'Until that night with you I had never even… I don't know why I'm telling you this.'

Rigo let a harsh breath escape his lungs. 'You had never even *what*, Nicole?' He watched as she visibly tensed at his words. He didn't care if he was being cold. What she was saying was so absurdly far from what he knew about her he found it impossible to believe.

'You were the first man I actually slept with.' She shrugged self-consciously. 'The others were all lies and scandals, drummed up for publicity.'

'Excuse me if I find that hard to believe. You were hardly innocent that night.'

She bit her lip. 'I almost told you—just before we got to your apartment. But then you were saying such wonderful things I just lost my nerve. I was selfish. I worried that it might make you stop, and I didn't want you to see me differently just because of one small detail.'

'That "detail" being your supposed virginity,' Rigo said coldly.

His memory of their night together surfaced painfully. She *had* been nervous. The revelation of what she was telling him now made his stomach clench. Her unashamed response to their lovemaking that night had driven him wild…the way she had been so amazed by her own pleasure. He had been surprised at her shyness about her body, her seemingly unpractised explorations of his body. But once he had found out who she was he had assumed it had all been just a part of her act.

'You're telling me that you were a *virgin*?' he said incredulously, his voice harsher than he'd intended.

'Don't say it like that.' Nicole tugged her wrist out of his grasp, walking away from him into the dim light of the suite's dining room.

'*Dannazione*, Nicole,' he gritted, stepping inside and shutting the door hard behind him.

She turned around, eyes wide at his sudden display of anger.

'Don't just walk away from me after all that.'

'"All that" is my life, Rigo. My truth. I'm not trying to make you feel guilty, or gain sympathy. I just needed to talk about something real for once!' she exclaimed. 'Do you know what? Let's just forget this conversation ever happened and you can go back to whatever you thought of me before. Whatever makes you feel better.'

'You honestly think I could *forget* knowing that I took your virginity and then threw you out on the street?' Agitated, he ran a hand through his hair. 'You walked away that morning after I practically called you a whore. Then, even when you knew that the child you carried was mine, you walked away again.'

'Oh, no. You don't get to turn this around on *me* just because you've realised how callous you actually are. I walked up to you in the middle of a crowded nightclub, Rigo, because you refused to answer any of my calls. I was honest about my pregnancy. The only reason I chose not to push any harder was because you made it brutally clear what you thought of me—and of the child I carried.'

Her words were like cold water over his temper. He

had been abrupt and forbidding, refusing to entertain her from the moment she had shown up unannounced at his favourite club. The thought suddenly filled him with cold shame.

'You *laughed* at me, Rigo. You humiliated me in front of all your rich, sophisticated friends. It's probably best that this sham doesn't go ahead, because I don't think I could survive being married to a man I know doesn't respect me.'

'Nicole…' He shook his head, needing her to stop talking so that he could process the reshuffling of the facts in his mind.

'I need to leave, Rigo. Please don't follow me.'

He caught a glimpse of the tears in her eyes for a split second before she turned and walked away, disappearing through the suite in a blur of long legs and pale blue silk.

With every passing second he felt his temper ebb and the cold realisation of his own actions set in. He had made presumptions about her character from the moment they'd met, just as she had accused him of doing. But was it entirely his fault when she had worked tirelessly to make the media believe she was someone else?

He thought of the woman he had bedded that night, of her hushed moans and the momentary cry of pain that he had presumed was some sort of theatrical move. He had been so blind, and he had coldly brushed the intense feelings from their lovemaking aside once he'd learned her name the next morning.

He had rushed things. He hadn't known her from the

English tabloids so he had powered ahead, giving in to the ridiculous heat that had burned between them. He knew that his reaction on finding out who she was had been exaggerated. But after being fooled by a woman once before on such an enormous, soul-wrenching scale, his pride wasn't something he took lightly. He had called her a gold-digging whore. And then he had humiliated her.

The memory sat heavily in his gut.

This arrangement was proving more complicated than he had ever imagined. The waters had grown murky and he didn't like it one bit. He would have to find a way to make peace with his wife-to-be or this marriage was never going to work.

Nicole sat cross-legged in the middle of the nursery. Anna's chubby legs kicked hard in the air as she tried to roll over on the carpet. It was already midmorning and there had been no sign of Rigo coming home since last night. She tried to focus on folding Anna's belongings into her small case, hoping it might calm the storm of emotions going through her brain. She hadn't planned on letting things get so personal last night. And she hadn't meant that kiss.

What on earth had been going through her head to let Rigo know that she had been a virgin? It didn't really make a difference to their situation. It had been her own private secret, along with the memories she held close of the one night when she had trusted a man enough to completely let go and take her own pleasure. She didn't know why she had waited so long, but there it was. And now the look of horror on his face would ruin that memory for her forever.

Anna squealed, looking at a spot directly behind her. Nicole knew she would find Rigo standing at the door even before she smelled his cologne on the air. His hair was wet, as though he had just stepped out of the shower. His blue eyes were darker than usual—or was it the faint shadows under his eyes that made them seem so? Either way, he looked both terrible and devastatingly handsome at the same time. It was quite an accomplishment.

He was silent for a moment, his gaze trained on Anna as she continued to try to roll onto her stomach, laughing as she fell back each time. 'The housekeeper told me that you were packing,' he said finally.

'I asked her to help but she said she had to clear it with you first.' Nicole sighed. 'Thankfully I am under no such obligation.'

'Can we at least talk before you go barrelling out of here?' he said darkly. 'Do you even know where you will go?'

Nicole steeled her resolve. He knew that she had very few options here. But her pride wouldn't let her stay a moment longer.

She stood up, facing him with her chin held high. 'I won't talk to the press. You can pretend the engagement still stands if you want. We can keep this quiet for as long as you need for your deal to go through. Pretend the wedding has been postponed or something.'

'What can I do to make you stay?' He stood absolutely still, his hands deep in his pockets as he held her gaze.

Nicole shook her head, looking away from him and trying to find the right combination of words to let him know she couldn't do this any more.

Rigo's phone sounded, startling Anna with its shrillness. The baby began to sob. Nicole bent down to scoop her up in her arms, holding her close as Rigo began having what sounded like quite an urgent conversation in Italian.

He ended the call, looking up at her with the closest thing to panic as she had ever seen on his face. 'Alberto has just called to say that the magazine team is on its way up in the lift.'

'The interview… It's today?' Nicole felt her heart beating hard in her chest.

She had been gearing up for this all week. They were to present the world with an intimate portrait of them in their home to go along with the photographs of their engagement party. The prep work had been done with the PR team, and her pre-approved outfit hung pressed and waiting in the dressing room. It was a vital piece of this facade to set the scandal straight and get the media on their side.

'I've had my phone turned off since last night.' He pinched the bridge of his nose hard. 'Nicole, I know that I have no right to ask you for help but…I need you by my side.'

Nicole bit her lip. *I need you.* She must be mad, but she didn't want to let him down. She nodded, watching his shoulders sag with relief.

\* \* \*

The magazine that would cover their entire sensational love story had competed against countless others to win the contract. In the end it had all come down to privacy for Rigo. He wanted a respectable British publication to take charge of the coverage, with the money raised from the deal going straight into his parents' charity.

The team was busy setting up lighting around the seating area. Nicole sat by his side, dressed in jeans and a soft pink top that cut across her collarbone to sit at the tops of her shoulders. She looked deceptively relaxed in the soft morning light.

While they waited Anna sat propped on her lap in pink baby pyjamas, all ready for her afternoon nap.

The make-up artist came over, with her belt filled with brushes. 'I just want to touch up a few bits, Miss Duvalle, if that's okay?' She gestured to a stool set up across the room.

Nicole looked at him for a moment, her expression strange. 'Would you...hold her?' she asked quietly, looking up briefly to where the journalist sat near them, taking notes and preparing for their interview. Anna might not be featuring in the photo shoot—both Nicole and Rigo had been clear about that—but even behind the scenes they were on show.

Rigo cleared his throat, nodding as casually as he could before accepting the pink bundle into his arms. He probably wasn't holding her correctly, he thought suddenly. He looked to Nicole, but she was already sitting on the stool with her eyes closed as the make-up woman deftly swept a brush over her cheeks.

He looked back down at the child. She sat facing away from him, looking towards the window. He hadn't been around babies much in his lifetime—not at all, really. She shifted her weight, almost jumping off his lap as a bird flew down to land on the balcony outside. Her excitement was instantaneous, and her features lit up with glee as she pointed one chubby finger towards the creature.

Rigo smiled. He couldn't help it. Her laughter was infectious, just like her mother's.

He stood up, walking closer to the window and holding her tight against his chest. She sat relaxed in his arms, her attention entirely focused on the creature pecking at the moss on the balcony ledge.

A bright flash drowned them both in sudden blinding light. Anna's tiny features scrunched up with surprise before she let out a piercing wail. The cameraman stood guiltily a few feet away. Rigo felt the sudden urge to punch the man full force in the face. He controlled himself, not shouting at the oaf for fear of upsetting the baby further.

He looked across the room to Nicole, silently begging her to help. Anna was inconsolable now.

Nicole stood swiftly, crossing the room to take Anna into her arms. The child was instantly soothed, looking briefly up at him with a mixture of fear and recrimination. He took the chance to retreat, speaking sternly to the cameraman so that they didn't have a repeat incident and making sure he deleted the photo from his camera.

As the director announced that they were all set Nicole handed the child over to the nanny for her nap. The twenty-minute photo session drained them, with all the forced poses and orders to smile on cue. They took a few romantic 'couple' shots before beginning the interview.

Rigo kept his arm slung around Nicole's shoulders on the back of the sofa. They needed to seem at ease with each other, but she was as tense as an ironing board. When he'd leaned over to lay a kiss on her lips at the photographer's suggestion he might as well have kissed a block of ice.

'So let's start with what exactly are the boundaries for the big day?'

The female journalist's husky Scottish accent interrupted the tense silence in the aftermath of the disastrous photo shoot. She placed a digital recorder on the futon between them, its red light blinking.

Rigo spoke, his answers all pre-rehearsed. 'We expect discretion at all times, with only a prearranged time slot for photographs.'

The woman nodded, ticking a box on her list. 'Will we be allowed access to the bride as she prepares? We would love to get some candid shots of all aspects of the day.'

'No,' Nicole said suddenly. 'I mean…I don't think I would be comfortable with that.'

Rigo looked at her pointedly, laying his hand gently on her thigh. 'What my beautiful fiancée means to say is that she'll likely be too nervous for that on the day.'

The journalist narrowed her eyes, clearly unimpressed at the answer. She flipped through some of the photographs from the engagement party the night before, pausing on one.

She looked up, a gleam appearing in her eyes. 'Your mother wasn't invited to the party last night, Nicole?' she asked in her simpering voice. 'Why was that?'

'She was invited. There was simply a mix-up with the list,' Rigo said quickly.

'And yet these photos clearly show Nicole and Goldie having what looks like a heated argument.' She raised her brow.

Rigo looked to Nicole, noticing the sudden look of horror on her face. She masked it quickly, taking a sip from her glass of lemon water.

'There was no argument, Diane. Move on, please,' she said harshly.

Rigo frowned at Nicole's use of the woman's first name. He had noticed the immediate tensing in Nicole when they had been introduced to the woman who would write their article, but he had put it down to nerves. Now, looking at the two women staring each other down, he wasn't so sure.

'From what I hear, you should be *thanking* your mother. Not arguing with her.' The woman continued to pout in that same ridiculous way, staring at Nicole like an eagle watching her prey.

'You're here to ask questions about the wedding. Do your damned job,' Nicole said quickly, before moving a hand to her mouth with instant regret.

Rigo sat forward, pressing a button on the digital recorder swiftly. 'I think we need to take a break.' He stood, gesturing for Nicole to follow him.

The woman—Diane—spoke quickly. 'Oh, no, I *am* here to do my job after all. So as a matter of interest for the article, does your fiancé know the kind of family he's marrying into?'

'Diane…' Nicole shook her head sadly, a bleak look in her eyes.

'This is not proper conduct when in the home of your subjects.' Rigo walked towards Diane, using his height to appear imposing towards the woman.

'I just thought that you might want to know a few things about your wonderful bride-to-be. Like the fact that she and her mother are the most slippery creatures to walk this planet.'

'You have personal experience with my fiancée that gives you this opinion?' Rigo asked.

Diane spluttered at his challenge. 'Her mother is a witch, a horrible—'

'Goldie Duvalle is not in this room, and I would like to know why you are attacking her daughter—unless you have some personal reason.'

The woman froze, her mouth opening and closing twice in quick succession.

'That's what I thought.' Rigo shook his head, looking down at his designer watch. 'I don't have any more time for this. Leave now. All of you. You've got what you came for.'

Nicole sat completely still, with her shoulders down so far he thought she might be trying to disappear into the settee. As the magazine crew packed up their things and filed out into the hall, the interviewer looked pointedly at Nicole one last time.

'Oh, and, Diane, was it?' Rigo said darkly. 'I'd expect a call from your superiors this afternoon if I were you. You'll want to start job-hunting.'

'You people think you run the world!' she said angrily as Rigo herded her out through the door. He closed it with a resounding snap as she continued to curse him from the other side.

Rigo looked down at his fiancée, his gut tightening as he noticed her pale face. He refilled her glass of lemon water, offering it to her.

She took a sip, looking away from him towards the windows. 'I didn't know it would be her doing the interview.'

'I take it from that display of hostility that you are previously acquainted?'

'Yes. You could say that.' Nicole shook her head sadly. 'The man my mother is currently getting a divorce from is Diane's seventy-year-old father.'

# CHAPTER SIX

NICOLE FELT THE tension in her temples rise to breaking point. 'That's the third time she has confronted me like that and I still never know what to say to her.'

'Why would you say anything at all?' Rigo shrugged. 'She is clearly angry at your mother and using you as a scapegoat.'

'I sympathise with her. I feel guilty about what my mother did to her family. Her parents had been happily married for decades before…' She felt sadness encompass her, knowing exactly what it felt like to have your parents disappoint you that way. 'My mother has this uncanny knack for taking someone's life and turning it completely upside down.'

She had been sure that Diane knew about her mother giving that interview, had braced herself for the other woman to announce it and ruin the shaky friendship that she and Rigo seemed to have come to. But now she was gone, and they were standing here discussing her mother. She knew the time had come to tell him.

'You are not your mother's keeper, Nicole. Do you

realise that?' Rigo said softly. 'She is a grown woman who is responsible for her own actions.'

'Most of the time her actions directly affect me in some way or another.' Nicole cleared her throat, looking up at him. 'Diane was right. I *was* arguing with her last night.'

'That's why you ran out?'

She nodded, swallowing the lump in her throat. 'She told me something so awful that I just couldn't bear to stand across from her a moment longer.' She stepped away from him, taking a deep breath as she tried to find the right words. Wringing her hands, she turned back to face him. 'Goldie was the anonymous source, Rigo. She's the one who leaked the story.'

He was completely silent for a moment, looking at her with something akin to curiosity. 'Why didn't you tell me this last night, when you were confessing all your sins?'

'I was afraid of how you might react.'

'In other words, you thought I would believe you had a part in it?'

Nicole paused, her eyelids fluttering up to meet his gaze. 'Well, don't you?'

Rigo shook his head, shoving his hands deep into his pockets. 'Before last night, maybe. But I'm coming to see that I've been very quick to judge you.'

'Well, I suppose I should be thankful for that, at least.'

'Nicole, I can see why you want to walk away from this marriage now. But I'm asking you to reconsider. For Anna, if nothing else.'

'We proved to each other last night that we can't be civil or separate in this arrangement. We're just not good for each other,' she said quietly.

He was quiet for a moment, looking out the window. 'Nicole, I want this marriage to work. If that means me staying as far away as possible then I will do it. To keep you and Anna safe.'

She looked into his eyes. He was being earnest. But she didn't want him to stay away at all—that was the problem. She walked away from him, crossing her arms over her chest as she followed the progress of one errant raindrop down the window. Within a matter of seconds it had begun to pour, the landscape turning a dull grey.

She knew that backing out of their arrangement had been a decision made in the heat of the moment. Marrying Rigo *was* the best choice for Anna and it always would be. Looking into his eyes, she could feel the shift between them—not quite enemies any longer, but it had put them in a kind of limbo. He made her feel off balance…as if simply being around him for too long put her at risk of making a fool of herself all over again.

'Send the staff away,' she said suddenly. 'Just until we leave for the wedding. Give them extended holiday leave. Then there will be no need for us to share a bed. We can each have our space until the wedding is over.'

'Consider it done.' Rigo nodded once, his face completely unreadable.

'Thank you.' Nicole took a deep breath, feeling decidedly less filled with dread than she had this morning. And yet she still felt that same tug of unease in the back of her mind. As if somehow by putting more distance between them she was denying herself something vital. But she didn't need Rigo's kisses in her life, and she definitely didn't need him in her bed. Sleeping or otherwise. Boundaries were the only thing protecting her from the damage this man could do to her if she ever let him close again. This was safe.

Nicole looked down at the slim diamond-encrusted watch on her wrist and felt her anxiety peak. The rehearsal dinner was due to start in twenty minutes and Rigo hadn't arrived yet. His entire family was downstairs, waiting to meet his bride-to-be for the first time, and she couldn't hide up here a moment longer.

She hadn't seen him for more than a passing greeting in the past weeks, since the magazine debacle. True to his word, he'd had Diane fired and a new journalist had taken her place. The interview had gone without a hitch and now the whole world was geared up and waiting with bated breath to witness the wedding of the decade.

She took in her reflection in the mirror, frowning at the lines between her brows. Her mother had always told her that frowning and laughing too much was a recipe for crow's feet. She shrugged off the thought. Her mother was the last person she needed to be thinking of right now. She was probably down there already, guzzling champagne and on the lookout for husband number eight.

As expected, the PR team had advised that Goldie should not be kept out of the celebrations, to avoid any negative speculation. Well, that was their official standpoint, but Nicole had a feeling that Rigo didn't want her mother tempted to do any more anonymous interviews before his Fournier deal was put through. The last thing they needed was more scandal.

The secret location for their wedding had been leaked in the past week, but Rigo had assured her that an increased security presence would deter any would-be paparazzi gatecrashers. Truth be told, it didn't worry her too much. Anna was staying put in Paris until Nicole returned to collect her for their honeymoon.

Forty-eight hours apart seemed like a lifetime right now, but she knew she had done the right thing. Rigo had told her his parents were waiting impatiently to meet their first grandchild, having just returned from the Indian Ocean that morning. He hadn't spoken of his father much, but she'd got the impression that his family dynamic was one of ease. She just hoped that she gave a better impression to them than she had given to his brother on their first meeting.

Nicole walked down the sweeping staircase, taking in the throng of guests in the chateau's large reception area. She stood alone at the bottom, looking around for a familiar face and cursing her fiancé. She recognised some of the faces from their engagement party, but without Rigo to smooth the way she felt small and insignificant. Technically, she was the hostess—she should be commanding the event. And yet she wanted nothing more than to run back up the stairs and hide.

A man stood in the centre of the gathering, his presence seeming to make the guests flock around him. His resemblance to her future husband was remarkable—

the only difference being the mop of grey waves that crowned his head and his slightly age-weathered features. A small, elegantly dressed woman stood by his side. Valerio Marchesi stepped close to the woman and smiled, dropping a familiar kiss on her cheek before she took him into a warm embrace.

Nicole forced herself to walk the few steps across the room, noting Rigo's brother tense as he spotted her.

'I wonder if my brother has decided to bolt,' he said wryly, looking down at her with moderate disapproval. 'It would be an awful pity to leave you jilted, Nicole.'

The older brunette stepped forward, taking her in from head to toe. 'You must be my future daughter-in-law,' she said, her voice heavily accented. 'I must apologise that you're being left to introduce yourself alone. I can imagine this is quite intimidating.'

'Rigo has likely been delayed at the office,' she said, her voice shaking slightly with nerves. 'But I'm sure he'll be here soon.'

Rigo's mother made no move to embrace her nor did she formally introduce herself. His father was deep in conversation and made no move to greet her. Nicole stood in awkward silence, not quite knowing what move to make next.

Her relief when the main door opened was palpable, and the small gathering turned as Rigo entered. He was commandeered instantly by a group of friends near the doorway.

'My son likes to make an entrance.' A deep male voice boomed next to her. 'My apologies for not greeting you straight away. These buffoons still think I hold

some power in the fashion industry.' The man chuckled, the scent of red wine on his breath as he leaned
forward. 'I'm Amerigo Marchesi Senior. You've met
my wife, Renata?'

He embraced Nicole with the force of a bear, dropping a warm kiss on each cheek before motioning for
his wife to do the same.

Nicole noted the tightness around Rigo's mother's
mouth as she leaned forward to embrace her. She got
the distinct impression that the woman already disliked
her. Wonderful.

'We are quite eager to meet little Anna, aren't we,
*tesoro*?' Amerigo smiled.

Renata raised a brow, unimpressed. 'Rigo has been
very tight-lipped about it all. We were only told this
week, as a matter of fact. Our only grandchild and we
haven't even seen a photograph.' Renata pursed her lips,
looking across to where her son stood.

Nicole saw a telltale tremor in Renata's lower lip
for a brief moment before the woman covered it up by
taking a sip from her wine glass. She was hurt at being
kept out of the loop. Nicole felt a pang of sympathy for
the woman.

She opened her purse, taking out the photograph of
Anna that she carried with her for good luck. She held
the glossy image out to the older woman, noting how
her eyes softened as she accepted it and cradled it in
her hands.

'She has the Marchesi eyes,' she whispered with awe.
'I can hardly believe that she is real—she looks like a
little doll.'

'She is very like Rigo,' Nicole agreed, missing her daughter intensely.

'Ah, but she has hair like her mother.' Amerigo smiled, taking her hand in his own. 'You will make a beautiful bride, Nicole. And I wish you both great happiness.'

Nicole felt her throat tighten at the man's words. He was nothing like she had imagined. Neither of them were. She shook her head as Renata made to return the picture. 'No, please keep it. I have plenty more.'

As Amerigo moved away to go and greet his son Renata took her hand, gesturing for them to move to the side of the room together. Nicole waited for the disapproval, the scorn that she expected as the woman who had brought scandal on this ancient family. She was completely taken by surprise when Renata leaned forward and hugged her—a real embrace, unlike the formal one before. She relaxed her shoulders, feeling the warmth seep into her bones.

The older woman pulled back a fraction. 'I'm sorry if I'm giving you mixed signals, my dear. But I wasn't sure…'

What she had been about to say was drowned out by a familiar high-pitched voice. Nicole's mother was making her way towards them across the hall. 'I simply *must* introduce myself to the mother of the groom.' Goldie fawned over Renata, laying an exaggerated kiss on each of her cheeks. 'Isn't this all just so heartbreakingly romantic?'

'Yes, I suppose so,' Renata said demurely, taking a discreet look down at the photograph in her hand and smiling. 'I'm looking forward to having them both in Tuscany once this has all died down. I can't wait to get my hands on this little *piccolina*.'

Nicole saw the light die in Goldie's eyes as they narrowed in on the photograph. 'Oh, how *delightful*. May I see?'

Before Nicole could intervene, Goldie had reached out and grabbed it from Renata's hands.

'*So* nice of you to make plans with the grandparents, Nicole.' Goldie's lips pursed as she stared at Anna's picture. 'I'm not privileged enough to meet the little princess, you see,' she said darkly.

'Mum, why don't we go outside?' Nicole stepped forward, taking hold of her mother's elbow gently.

Goldie shrugged her off. 'I thought she'd have nice tanned skin, like her father,' she mused, looking closely at the picture. 'Thank goodness she didn't get his nose, though.'

'I'll take that back, thank you.' Renata reached out and plucked the photograph from Goldie's hands just as Rigo appeared beside them.

'Is everything all right here, ladies?'

'Oh, here he is—the knight in shining armour,' Goldie spat. 'I've just had the privilege of meeting your mother, Signor Marchesi.'

She exaggerated the *r*'s with a roll of her tongue and Nicole suddenly realised her mother was roaring drunk.

'Mum, perhaps you should go and drink some water,' Nicole suggested weakly, seeing that her mother's mood had shifted for the worse.

'Oh, shut up, Nicole,' Goldie said, pushing her hand

away with vehemence. 'Look at you—pretending to be all sweetness and sophistication.' Goldie continued to raise her voice, looking to Renata, who was frozen in shock. '*I'm* the one who did all this for her. *Me!* You'd still be hiding away if I hadn't drawn you out.' She stepped dangerously close to Nicole, the smell of sour champagne heavy on her breath. 'And suddenly you're too good for me? You are nothing but an ungrateful little—'

Rigo caught Goldie's hand just as it flew up into the air. The look of thunder on his face made Nicole's stomach flip. 'That will be enough,' he said darkly.

The entire room full of guests had turned to watch the altercation. Nicole felt hot embarrassment sweep up her neck and into her cheeks. Rigo was fully prepared to deal with Goldie and send her out on her ear—she could see that clearly. But something in his face prompted her to step forward, placing her hand on her mother's arm.

'I would advise you to leave now if you ever hope to meet your grandchild at all,' she said quietly, knowing Renata was still within earshot.

'You owe me…' Goldie slurred. 'You know what I did—'

'I owe you *nothing*,' Nicole said with cold finality. 'You are lucky that I'm still speaking to you after the way you've treated me. Now please leave before we have to do this the hard way.'

Goldie looked as if she was going to fight, and her eyes narrowed horribly on Rigo's mother. But finally, with a heaving sigh, she shook her head and allowed Rigo to guide her across the hall.

'I'm sorry you had to witness that.' Nicole turned to Renata.

'She is the one who should be sorry, my girl.' Rigo's mother shook her head. 'You shouldn't have to tolerate that kind of intimidation—least of all from your mother.'

'She means well...I think,' Nicole said.

Renata sighed. 'You have a kind heart, Nicole. Take my advice and protect it from people who don't take care with it.'

Nicole smiled, still preoccupied with watching Rigo's progress across the room. It was a strange feeling, knowing she suddenly had someone looking out for her. That he was prepared to stand in her corner and fight. She had grown used to conceding defeat time and time again. The comfort of telling herself that she didn't care had always been like a blanket, stopping her from changing or growing. Somehow knowing that he thought she was worth defending gave her the confidence to want to defend *herself.* She didn't want to be weak anymore. She wanted to care enough about being treated badly that she would stand up and fight her own ground.

'I want to wish my brother and his beautiful bride-to-be a long and happy marriage.' Valerio Marchesi clapped his older brother hard on the back. '*Cent'anni*—to one hundred years!' He shouted the traditional Italian toast, which was quickly repeated by the intimate gathering of guests at the rehearsal dinner.

'*Grazie*, little brother.' Rigo raised his glass briefly, before downing the champagne in one go.

All his senses were heightened by the presence of the woman by his side. Nicole looked so quietly radiant in her strapless black dress that anyone might think her silence all evening was simply a result of bridal nerves. But he knew better.

He silently cursed Goldie Duvalle for being such a callous, selfish human being. It had taken all his will-power to step back. Nicole had handled the situation with infinitely more grace than he would have. Rehearsal dinner be damned—he'd wanted nothing more than to have the woman dragged out of the room by security and thrown on the first flight back to wherever she'd come from.

He half listened to his father and brother, who were deep in conversation comparing their latest travel stories. Valerio Marchesi was a wild card. He had declined their father's invitation into the family business in order to pursue his own career, chartering yachts and luxury sailing boats around the Caribbean. Now, ten years later, he was a success in his own right, co-owner of one of the biggest luxury maritime-vessel charter companies in the world.

Rigo envied his younger brother his freedom, his lack of responsibility. Normally he would have been eager to hear about Valerio's pirate-like exploits on the high seas, but tonight his mind just wasn't focused. Try as he did to stop them, his eyes kept straying to Nicole.

Once the dinner had ended and all the wine had been drunk, the guests began to filter up to their rooms. He stood in the hallway with his parents to say goodnight. Nicole was deep in conversation with his mother and aunts. Valerio stood by his side, arms crossed, filled with the same tension he had seen in him all evening.

'You look s if you've sucked on a lemon.' Rigo raised a brow at his younger brother. 'Careful, or I might think your speech was insincere.'

'I just can't get my head around your logic, that's all.' Valerio shrugged. 'But just because I don't agree with it, it doesn't mean I don't wish you happiness.'

'If you're worried I haven't learned something in the past ten years, then you can relax. This is nowhere near the same situation,' Rigo warned him, not wanting to get into a conversation about his disastrous relationship history. He knew his family had been affected by his relationship with Lydia, but seeing the tension in his brother's face made it clear that he should have been more considerate in breaking the news this time.

'No, it's not. At least this time you knew the woman was a gold-digger *before* you arranged the wedding.' Valerio looked at him. 'I just don't want to see you go through the same hell you did with Lydia. That she-beast changed you.'

'I learned a valuable lesson from that "she-beast".' Rigo smiled darkly. 'Never trust a woman with anything more than your credit card. And even then at least check the bills.'

His smile died on his lips as he turned to see Nicole standing by his side, a mask of hurt on her face.

Valerio cleared his throat, taking his mother's arm and ushering her up the stairs with a murmured good-night.

Nicole narrowed her eyes at him, her shoulders squared. 'She-beast?' she said quietly.

'That conversation wasn't about you.' He forced an easy smile, taking her hand into his. She pushed it away. 'We were talking about someone else.'

She nodded once, not quite seeming to relax. 'Charming. Your brother doesn't like me at all.'

'My not-so-little brother has a very large, very annoying sense of protectiveness towards me.' Rigo sighed, looking up at where Valerio and his mother were just disappearing around the corner at the top of the stairs. 'You're not the only person I've hurt in the past due to my own stubbornness.'

She looked up at him. 'That doesn't explain why he's taking it out on me.'

'It's this situation we're in. This whirlwind wedding. It's an uncomfortable reminder for them all of the last time I told them I was engaged.'

Rigo continued, oblivious to the horrified expression she knew must be on her face. 'I was engaged to be married ten years ago and it ended…badly.'

'What happened?' Nicole asked, even though a part of her didn't want to believe he'd been engaged to someone else at all.

'Just the usual stuff.' He shrugged, looking down at the floor briefly. 'The break-up was rather messy, and my mother took it quite hard. The wedding had been planned, invitations sent out.'

'That sounds like a nightmare,' she breathed.

A strange look came over his face—a mask of emotion so intense it took her breath away. All of a sudden it was gone, replaced by a blank stare.

'It was many years ago, Nicole.'

He reached down to take her hand in his once more and this time she didn't push it away. Knowing he had a heart after all, knowing he had been affected on some level by heartache, made her want to be the one to heal him.

She had felt it all evening—this tingling sensation in her chest that increased as their wedding day grew nearer. She'd kept telling herself that this was just another promotional appearance, that it meant nothing. But meeting his family and presenting them with this show of love and devotion had made her begin to wish it wasn't all an act.

But she knew from experience that hope was a dangerous emotion.

The next morning Nicole stood in front of the full-length mirror with a sense of overwhelming awe. Her wedding gown truly was a work of art, with the fitted bodice hugging her curves like a second skin before flowing out in an elaborate skirt from just above her knee.

It was everything she had never dared to imagine for herself. She turned to the side, taking in the intricate lace beading down her back and the long train of silk and tulle that flowed out behind her. Women should be able to wear gowns like this every day, she thought, smiling to herself. She felt like royalty.

Rigo's mother stepped closer to her side. 'My mother

stood with me like this on the morning of my wedding, you know.' Her deep blue eyes were filled with warmth. 'She and her sisters had spent weeks making my dress, but this veil was her own personal project.'

She held out a length of delicately embroidered vintage lace.

'She poured her heart and soul into it, and told me it would bring me and my new husband strong love and strong sons…daughters in your case.' She smiled, brushing away an errant tear. 'I didn't have any daughters of my own, so I'm passing down this gift to you. Don't worry—the stylists know not to cross me.'

'Oh, Renata, that's such a beautiful gesture.' Nicole's hands traced the delicate pattern of hand-sewn embellishments.

'It's my pleasure. And I hope one day you will have the gift of placing this on your own daughter's head when she marries the one she loves.'

Nicole dipped down as her future mother-in-law pinned the delicate veil in place and the stylists began to tease out the loose waves of her hair underneath. The overall effect was so classically stunning she was speechless.

'Love him with all your heart, Nicole. And I'll never have to worry about him again.'

Renata kissed her lightly on each cheek before disappearing out the door.

Nicole frowned at the woman's words, feeling them settle in her chest. His mother believed them to be deeply in love. She was happy for them. If she knew the truth it would probably break her heart.

Nicole took a deep breath and tried to calm her nerves as she was left alone for a few moments in the bridal suite. This was just another day—nothing special, she told herself.

As she made her way down the staircase to meet the events team she became conscious of the fact that she had no bridesmaids and no flower girls to stand with. Only the kind-faced event co-ordinator, who now stood on the steps to escort her outside to the grounds of the chateau, where a beautiful chapel nestled halfway into the forest.

The co-ordinator and her staff hurriedly adjusted her train before the door to the chapel was thrown open. Nicole stood still at the entryway, having chosen not to have anyone walk her down the aisle. She was making her own choices now, so it seemed fitting to give herself away.

As the doors opened and she began to walk slowly down the aisle she was aware of the guests' hushed breaths and sighs of approval.

She held her breath as Rigo turned to face her. The look of silent awe in his eyes almost brought her to a grinding halt. She reminded herself to keep moving towards him, to focus on his face and forget about everything else.

He wore a sleekly cut designer tuxedo, and his brother stood by his side in the same. She was completely on show and yet she didn't feel exposed. She felt confident with his eyes on hers. She felt a sense of anticipation as she got closer and closer to him. But as she came to a stop by his side and looked up at him the enormity of what they were about to commit to was overwhelming.

Rigo's hand enveloped hers as the priest began the ceremony and she fought to focus on the various prayers, then automatically repeated the phrases.

When the moment finally came for her to slide a thick gold band onto Rigo's third finger as a symbol of their eternal devotion, to her embarrassment she felt her fingers shake uncontrollably. His tanned, muscular fingers covered hers and she saw the spark of possession in his eyes as he placed an identical gold band onto her finger.

The priest pronounced them husband and wife.

Nicole felt her breath catch in her throat at the look of dark possession in Rigo's gaze. He took no time in pressing his lips to hers, moving his hand to her waist as he pulled her close. The kiss was a part of the ceremony, she told herself. But as he released his breath slowly she felt his fingers tremble against her waist. That one sign of weakness made her wonder if perhaps she wasn't the only one struggling not to be affected.

He broke the kiss after a respectable amount of time—they were in a church after all—but the heat in his gaze was just for her. She knew with sudden clarity that this moment would be scorched on her memory forever, no matter what came after.

The wedding reception passed in a blur of wine and dancing. By the time Rigo's father swept her up on the dance floor for the third time her feet were aching to escape from their designer shoe prisons.

'May I cut in?'

Rigo's voice came from somewhere behind her left ear as the music slowed down to a steady beat. They had shared a first dance already, earlier in the evening. The memory of it still clung to her skin, where he had pressed his face against her neck.

The photographers had been present then, trying their best to melt into the background but not really succeeding. All day he had touched her and kissed her, their charade successfully convincing the world of their marital bliss. But her traitorous body didn't seem to realise that this wasn't real. That he was playing a part.

Rigo's hands rested low on her waist, his fingertips pressing just above her hips. As he pulled her close she thought she heard him release his breath on a deep sigh. But when she looked up he was looking away from her. She laid her head against his chest, her hands gripping on to the back of his jacket as she breathed in the scent of him.

All too soon the guests had formed a line to wish them well as they made the traditional exit through the arched arms of Rigo's family and friends.

They made their way in silence up the stone steps to the master suite at the top of the chateau. Nicole stopped for a moment in the middle of the corridor to slip her shoes off her feet. She moaned with relief as her aching toes lay flat on the carpeted floor.

'Better?' Rigo said huskily.

She nodded. 'It's a long walk up here. Especially in heels.'

He took a step towards her, cupping her face in one hand. 'I can carry you if you like?'

When she didn't immediately respond he stepped closer again, his mouth lowering to lay another kiss on her neck. 'I haven't been able to stop inhaling this delicious scent all day.'

'The photographers are gone, Rigo,' she breathed, trying to ignore the immediate frisson of arousal that coursed through her body.

'Let's pretend they're not.'

Those words seemed to unlock a tension inside her that she hadn't known was there. This kiss was different from the others—more urgent. His hands cupped her jaw, holding her in place as his tongue moved against hers. Their breath mingled into one as the rest of the world fell away. There was no one watching them now, no one to perform for. This was just for them.

She stopped holding back and gave in to the arousal that threatened to burn her up, grabbing a fistful of his hair and groaning into his mouth as he pressed the evidence of his arousal against her. She wanted him. She wanted everything that she knew he couldn't give her. And yet maybe just having tonight might make whatever came after easier to survive.

It suddenly seemed impossible to stop.

She took a deep breath, their eyes locked in the dim light of the corridor. 'Rigo… If we go into that bedroom together, I want it to be real.'

Rigo took her hand, pressing it to the hard beating of his heart through his shirt. 'Do you actually doubt that it is?'

She bit her lip, holding on to his hand as he led her down the hall and into the honeymoon suite. His lips were on hers as soon as the door had closed behind them. She barely had a moment to appreciate the romantic candlelight that glowed around the room before he was burning her up all over again. And, oh, it was good to burn.

She turned and swept her hair to the side so that he could access the row of tiny pearl closures that ran down to the base of her spine.

'*Per l'amore di Dio*—is this a dress or a straitjacket?' Rigo breathed, popping open the tiny buttons one by one at a torturously slow pace. 'It would be easier to just rip them open.'

'It would. But you won't.' She bit her lip. 'At least I hope you won't.'

'I can tell that you love this dress, so I will try to control myself.'

He continued popping the tiny pearl fastenings until the dress was loose enough for her to shimmy it down. She did love this dress—not because it was haute couture, or because it was miles ahead of the fashion trend. She loved it because *he* loved it. And it would remind her forever of the awestruck look on his face as she'd walked down the aisle to become his wife.

Nicole let the material fall slowly down her body to the floor before stepping out of the mountain of silk and chiffon. With his eyes firmly fixed on her half-naked body, she became painfully aware of how utterly on show she was.

He stood back, undoing the knot of his tie and unbuttoning his shirt slowly. Nicole's throat dried as his deliciously bronzed skin was revealed inch by inch, before he removed the shirt completely and dropped it to the floor.

'Do you want me to fold that up?' she asked coyly, unnerved by the crackling tension. 'We wouldn't want it to crease.'

'No jokes, Nicole,' he growled, grabbing her by the waist and holding her against him.

'I'm nervous,' she admitted, her voice barely a whisper.

'*Dio*, how can you not see how beautiful you are?'

'You're the only person to ever actually make me want to believe that.'

'That sounds like a challenge, *tesoro*.' His eyes gleamed.

# CHAPTER SEVEN

SHE REACHED OUT, boldly running her hand across his bare chest, just as she had done that very first night in Paris a lifetime time ago. Only that time the room had been too dark for her to appreciate his perfection. Right now the faint glow of the candles bathed the room in just enough light.

Her sense of exposure intensified, but with his eyes locked on hers and the heat she saw there some of her self-consciousness melted away. He was just as turned on as she was—just as wild with anticipation as he seemed to drink in every inch of her body. She leaned her head back, closing her eyes as he ran his hands down her body. He cupped both her breasts, teasing her hardened nipples through the silk and lace of her delicate bridal corset.

The structured silk garment had originally been designed for practicality, not seduction. But as Rigo turned her around and she caught a glimpse of herself in the mirror she began to understand the appeal of such feminine lingerie. She watched his eyes darken as he slowly pulled the laces loose. The fabric brushed against her already sensitive breasts as the whole thing loosened and came to rest around her hips.

Rigo moved against her, the heat of his erection pressing on her lower back as his tongue licked a path up from the sensitive spot between her neck and shoulder. Their eyes met in the mirror as his fingers explored her bare breasts, and Nicole couldn't resist moving herself back against the hardness of him.

Her hand seemed to reach down of its own accord to touch him through the fabric of his trousers. The pace of his breathing increased as she squeezed his length, then ran her fingernails down the hard ridge of his erection. The sound of his guttural moan filled her with pleasure, and her own heartbeat was now thumping powerfully in her chest.

Rigo suddenly grabbed her hand, pulling her with him across the room to the king-size four-poster bed. He sat on the coverlet and positioned her so that she stood facing him, trapped between his thighs. Her corset was dropped to the floor entirely, followed swiftly by her underwear.

Nicole instinctively moved to cover her abdomen, knowing that the faint marks from her pregnancy were now in full view for him to see.

Rigo moved Nicole's hands away, holding them by her sides as he looked his fill.

'Don't hide yourself from me.'

He leaned forward, taking one taut nipple in his mouth, his hands roaming on a path down her sides to cup her behind. And what a behind it was, he thought as he squeezed tight.

Nicole began to relax, her body leaning into him as he kissed a trail between her breasts. She was unsure of herself, of her appearance. Why, he had no idea. He couldn't make it any clearer how sexy he found her, how ridiculously turned on he was.

So he stopped talking, instead focusing on showing her with his tongue, running it down her abdomen. With the way his hands caressed the front of her thighs, spreading them apart so that he could stroke his knuckles along the soft dark hair between. He slipped one fingertip inside the crease to tease her with gentle touches before running a smooth rhythm up and down the crease of her lips.

Every one of her husky moans made it harder and harder not just to bury himself deep inside her and end the torture. He settled for moving a finger to her slick entrance, sliding it deep and setting a slow rhythm before adding a second. Nicole groaned deep in her throat, whispering something incoherent as he continued pleasuring her.

He bit hard on his lip, knowing he was the only man who had ever brought her this kind of pleasure. She was destroying his control with her unschooled responsiveness. There was no pretence in the way she dug her fingernails into his shoulders and let a harsh breath hiss out from between her teeth as her climax began to build.

He felt her muscles tighten and slowed his pace, wanting to draw out the torture a little longer. He had

waited long enough to want to take his time. He wanted
to tease her right to the brink, then feel her come apart
on his tongue. Without hesitation he moved her back a
pace and dropped to his knees in front of her. She didn't
have a moment to protest before his tongue was sliding
against her centre, stroking her in long, slow movements
in time with his fingers.

Nicole grabbed a fistful of his hair as she moaned
her release, each delicate spasm sending tremors against
his tongue as he rode it out with her. He stood up, then
laid her down on the bed, covering her body with his.
She felt like hot silk… A man could drown in pleasure
like this. It was like nothing he had ever felt and they
had barely even got started.

She opened her legs for him, pressing herself against
his erection without any of the nerves from earlier. A
good orgasm apparently made his wife brave. He smiled
to himself. He must make note of that for future ref-
erence.

He lowered his mouth to hers, kissing her hard and
deep, knowing she could taste herself on his tongue.
That fact only served to make him harder as he lay back
on the bed beside her and grabbed her by the waist. He
wanted her on top of him, so that he could watch her
as he made them both come.

Nicole tensed, her hand on his chest as she half
leaned over him. 'Rigo…' She bit her lip, her voice
hesitant.

'Just trust me.' He pressed a kiss to her lips, holding her waist and guiding her on top of him so that her
thighs cradled his hips completely. He held his breath as

she slowly lowered herself to him, capturing his erection in a vice-like grip of molten heat.

Rigo head tilted his head back against the pillow, the sensation of delicious tightness almost more than he could bear. Nicole lifted her hips slightly, sending fresh waves of pleasure up his spine.

'*Yes*—just like that,' he urged, groaning as she repeated the motion and circled her hips in a slow, tortuous rhythm.

From this angle he had a full view of every tantalising curve of her body. The full high peaks of her breasts, the inward curves of her waist. She was like something that had walked straight out of his wildest fantasy. He took a moment to relish the fact that she was entirely his. The knowledge that he had been the only man to see her this way, to feel her as she lost control of herself…

He sucked in a breath as she leaned over him, giving him the perfect opportunity to claim her breasts once more. She was fast gaining pace, sliding against him in a steady rhythm as she braced her hands on the bedposts above them. Rigo thrust upwards in time with her, feeling his pleasure intensify. He had never felt an orgasm build this slowly, seeming to thrum up the tension in every nerve ending of his body.

He took one of her hands from the bedpost and guided it to her clitoris. 'Show me how you like it…'

Nicole's eyelids fluttered down as her fingertips drew a slow circle on her clitoris. Knowing he was watching her touch herself was both shocking and intensely sexy. She forced herself to open her eyes, to look down at him as she brought them both closer to their release. The pleasure was so intense she almost stopped, her breath coming hard and fast as she rode him.

Rigo seemed to sense her uncertainty. 'Harder,' he growled, sinking his fingertips into her hips.

He thrust upwards, filling her so completely that she cursed. His eyes widened, and his hands tightened on her hips as he repeated the motion, over and over. She could tell that he was close—just as she was. Her fingers worked faster. Her orgasm was building with such intensity it took her breath away. When she finally shattered into a million pieces Rigo wasn't far behind her. A few sharp thrusts were all it took for his muscles to tighten beneath her and spasms to ripple through his powerful body.

Nicole tried to move, not wanting to collapse on top of him, but Rigo kept his grip on her hips. He groaned low in his throat as he buried his mouth in the valley between her breasts and pulled her down to cover him. She relaxed her muscles, unable to hold herself up any longer, and gloried in the aftermath of their lovemaking.

'I have been thinking about doing that for weeks,' Rigo whispered in her ear. 'Watching you ride me while you touch yourself…'

Nicole shied away from his erotic words, her bravery fast waning.

He nipped the skin just below her ear, his voice a low rasp. 'You have no idea what it does to me to have you in control like that…' His words were slurred with tiredness as his body turned so that they lay on their sides, his arm around her waist, holding her close against his chest.

Nicole heard the moment his breathing slowed and sleep claimed him. She felt his heat surrounding her, protecting her, and as she looked down she caught the glint of his gold wedding band in the dim light. After all the pleasure she had just experienced she had almost forgotten that they were married. She was someone's wife now.

And this man—this utterly sinful, passionate man— was her husband. The concept of man and wife had never truly held any weight with her until today. But as she had stood in the church and made a vow to love and honour the man beside her she had been jarred by an errant thought.

She wasn't quite sure if she had been acting.

Rigo lay on his stomach, his face completely relaxed in sleep and mere inches from hers. Nicole had no idea what time it was, but judging the brightness of the sun at the windows it was late morning. She turned on her side, taking in the sheer presence of him. A strange tingling sensation began in her stomach as she raked her gaze down over his muscular shoulders, over the smooth olive-toned skin that lay bare down to his hips before being covered by the soft white sheets.

If she moved her foot ever so slightly the sheet would slip down further, revealing just a little more… She bit her lip, smiling at her own wayward thoughts.

She tested her theory, shifting her foot and watching as the sheet slipped down an inch. One tanned, toned buttock was revealed and she felt her breath catch. Her eyes darted up to his face. Thankfully he was still sleeping. Her throat was painfully dry, her heartbeat quickening, but still she got braver. With one smooth flick she pulled her foot away completely. The sheet came away, too, bringing every hard, muscular plane into view.

His body shifted suddenly, and Nicole froze as his muscles flexed before his entire body turned so that he lay on his back. She looked up, and sure enough he was wide-awake, watching her with a mischievous glint in his eyes.

'Please, by all means carry on. Don't let me disturb you.'

Rigo's husky drawl made her cheeks warm as he reached out to stroke a hand lazily down her ribcage.

Of course, him being on his back now meant that an entirely different plane of muscles was on show. Nicole looked away, focusing instead on his face. His eyes were crinkled at the sides with the effort of holding in his amusement.

'I have absolutely no idea what the etiquette is for this situation.' She looked up at the ceiling, trying not to smile herself.

'This is new territory for me, too, Nicole.'

She looked back at him, one brow raised. 'Oh, come on—you've probably done the "morning after" routine so many times you've lost count.'

'None of those women were my wife.'

She was his wife.

Nicole's brain seemed to trip over the words uncomfortably. It all just seemed so surreal. Here she was, lying in bed with him after a night of the most intense lovemaking she had ever experienced. Granted, it had only been her second time, and with the same guy. But still…

She bit her lip. 'We should probably talk about how this affects…everything.'

'Is that what you want to do?' he asked.

He was looking at her with a gaze so heated it made her skin prickle. He rolled over, pushing her down to the bed and covering her body with his own. His skin was deliciously bed warm, and hard against her. She realised she had been waiting for him to do just this— that her body had been craving contact with his from the moment she'd opened her eyes.

'If you want to talk, by all means go ahead. But I can't promise I'm going to pay attention.'

His head bent down to trail kisses past her collarbone. Nicole felt the scorching heat of his tongue make a trail down the sensitive underside of her breast. He wasn't playing fair at all.

'I'm just not sure what we're doing, that's all…' she breathed, groaning as his tongue darted across her nipple in one harsh flick.

'Clearly I'm not doing it correctly.'

His gaze held hers captive as he took her whole nipple into his mouth, caressing it with his tongue and lips until she moaned low in her throat. He moved her legs apart, settling his body between her thighs. He fitted perfectly there, the dark hairs on his abdomen trailing down to where his erection pressed, hot and heavy. She looked up at him, finding his eyes trained on her.

'I want you, Nicole.' His voice was a husky whisper. 'God help me, but I want my wife in my bed. I can't think of anything but having you underneath me, crying out with pleasure.'

He moved a fraction of an inch. She sucked in a breath as the tip of him slid ever so slightly against her most sensitive spot. Her eyes drifted closed. The delicious pressure was taking over.

'Look at me,' he said, lowering his body weight onto his forearms so that his chest lay against hers. 'Tell me that you want this.'

It wasn't a demand, but also not quite a question. She urged her sex-hazed brain to respond, but couldn't find the words. Every inch of her skin was being burned up with his heat. Her legs rose to grip his hips, silently begging him to end the torture. He was still waiting, watching her intently.

'I want this,' she whispered, pulling his head down to close the final gap between them.

Her kiss was hungry and filled with the need that consumed her. He was just as out of control. She could feel it in the way his shoulders trembled under her touch. This felt different from last night somehow. Maybe it was the light of the day that made it more real.

She forced herself to open her eyes as he pulled away, grabbing a foil pack from the bedside cabinet and sheathing himself.

His eyes never left hers as he entered her. Her body stretched and moulded to him, heat filling her and travelling up in waves across her abdomen. The angle of his erection sliding against her seemed to increase the pleasure almost to breaking point. It was overwhelming and yet not enough, all at the same time. He lay flush against her, his mouth and tongue devouring hers as he moved his hips in a slow rhythm that was blissful torture.

Nicole felt the tension in her sex building, felt the pleasure radiating through her in long waves but not quite seeming to crest. She clutched a fistful of the hair at the nape of his neck, willing him to go harder, to end the torture. Rigo kept his pace, his face buried against her neck, whispering something she vaguely recognised as Italian.

When she finally reached the peak she fought the urge to sink her teeth into his shoulder as molten heat coursed through her body in magnificent waves. With one final thrust he sank himself deep inside her and groaned his own release.

Rigo smiled as Nicole released her death grip on the armrest as soon as the 'fasten seat belts' sign was switched off. The bright light in the cabin seemed to exaggerate her pallor as she leaned her head back and exhaled softly.

The child, on the other hand, had been asleep in her car seat since they'd arrived at the airport an hour before. Nicole had anxiously confided her worries over cabin pressure to the stewardess, but he could see now that her worry was only partly about Anna.

'You are a nervous flier?' He raised a brow, thanking the attendant as she laid down two glasses of sparkling water and an assortment of light snacks.

Nicole moved to fuss over the blankets that cocooned the child, checking the belt that held the seat in place. 'I'm not usually, but it's Anna's first time on a plane.'

'And she is looking a damned sight better than you do right now.' He smiled. 'Relax, it's a short flight to Siena, and I assure you my jet is well maintained and completely safe.'

'I know that.' She forced a wan smile, letting out one long breath. 'I'm fine—honestly. I'm looking forward to getting a break from the publicity. That's enough to get me through this flight.'

'We won't be disturbed at the estate—that much I can guarantee.'

He had made sure to organise security for their stay, knowing that there were no real boundaries for the paparazzi. He had also arranged for the nanny to fly over for a few days, to facilitate some alone time with his new wife. He realised he was looking forward to taking some time off from work, and the thought made him pause. He had woken this morning more relaxed and satisfied than he had been in a long time. And yet on their drive back to Paris he had found himself tenser than ever.

The wedding photos had been on the magazine's website, setting off a storm of publicity he knew would be the final step in undoing any damage to the Fournier deal. The original scandal had all but disappeared from the most prominent tabloids once the news of their engagement had filtered through.

He looked down at his sleeping daughter, now legally a Marchesi by name as well as blood. He should be relieved that things were going to plan. The new developments in his relationship with Nicole would only strengthen their partnership—or so he hoped. She didn't seem the type to believe in the fairy tale of marriage. She had said herself that love was just a romantic notion, hadn't she?

He sat forward. 'Nicole, I was thinking about—' He stopped, noticing the faint yellow tinge to her cheeks. 'Are you sure you're okay?' He leaned across the table between them, pressing his hand to her forehead. She was cold and clammy.

She pushed his hand away, shaking her head as she took another deep breath, this time groaning openly. Without another word she stood up and moved like lightning down the luxurious cabin, shutting the bathroom door behind her with a loud click.

Anna let out a small cry in her sleep. The commotion had been enough to disturb her. He silently willed the child not to stir, but of course her eyelids began to flutter before she opened her eyes wide and settled them straight on him.

He had chaired intense, high-risk meetings between multi-billion-euro corporations in the past. He had given keynote speeches in front of tens of thousands of people. But this… He winced as his daughter's face scrunched up and her eyes filled with tears. *This terrified him.* He stood as Anna began to sniff, the tears welling in her eyes as she looked up at him.

'I'm not your *mamma*—I know,' he said, feeling utterly ridiculous. She didn't understand a word he was saying.

The sniffs turned to sobs, and after a moment of in-decision he hurriedly undid the seat belt and lifted the small bundle into his arms. She was light as a feather and fitted neatly against his chest. The cabin was cool, so he kept a blanket wrapped tightly around her. He was probably doing it all wrong, but at least she wasn't cry-ing anymore. He smiled as he felt a tiny fist grab on to his shirtfront. Two perfectly round blue eyes took him in, unapologetically curious.

The bathroom door opened and Nicole emerged, looking slightly less pale. She stood frozen for a mo-ment, watching him with a strange look on her face. As soon as the baby caught sight of her *mamma* she was wriggling and craning away from him. Nicole made quick work of taking her into her arms and holding her close.

'Sorry about that,' she said quietly. 'I suffer from travel sickness from time to time. The worrying prob-ably didn't help.'

'It's fine. I seem to have avoided breaking her for the time being.'

Nicole smiled, hugging Anna close to her chest. 'She's quite sturdy now, really. She was actually five weeks premature—you should have seen her when she was born…'

Nicole's voice died away, her words hanging between them, heavy and uncomfortable. Then Anna laughed, reaching up to grab a handful of her mother's dark hair.

'I should probably go and freshen up,' Nicole con-tinued awkwardly. 'I'll take her with me this time. You probably have work to do.'

Rigo nodded, glancing at from his emails onscreen as she gathered up a bag of toiletries and disappeared into the bedroom at the back of the plane. Something dark and uncomfortable began to uncoil in his chest.

She was beautiful, his daughter. How he hadn't seen the resemblance straight away he would never understand. But the mind played cruel tricks when it was angry, and he had most definitely been angry. He had missed so much already. He wondered if the little girl would somehow have already erected a great big wall between them. Or if she would remember his absence and think of him forever as somehow lacking as a father.

As Rigo stepped out onto the veranda of his Tuscan villa he was once again filled with a sense of bone-meltingly deep calm. He nursed a cup of freshly brewed espresso in his hands and sat down to watch as pink fingers of sunlight spread across the dawn sky above the vineyards. The villa sat on acre upon acre of sprawling lush green hills and farmland. He listened to the glorious absence of traffic noise, pedestrian voices and all the other sounds he associated with his life in Paris.

Nicole appeared beside him, dressed in only a light silk robe, her hair spread over her shoulders in a tumble of loose errant waves. He had made love to his wife once more in the night, after waking to feel her long limbs tangled with his own, and then again just before they had decided to get up early for breakfast.

'This view is breathtaking.' She sighed, leaning forward against the balustrade as she cradled her own steaming cup of coffee in her hands. 'If it were mine I would never leave.'

'Technically it *is* yours now.' He stirred his coffee thoughtfully. 'I bought this place to help drum up profit in the local area, with the vineyards and the stables, but I don't think I've set foot here more than twice in the past few years.'

'Don't you ever take time off?' she asked. 'Wait—I already know the answer to that question.'

'I live a very busy life, as you know. But I have been ordered by my PR team to take this honeymoon so I plan to make the most of it.'

'You make it sound like such a chore.' Nicole's expression dropped a little, her eyes drifting away to gaze out at the sudden sparkling fountains of water that had begun to fly through the air as the sprinkler system began to drench the land.

'I'm sorry if my lack of enthusiasm offends you, but I'm simply not built to be idle. It makes me feel edgy.'

She looked up at him. 'That's possibly the first spontaneously personal thing you've ever said to me,' she said. 'I was beginning to wonder if you might be made of stone under all that muscle.'

'I think we both know that I don't run cold with you, *tesoro*.' He reached out to trap her in the circle of his arms, pulling her close.

Nicole laid her coffee down on the table beside them, placing her hands flat on his chest. 'We communicate well in bed—that much is true. But I'm talking about when we're not in bed, Rigo. It makes me uncomfortable to think that you know practically everything about me while I still know so very little about you.'

'What would you like to know?' he asked, leaning back against the balustrade.

'I don't know.' Nicole laughed. 'That's like asking me how many grapes grow in this vineyard.'

'About five and a half tons per acre, give or take.' He smirked at her answering glare. 'I'm joking—that's just a guess.'

'Isn't there a Rigo Marchesi that you have never shown to the world?'

His expression faltered for a moment, and the emotion in his eyes was so intense it made her breath catch. But just as quickly as it had appeared it was gone, making her wonder if she had simply imagined it.

'I have never lived under any pretence like you have, Nicole. The Marchesis don't have the luxury of keeping secrets,' he said nonchalantly, taking another sip of his coffee. 'If you want to know more about my secret wine collection, now, *that* is something I can do.' He smiled—a brilliant expression that transformed the previous shadows in his face.

Nicole looked at his smile and felt something bloom inside her. That small little seed of silly hope that she knew she was clutching tight to her chest. He was still holding back a lot of himself. But was she naive to hope that their attraction might bloom into something deeper if given the chance? They would be here together for the next couple of weeks, and she was determined to make the most of her chance to dig under the protective armour he seemed to wear.

After they'd washed and dressed they spent the day exploring the grounds of the estate, with Rigo seeming more at ease holding Anna as he pointed to all the different types of grapes that grew in the massive vineyard.

Nicole tried her best to step back and let him take the lead. She hadn't expected him to be so interested in his daughter. She didn't want to get her hopes up that he would be an involved father when she had already seen how much he worked. But as Rigo leaned down and dropped a kiss on Anna's cheek she felt another layer of the armour around her heart crack apart. Anna nestled her face into his shoulder and Rigo's brows rose in surprise.

'I think she's starting to like me.' He looked to where Nicole stood, watching them.

She tried to laugh, ignoring the way her heart soared at the sight of him holding his tiny daughter. That pesky glimmer of hope bloomed once more in her chest, making her want things she couldn't have.

# CHAPTER EIGHT

RIGO MOVED AWAY from the doorway after watching Nicole lay their daughter down. She had fallen asleep in her arms. The little girl was exhausted after a morning of paddling in the pool followed by an afternoon visiting the stables. The past week, since they'd landed in Tuscany, had passed for him in a comfortable routine of long days exploring the surrounding towns followed by long, hot nights with his wife.

Nicole followed him out to the veranda, plugging the monitor in nearby as Rigo grabbed two glasses of wine.

'I don't think I will ever settle for another wine again after tasting this.' Nicole sighed deeply, leaning her head back as they sat down on one of the loungers, side by side.

'All the wine from this vineyard is exceptional. But this particular one is from their vintage collection—my personal favourite.'

'So are you going to explain your behaviour earlier?' Nicole smirked, a knowing smile playing on her lips.

'You mean when I saved Anna from having her fingers bitten off?' Rigo shook off the sheer anxiety he'd felt at having the small child in the stables, surrounded by his huge stallions.

'The horse was at least two feet away, Rigo. And I was holding her tightly.'

'She was getting too excited—flapping her tiny fingers in front of it. It was only a matter of time before something happened.'

'Oh, Mr Serious, you really do need to learn how to relax.' Nicole tutted. 'Anna was in no danger today. You seem to have bonded with her a little over the past week. Am I sensing some kind of overprotective-father syndrome?'

'It's hardly overprotective to want to make sure she doesn't get hurt, is it? I mean, maybe I was a little over-cautious. But what was I supposed to do? Just let her have her hand bitten off?'

Nicole burst out with low laughter, her shoulders shaking from the force of it. 'Welcome to parenthood, darling.' She smiled at him. 'One long endless road of worry and self-doubt.'

Rigo paused, absorbing her words. Was that what had been wrong with him today? The tension in his body at having his tiny daughter so close to the animals had almost driven him insane. In the end he had just herded them all back to the house so they could swim in the pool while he caught up on some emails.

Nicole had been pushing and pushing for him to spend more time with Anna, and he knew he was being unreasonable by keeping himself at a distance. So all week long he had tried to be more interactive—swimming and talking and trying to form some sort of bond. But he was beginning to think that maybe he just wasn't built for fatherhood.

'Rigo, can I ask you something?' she asked, turning to him. 'It's just something that's been playing on my mind after meeting your family and seeing you here with Anna.'

He nodded and took a sip of wine, waiting for the question he had known she would ask eventually.

'Why did you decide not to have children at such a young age?' She frowned. 'You come from such a tightly knit family, it just doesn't make sense.'

'Nicole…' he began, not quite knowing what to say. He didn't want to talk about the past—that was for sure. But the look in her eyes told him that she was serious about this.

'I just want to understand the man I'm married to. Is that so terrible?'

'I had a vasectomy because I came to the decision that fatherhood was not for me. Is that so hard to believe?'

'And now…?'

He paused. And now he could feel himself caring more and more for his wife and daughter every day. He'd spent this whole week with Nicole and Anna, doing various activities around the countryside. And each night he had lost himself in his wife's passionate embrace, making love to her until they were both spent. He had never slept so well as he had since coming to his villa. The place rejuvenated him. That could be the only answer for his sudden heightened sense of well-being.

Nicole was looking at him expectantly. He took another sip of wine, eyeing her over the rim of his glass. 'I don't quite know what you want me to say.'

'Do you still feel the same about fatherhood now that you have Anna?'

'I didn't really have a choice, to be fair,' he said quickly, and then saw the hurt in her face. 'I didn't mean it like that.'

'Never mind. I don't know why I even bothered asking.' She sat back, turning to look at the still bright evening sky.

'I told you—I don't like to live in the past.'

'There's a difference between living there and pretending it never happened.' She looked at him. 'The night of the rehearsal dinner you mentioned having a fiancée before me…'

'If you insist on knowing ancient history, far be it from me to deny you.'

He put his glass down, clearing his throat. He felt his thumb begin to tap nervously on the side of his chair, and stilled the movement before it became too pronounced.

'Her name was Lydia. We met when I was in my final year of college in the States. She was a year older than me…worked in a coffee shop on campus. I met her at a bar one Friday night and before I knew it we were living together.'

'That fast?' Nicole asked.

'Too fast. But I couldn't have known that at the time. I was too madly in love to see the warning signs all around me.' He stood up, walking over to perch against the balustrade of the terrace. 'We were barely together six months before she told me she was pregnant.'

Rigo took in a deep breath, hating the effect this was having on him. He hated thinking of that time in his life. When he had been so utterly young and naive.

'I was a romantic fool. I proposed instantly and flew us both here to meet my family. I didn't tell them about the baby, of course. That was to be our secret until after the wedding.'

He laughed—a cruel sound, deep in his chest.

'She had me wrapped around her finger. If my mother hadn't taken an instant dislike to her, who knows what way things might have gone? My mother arranged for some security checks—just a precaution before the wedding. I remained here while Lydia flew back to the States to continue the wedding plans. With my credit card, of course.'

Nicole looked up at him, her face tight with tension as he continued.

'I remember I was sitting outside the chapel after booking our wedding date when she called me, crying. She had lost the baby.' He shook his head. 'I sat on the steps of that church and I cried with her, utterly heartbroken for the life we had lost. I got on the next available flight and rushed to her side. I cared for her, comforted her. I told her we would try again—that I would give her as many babies as she wanted.'

He sighed.

'My mother arrived at my apartment unexpectedly a few weeks later. Lydia was at a spa. I'll never forget the look on her face as she told me about the security checks she'd had performed. I was furious. I almost ordered her out. But then she showed me a copy of a medical document from one month before. It had Lydia's name on it. And there was a picture of her from security footage. In an abortion clinic.'

Nicole clapped her hand over her mouth in horror. 'Rigo…'

'I confronted her the moment she got home. Naturally she denied everything until I showed her the proof.' He shook his head. 'She told me she was scared of having the baby, that she was worried it would make me love her less. But by that point my mother had already shown me the massive bills she had run up on my accounts and I had lost the lovesick blinkers that had blinded me to who she truly was.'

Nicole sat silently, processing the revelation that Rigo had once been in love. He had said that he didn't believe in love and romance, but clearly at that stage in his life he had. And this woman had stomped all over that.

He continued unprompted, his face a tight mask of hurt. 'When I was having her things removed from my apartment I found a safety pin at the bottom of the same drawer I used for my condoms. She had often urged me not to use protection, claiming she was on the pill. But I was rigorously safe, even then.'

'She got pregnant on purpose?' Nicole breathed.

'She admitted it all eventually—once she realised it was over. It was hard, seeing the pretence fall away and finding that she wasn't the person she'd said she was. She had lied about almost everything in order to take me in.'

'So you chose to get a vasectomy because of what happened?' Nicole asked, still struggling to get her head around it all.

'I got over the break-up soon enough—the anger helped. I graduated and moved back to Italy to start working for my father. I was so lost I just wanted to run wild, to party and sleep around to blow off some steam. But every time I looked at a woman I wondered if she was just like Lydia.'

He raised his brows, sitting down beside her heavily.

'I couldn't sleep with anyone for more than a year. It tortured me. Then I heard my uncle having a conversation with my father about his mistresses and laughing about how they often tried to get pregnant, not knowing he'd had a vasectomy.'

'So you went and got one, too?' Nicole said quietly.

Rigo shook his head. 'It wasn't so simple as that. I truly agonised over it. When Lydia first told me she was pregnant I was terrified, but fear soon paved the way for excitement. I had always wanted to be just like my father, you see.'

'You still went through with it, though?'

'Yes. I decided that I would never risk giving myself like that ever again anyway, so children wouldn't be a possibility. I had the procedure, and only had attachments with women I knew were career driven and independent. Nothing close to a gold-digger.'

'Until you met me.' Nicole looked up at him, feeling the emotion of his revelation sitting heavy on her chest. 'It's very clear to me now why you reacted to me the way you did that morning. I reminded you of her, didn't I?' Nicole said sadly.

'I was unnerved by my oversight, yes. But I know different now. I know the truth about your past.'

'And yet still you're determined never to let anyone in ever again?'

'Nicole…I told you this to help you understand me…'

'And now I do. Very clearly.' She stood up, walking as far as the balustrade before turning to face him. 'What happened to you was painful and scarring. I can't imagine how difficult it must be to trust a woman again.' She shook her head. 'But here we are, married a little over a week now, and I'm only just finding this out.'

'I should have told you before. But we had agreed to keep our distance, I didn't think you needed to know.'

'I thought that you were distant with me because of *our* past. That you were still learning to trust me. I've been hoping that maybe with time… That some day we could have more.'

'I do trust you, Nicole.' He stood up, taking her hands.

She shook him off, turning away. 'You trust me not to steal your money, perhaps. But you'll never trust me with your heart, will you?' She turned back, seeing his face twist in confusion.

'My *heart*? What does that have to do with trusting one another?' He raised his voice.

*'Everything!'* she said, emotion pouring out of her with every word. 'How can you not tell that I'm head over heels in love with you?' She refused to let the tears fall from her eyes. 'I've been falling for you since the

night I opened up and told you about my past. I spoke the truth for the first time and you listened. You're the only person in this world who truly sees me for who I am. What we have together is real—can't you see that?'

'I know it's real. We have a great thing here, Nicole.'

'But you don't love me.' She let the words fall heavily between them. Creating a gap that she knew now would never be filled no matter how hard she tried.

Rigo ran a hand through his hair, his blue eyes darkening with frustration. 'It's not that I don't—it's that I can't. You're asking for something from me that doesn't exist.'

Nicole shook her head. 'Of course it exists. You're not a robot just because you've been burned badly. You're afraid to give yourself fully to anyone, and I understand that.'

'Nicole, let's just take a breather here...' He took a few steps away from her, his body tense and unyielding.

'This conversation was always going to happen,' she went on. 'And I'm glad it's happening now. I won't settle for half a relationship—not when I know now that I deserve more.'

'So I don't deserve you? Is that what this is? You're trying to force me to say things when you don't even understand what you're asking of me.'

'You don't have to say anything. I won't push you, or walk away in a storm of tears.' She cleared her throat. 'I'm giving you the option to go back to our previous arrangement.'

'Nicole...'

'That is all I'm prepared to give, Rigo. If we continue

down this road someone will end up getting hurt. And we both know that someone will be me.'

Rigo remained silent, watching her with the coldest look she had ever seen him give. It was as though she could almost literally see shutters coming down in his eyes. Blocking him away from her words.

'I will still be your wife. But in name only.' Her voice was stiff and scratchy with the effort of holding off the flood of emotion she knew was imminent.

'If that's what will make you happy, then by all means move your things into one of the guest bedrooms.' He sat down, pouring himself another glass of wine.

Nicole stood there for longer than she should have, staring down at the man she loved, willing him to come to his senses.

As she walked back indoors and moved silently up the stairs she willed him to follow her. Just as she had willed him to follow her on that day she had told him she was pregnant a lifetime ago. But this feeling was so much worse. Before, she hadn't loved him. She hadn't even known what love was. Now she felt as though her heart was breaking with every step away from him, even though she knew it was for the best.

She couldn't give everything to him knowing that he would never feel the same. That he would always be holding back some part of himself from her.

By the time she stood in their bedroom, packing her things into her case before moving them to another room, the tears had begun flowing in earnest. She continued to pack, wiping each tear away, furiously trying to hold it together.

Then she heard a loud engine roar to life outside the window and she looked down to see Rigo's car speeding down the driveway, its headlights disappearing into the night.

She sat down on the bed and finally admitted to herself what she had refused to believe completely. There was no hope to hold on to anymore.

Loud, whimpering sobs racked her chest as she leaned forward, wrapping her arms around herself.

It was over.

Rigo stood in the makeshift office at the villa, waiting for the call to tell him that his jet was ready to go. He still had five days left of his honeymoon, but he couldn't stay here a moment longer. Not now that Nicole was refusing to speak to him.

Her anger he could take easily. But her silence was more than he could bear.

He should have known it would end this way. Things had been going far too well. At least before they had been able to be civil at times. Now here they were, married a mere week and absolutely miserable, just as she had predicted. Divorce wasn't only a possibility now. It was inevitable.

He thought of his parents' marriage: thirty-five years strong without a single separation. How on earth did they do it?

He hadn't been able to find her all morning, but it was likely she had been collected by his parents' chauffeur and had forgotten to tell him. She had been regularly going to his parents' estate so that they could spend time with Anna.

They had probably spent more time with his daughter than he had at this point. He didn't know why he couldn't just be natural, like his father. Not that it mattered now. Once Nicole had left him completely he would probably only get limited visitation anyway.

The thought of them living apart from him filled him with emptiness, but he knew it was for the best. He couldn't give Nicole what she wanted. He would never be able to.

Nicole was fast regretting her decision to take Anna for a picnic without the stroller. The little girl's weight in her arms was like lead after a mere ten minutes of carrying her up the hill outside the villa. But the oppressive atmosphere in the villa was more than she could take. Rigo would be leaving today, and she didn't want to be there when he did.

She'd done enough crying over the past twenty-four hours to last her a lifetime. And it was time she got used to living here alone now that she had chosen to stay.

She loved this place. The views and the smells. It was the perfect place to raise Anna. The people here were used to the Marchesis, and they didn't bother them. It would be a quiet life.

She stopped at the top of the hill, finding a nice leafy tree for them to seek shade under. It was still early morning but it was already a balmy twenty-five degrees. She set about propping Anna on a blanket and kicking off her shoes. She had brought some fruit and bread as a midmorning snack, and laughed as Anna grabbed a piece of melon from her hand and sucked on it greedily.

She would be all right here, she told herself as she munched on her own fruit. She had her daughter and her privacy and that was all that mattered right now.

Once they had finished eating it was nearing eleven, and much hotter. She stood up, stretching her leg muscles from being cramped underneath her for so long. She looked further ahead of her, to the hill that led to the church. For some reason she felt suddenly unnerved by the quiet that usually calmed her.

A man was standing there, beside a black car, his face partially obscured by a wide straw hat. He looked like a local, she thought, her mind working overtime to process her sudden feeling of unease.

Without warning the man pulled a dark bag out of the car, unclipped a large telescopic camera and began walking down the hill towards her.

Paparazzi. Nicole didn't waste a moment. Abandoning her picnic and the blanket, she covered Anna's face and walked as fast as she could manage in the opposite direction. She looked over her shoulder, and sure enough the man was pulling out the high-scope lens and breaking into a run. Her heart beat hard in her chest as she fought to hold Anna close, still shielding her face.

She broke into a run down the hill but, having abandoned her sandals with their picnic, found her bare feet soon ravaged by the rough terrain. Every step proved to be pure agony as she tried frantically to stay ahead of her pursuer.

Her steps faltered as she heard a scuffling behind

her. Turning to check he wasn't gaining on her, she lost her footing and caught her heel on a sharp rock. Anna began to cry—a sharp, piercing sound that sent waves of pain straight to Nicole's heart. The man was gaining on them—fast.

He didn't care if her daughter was terrified, she thought angrily. All he wanted was a million-euro picture of her child. There was no way in hell he was getting it.

Hissing with the pain, she stood straight and forced herself to put pressure on her foot, feeling tears prick her eyes. They were almost at the gates, she told herself. They were almost safe. She shouted for the security guards who stood sentry there, her voice shaking with adrenaline. Anna was crying in earnest now, her little body shaking as she clung to her blouse.

Mercifully the men responded quickly, running out of their hut to meet her. But they were quickly overtaken by the appearance of her husband, his face a mask of pure rage.

# CHAPTER NINE

RIGO'S FIST CONNECTED squarely with the photographer's fleshy jaw, sending him to the ground instantly, where he lay cowering. He grabbed the camera, hurtling it at the boundary wall of the estate with a satisfying smash.

'You're going to regret this, Marchesi.' The man spat blood onto the ground, groaning as he held his rapidly swelling jaw.

Rigo leaned down, grabbing him by the collar and watching him wince in preparation for another punch.

Nicole's hand on his arm was the only thing that stopped him from pummelling the man to within an inch of his life. The red rage lifted and the sound of his daughter's terrified cries was suddenly all he could hear.

His security guards stepped in, pulling the man to his feet and holding him in their grasp while one began contacting the local law enforcement.

Rigo reached out, taking Anna from Nicole's shaking arms. The little girl nestled into him, her cries still fearful but not as piercing now that he held her close. Holding Nicole by the arm, he guided her away from the ugly scene, back towards the villa as his heart hammered painfully in his chest.

Once inside, Rigo calmed Anna with quiet shushing until she was laughing once more. He set her down in her playpen and surrounded her with toys. He had to tend to Nicole's injured feet. The sight of her panic-stricken face flashed through his mind, making his fists clench. He blocked it out. Needing to do something practical to calm himself, and to stop himself from running out and physically attacking the rat once more, he grabbed a first-aid box from the kitchen, getting to work cleaning her raw wounds and bandaging the more open cuts.

Nicole hissed with pain. 'I lost my shoes when I ran from him.'

Rigo clenched his jaw. 'He's going to be taken care of—don't worry.'

'He's going to sue you for attacking him,' Nicole whispered, looking past him to the windows.

'I'd like to see him try,' Rigo gritted, putting one last rub of salve on her skin before closing up the kit with a dull click.

He stood up, needing to move, needing to rid himself of the awful sensation of his control slipping further and further away. He had acted rashly in punching the bastard, but he would do it again—countless times.

'Rigo, this is bad.' She looked up at him. 'You have basically just started a war with the very people we've worked so hard to sway.'

'Would you have preferred that I let him walk away with pictures of our child?'

'No, of course not.' She winced as she put pressure on her foot. 'I'm just worried about how this will affect your deal...your company.'

Rigo's chest tightened. He hadn't been thinking about the company at all. If he was honest with himself he hadn't thought about it in days. He had acted on instinct, protecting what mattered most to him. For the first time in his life that hadn't been his own interests or the bottom line. When had Nicole and Anna become more important?

He stood up, pacing away from her to the window. In the distance he could see the repugnant photographer being bundled into a *polizia* car. Alberto stood at the gate, turning to look up at him with an expression he knew mirrored his own.

He had messed up—royally.

Nicole sat in the breakfast nook the next morning, watching as Rigo paced on the terrace and continued his phone call with the legal team. It unsettled her that she didn't know whether to reach out to her own husband or leave him be. Seeing him lose his temper so completely yesterday had been terrifying—like watching a stranger.

He returned inside, laying the phone down on the counter with a click and taking a long sip of his espresso.

'The photographer has started a lawsuit,' he said, clenching his fist tightly on the counter. 'He is claiming that because he was on a public road he should have had the freedom of the press. The media are pressing to have our injunction turned around.'

Nicole's hand froze, her croissant dropping back to her plate. 'He can't do that. He's just one man.'

'It's never "just one man" when it comes to the paparazzi and what they see as their God-given right to give the public what they want.'

Nicole felt suddenly cold, even though the morning sun shone in brightly through the windows. If their injunction was overturned it would mean that every detail about their relationship, their child, would be fair game.

'We will need to leave for Paris immediately,' he said, turning back to her, his hands thrust deep into his pockets.

'I am *not* going to Paris.' Nicole looked at him in amazement that he could even suggest such a thing.

'We need to tackle this, Nicole. If the Fournier deal falls through now thousands of jobs will be at stake. Not to mention the effect it will have on the Marchesi Group.'

'Your company is not my priority right now.' She bit her lip hard.

'Nicole, I need you by my side if we're to stand any chance of braving this,' he said earnestly. 'You're my wife.'

'Exactly. I'm your *wife*. So stop thinking of me as a media device and consider my *feelings* for a change.' She stood up, ignoring the pain it brought. 'That man chased me down a hill to get pictures of my child, Rigo. Do you have any idea how terrifying it is to know that I still can't protect her?'

Rigo raised his voice. 'You agreed to this when you married me. You knew what a high-profile relationship involved.'

'I didn't agree to walking right into the heart of a fresh scandal. I can't go back to Paris. I can't put myself back out there for you. I'm sorry.' She shook her head, walking into the living room.

Rigo followed her, backing her up against the door. 'I did what I did to protect my family. I stood up for you. And now you are running away like a coward.'

'You know…that's exactly what my mother always said whenever *she* had done something that made my life more difficult,' she spat, and saw him react as though she'd slapped him.

Rigo frowned. 'That's unfair. You know that I care about you—and about Anna.' He stepped away from her, giving her some breathing room. 'I need you both with me in Paris, and that is final.'

'If you cared about us you wouldn't make us leave this estate ever again.'

'Nicole, listen to me. I will protect you both from the media.' He took her hands in his. 'I made that vow and I have already proved that I meant it. Let me protect you.'

Nicole shook her head sadly. 'You can't use me again and again to protect your company from scandal and still make out as though you're putting family first.'

He dropped her hands hastily, stepping away as though she'd burned him. 'So what? You're going to hole yourself up here and raise my daughter alone in this house like bloody Rapunzel? You think *that's* better than risking a photo of her being leaked?'

Nicole remained silent. Refusing to look at him.

He shook his head with finality. 'The only person

being unreasonable here is you. I hope you're happy here in your own personal prison.'

He stormed out, leaving Nicole to stare at the door blankly.

Rigo remained completely silent in the conference room as all hell broke loose around him. The PR team had worked furiously for three days now to uphold the injunction, but with the story gaining steam on social media it had become akin to holding sand in their bare hands. The paparazzi were banding together, demanding blood, and the story was making waves across the globe.

Nobody cared that the man had ambushed his wife and child. He had been on public land and therefore within his rights. The fact that a billionaire had assaulted him and damaged the property of one of the 'little guys' was far more interesting than a case of child protection. The case would go to court, and the directors at Fournier had already called for an emergency meeting with the board.

They were going to jump ship, and there was nothing Rigo could do to stop his entire world from unravelling.

If only Nicole had trusted him enough—maybe together they could have swayed the public in their favour. But instead she had chosen to stay hidden away.

'Rigo, are you even listening to this?' The senior director of his legal department was looking at him expectantly, along with the rest of the room.

He sat up, suddenly very tired of the whole situation. All these people had been working tirelessly for him, likely neglecting their loved ones in the process, and all for what? These past five years had been devoted to growing his family company into the biggest fashion corporation in Europe. He had absorbed countless smaller companies, and with each one he had felt that same rush as when he'd first pursued Fournier. Now, with the deal set to crash and burn spectacularly, he felt nothing but emptiness.

The realisation than he no longer cared was so unsettling that he stood up and left the meeting without a single explanation, ignoring the shouts of concern as he shut the door behind him and ordered the car to take him home.

The drive through the busy streets of Paris passed in a blur. His mind was foggy and he felt subdued—likely to do with the fact that he hadn't slept or eaten properly in the days since he'd returned to Paris.

As the car pulled up to the kerb he noted the gangs of photographers still camped outside his apartment building. The abuse he had endured from their angry mouths for the past three days had opened his eyes to the kind of life Nicole must have lived. As Rigo Marchesi, golden boy CEO, he had never known anything but professionalism from the press. But now, branded a paparazzi attacker, he was subject to threats, taunts and worse from these men and women who hounded him day and night.

It was an eye-opening experience.

He entered his apartment, immediately noticing the vibrant blue fedora that lay on the kitchen counter. His father sat on the sofa, nursing a brandy, and looked up as Rigo walked into the living area.

'I came straight here as soon as I saw the news.' He stood up, pouring a second glass and handing it to his son with a half-smile.

'Aren't you meant to be in the rainforest somewhere right now?' Rigo raised a brow. 'Or did Uncle Mario send for you the minute he realised how badly I'd messed up?'

'Mario did call.' Amerigo nodded, looking down at his glass. 'But I'm here for my son—not for the CEO of the Marchesi Group.' He sat back, eyeing Rigo intently. 'Before this wedding, when was the last time you took a break, huh?' he rasped.

'I've got bigger things to worry about than that right now.'

'Another vital acquisition, I heard?' The older man shook his head. 'I admire everything that you have accomplished, Rigo. You have brought our family business to levels I never dreamed of achieving myself. But when is it going to be enough?'

Rigo looked at his father blankly. 'If everyone stopped after a certain level of success the world would grind to a halt. I believe in constant progress.'

'Progressing? Is that what you think you're doing? Because from here it just looks as if you're running on the spot.'

'Papà, I'm under a lot of pressure right now and I don't appreciate your taunts,' he gritted.

'You *need* to be taunted every now and then. You're so bloody stubborn—just like your mother…' he mused.

'Ever since that damn girl took you for a ride you've been like this. Running and running from the pain.'

'I have been getting on with my life. Why is that so hard to believe?'

'Because it's absolute crap.' His father sighed. 'And once you realise that maybe you will finally get over yourself and see that it is more important to leave this mess to fizzle out and go and enjoy the rest of your honeymoon. The company will survive the loss of Fournier.'

'It's not that simple.' He took a long swallow of the amber liquid and felt it scorch his throat. 'If I lose this deal the board will react. They have already expressed their anger.'

'Son, if I could impart to you one life lesson, it's this. Don't waste valuable time on what the board or anyone else thinks you should do. Live your life.'

His father's words echoed in his mind long after he had left him alone with his thoughts. He had told Nicole not to let the media dictate her life, but here he was, doing the very same thing. He had told her to trust him, that he would protect her from her fears. And yet the moment things got tough he had asked her to throw herself under a bus for his company.

He had treated her no better than her mother had for all those years and the realisation made him suddenly nauseous.

As the town car rolled slowly along the streets of Paris, Nicole wondered for the millionth time if she was doing the right thing. Once she had heard that the court case was today she'd known she couldn't stay away any longer. She had to try to do something.

She stepped out of the car and looked up at the steps of the courthouse, seeing Rigo standing near the top, finishing up his statement to the press. He stood alone as the cameras turned away to move towards the prosecution group, who had just emerged from the building.

She felt her stomach tighten as Rigo turned and saw her. She suddenly felt a lot less brave. His face tightened with surprise and he powered down the steps towards her, his eyes darting towards the cameramen, who hadn't yet seen her.

'What the hell are you doing here?' he asked harshly. 'Get back into the car *now*—before they see you.'

'I'm here to give my statement,' Nicole said. 'I'm here to stand by your side.'

'It's all over.' Rigo exhaled harshly. 'I paid them off and the case has been thrown out. If you had told me you were going to come I would have told you to stay exactly where you were.'

'In my prison?' she asked quietly.

'I was angry at myself when I said those words.'

He took her hand, looking down at her with such fierce sincerity she thought her heart might break.

'No, you were right, Rigo. I can't live my life running away and hiding from these people or my voice will never be heard. I can't teach my daughter to be fearful.'

'When I said those words all I was thinking of was myself. I've been living under a microscope for days now and it's already driven me halfway to madness.

But it was my actions that got us into this mess and I will face it alone.'

'I'm not just here for you, Rigo. I'm here for me, too. To prove to myself that I'm strong enough to protect my daughter.'

'You *are* strong enough, Nicole. You are the strongest woman I have ever known.'

A cameraman turned, catching sight of the candid discussion he was missing out on, and soon the whole press camp was descending upon them.

'Last chance,' Rigo warned, his fingers holding in a tight grip on her arm, as though he wanted to haul her away from the crowd.

She looked up at him, her eyes gravely serious. 'No more running.'

The crowd of cameras and microphones surrounded them with an excited hum.

One 'respectable' news journalist took an immediate jab. 'Nicole, what have you to say on the allegations that your marriage is a complete sham?'

Nicole took a deep breath, remembering the speech she had prepared and memorised on the plane journey. The words seemed to swim in her head, moving just out of her reach for a millisecond, before she squared her shoulders and grabbed them with both hands.

'Marriage is a deeply private affair for my husband and I,' she began, 'and just because we both may have previously courted the media it does not somehow make our private lives fair game.'

'What do you have to say about your husband's ferocious attack?'

'My husband acted instinctively, to protect my daughter and me from a stranger's harassment. I ask you this. In what world is it okay for a man to pursue a lone woman and an innocent child for the purpose of entertainment? Does his occupation give him the right to disregard the safety of those unable to protect themselves? Until my child is old enough to make the choice herself, I will be upholding her right to privacy.'

# CHAPTER TEN

Rigo was in awe of the strong, confident woman who stood poised on the steps of the courthouse. She held the media in the palm of her hand. Her words were unpractised, imperfect and deeply emotional, but they held all the more weight for it. What had begun as a press statement had somehow morphed into a public shaming of the paparazzi and their careless disregard for children.

He was seeing his wife transformed before his very eyes. Gone was the passive girl who had lived her life according to everyone else, and in her place was this fiery woman, poised and ready to wage war on those who dared to oppose her.

As she finished speaking a crowd of onlookers erupted into applause, and then the press began to ask more questions, one after another.

Rigo motioned to his guards to move forward as he carefully guided Nicole away.

'That was quite possibly the most terrifying, exhilarating thing I have ever done.' She smiled as they walked towards the street. 'I feel as if I could take on the world.' Her smile faded as he held open the door of his limousine. 'I'm not going with you, Rigo. I came straight from the airport,' she said quietly, gesturing to the town car parked just behind them. 'I'm flying back to Tuscany straight away.'

'We need to talk, Nicole. Please—just come back to the apartment with me.'

She shook her head. 'There's nothing else to say.'

'Nicole…'

Rigo fought past the strange tightness in his chest. He was trying to tell her how proud he was. How lucky he was to have her by his side. But the words wouldn't come, so instead he leaned forward and captured her lips with his. His hands tangled in her hair as he took his time, not caring about the people around them. He kissed her deeply, trying in vain to show her how much she meant to him.

When he ended the kiss she was breathless, and his chest was tighter than ever.

Nicole's eyes were guarded as she pulled away from him. 'Rigo…'

He held his breath as he watched her war with herself, but when she raised her eyes and he saw the solemn look in them, he knew the answer would be no even before she turned and walked away to her car.

As the pilot made his final checks Nicole took her seat and looked out the window with unseeing eyes. She should have just gone with him and drowned in his kisses. They would have gone back to the apartment under the pretence of talking and ended up falling straight into bed.

She bit her lip, swallowing past the lump in her throat that hadn't eased since she had walked away from him outside the courthouse.

She had told him that she loved him and he'd made it clear that he didn't feel the same. He cared about her. She knew he did. But she couldn't stay in a relationship in which she was the only one with both feet in the boat. Watching him walk away from her in Tuscany had broken her heart all over again, and she knew that she couldn't keep going round in circles when she was the only person who kept getting hurt.

There was a commotion at the door of the plane and suddenly the stairs were being lowered to the tarmac once more. Heavy footsteps banged hard on the steps and Rigo's hulking form appeared in the entryway.

'What are you doing here?' She unbuckled her seat belt and moved to her feet, facing him off in the bright cabin. The stewardess tactfully disappeared into the cockpit, giving them privacy.

Rigo stepped forward, his eyes dark with some unknown emotion. For the first time she noticed the dark circles under his eyes and the way his jaw was overgrown with dark stubble. Had he looked so tortured outside the courthouse?

'I shouldn't have kissed you like that.' His voice was deep with emotion as he fought to regain his breath.

Nicole crossed her arms. 'No, you shouldn't have.'

'I don't know what's wrong with me. It's like I just keep saying or doing the wrong thing with you. Time after time.'

Nicole bit her lip, silently willing him to leave so that

she wouldn't be tempted to forget why she'd left in the first place. 'There's no need to say anything. I told you to go and live your life separately.'

'That's the problem, Nicole.' He shook his head. 'I don't want to be anywhere else but right here with you.'

The air in the cabin seemed to thicken around them as his words echoed in her mind.

He continued, watching her intently. 'That day with the photographer, when I walked out and saw you terrified and bleeding, I swear to God something seemed to rise up and choke me from inside. I'm a grown man, and yet I was afraid of how utterly helpless that made me feel. You had already told me to either love you or leave, Nicole. But what I didn't realise is that I've been trying not to lose my mind over you from the moment I first saw you.'

'Rigo, I meant it when I said I wouldn't settle for half a relationship...' Nicole breathed, her mind swimming with the effect his intense gaze was having on her.

He closed the gap between them, taking her hands in his and making her look at him. 'I won't settle, either. I want it all, Nicole.'

This was an entirely different side to him than she had ever seen before. He was completely bared to her, saying things that she had only ever dreamed he might say. She didn't dare to speak, fearing she might break the spell.

'I was a complete fool to think that I had lost myself after my relationship with Lydia. The truth was I was shielding myself from ever being hurt like that again. Even from Anna.' He shook his head. 'I know I don't deserve it, after all I've done, but I couldn't let you get on this plane and fly away without taking a chance and risking rejection. I want to be your husband, Nicole, in every sense of the word. Let me love you like you deserve to be loved.'

'Are you telling me that you *love* me?' Nicole breathed, her heart soaring in earnest.

'*Tesoro*, I've been in love with you since the moment I slid that ring on your finger and made you my wife. I was just too much of a stubborn fool to realise it.'

Nicole felt her heart melt completely as she looked into his deep blue eyes. She couldn't think of a single coherent thing to say. She settled instead for wrapping her arms around his neck and kissing him with all the passion she had to offer.

Rigo felt Nicole's lips touch his and his heart almost burst right then and there. He lifted her up from the ground, kissing her with all the love he possessed. She felt so good in his arms, so right. How had he ever thought he would be happier without this woman in his life?

The thought of how he had hurt her so many times made his gut clench. He broke the kiss and slid her down to the ground, smiling as she groaned in protest.

'Nicole, I understand if I have messed up too many times for you to trust me, but I want to make that right. If you give me the chance I promise I will never walk away from you again for as long as I breathe.' He laid his forehead on hers. 'I want to spend more time with my family and stop working myself into the ground.'

'You would do that for us?'

'For all three of us,' he said earnestly. 'I never want to be away from my family for longer than I need to be.'

'Not even if I leave my underwear strewn all over the bedroom floor?' She raised a teasing brow.

'Especially then.' He smiled. 'I love you, Nicole. So much.'

'I don't think I'll ever get sick of hearing you say those words.' She draped her arms around his neck, nestling her face into his collar.

# EPILOGUE

'I'M FINDING IT hard to adjust to the sight of my husband driving his own car.' Nicole smiled, resting on her hand on Rigo's forearm as he guided the SUV around another tight bend in the narrow French country road.

'I'm probably taking the concept of Sunday driving a bit too literally.' Rigo gestured to the leisurely speed on the digital panel. 'I chose luxury over speed, seeing as the Ferrari wasn't an option.'

He looked briefly over his shoulder and smiled.

Nicole followed his gaze to where Anna slept peacefully in her car seat. How had an entire year passed since she had first laid eyes on her baby girl? When she thought back to that day in the hospital, holding her daughter's tiny hand and wondering if Rigo had any idea he had just become a father...

Never in her wildest dreams would she have expected to be sitting next to him on their daughter's first birthday, married and planning a long, happy life together.

The object of her thoughts laid his hand on her thigh, jolting her from her smiling reverie.

'Do you recognise the road yet?' He raised a brow, a devilish smile on his lips.

Nicole shook her head and peered out at the rolling French countryside, trying in vain to spot anything familiar. They had headed away from Paris on one of the many motorways that wove in networks across the country. Her attention had been monopolised by Anna for the first half of the journey, so she had no idea where they were.

Rigo gestured to the road ahead of them, where a sign was appearing on the horizon. Nicole squinted, trying to make out the small black lettering. Suddenly her breath caught. Her eyes darted to her husband's face before flying back to the road as a tiny town came into view.

'You've brought me to L'Annique?' she whispered. 'Oh, Rigo…'

'I thought it would be a nice tradition to spend Anna's birthday here every year.'

Nicole fought against the wave of emotion rising in her chest as they passed the small church on top of the hill and looked down on the place that had been her first slice of normality. La Petite was the farmhouse where she had started to become her true self—where she had let go of the pretences of her old life and embarked upon a new adventure.

'You are a true romantic, Rigo Marchesi, do you know that?' She smiled, grabbing his hand and putting it to her face, feeling an overwhelming love for the powerful man by her side. 'We could have lunch in Madame Laurent's café. It's nothing special, but I used to eat there regularly.'

'Actually, I had something else in mind.'

He guided the car around a corner and began driving up a familiar road. The last time Nicole had seen this laneway it had been filled with paparazzi, but today it was blissfully clear and lined with beautiful summer wildflowers. The gate to her rented house came into view, along with the familiar blue-grey roof of the farmhouse that had been her home.

She fought the urge to jump with excitement when Rigo drove into the courtyard and brought the car to a stop. They stepped out into the glorious sunshine, and the familiar smell of cut grass and bluebells washed over her. This place was like a balm to her soul, reminding her of that first choice she had made on the path to becoming the woman she was today.

She walked over to the small fountain on the lawn and ran her fingers across the ageing stone. 'I'm not sure the owner would like us trespassing, but I'm glad you brought me here. Thank you, *amore*,' she whispered, walking back to lay a single kiss on his lips.

'Oh, I'm sure the owner won't mind,' Rigo said, turning to peer through the window of the car. 'She seems to be sleeping at the moment, but you can ask her once she wakes.'

It took a moment for his words to sink in to her love-clouded brain. Then Nicole looked up at him in disbelief. 'The owner is Anna? Wait…you *bought* the farmhouse?'

Rigo nodded once, gesturing to the grand old building. 'It's kind of her birthday present.' He smiled. 'I thought it could be our weekend getaway. Somewhere we can just be together. No housekeepers or chauffeurs. It's probably a little too extravagant for a first birthday, but…'

'It's perfect.' Nicole shook her head, feeling happy tears threaten behind her eyelids. Swallowing hard, she wrapped her arms around his neck. His eyes were so mesmerisingly blue in the sunshine that she almost forgot what she wanted to say.

He took her silence as a chance to continue. 'I remembered how fondly you spoke of this place and all the memories you'd made here together.' His voice trailed off, a strange look entering his eyes. 'I wanted to give that back to you—even if it reminds me of the time you both spent together without me. A time that I'm not proud of.'

'Rigo, you were always a part of this place.' Nicole sighed, stepping back and looking up at the picturesque whitewashed facade of her old home. 'A day never passed here when I didn't think of you, or talk to Anna about her *papà*. I had always planned to tell her about you some day.'

Rigo took a step towards her, taking her face in his hands. 'I hate to think of you here alone. Cursing me for being such a stubborn fool.'

Nicole looked up into the troubled eyes of the man she loved with all her heart. She knew he still struggled with missing the first months of his daughter's life.

'Rigo, our past is only there to pave the way for our future. Look at what we have now—look at the family we have built together. I for one wouldn't change a single thing.'

\* \* \*

Rigo felt her words soothe the tightness in his chest. The look of pure love on her face made him hold her even tighter as he kissed her. It was one of maybe a thousand kisses they had shared since becoming husband and wife, and yet it was different. With this kiss the last piece of their past seemed to melt away, leaving in its wake only this one glorious moment. She was his and she always had been, from the moment he had taken her hand on that ballroom floor.

Rigo ended the kiss, looking back towards the open car door as a familiar gurgle could be heard breaking the calm. With a few strides he bent to scoop his daughter from her seat and deftly placed a small sun hat on her tiny head. Anna smiled up at him, her cheeks rosy from slumber. He had never expected for this to feel so right—holding his child in his arms and wanting to spend every moment of every day with her. But once he had given in to the overwhelming love his natural paternal instincts had soon followed.

'Happy birthday, *piccolina.*'

He dropped a kiss on Anna's cheek, wrapping his other arm around his wife. All that time he had spent trying to conquer the world from the boardroom meant nothing compared to holding his whole world in his arms at that moment.

'*Cent'anni,*' he whispered to them both. 'To a hundred years.'

\* \* \* \* \*

# MILLS & BOON®

## Why shop at millsandboon.co.uk?

Each year, thousands of romance readers find their perfect read at millsandboon.co.uk. That's because we're passionate about bringing you the very best romantic fiction. Here are some of the advantages of shopping at www.millsandboon.co.uk:

* **Get new books first**—you'll be able to buy your favourite books one month before they hit the shops

* **Get exclusive discounts**—you'll also be able to buy our specially created monthly collections, with up to 50% off the RRP

* **Find your favourite authors**—latest news, interviews and new releases for all your favourite authors and series on our website, plus ideas for what to try next

* **Join in**—once you've bought your favourite books, don't forget to register with us to rate, review and join in the discussions

Visit **www.millsandboon.co.uk**
for all this and more today!

# MILLS & BOON®

# MODERN™

**POWER, PASSION AND IRRESISTIBLE TEMPTATION**

## A sneak peek at next month's titles...

### In stores from 7th April 2016:

- **Morelli's Mistress** – Anne Mather
- **Billionaire Without a Past** – Carol Marinelli
- **The Most Scandalous Ravensdale** – Melanie Milburne
- **Claiming the Royal Innocent** – Jennifer Hayward

### In stores from 21st April 2016:

- **A Tycoon to Be Reckoned With** – Julia James
- **The Shock Cassano Baby** – Andie Brock
- **The Sheikh's Last Mistress** – Rachael Thomas
- **Kept at the Argentine's Command** – Lucy Ellis